Organic Chemistry Experiments

有机化学实验
Youji Huaxue Shiyan

Wang Mei   Wang Yanhua   Gao Zhanxian

高等教育出版社·北京
HIGHER EDUCATION PRESS   BEIJING

Capsule summary

This book is compiled on the basis of "Organic Chemistry Experiments" (fourth edition, edited by Zhanxian Gao) and with combination of the bilingual teaching experience.

The book encompasses six sections: introduction, basic techniques for organic experiments, basic preparation experiments of organic compounds, comprehensive experiments, self-designing experiments, and investigative experiments. Tables of commonly used data, index, and the Chinese-English professional glossary are attached to the end of the book.

The book was written with emphasis on (1) basic techniques for organic experiments, including some advanced experimental techniques such as microwave reactions and the resolution of racemates; (2) common-scale and miniscale experiments, also taking account of semimicro- and microscale experiments; (3) traditional and representative organic reactions, meanwhile, introducing the concept of "green" synthesis; and (4) training students in basic experimental skills, including developing their ability in experimental design and scientific research as well.

This book can be used as a textbook for the bilingual course of organic chemistry experiments. It can also be used as a teaching reference book for the experiment courses of other related majors.

图书在版编目（CIP）数据

有机化学实验 = Organic Chemistry Experiments：英文 / 王梅，王艳华，高占先编 . -- 北京 : 高等教育出版社，2011.11

ISBN 978-7-04-030093-2

Ⅰ. ①有… Ⅱ. ①王… ②王… ③高… Ⅲ. ①有机化学－化学实验－高等学校－教材－英文 Ⅳ. ①O62-33

中国版本图书馆CIP数据核字 (2011) 第217431号

策划编辑	付春江	责任编辑 刘 佳	封面设计 于 涛	版式设计 马敬茹
插图绘制	尹 莉	责任校对 张小镝	责任印制 刘思涵	

出版发行	高等教育出版社	咨询电话	400-810-0598
社　　址	北京市西城区德外大街4号	网　　址	http://www.hep.edu.cn
邮政编码	100120		http://www.hep.com.cn
印　　刷	山东省高唐印刷有限责任公司	网上订购	http://www.landraco.com
开　　本	787mm×1092mm 1/16		http://www.landraco.com.cn
印　　张	15.25	版　　次	2011年11月第1版
字　　数	370千字	印　　次	2011年11月第1次印刷
购书热线	010-58581118	定　　价	21.20元

Preface

To facilitate the bilingual teaching in the colleges and universities of the whole country, the Ministry of Education put forward a program in 2007 to build 500 state-level model courses of bilingual teaching in five years. The project, "Construction of a model course for bilingual teaching of organic chemistry and experiments" in Dalian University of Technology, is one of the first hundred projects granted by the Ministry of Education for setting up model courses of bilingual teaching. With support from the project of the Ministry of Education, we compiled this textbook of English version for the course of organic chemistry experiments. We translated the main parts of the first and second chapters on comprehensive introduction of organic chemistry experiments and selected 30 representative experiments from Chapters 3 to 6 of the Chinese textbook, "Organic Chemistry Experiments" (fourth edition, edited by Zhanxian Gao, as one of the "Eleventh Five-Year" national planning teaching materials for ordinary higher education),. The book encompasses six sections: introduction, basic techniques for organic experiments, basic preparation experiments of organic compounds, comprehensive experiments, self-designing experiments, and investigative experiments. Tables of commonly used data, index, and the Chinese-English professional glossary are attached to the end of the book.

The book was written with emphasis on (1) basic techniques for organic experiments, including some advanced experimental techniques such as microwave reactions and resolution of racemates; (2) common-scale and miniscale experiments, also taking account of semimicro- and microscale experiments; (3) traditional and representative organic reactions, meanwhile, introducing the concept of "green" synthesis; and (4) training students in basic experimental skills, including developing their ability in experimental design and scientific research as well.

There are 6 Chapters in the book. Chapters 1 to 3 and Section 6. 4 were compiled by Mei Wang and Chapters 4 and 5 as well as Sections 6. 1 to 6. 3 were compiled by Yanhua Wang. Mei Wang checked and revised the whole content of the book. Zhanxian Gao of Dalian University of Technology and Yanmei Li of Qinghua University successively reviewed the manuscript of the book and gave many valuable comments and suggestions; Xiaoan Zhang of Jilin University polished parts of the content; Yi Zhai, Jia Liu, and Chunjiang Fu of Higher Education Press did lots of work for putting out this book. Here we would like to express our thanks to all of them.

As the knowledge of the editors is limited, there might be some improper parts in the book. We sincerely welcome corrections and comments from experts, peers, as well as teachers and students using this book.

Editors
Spring, 2011

Contents

Contents

Chapter 1

Introduction

The course of experimental organic chemistry will introduce you to the techniques and procedures used in organic chemistry. You will learn how to handle a variety of chemicals safely and how to manipulate apparatus properly. Along with becoming more skilled in the technical aspects of laboratory work, you should also develop a proper scientific approach to the execution and interpretation of experiments. The "hands-on" experience gained in the laboratory, as you gather and interpret phenomena and data from a variety of reactions, will provide a sense of organic chemistry that is nearly impossible to communicate in classes. Performing reactions in practice will give you a deep impression and better understanding on the theoretical concepts, functional groups, organic reactions and methods you have leant in organic lectures.

1.1 General Rules for Organic Chemistry Laboratory

When entering, working, and leaving the laboratory, you should be clearly aware of and strictly observe the following basic rules to keep good order in laboratories and to ensure laboratory safety.

(1) You should be aware of safety rules and first-aid procedures, and familiar with the layout of the laboratory room. Know the locations of the fire extinguishers, fire blankets, safety showers, gas valves, and electric switches.

(2) Wear laboratory coat when working in the laboratory. Do not wear shorts and scandals in the laboratory. Wear latex gloves when working with concentrated acids, bases, bromine and other particular hazardous chemicals. Never bring food and drink to the laboratory.

(3) Make a theoretical preparation in advance for each experiment by reviewing the basic knowledge related to the experiment, studying the entire experiment procedures, learning the operation rules for the apparatus and equipment you will use and understanding the toxicity and other potential hazards of the chemicals used in experiment. Never begin any experiment until you understand its overall purpose and the reasons for each operation that you are to do.

(4) Strictly observe all the rules and regulations for organic chemistry laboratory. Follow the guidance of your teachers and instructors, and follow the experiment procedures in the textbook. Do not make any modification in experiment without a permission of your instructor. Never work alone in the laboratory and never leave an ongoing experiment unattended.

(5) During experiment, keep the laboratory clean and tidy. Handle the glassware with care and clean it after experiment. Put all glassware and apparatus in good order either on your bench top or in your kit. Keep sinks clean. Do not pour and throw other things into sinks except for neutral and nonhazardous aqueous solution.

(6) After using the chemicals, cover the stopper of the container immediately and put it back to the original place. All reagents prepared should be stuck on a label with name, concentration and date. Always pay attention to economize chemicals, water, electricity and gas.

(7) Read the manuals for instruments and gauges to understand their working principles and operation methods before manipulating them. Operate precision instruments and gauges with care and strictly follow the operation rules. Do not dismantle and remove the instruments without a permission of your instructor.

(8) All solid wastes and organic liquid wastes should be placed in designated containers, respectively.

(9) After experiment, clean the laboratory thoroughly. Before leaving the laboratory, carefully check whether all switches and valves for water, electricity and gas are switched off safely.

1.2 Safe Laboratory Practice and First Aid in Case of an Accident

Chemistry laboratories are potentially dangerous because organic chemistry experiment commonly uses fragile glassware, flammable liquids, toxic chemicals and equipments under vacuum or high pressure. Most organic solvents, such as benzene, alcohols, gasoline, ethers, acetone, and so on, are volatile and highly flammable, and some chemical substances are explosive if handled improperly. Incorrect operations may cause experimental accidents or even disasters. Therefore, you should have a sound knowledge of how to perform experimental work in a safe manner and strictly follow standard safety protocols.

1.2.1 Prevention of Fires and First Aid in Case of a Fire

Occasionally, open flames may be used for heating a reaction mixture or distilling a highboiling point liquid. In such cases, give special precautions for the open flames and strictly follow the guidelines in the "Safety Alert" section.

(1) Always check carefully for cracks, chips or other imperfections in the glassware that you will use, and equip the apparatus with all joints tightly fitted.

(2) Never use a flame to directly heat a flammable liquid. Use a water or steam bath or electrical heat device instead.

(3) Flammable chemicals must be kept and handled in a place away from an open flame.

(4) Do not pour flammable and water-insoluble organic solvents into drains or sinks. They must be recovered after experiment.

(5) Do not store a large amount of flammable liquids in the laboratory.

In case of a fire, quickly turn off the power and gas, and call for help. Remove all flammable liquids and materials from the immediate area, and then extinguish the fire with a fire extinguisher, sand or asbestos cloth. If your clothing is on fire, do not run. Roll on the floor to smother the fire and to keep the flame away from your head. Your neighbors can help to extinguish the flame by using fire blankets, laboratory coats or other items that are immediately available. A laboratory shower, if close by, can be used to extinguish burning clothing.

If burns are minor, apply a burn ointment. In the case of serious burns, do not apply any ointment; seek professional medical treatment at once.

1.2.2 Prevention of Explosions

(1) Some chemicals are explosive if handled incorrectly. For example, peroxides, multi-nitro aromatic compounds and nitrates may explode when heated or knocked. Ethers may contain peroxides, so do not distill them to dryness and it is recommended to remove peroxides from ethers before distillation. Do not dry multi-nitro aromatic compounds in an oven. Mixing alcohol with concentrated nitric acid may cause a fierce explosion.

(2) Wrong assembly of apparatus and incorrect operations can also cause explosion. Do not heat an air-tight system for common distillation or reflux. Always wear safety glasses or goggles in the laboratory.

(3) Immediately turn off the gas when it leaks out, open the windows, and inform your instructor to check and repair it.

1.2.3 First Aid for Cuts and Scalds

Handle glassware with care and be cautious of hot apparatus and solutions to avoid hurt by cuts and scalds. If you are unfortunately injured by broken glass, for minor cuts, squeeze the contaminated blood out immediately, pick out the pieces of broken glass, and rinse the cut thoroughly with distilled water. After this, wipe the cut with tincture of iodine or merbromin, and bind it up with gauze or apply with adhesive bandages. For severe cuts, first bind up the cut with gauze. If the cut bleeds, attempt to stop the bleeding with compress and pressure. Seek the professional medical treatment at once.

In case of scalds, smear some scald ointment on the affected area and coat the injured area with gauze. If the scald is severe, go to the clinic for further treatment.

1.2.4 Prevention of Damages from Hazardous Chemicals and First Aid for Chemical Burns

The variety and potential danger of chemicals used in the organic chemistry laboratory probably exceed that of any laboratory course you have had. It is imperative to understand the properties of the substances with which you are working, and to take a proper precaution.

(1) Make reactions that will release toxic gases, such as chlorine, bromine, nitrogen oxide and hydrochloride in a hood or in a well-ventilated area, and absorb the toxic gases with a gas trap. Avoid inhaling vapors of organic and inorganic compounds. Work in a hood when handling particularly volatile and noxious chemicals.

(2) Wear latex gloves when handling particularly toxic and corrosive chemicals to avoid contacting with your skin. Do not drop them on the bench and the floor, and never pour or throw them into the drains or sinks. Concentrated acids and bases and bromine are very corrosive and could cause chemical burns, so handle them with great care.

(3) If corrosive chemicals accidentally come in contact with your skin or eyes, wash the affected area immediately with large amounts of running water, and then treat the affected area in the following ways:

For acid-burn, first wash the eyes with 1% sodium bicarbonate solution and wash the skin with saturated sodium bicarbonate solution, and then wash the eyes or skin with water. Finally, apply burn ointment on the affected area.

For base-burn, first wash the eyes with 1% boric acid solution and wash the skin with 1% acetic acid, and then wash the eyes and skin with water. Finally, apply burn ointment on the affected area.

In all instances where eye tissue is contacted with bromine, consult an ophthalmologist as soon as possible after immediately flooding the eyes with water; for bromine-burn of skin, sequentially wash the affected area with petroleum ether and 2% sodium thiosulfate solution, and then smear with glycerol and apply cod liver oil ointment on the affected area.

For treatment of serious burns, see a surgeon after first aid.

1.2.5   Toxicity and Safety Data of Chemicals

Common chemicals are more or less harmful to the health of human beings. Even compounds with pleasant smell are harmful if inhaling too much vapors of the compounds. Some nitrogen-containing and fused ring compounds are very toxic, exhibiting a relatively low lethal dose, and some chemicals are possibly carcinogenic. One of the principles to choose experiments for this textbook is to avoid using particular toxic chemicals in the teaching laboratory. Your actions and those of your labmates, will determine whether you can do experiment in a safe environment.

The increased emphasis on the proper handling of chemicals has led to a number of different types of publications containing key information about the chemical, physical and toxicological properties of the majority of organic and inorganic compounds. The data provided by such references are basically a summary of the information contained in the Material Safety Data Sheets (MSDS) published by the suppliers of chemicals. MSDS data include physical constants,

Safe Laboratory Practice and First Aid in Case of an Accident

inflammability and explosibility, reactivity, treatment measures in case of leaking, handling and storage knowledge, health hazards, toxicity data, and so on. From a standpoint of environmental protection, the threshold limit values (TLV) of many chemicals in the area of chemical factories and laboratories have been stipulated by labor and health administrations and the permissible levels of chemicals in the area of laboratories have been set by the occupational safety and health administration (OSHA). The threshold limit values for some commonly used compounds are given below. Before experiment, you should know the properties of the chemicals used in the experiments and refer to MSDS to learn about toxicity and other potential hazards associated with the chemicals.

(1) Toxic solids

compound	TLV[1]/(mg·m^{-3})	compound	TLV/(mg·m^{-3})
osmium trioxide 三氧化锇	0.002	arsenium 砷化合物	0.5 (based on As)
mercury compounds, especially mercury alkylides 烷基汞	0.01	vanadium pentoxide 五氧化二钒	0.5
thallium salts 铊盐	0.1 (based on Tl)	oxalic acid and oxalate 草酸和草酸盐	1
selenium and its compounds 硒和硒化合物	0.2 (based on Se)	inorganic cyanides 无机氰化物	5 (based on CN$^-$)

① TLV (threshold limit value): To work in a safe environment, the concentration of the vapor or bug dust of the toxic compound should be kept below the limit value.

(2) Toxic and hazardous gases

compound	TLV/(μg·g^{-1})	compound	TLV/(μg·g^{-1})
fluorine 氟	0.1	hydrofluoride 氟化氢	3
phosgene 光气	0.1	nitrogen dioxide 二氧化氮	5
ozone 臭氧	0.1	nitrosyl chloride 亚硝酰氯	5
diazomethane 重氮甲烷	0.2	cyanogen 氰	10
phosphine 磷化氢	0.3	hydrogen cyanide 氰化氢	10
boron trifluoride 三氟化硼	1	hydrogen sulfide 硫化氢	10
chlorine 氯	1	carbon monoxide 一氧化碳	50

(3) Toxic, hazardous liquids and irritant materials

Contacting with the following compounds for a long time can cause chronic intoxication. The vapors of most of the following compounds are strongly irritant to eyes and respiratory tract.

Introduction

compound	TLV/($\mu g \cdot g^{-1}$)	compound	TLV/($\mu g \cdot g^{-1}$)
carbonyl nickel compounds 羰基镍	0.001	dimethyl sulfate 硫酸二甲酯	1
methyl isocyanate 异氰酸甲酯	0.02	diethyl sulfate 硫酸二乙酯	1
acraldehyde 丙烯醛	0.1	tetrabromoethane 四溴乙烷	1
bromine 溴	0.1	propenol 烯丙醇	2
3-chloropropane 3-氯丙烷	1	2-butenal 2-丁烯醛	2
chlorophenylmethane 苯氯甲烷	1	hydrofluoric acid 氢氟酸	3
bromophenylmethane 苯溴甲烷	1	tetrachloroethane 四氯乙烷	5
boron trichloride 三氯化硼	1	benzene 苯	10
boron tribromide 三溴化硼	1	bromomethane 溴甲烷	15
2-chloroethanol 2-氯乙醇	1	carbon disulfide 二硫化碳	20

（4）Other toxic materials

some halogen-containing compounds 含卤素化合物

compound	TLV	compound	TLV
bromoform 溴仿	0.5 $\mu g \cdot g^{-1}$	1,2-dibromoethane 1,2-二溴乙烷	20 $\mu g \cdot g^{-1}$
iodomethane 碘甲烷	5 $\mu g \cdot g^{-1}$	1,2-dichloroethane 1,2-二氯乙烷	50 $\mu g \cdot g^{-1}$
carbon tetrachloride 四氯化碳	10 $\mu g \cdot g^{-1}$	bromoethane 溴乙烷	200 $\mu g \cdot g^{-1}$
chloroform 氯仿	10 $\mu g \cdot g^{-1}$	methylene chloride 二氯甲烷	200 $\mu g \cdot g^{-1}$

aromatic and aliphatic amines 芳香和脂肪胺

compound	TLV	compound	TLV
phenylenediamines 苯二胺	0.1 mg·m^{-3}	aniline 苯胺	5 $\mu g \cdot g^{-1}$
methoxyanilines 甲氧基苯胺	0.5 mg·m^{-3}	methylaniline 甲基苯胺	5 $\mu g \cdot g^{-1}$
nitroanilines 硝基苯胺	1 $\mu g \cdot g^{-1}$	dimethylamine 二甲胺	10 $\mu g \cdot g^{-1}$
N-methylaniline N-甲基苯胺	2 $\mu g \cdot g^{-1}$	ethylamine 乙胺	10 $\mu g \cdot g^{-1}$
N;N-dimethylaniline N,N-二甲基苯胺	5 $\mu g \cdot g^{-1}$	triethylamine 三乙胺	25 $\mu g \cdot g^{-1}$

phenols and nitrobenzene derivatives 酚和芳香族硝基化合物

compound	TLV	compound	TLV
picric acid (trinitrophenol) 苦味酸	0.1 mg·m^{-3}	nitrobenzene 硝基苯	1 $\mu g \cdot g^{-1}$
dinitrophenols 二硝基苯酚	0.2 mg·m^{-3}	phenol 苯酚	5 $\mu g \cdot g^{-1}$
chloronitrophenols 硝基氯苯	1 mg·m^{-3}	methylphenols 甲基苯酚	5 $\mu g \cdot g^{-1}$
m-dinitrobenzene 间二硝基苯	1 mg·m^{-3}		

(5) Carcinogenic materials

biphenylamines and their derivatives 联苯胺及其衍生物	β−naphthylamine β−萘胺
dimethylaminoazobenzene 二甲氨基偶氮苯	α−naphthylamine α−萘胺
N−methyl−N−nitrosylaniline N−甲基−N−亚硝基苯	N−nitrosyldimethylamine N−亚硝基二甲胺
N−methyl−N−nitrosylurea N−甲基−N−亚硝基脲	N−nitrosylhydropyridine N−亚硝基氢化吡啶
bis(chloromethyl) ether 双氯甲基醚	dimethylsulfate 硫酸二甲酯
chloromethyl methyl ether 氯甲基甲醚	iodomethane 碘甲烷
diazomethane 重氮甲烷	β−hydroxypropalactone β−羟基丙酸内酯
benzo [a] pyrene 苯并[a]芘	dibenzo [c,g] carbazole 二苯并[c,g]咔唑
dibenzo [a,h] anthracene 二苯并[a,h]蒽	7,12−dimethylbenzo [a] anthracene 7,12−二甲基苯并[a]蒽
thioacetamide 硫代乙酰胺	thiourea 硫脲
asbestos dust 石棉粉尘	

(6) Toxic materials that have a chronic accumulation effect

Once the following toxic materials are assimilated, they are difficultly discharged from human body, resulting in chronic poisoning.

(a) Benzene.

(b) Lead compounds, especially organic lead compounds.

(c) Mercury and its compounds, especially divalent mercurate and organic mercury compounds.

Proper protecting measures should be adopted when using the afore-listed toxic materials. Avoid inhaling the vapors or the dust from these toxic materials, and do not allow them to come in contact with your skin. Toxic gases and volatile toxic liquids should be handled in a hood or in a well-ventilated area. The surface of mercury should not be exposed to air and it must be covered with water for storage.

1.2.6 Disposal of Chemical Wastes

The proper disposal of chemical wastes is one of the biggest responsibilities that you have in the organic laboratory. The experimental procedures in this textbook have been designed at a scale that should allow you to isolate an amount of product sufficient to see and manipulate, but they also involve the use of minimal quantities of reactants, solvents and drying agents to reduce the amount of chemical wastes. For environmental protection, chemical wastes generated from the organic laboratory must be classified and recovered. Only the nonhazardous, water-soluble, neutral, nonflammable and biologically degradable chemical wastes can be flushed down the drain with excess water. Solid chemical wastes should not be thrown in a trash can.

The recommended procedures that should be followed are described under the heading, "Finishing Touches". The organic laboratory should be equipped with various containers for disposal of hazardous solids, nonhazardous solids, halogenated organic liquids, hydrocarbons and oxygenated organic liquids. The containers must be properly labeled as to what can be put in them. It is very important for safety and environmental reasons that different categories of spent chemicals are segregated from one another. Following is the general rules for disposal of chemical wastes:

(1) All inorganic acids and bases used in this textbook should be neutralized first and diluted with copious water before flushing down the drain.

(2) Different organic liquid wastes should be classified and poured into properly labeled containers, respectively. Waste containers should be stored in a well-ventilated place. Never pour flammable and water-insoluble organic liquids into drains or sinks.

(3) Nonhazardous solid wastes such as alumina, silica gel, drying agents, and so on, should be placed in a designated container after solvents are evaporated in hoods.

(4) Hazardous solid wastes should be disposed of in a specially labeled container. The exact name of the solid wastes should be written on the label.

(5) Broken thermometers are a special problem because they usually contain residue mercury, which is toxic and relatively volatile. Collect all mercury for the broken thermometer and place it in a specially labeled container. The mercury should be covered with water and the container should be tightly closed. If mercury has spilled as a result of the breakage, it should be cleaned up immediately. Consult your instructor about appropriate procedures for doing so.

(6) Chemical wastes that react violently with water such as Grignard reagent, aluminium chloride, acetic anhydride should be decomposed with proper reagents in a hood before disposal.

1.3　Information Sources for Experimental Organic Chemistry

There are varieties of the literature on experimental organic chemistry available in print and online. To be familiar with the literature and handbooks of experimental organic chemistry is important for designing and making organic experiments. This section provides you with a general knowledge about four major categories of the important information sources of organic chemistry, which may be used as valuable lead references to initiate a specific search.

1.3.1　Important Handbooks and Dictionaries

(1) **Beilstein's Handbuch der Organischen Chemie (Beilstein Handbook of Organic Chemistry).** It is perhaps the most complete reference work on organic compounds. It provides full access to the database of over eight million compounds and five million reactions. The records in the Beilstein handbook include molecular structures, chemical and physical properties and constants,

spectral identification, synthetic procedures and relevant references. The printed Beilstein handbook is published in German, but the Beilstein Online database gives information in English. The easier and faster way to get the needed information is to access the CrossFire Beilstein Online database if your library has paid to the online vendor. The CrossFire Beilstein indexes three primary types of data. The substance domain stores structural information with all associated facts and literature references. The reaction domain details the preparation of substances with reaction search queries, scientists can investigate specific reaction pathways. Chemical literature citations, titles, and abstracts, which are hyperlinked to substance and reaction domain entries, are stored within the citation domain.

(2) **Merck Index of Chemicals and Drugs**, 12th ed. , Merck and Co. , Rahway, NJ. It provides a concise summary of the physical and biological properties as well as uses, toxicity and hazards of more than 10 000 compounds and some literature references. Organization is alphabetical by names, synonyms and trade names. Formula and subject indexes, and a Chemical Abstracts Service registry number index are available for this handbook.

(3) **Dictionary of Organic Compounds**, 6th ed. , Buckingham, J., Ed. Chapman and Hall, New York. This dictionary is in nine volumes. Volumes $1 \sim 6$ contain the data for the compounds, Volume 7 is a name index with cross-references, Volume 8 contains a formula index, and Volume 9 is a Chemical Abstracts Service registry number index.

(4) 有机化学实验常用数据手册,第三版,吕俊民编,大连理工大学出版社,1997. The first part of this handbook contains physical properties of common organic and inorganic compounds, including the Chinese and English names of compounds, their chemical formulas, relative molecular weights, color and crystal shapes, relative densities, melting points, boiling points, refractive indices, solubilities in water, alcohols and ethers, as well as the original sources of all items. The second part contains the thermodynamic data related to the experiment of organic chemistry, and the third part contains the safety data of chemicals. There is a chemical formula index in the end of the handbook.

1.3.2　Important Journals Involving Organic Experiment

Primary research journals are the ultimate source of most of the information on organic chemistry. Some of the important journals and a brief description of their contents are given below.

(1) *Journal of the Chemical Society , Perkin Transactions* , published by the Royal Society of Chemistry (UK). It publishes articles and a few communications in all areas of organic and bioorganic chemistry.

(2) *Journal of Organic Chemistry* , published by the American Chemical Society. It publishes articles, communications and notes covering all areas of organic chemistry.

(3) *Journal of European Organic Chemistry* , published by Join Welly in English. It publishes articles covering all areas of organic chemistry.

(4) *Journal of American Chemical Education* , published by the division of chemical educa-

tion of the American Chemical Society.

(5) 有机化学 (Chinese Organic Chemistry), published by the Chinese Chemical Society. It publishes articles, communications and reviews covering all areas of organic chemistry.

1.3.3　Important Online Resources

It is a fast and convenient way to search information online. The following are the most useful websites providing various chemical information.

(1) Online libraries

http://www.nlc.gov.cn

http://www.lib.tsinghua.edu.cn

http://www.lib.pku.edu.cn/html

(2) Online periodical resources

http://www.interscience.wiley.com

http://pubs.acs.org

http://www.rsc.org

http://www.chinajournal.net.cn

http://www.isiknowledge.com

(3) Database resources

http://www.chemfinder.com (property of compounds)

http://riodb01.ibase.aist.go.jp (NMR, IR, MS, ESR and Raman Spectra database)

1.4　Common Glassware and Apparatus

This chapter introduces the glassware and apparatus that are commonly used in organic chemistry laboratory. When you are preparing for an experiment, have a look at the appropriate figures of this chapter.

1.4.1　Names and Uses of Common Glassware

Standard-taper glassware with ground-glass joints is commonly used for performing reactions at mini-and micro-scale levels. Standard-taper joints come in a number of sizes, 14, 19, 24, 29 and 34. This number represents the diameter of the joint in millimeters at its widest point.

(1) Flasks (Figure 1.4−1)

(a) **Round-bottom flasks** are the most useful containers for organic reactions and distillation, and they can also be used as receivers for distillation. The capacities of common round-bottom flasks are 1000 mL, 500 mL, 250 mL, 100 mL, 50 mL, 10 mL, and 5 mL.

(b) **Two-neck round-bottom flasks** are usually used for semi-micro-and micro-scale preparation. The middle-neck can be jointed to a cooling condenser, a still head or a short fractionating

Common Glassware and Apparatus

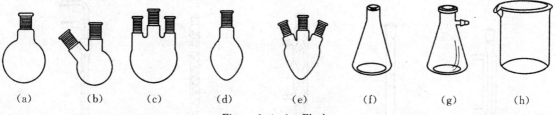

Figure 1. 4 −1   Flasks

(a) Round-bottom flask   (b) Two-neck round-bottom flask   (c) Three-neck round-bottom flask
(d) Pear-shaped flask   (e) Three-neck pear-shaped flask   (f) Erlenmeyer flask   (g) Büchner flask
(filter flask)   (h) Beaker

head, and the side-neck can be jointed to a thermometer or an addition funnel. The capacities of common two-neck round-bottom flasks are 50 mL and 10 mL.

(c) **Three-neck round-bottom flasks** are normally used for the more complicated reactions and for the reactions that need refluxing and mechanical stirring simultaneously. The middle-neck can be equipped with a stirrer and the two side-necks can be installed with a cooling condenser, an addition funnel or a thermometer. The capacities of common three-neck round-bottom flasks are 1 000 mL, 500 mL, 250 mL, 100 mL and 50 mL.

(d) **Pear-shaped flasks** are used for reactions in a small amount. The advantage of this kind of flask is that most of the liquid in the flask can be distilled out. The capacities of common pear-shaped flasks are 100 mL and 50 mL.

(e) **Three-neck pear-shaped flasks** are used similarly as three-neck round-bottom flasks for semi-micro-and micro-scale experiment. The capacities of common three-neck pear-shaped flasks are 50 mL and 25 mL.

(f) **Erlenmeyer flasks** are used for titration, crystallization and synthetic reactions that generate solid products. They can also be used as receivers for common distillation but not for vacuum distillation. The capacities of common Erlenmeyer flasks are 500 mL, 250 mL, 100 mL, 50 mL, 25 mL and 10 mL.

(g) **Büchner flasks (filter flasks)** are used together with a Büchner funnel for vacuum filtration of solid products.

(h) **Beakers** are used as containers for solid dissolving, liquid mixing and heating or condensing aqueous solution.

In general, the reactants or the solution added should occupy 1/3 to 1/2 of the total capacity of a flask, but should not exceed 2/3 of the total capacity.

(2) Condensers (Figure 1. 4 −2)

(a) **West condenser** is normally used for distillation and also for reflux of a micro-scale synthetic reaction. Use water-cooling condenser when the boiling point of the distillate is below 140 ℃. If it is higher than 140 ℃, do not inlet water into the condenser. Otherwise, the joints of the inner and outer tubes may burst.

Introduction

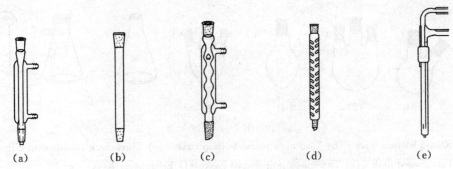

Figure 1.4-2 Condensers

(a) West condenser (b) Air condenser (c) Reflux condenser

(d) Fractionating column (e) Cold finger

(b) **Air condenser** is used for distillation of liquids with high boiling temperatures. Use an air-cooling condenser when the boiling point of the distillate is higher than 140 ℃.

(c) **Reflux condenser** is more effective than West condenser for condensation of vapors. It is used for refluxing experiment. The lengths of common condensers are 300 mm, 200 mm, 120 mm, and 100 mm.

(d) **Fractionating column** is used for efficient separation of liquids by distillation.

(e) **Cold finger** is used for vacuum micro-distillation and for sublimation of solid products.

(3) Funnels (Figure 1.4-3)

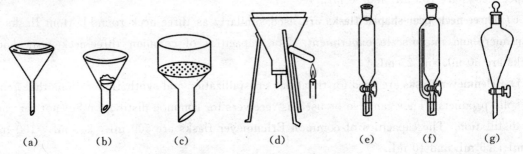

Figure 1.4-3 Funnels

(a) Long-stemmed funnel (b) Hirsch funnel (c) Büchner funnel (d) Hot filtration funnel

(e) Addition funnel (f) Pressure-equalized addition funnel (g) Pear-shaped separatory funnel

(a) **Long-stemmed funnel** is used for common filtration.

(b) **Hirsch funnel** is used for vacuum filtration of a trace amount of solid products.

(c) **Büchner funnel** is used for vacuum filtration of solid products.

(d) **Hot filtration funnel** is used for recrystallization. Decolorizing carbon or other solid impurities can be removed by hot filtration from an organic compound that is only sparingly soluble in the solvent at room temperature.

(e) **Addition funnel** is used for dropwise addition of liquids into a container.

(f) **Pressure-equalized addition funnel** is used for dropwise addition of liquids into an airtight

Common Glassware and Apparatus

container.

(g) **Pear-shaped separatory funnel** is used for extraction, washing and separation of liquids.

(4) Joint heads and adapters (Figure 1.4-4)

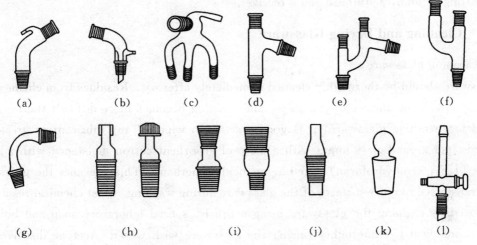

(a)   (b)   (c)   (d)   (e)   (f)

(g)   (h)   (i)   (j)   (k)   (l)

Figure 1.4-4   Joint heads and adapters

(a) Distillation adapter   (b) Vacuum distillation adapter   (c) Swallowtail-shaped distillation adapter   (d) Stillhead   (e) Claisen head   (f) Claisen adapter (Y-tube)   (g) 75° Elbow   (h) Thermometer adapter   (i) Reduction/expansion adapter   (j) Casing tube for stirrer shaft   (k) Stopper   (l) Two-way cock

(5) Drying tube and water segregator (Figure 1.4-5)

(a) **Straight and bent drying tubes** are filled with drying agents and used for protecting the water-susceptive reaction system from humidity.

(b) **Water segregator** is used for removing the water as it forms from a reaction system.

(a)   (b)

Figure 1.4-5   Drying tube and water segregator

(a) Straight and bent drying tubes

(b) Water segregator

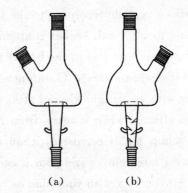

(a)   (b)

Figure 1.4-6   Special glassware used for micro-scale organic experiment

(a) Hickman stillhead with port

(b) Hickman fractionating head with port

(6) Special glassware used for micro-scale organic experiment (Figure 1.4-6)

(a) **Hickman stillhead with port** is used for micro-scale distillation, which acts as both a still-head and a receiver.

(b) **Hickman fractionating head with port** is used for micro-scale fractionation, which acts as a fractionating column, a stillhead and a receiver.

1.4.2　Cleaning and Drying Glassware

(1) Cleaning glassware

Glassware should be thoroughly cleaned immediately after use. Residues from chemical reactions may attack the surface of the glass, and cleaning becomes more difficult the longer you wait. Before washing glassware, it is good practice to wipe off any lubricant or grease from standard-taper ground-glass joints with a piece of absorbent cotton moistened with a solvent such as THF (tetrahydrofuran), acetone or dichloromethane. This prevents the grease from being transferred to inner surfaces of the glassware during washing. Most chemical residues can be removed by cleaning the glassware using a brush, special laboratory soap and household cleanser, followed by thoroughly rinsing the glassware with water. Acetone dissolves most organic residues and thus is commonly used to clean glassware; use as little solvent as possible to do the job. The acetone used should be transferred to an appropriately marked container for disposal. However, acetone should not be used to clean the glassware that contains residual amounts of bromine since a powerful lachrymator, bromoacetone (a tear gas), may form. Never use chemical reagent or organic solvent thoughtlessly to clean the glassware. This may cause a hazardous situation.

Stubborn residues may sometimes remain in the glassware. Often these may be removed by ultrasonic oscillation in the presence of soap and water or acetone. If this technique fails, more powerful cleaning solutions may be required. Chromic acid solution is an effective cleaning agent, which is made according to the following procedecures: add 5 g of potassium or sodium dichromate to a 250 mL beaker containing 5 mL of water, and then slowly decant 100 mL of concentrated sulfuric acid to the beaker while stirring the mixture. The temperature of the mixture will increase to $70\sim80$ ℃ during addition of acid. Decant the mixed solution to a dry glass container with an airtight ground glass stopper when it cools to 40 ℃. The chromic acid solution loses efficacy when it turns from red-brown to green after stored for a long time. Since chromic acid is highly corrosive, it must be used with great care. When handling chromic acid, always wear latex gloves and pour it carefully into the glassware to be cleaned. Do not allow it to come into contact with your skin or clothing; they will cause severe burns and produce holes in your clothing. After the glassware is clean, pour the waste chromic acid solution into a specially designated bottle, not into the sink or the drain.

Because the toxicity of chromium compounds, some other powerful cleaning solutions such as alcoholic potassium hydroxide are used to replace chromic acid solution. Immerse the glassware in the alcoholic potassium hydroxide solution for several hours or overnight, and then rinse the glassware thoroughly with water to complete the washing process.

After the glassware is cleaned and dried, put a piece of paper between male and female ground-glass cocks to avoid difficulties in moving off the cock.

(2) Drying glassware

In most organic experiments, dry glassware must be used. The following are the usual methods to dry the glassware:

Air dry: Make the widest use of air dry method. After washing, place the glassware upside down on a drying rack, and the condensers should be clamped vertically on a drying rack. The air dry of the glassware needs one or two days.

Oven dry: The glassware can be dried by placing it in an oven at $110 \sim 120$ ℃ for several hours. Using a blow oven can shorten the drying time. Completely decant water from the glassware and place it into an oven with mouth up to avoid dropping water onto the hot glassware in the oven. It may cause the burst of the glassware. The thick-wall glassware, such as graduated cylinder, graduated pipette, Büchner funnel, condenser, and so on, cannot be dried in an oven. Separatory funnel and dropping funnel should be dried in an oven after dismounting the male cock and wiping off any lubricant or grease from the cock.

Blow dry: After washing, shake off residual water from the glassware, and then place the glassware upside down on the porous metal bars of an air-flow dryer. Control the temperature of the flow air. The blow dryer should not be continuously used for a long time; otherwise, the motor and heating wire may be damaged.

Organic solvent dry: The fastest method for drying the glassware is to rinse it first with a small amount of 95% ethanol and then with acetone. Flasks and beakers should be inverted to allow the last traces of solvent to drain. Final drying is also aided by blowing the glassware with dry compressed air or with a hair blower. The used alcohol and acetone should be poured into an assigned container.

1.4.3 Common Organic Lab Apparatus

The usually used reaction apparatus are shown in Figures 1.4−7 to Figure 1.4−11.

(1) Reflux apparatus

Some reactions undergo very slowly at room temperature. To shorten the time required for completion of a reaction, the reaction mixture is often heated under reflux for a certain time. Figure 1.4−7a shows the simplest reflux apparatus. The solvent, if any, and reactants are placed in a flask, together with a stirbar; this flask should be set up about 15 cm or more from the bench top to allow for fast removal of the heating source if necessary. The flask is then fitted with a reflux condenser with water running slowly through it from its inlet to outlet. Do not stop the top of the condenser. *A closed system should never be heated*. A proper and safe heating source should be used to slowly heat the reaction mixture to the boiling point. Slow heating makes it possible to control any sudden exothermicity. The heating should be controlled to ensure that the rising height of vapors in the condenser does not exceed 1/3 of the total height of the condenser. The volatile components of the mixture vaporize and reliquefy in the condenser, and the condensate returns to the boiling flask; in this manner no solvent or react-ant is removed or lost.

If reactants are susceptive to water, equip a drying tube filled with anhydrous calcium chlo-ride on the top of the condenser to prevent humidity going into the flask (Figure 1.4−7b). If the reaction releases some toxic gas such as hydrochloride and hydrobromide, a gas trap must be connected to the outlet of the drying tube (Figure 1.4−7c). Figure 1.4−7d shows a reflux apparatus for a micro-scale reaction.

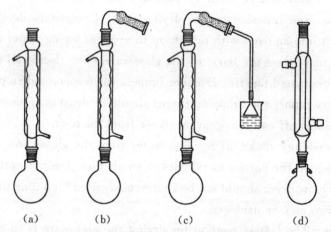

(a)   (b)   (c)   (d)

Figure 1.4−7   Reflux apparatus

(a) Simple reflux apparatus   (b) Reflux apparatus equipped with
a drying tube   (c) Reflux apparatus equipped with a drying tube
and a gas trap   (d) Reflux apparatus for micro-scale experiment

(2) Reflux-addition apparatus

Many chemical reactions are strongly exothermic. In these cases, the reaction rate may be controlled by adding one of the reagents slowly. Some reactions may require that one of the rea-gents should be present in high dilution to minimize the formation of side products. Figures 1.4−8a and b show typical apparatus that allow a liquid reagent or solution to be dropped to the reaction flask using an addition funnel, which are usually used for mini-scale reactions. For mi-cro-scale reactions, a dropping pipet or a syringe can be used for dropwise addition of a reactant (Figures 1.4−8c and d).

(3) Reflux-water segregation apparatus

For a reversible reaction, products or one of the products must be continuously removed from the reaction mixture to drive the reaction to completion. A water segregator is usually used for removing water from the reaction system as it forms. Figures 1.4−9a and b show reflex appara-tus with a water segregator. A condenser is equipped on the top of the segregator. When

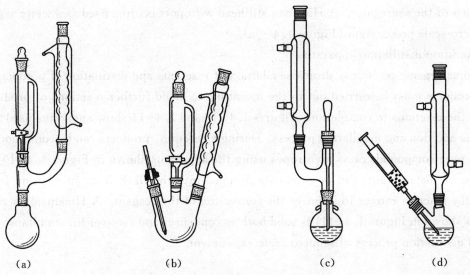

Figure 1.4−8   Reflux-addition apparatus

(a) and (b) for mini-scale experiment   (c) and (d) for micro-scale experiment

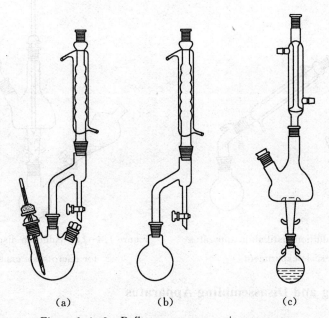

Figure 1.4−9   Reflux-water segregation apparatus

(a) and (b) for mini-scale experiment   (c) for micro-scale experiment

organic reactants and water formed in the reaction are refluxed at an azeotropic point, the vapors are liquefied in the condenser and the condensate drops to the segregator. The azeotropic mixture separates into two layers. The upper layer of organic compounds will spontaneously flow back to the flask and the water layer is occasionally drained from the two-way cock of the segregator. The level of the water in the segregator should always be kept slightly lower than the branch of the segregator. A Hickman stillhead with port is often used as a water segregator for a micro-scale preparation (Figure 1.4-9c).

(4) Addition-distillation apparatus

For some organic reactions, dropwise addition of reactants and distillation of products or one of the products must be carried out in the meantime to avoid further reactions of products and to drive the reactions to completion. Figures 1.4-10 and 1.4-11 show apparatus used for simultaneous addition and distillation process. During a reaction, products can be continuously distilled as pure compounds or as azeotropes using the apparatus shown in Figure 1.4-10, meanwhile one of the reactants can be gradually dropped into the flask from an addition funnel to control the reaction rate or to improve the conversion of the reagent. A Hickman fractionating head, as shown in Figure 1.4-11, is used both as condenser and receiver for simultaneous addition and distillation process of a micro-scale experiment.

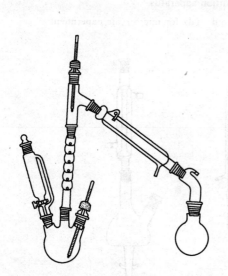 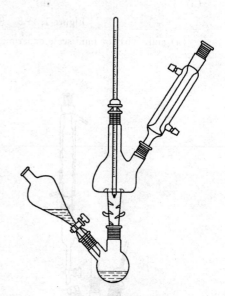

Figure 1.4-10   Addition-distillation apparatus
for mini-scale experiment

Figure 1.4-11   Addition-distillation apparatus
for micro-scale experiment

1.4.4   Assembling and Disassembling Apparatus

(1) Connecting apparatus

In the experiment of organic chemistry, the individual pieces of equipment are connected either with glass tubes or with standard-taper ground-glass joints.

Connection with glass tubes: If standard-taper joints are not available, rubber stoppers and glass tubes have to be used for connecting glass apparatus. The proper size of the rubber stopper is that 1/2 to 2/3 of the stopper can be inserted to the mouth of the glassware. Bore a rubber stopper and insert a glass tube to the stopper through the hole. Apparatus are then assembled by connecting the individual pieces of equipment with glass tubes. Because connection with glass tubes is time consuming and many chemicals are reacted with or absorbed by rubber stoppers, nowadays standard-taper glassware with ground-glass joints is commonly used in organic chemistry labs.

Connection with standard-taper joints: Except for a few glass apparatus such as separatory funnels, most of the glass apparatus feature standard-taper ground-glass joints. The joints are tapered to ensure a snug fit and a tight seal. The sizes of commonly used standard-taper joints are 14 mm, 19 mm, 24 mm, and 29 mm, which represent the diameter of the joint in millimeters at its widest point. A given size of a male standard-taper joint will fit with a female joint of the same size. Joints with different sizes can be connected with a reduction or an expansion standard-taper adapter.

Following matters should be noticed when using standard-taper glassware with ground-glass joints:

(a) The ground-glass joints must be clean. If there is any solid between male and female joints they cannot be tightly fitted. The hard solid may permanently damage the surface of the ground-glass joints.

(b) When using glassware with standard-taper ground-glass joins, especially for vacuum distillation, the joints should be properly lubricated so that they do not freeze and become difficult to separate. Lubrication is accomplished by spreading a thin layer of joint grease around the outside of the upper half of the male joint, mating the two joints, and then rotating them gently together to cover the surfaces of the joints with a thin coating of lubricant. Before decanting the reaction solution from the female joint, completely wipe off the lubricant from the joint with a piece of absorbent cotton moistened with a solvent such as acetone, THF (tetrahydrofuran) and dichloromethane to avoid contamination of products by lubricant.

(c) As soon as you have finished the experiment, disassemble the glassware to lessen the likelihood that the ground-glass joints will stick. After cleaning, standard-taper male and female joints should be placed separately, while a pair of male and female non-standard joints should be placed together with a small piece of paper between them to avoid fixation of the joints.

(d) Saline solutions may come to the joints and make them stuck and basic solutions can corrode the surfaces of ground-glass joints. So, saline and basic solutions cannot be stored in containers with ground-glass joints for a long time. If saline or basic solution is handled using glassware with ground-glass joints, spread a thin layer of grease on the surfaces of the ground-glass joints.

(e) If the pieces of glass do not separate easily, the best way to pull them apart is to grasp the two pieces as close to the joint as possible and try to loosen the joint with a slight twisting motion. Sometimes the pieces of glass will still not separate. In these cases there are a few other tricks that can be tried. These include the following options: Tap the joint gently with the wooden handle of a spatula, and then try pulling the joints apart as described earlier; heat the joints in hot water or boil them in water before attempting to separate the joints; as a last re-sort, heat the joints gently in the yellow portion of the flame of a Bünsen burner. Heat the joints slowly and carefully until the outer joint breaks away from the inner section. Wrap a cloth towel around the hot joints to avoid burning yourself, and pull the joints apart as de-scribed earlier.

(2) Assembly of apparatus

In an organic laboratory, students normally use standard-taper glassware with ground-glass joints of the same size (e. g. 19$^\#$) for a mini-scale experiment. In this case, various apparatus for different purposes can be conveniently assembled with a few pieces of glassware.

To perform most of the experiments in the organic chemistry laboratory, you must set up the appropriate apparatus. The following section will introduce you to the proper techniques for erecting and supporting apparatus. A general rule for assembling the apparatus is "bottom-to-top" and "left-to-right". It is best to begin assembling the apparatus with the reaction or distil-lation flask and to use a single ring stand if the apparatus must be moved. For example, when assembling an equipment for an addition-distillation process (Figure 1.4-10), first fix the flask at a proper height, and then equip the flask with a dropping funnel, fractioning column, still-head, West condenser, distillation adaptor and receiver step by step in their given order. If the experimental technique requires heating or cooling the apparatus, the flask should be assembled about 15~25 cm above the base of the ring stand or bench top and supported by a laboratory jack. In this case, you can quickly lower a heating source or cooling bath when necessary, without moving the apparatus itself.

Adequate supports should be provided for the apparatus to preventing breakage, especially for apparatus equipped with a mechanical stirrer. Figure 1.4-12 shows the stands and various clamps that may be used for setting up apparatus. The apparatus should be clamped to a ring stand or other vertical support rod using a jaw clamp (Figure 1.4-12d). All clamps must have soft pad such as a piece of cork, cloth tape and some rubber, and do not let the metal of the clamps directly contact the glassware. The proper way to tighten a rigid clamp is to place the neck of the flask or other piece of glassware being secured against the stationary side of the clamp into contact with the glassware so that the piece of glassware fits snugly in the clamp. To avoid breaking the glassware, do not overtighten the clamp. Other clamps should be posi-tioned to support the remainder of the apparatus and should be loosely tightened to avoid strai-ning the glassware and risking breakage. Alternatively, for small glassware such as distillation adaptor, plastic Keck clips (Figure 1.4-12e) or rubber bands may be used in place of additional rigid clamps. The receiver should be supported by a laboratory jack. The glassware with ground-glass joints of 14$^\#$ is usually used for micro-scale experiment and should be fixed by rig-id three-finger clamps. A well-assembled apparatus should be stable, safe and without any strains; the central column is vertical to the bench top and all pieces of glassware are located in the same plane.

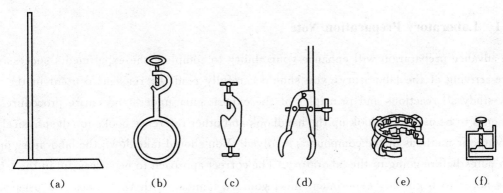

Figure 1.4-12   Commonly used standers and clamps
(a) Support stand   (b) Metal ring   (c) Clamp holder
(d) Jaw clamp   (e) Keck clamp   (f) Screw clamp

An apparatus used under ordinary pressure must have an opening to the atmosphere to avoid development of a dangerous high pressure within the reaction of distillation system when it is heated.

(3) Disassembly of apparatus

As soon as the experiment has been completed, disassemble the pieces of glass one by one according to the rule of "right-to-left, up-to-down". The apparatus must be supported with the hand when its holding clamp is loosened, especially for the slantingly installed apparatus. Do not let joins bear any force from apparatus; otherwise, the glassware is easily broken. For an apparatus used for vacuum distillation, first vent the equipment and then disassemble it. Wash all glassware thoroughly and immediately after use, and place the dry glassware into your laboratory kit in good order.

1.5   Preparation and Notebook for the Laboratory

You will undoubtedly be required to maintain a laboratory notebook. Use a bound notebook with printed page numbers for your permanent laboratory record to minimize the possibility that pages will be lost. If a number has not been printed on each page, do so manually. Do not use a loose-leaf notebook or a piece of paper for laboratory record.

You should take down the laboratory preparation notes, experimental record as well as results and some discussions in the laboratory notebook. The content of experimental record must be accurate and complete, and the writing must be neatly and legibly. The habit of keeping a complete and understandable record of the experimental work that has been done is one of the most important characteristics of successful scientists. After finishing the experiment, turn over your laboratory notebook and product (for a preparative experiment) to your instructor.

Introduction

1.5.1　Laboratory Preparation Note

An advance preparation will enhance your ability to complete the experiments successfully. Before arriving at the laboratory, you should carefully read the relevant content in the textbook, study all reactions and principles of the experiment, understand entire procedures and techniques to be used, and look up the handbook and other reference books for the physical data and synthetic methods of the compounds involved. You should take down the laboratory preparation notes before going to the laboratory. The correct approach to be successful in the laboratory is never to begin any experiment until you are familiar with the names and uses of the glassware and equipment, know the working principle and operating method of the instrument, and understand the overall purpose of the experiment as well as the reasons for each operation that you are going to do. Inadequate preparation for the laboratory may lead to inefficiencies, accidents, and minimal educational benefit and enjoyment from the laboratory experience.

In general, the laboratory preparation notes should include the following contents:

(1) The title of the experiment;

(2) The general statement of the experimental purpose and process to be done;

(3) The balanced chemical equations of the main reaction and the major side-reaction(s);

(4) The physical data of the reagents, products and possible by-products;

(5) The amount of the reagents to be adopted in grams, milliliters or moles, the excessive percentage of the reagent and the theoretical yield;

(6) The chemical or biological hazards of the reagents and the required precautions for reagents and operations;

(7) A correct and clear diagram of the equipment and apparatus;

(8) A flow chart for entire experimental procedures.

1.5.2　Experimental Record

As the main criterion for what should be noted in the experimental record, adopt the rule that the note should be sufficiently complete so that anyone who reads it will know exactly what you have done and can repeat the work in precisely the same way as it was done originally. The experimental record is an original and permanent document of your accomplishments in the course, and you should pay great attention to its quality and completeness. The following list is representative of a good notebook.

(1) Reserve the first page of the notebook for use as a title page, and leave several additional pages blank for a Table of Contents.

(2) Do not use a pencil for experimental record, and do not tear any page from the laboratory notebook, and do not delete anything you have written in the notebook. It you made a mistake, cross it out and record the correct information. Using erasers or correction fluid or tapes to modify entries in the laboratory notebook is unacceptable scientific practice.

(3) Jot down the date and the time when you did the work, and also the whether of that day. Record all experimental observations such as the precipitation and the color change during the entire course of the reaction, the exact temperature at which the reaction was performed, the starting and ending time of the reaction, etc. It is important to record the observations directly in the notebook while the experiment is performing. Do not record the observations after experiment relying on your memory. You may have forgotten a key observation that is critical to the success of the experiment.

Do not just transcribe the experimental procedures provided in your textbook or elsewhere. The record should realistically and accurately reflect the authentic situation of your own experiment. When the phenomena observed are different from that predicted, or the manipulations you did differ from those written in the textbook, clearly and completely take down the realistic observations and operations.

(4) The other matters, such as explanations for experimental phenomena, weight data, and other things that should be remembered, can be written down in the remarks column.

(5) Start the description of each experiment on a new page titled with the name of the experiment.

1.5.3 Sample Calculation for Notebook Records

In most preparative experiments, the added molar amounts of reactants are usually different from the exact molar ratio required by the balanced equation. One or two of the reactants may be used in excess. Which reactant should be used in excess depends on: ① the price of the reactant; ② whether the excessive reactant can be removed or recovered easily after reaction; ③ whether the excessive reactant can cause a side-reaction.

When calculating the yield, first determine which of the reactants corresponds to the limiting reagent. This is the reagent that is used in the least molar amount relative to what is required theoretically. In other words, the reaction will stop once this reactant is consumed. So its molar quantity will define the maximum quantity of product that can be produced, called the theoretical yield. The actual yield of the product is generally lower than the theoretical yield because of incompletion of the reaction, the side-reaction and the loss of the product during work-up. Once the isolation of the desired product has been completed, the percent yield can be calculated by the following equation. The percent yield is an important criterion to evaluate the overall efficiency of the experimental procedure and the working capability of the doer.

$$\text{Percent yield} = \frac{\text{actual yield (g)}}{\text{theoretical yield (g)}} \times 100\%$$

1.5.4 Laboratory Notebook Formats

| Experiment 2 | The S_N2 Reaction: Preparation of Ethyl Bromide (溴乙烷)

Purposes and main techniques of the experiment:

(1) Summarize the methods for preparation of alkyl halides from alcohols and review the acid-catalyzed nucleophilic substitution of alcohols, e. g. the mechanism of the reaction and the rearrangement of carbocations.

(2) Skillfully master the operation method of a separatory funnel and the technique of simple distillation.

Main reaction:

$$NaBr + H_2SO_4 \longrightarrow NaHSO_4 + HBr$$

sodium sulfuric sodium hydrogen
bromide acid sulfate

$$C_2H_5OH + HBr \underset{\triangle}{\rightleftharpoons} C_2H_5Br + H_2O$$

ethanol hydrobromic ethyl bromide
acid

Possible side-reaction:

$$2C_2H_5OH \xrightarrow[\triangle]{H_2SO_4} C_2H_5OC_2H_5 + H_2O$$

diethyl ether

$$C_2H_5OH \xrightarrow[\triangle]{H_2SO_4} CH_2=CH_2 + H_2O$$

ethene

Physical data of reactants and products:

compound	fw	relative density	mp/℃	bp/℃	solubility/(10^{-2} g/g solvent)
ethanol 乙醇	46.07	0.79	−117.3	78.4	∞ in water
sodium bromide 溴化钠	102.89		755		79.5 (0 ℃) in water
concentrated sulfuric acid 浓硫酸	98.08	1.84	10.4	340 (dec.)	∞ in water
ethyl bromide 溴乙烷	108.97	1.46	−118.6	38.4	1.06 (0 ℃) in water ∞ in ethanol
sodium hydrogen sulfate 硫酸氢钠	120.06				50 (0 ℃) and 100 (100 ℃) in water
diethyl ether 乙醚	74.12	0.71	−116.3	34.6	7.5 (20 ℃) in water ∞ in ethanol
ethene 乙烯	28.05		−169	−103.7	

Preparation and Notebook for the Laboratory

The weight of reactants used and the theoretical yield:

compound	the weight used	mole	excess/%	theoretical yield
EtOH (95%)	8 g (10 mL)	0.165	31	
NaBr (anhydrous)	13 g	0.126	limiting reagent	
H_2SO_4 (98%)	18 mL	0.32	154	
C_2H_5Br				13.7 g

Diagrams of the apparatus:

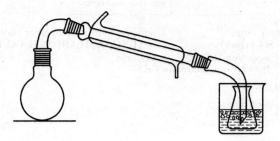

Figure 1.5-1   Reaction apparatus for preparation of ethyl bromide

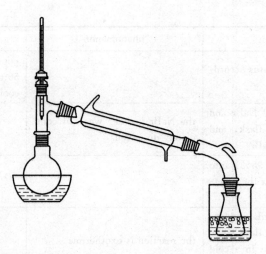

Figure 1.5-2   A shortpath distillation apparatus for distillation of ethyl bromide

A flow chart of entire experimental procedures:

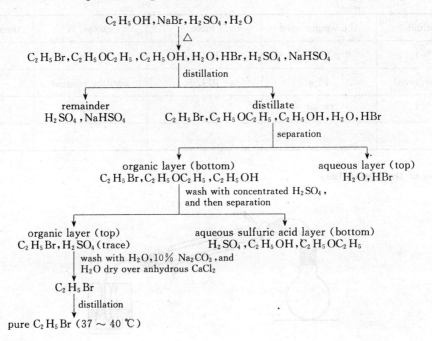

$$C_2H_5OH, NaBr, H_2SO_4, H_2O$$

$\triangle$

$$C_2H_5Br, C_2H_5OC_2H_5, C_2H_5OH, H_2O, HBr, H_2SO_4, NaHSO_4$$

distillation

remainder
$H_2SO_4, NaHSO_4$

distillate
$C_2H_5Br, C_2H_5OC_2H_5, C_2H_5OH, H_2O, HBr$

separation

organic layer (bottom)
$C_2H_5Br, C_2H_5OC_2H_5, C_2H_5OH$

aqueous layer (top)
H_2O, HBr

wash with concentrated H_2SO_4,
and then separation

organic layer (top)
C_2H_5Br, H_2SO_4 (trace)

aqueous sulfuric acid layer (bottom)
$H_2SO_4, C_2H_5OH, C_2H_5OC_2H_5$

wash with $H_2O, 10\%$ Na_2CO_3, and
H_2O dry over anhydrous $CaCl_2$

C_2H_5Br

distillation

pure C_2H_5Br ($37 \sim 40$ ℃)

Experimental record:

Date: March 18, 2009

time	manipulation	phenomenon	note
8:30	set up reaction apparatus according to Figure 1.5−1		pour 20 mL of water into a 50 mL Erlenmeyer flask and cool it with a cold water bath
8:45	add 13 g well-ground NaBr and 9 mL H_2O into the flask, and swirl it to dissolve NaBr	the NaBr powder was not completely dissolved	
8:55	pour 10 mL EtOH (95%) into the flask and well mix the reactants		
9:00	gradually drop 19 mL concentrated H_2SO_4 into the flask while shaking and cooling it in a cold water bath	the reaction is exothermic	
9:10	add 3 pieces of boiling clips and heat the mixture		
9:20		a large amount of foam appeared	
9:25		some distillate appeared in the condenser, and the milky white oil existed in the bottom layer of the aqueous solution	

Preparation and Notebook for the Laboratory

Continued

time	manipulation	phenomenon	note
10:15		all solid disappeared	
10:25	stop heating	no oily droplet appeared in the distillate. the cooled remainder in the flask turned to be colorless crystal	the test showed that crystal was soluble in water. It should be $NaHSO_4$
10:30	separate the oil layer		oil layer 8 mL
10:35	cool the oil layer with an ice-water bath, add 5 mL H_2SO_4, shake the funnel, and allow the layers to separate	the top oil layer turned clear	
10:50	drain the bottom aqueous layer		
11:05	set up a shortpath distillation apparatus according to Figure 1.5-2		
11:10	distill the oil layer with a hot water bath		the net weight of the receiver 53.0 g
11:18	the first drop of the distillate was recovered	38 ℃	the weight of receiver + C_2H_5Br 63.0 g
11:33	no more distillate came out	39.5 ℃	C_2H_5Br 10.0 g

Actual yield of product:

Ethyl bromide, colorless and clear liquid, bp 38~39.5 ℃. Yield: 10 g (Percent yield: 73%).

Discussion:

Self-explanatory.

1.5.5 Experimental Report

After experiment, you will be asked to write an experimental report as soon as possible. It should include the following parts:

(1) **Heading.** Provide information that includes the date and the title of the experiment.

(2) **Introduction.** Give a brief description on the purpose(s) of the experiment and the main technique(s) that you have used in the experiment.

(3) **Theoretical background.** Write chemical equations and give the main reaction(s) for conversion of starting material(s) to product(s) as well as the major side-reaction(s). Whenever possible, include the detailed mechanisms for the reactions that you have written.

(4) **Tables of reactants and products.** Set up Tables of Reagents and Products as an aid in summarizing the amounts and properties of reagents and products. The following items should be included in the Table:

Introduction

(a) The name of each reagent, catalyst and product;

(b) The relative formula weight of each compound;

(c) The weight used, in grams, of each reagent and the volume of any liquid reagent;

(d) The molar amount of each reactant used, the theoretical mole ratio for the reactants, and the theoretical yield of the product;

(e) Physical properties of the reactants and products; this entry may include data such as boiling or melting point, density, solubility, color, odor, etc.

(5) **Experimental.** Provide the types of all instruments used; draw diagram(s) of the apparatus and a flow chart of entire experimental procedures; describe the whole experimental procedures and observations including color change, precipitation, solubility, etc. ; give the weight of the product obtained and calculate the percent yield based on the limiting reagent; and give all data measured for the product such as boiling and melting point, IR, UV-Vis, NMR and MS data.

(6) **Results and discussion.** Discuss the quality and quantity of the product(s) on the basis of the results you have obtained, and analyze the problems existing in your experiment; try to explain the phenomena observed in the experimental process, and give answers to the problems for the experiment that have been assigned from this textbook or by your instructor.

(7) **Conclusions.** Summarize your findings in the experiment and make the conclusions from the experimental results.

(8) **References.** Provide a reference to the place in the laboratory textbook or other source where the procedure can be found.

Chapter 2

Basic Techniques for Organic Experiments

2.1　Working on Glass Tubes

Different shapes of glass tubes, Pasteur pipets as well as capillaries are usually used in organic experiment. Working on glass tubes is one of the fundamental operations in an organic laboratory.

2.1.1　Cutting and Bending Glass Tubes

(1) Cutting glass tubes

Place a clean and dry glass tube on a table or bench. Press the edge of a file (or a small sand wheel) on the proper position of the tube with strength, and make a single straight scratch on the surface of the glass tube by drawing the file and rotating the tube simultaneously on the opposite direction (Figure 2.1−1a). Hold the tube with your thumbs behind and close to the scratch as shown in Figure 2.1−1b. Then push the tube with your fingers to break it at the scratch in the direction of its length. If the scratch is moistened with a bit of water, it would be easier to break the tube with clean and even edges. Be careful with the sharp edges of the cut tube. Pass one end of the tube through the flame a few times. Heat one end of the tube on an oxidizing flame and continuously rotate the tube until the rough edge becomes smooth. Do not heat the edge of the tube on the flame for a long time. Otherwise, the orifice of the tube would shrink. Place the hot tube on an asbestos pad to cool. Do the same for the other end of the tube.

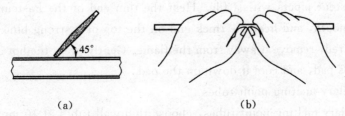

Figure 2.1−1　Cutting glass tubes

(a) Make a straight scratch on the surface of the glass tube

(b) Break a glass tube

Basic Techniques for Organic Experiments

(2) Bending glass tubes

First warm the glass tube by passing it through a weak flame a few times. Hold the tube with both hands; heat the part of the tube to be bended on an oxidizing flame and slowly rotate the tube. When the tube glows orange-red and becomes soft, immediately remove the tube away from the flame and gently bend it to the desired angle (Figure 2.1-2). Do not twist the tube while rotating and bending it. The two ends of the bent tube should remain in the same plane. If you need to bend the glass tube to a small angle, do not bend it in one time. Just repeat the above-described heating and bending procedure for several times. Each time bend the tube by a proper angle to avoid any kinks and constrictions on the bending part of the tube (Figure 2.1-3). Let the tube cool down before re-heating it and slightly shift the heating part of the tube. Ensure that the whole tube is in one plane after it is bended for several times. After bending, heat the tube on a weak flame for 1 or 2 min to anneal it, and then place the hot tube on an asbestos pad. Never put the hot glass directly on the table or a metal plate.

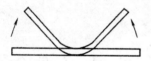

Figure 2.1-2   Bending glass tubes

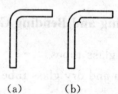

Figure 2.1-3   Bended glass tubes
(a) Well bended   (b) Incorrectly bended

2.1.2   Stretching Glass Tubes

(1) Making Pasteur pipets

Cut a clean and dry glass tube of 6~7 mm diameter to pieces of 200 mm. Heat the central part of the tube on the top of the flame, and in the meantime slowly rotate the tube. When the tube becomes soft, gently push two sides of the tube to make the wall of the central part thicker. Remove the tube away from the flame when it becomes dark red, and slowly stretch the tube to a tubule with rotating it back and forth to ensure that the thick and thin parts of the tube are located in the same axis. Place the tube on an asbestos pad to cool, and then cut the tubule into two Pasteur pipets with a file. Heat the thin end of the Pasteur pipet on a weak flame to make it smooth, and heat the thick end on the top of a strong blue flame. When the glass turns to dark red, remove it away from the flame. Gently press the hot end of the Pasteur pipet on an asbestos pad, and cool it down on the pad.

(2) Making capillary melting point tubes

For making capillary melting point tubes, choose thin-wall tubes of 10 mm diameter. Clean and dry the tube before heating. Heat and draw the tube to the capillary of 1~1.2 mm diameter according to the similar procedure as described for making Pasteur pipets. After cooling, cut the capillary to 100 mm pieces and seal the two ends of the capillary on a weak flame, respectively. Cut the capillary from the middle to obtain two melting point tubes.

(3) Making capillaries used for vacuum distillation

Choose thick-wall tubes to make capillaries used for vacuum distillation. The working procedure is similar to that described above. The noticeable point is that the hot tube should be drawn relatively quickly when removing away from the flame. To make long and thin capillaries, heat and draw the tube for two times. Draw the tube to the tubule of 1.5~2 mm diameter in the first time, and then cut the tubule after cooling. Re-heat the thin end of the tubule on a weak flame, and remove it away from the flame when it turns soft and quickly draw it to the capillary. Put the thin end of the capillary into diethyl ether or acetone, and blow the other end to test whether gas can go through the capillary.

2.2   Weighing, Measuring and Transferring Reagents

2.2.1   Measuring and Transferring Liquids

Knowing how to measure and transfer liquid reagents and products safely and accurately is important in organic labs. The weight of a liquid whose density is known is often most conveniently measured by transferring a known volume of the liquid to the reaction flask using a graduated pipet or a syringe. This is particularly practical when the amount of a liquid to be weighed is less than 200~300 mg.

Graduated cylinders (Figure 2.2-1a) are calibrated containers used to measure the volumes of liquids in the range of 2 mL to 500 mL, depending on the size of the cylinder. The markings on the cylinder shaft represent the approximate volume contained when the bottom of the meniscus of the liquid is at the top of the line. The accuracy of calibration is only about ±10%, so graduated cylinders are not used for delivering precise quantities of liquids.

In general, there are two styles of **graduated pipets** with different sizes. For a graduated "blow-out" pipet (Figure 2.2-1b), the full volume of liquid in the pipet is accurately calibrated only when the liquid remaining in the tip is blown out using a pipet bulb. The graduated pipet shown in Figure 2.2-1c is designed to deliver the full volume of liquid in the pipet without blowing out the liquid remaining in the tip. You should notice the difference of these two styles of pipets and use them properly. You should wash the pipet immediately with cleaning solutions, solvents or distilled water after use.

Plastic or glass **syringes** are often used to deliver liquid into reaction mixtures, especially for measuring and transferring air-sensitive solutions or liquid reagents. Syringes marked with graduations normally have an accuracy of volumetric measurement in the error range of ±5%. The syringes originally designed for use in gas chromatography and having volumes of 500 μL or less are more accurate. The needles on syringes are either fixed (Figure 2.2-1d) or

Basic Techniques for Organic Experiments

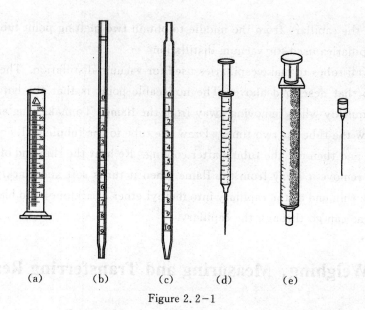

Figure 2.2-1

(a) Graduated cylinders   (b) "Blow-out" pipet

(c) Full volume delivery pipet   (d) Fixed syringe   (e) Demountable syringe

demountable (Figure 2.2-1e). There are different sizes of syringes, such as 10 mL, 5 mL, 2 mL, 1 mL, 0.5 mL, and so on. In general, the sleeve and core of a syringe are matched with each other, and they cannot be exchanged with that of other syringes. You should clean the syringe immediately after use. This is done by pulling some low-boiling solvent into the barrel. With the needle pointed upwards, slowly pull down the core to wash the inside of the sleeve, and then pull the washing solvent into a designated recovering container. The rinsing should be repeated several times.

The **Pasteur pipet** is comprised of a glass barrel, drawn out at one end to form a tip through which liquid is pulled with the aid of a latex suction bulb (Figure 2.2-2a). Pasteur pipets are not used for quantitative measurements of volumes, but they can be used for qualitative measurements. This requires calibration of the pipet. Do this by first weighing a specific amount of water into a test tube or by using a graduated cylinder to measure a given volume of liquid. Carefully draw the liquid into the pipet to be calibrated, and use a file to score the pipet lightly at the level reached by the liquid. Several ca-

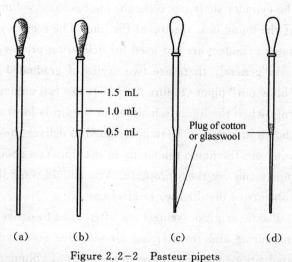

Figure 2.2-2   Pasteur pipets

(a) Pasteur pipet   (b) Graduated Pasteur pipet

(c) Pasteur filter-tip pipet   (d) Filtering pipet

libration marks, maybe at 0.5 mL, 1 mL, and 1.5 mL levels, can be scored on the pipet (Figure 2.2-2b). You can be calibrate several pipets at once since more than one may be needed in a given experimental procedure and they are easily broken.

The **Pasteur filter-tip pipet** (Figure 2.2-2c) and **filtering pipet** (Figure 2.2-2d) are two useful modifications of the Pasteur pipet. The filter-tip pipet is helpful for transferring liquids containing particularly volatile components. The filtering pipet has its plug at the base of the barrel rather than in the tip and is useful for operations such as removing solids from solutions. You may prepare a filter-tip pipet by first inserting a small piece of the packing material in the top of a Pasteur pipet and using a length of heavy-gauge wire or a narrow rod first to push it to the base of the barrel and then into the tip of the pipet. The second step is omitted when making a filtering pipet. Cotton is the preferred material for the plug because it packs more tightly than glasswool, making removal of finely divided solids more effective. However, glasswool is used in certain instances, such as when particularly rapid transfer of a liquid is desired or the particles to be filtered from a liquid are relatively large. Moreover, strongly acidic solutions may react with cotton, so glasswool is preferred in these cases as well.

2.2.2   Weighing Methods

It will be necessary to measure quantities of reagents and reactants for the reactions you will perform. For some liquids and all solids, weights are usually determined using a suitable balance. For quantities greater than 0.5 g, a top-loading balance that reads accurately to the nearest 0.01 g is usually adequate. When performing reactions in the microscale, it is necessary to use a top-loading balance that has a draft shield and reads to the nearest 0.001 g (Figure 2.2-3a) or an analytical balance (Figure 2.2-3b) that reads to the nearest 0.0001 g.

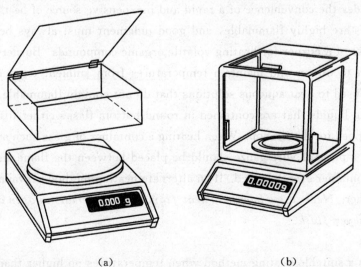

Figure 2.2-3

(a) A top-loading balance with draft shield   (b) An analytical balance with draft shield

Basic Techniques for Organic Experiments

With electronic balances, it is possible to subtract automatically the weight of a piece of paper or other container from the combined weight to give the weight of the sample itself directly. To weigh a liquid, tare a vial and remove it from the balance. Transfer the liquid from the reagent bottle to the vial with a pipet or syringe, and reweigh the vial. Be careful to avoid getting liquid on the outside of the vial or the balance pan. You should never weigh solids directly onto the balance pan. To weigh a solid, place a piece of glazed weighing paper on the balance pan and press the tare button. Using a microspatula, carefully transfer the solid from its original container to the weighing paper until the reading on the balance indicates the desired weight. Do not pour the solid directly from the original bottle because spills are more likely. You may also weigh the solid directly into the reaction vessel by first taring the flask or vial. After weighing, clean any spills promptly.

2.3　Heating, Cooling and Stirring Methods

2.3.1　Heating Methods and Precautions

Three general rules regarding heating should be noted. First, whatever device is used to heat a liquid or solid, to prevent accidents, you must arrange the apparatus so that the heating source can be rapidly removed from the apparatus if necessary. Second, the safest way to heat organic solvents is with a flameless heat source and in a hood. Third, do not heat a closed system unless an apparatus designed to withstand the pressure is used.

(1) Burner

A Burner provides the convenience of a rapid and inexpensive source of heat. However, many organic substances are highly flammable, and good judgment must always be exercised when considering the use of a burner for heating volatile organic compounds. Burners may be used to heat a water bath to obtain and maintain temperatures from ambient temperature to 90 ℃. They can also be used to heat aqueous solutions that do not contain flammable substances or to heat higher-boiling liquids that are contained in round-bottom flasks either fitted with a reflux condenser or equipped for distillation. When heating a container of glass such as flask and beaker with a burner, a piece of wire gauze should be placed between the flame and the glass container to let the container evenly heated. If an alternate heating method is available, choose it in preference to burner. *Never use a burner to heat flammable materials in open container such as beakers or Erlenmeyer flask.*

(2) Water bath

A water bath is a suitable heating method when temperatures no higher than a 90 ℃ are desired. The water contained in a wide-mouthed vessel can be heated either with an electrical hot plate or a Bunsen burner. It is helpful to cover the open portions of the bath with aluminum foil to minimize the loss of water through evaporation.

(3) Oil bath

Oil baths are commonly employed in the laboratory when reactions should be carried out at the range of 100 ℃ to 250 ℃. The advantages of heating baths are that a given bath temperature can be obtained by inserting a thermometer in the oil and accurately maintained by careful adjustment of the variable transformer. Although heat is transferred uniformly to the surface of the flask in the bath, there will be a temperature gradient of about 20 ℃ between the bath and the contents of the flask.

The maximum temperature that may be safely attained in an oil bath is limited by the type of heating liquid being used. Silicon oil is more expensive but is generally preferable to mineral oil because they can be heated to 200 ℃ to 270 ℃ without reaching their flash point. Mineral oil should not be heated to the temperature higher than 200 ℃ because it will begin to smoke and there is the potential danger of flash ignition of the vapors. Whiteruss should not be heated to the temperature higher than 220 ℃. After heating, lift the flask above the oil bath and let the oil drop down from the outer surface of the flask, and then wipe the flask with a piece of paper or with cloth.

The oil baths are commonly heated either by placing the bath container on a hot plate or by inserting a coil of resistance wire in the bath. Be careful when heating an oil bath. When the oil bath is heavily smoke, stop heating immediately. In the case of fire, stop heating, remove all flammable materials in the near area, and cover the oil bath with an asbestos cloth or slate.

(4) Heating mantle

Most heating mantles have a hemispherical cavity with different sizes. It is safe and convenient to heat a flask with the same size heating mantle. Electrical resistance coils are embedded in the fiberglass or ceramic core, therefore when using a heating mantle it is important not to spill any liquid on it. The mantle is normally equipped with a thermocouple so that its internal temperature can be monitored. A variable transformer connected to an electrical outlet provides the power for heating the mantle. The cord from the mantle itself must always be plugged into a transformer, never directly into a wall outlet! Do not overheat the mantle and do not heat an empty flask with a heating mantle. If the flask becomes dry or nearly so during a distillation, the mantle can become sufficiently hot to melt the resistance wire inside, causing the mantle to "burn out". Moreover, most mantles are marked with a maximum voltage to be supplied, and this should not be exceeded. A heating mantle can be used in conjunction with magnetic stirring, so that simultaneous heating and stirring of a reaction mixture is possible.

(5) Sand bath

Sand baths are convenient devices for heating small volumes of material in small flasks in a wide range of temperature up to 350 ℃. Sand is commonly contained in a dish of aluminum or stainless steel. The temperature can be monitored with a thermometer inserted into the sand bath with its bulb close to the flask or vial being heated. Because sand is not a good conductor of heat, there is an apparent temperature gradient in the bath. This gradient can be exploited: The flask or vial can be first deeply immersed in the sand bath for rapid heating, and once the mixture has begun to boil, the flask or vial can be raised to slow the rate of reflux or boiling.

2.3.2 Cooling Methods and Coolants

The most convenient cooling method is to immersing a flask or vial containing a reaction mixture in a cold water bath. If a reaction must be carried out at or below 0 ℃, ice-water can be used as cooling medium. Liquid water is a more efficient heat transfer medium than ice, because it covers the entire surface area of the flask with which it is in contact. Therefore, when preparing this type of bath, do not use ice alone. An ice-water bath has an equilibrium temperature of 0 ℃. For lower temperatures, an ice-salt bath can be prepared by mixing ice and sodium chloride or other salts in a certain ratio (Table 2.3-1). If the reaction is not affected by water, crushed ice can be directly added to the flask to effectively keep the reaction mixture at low temperature.

Table 2.3-1   Commonly used ice-salt baths and their corresponding temperatures

salt	the mass ratio of salt to ice	the lowest temperature of the medium/℃
NH_4Cl	25:100	-15
$NaNO_3$	50:100	-18
$NaCl$	33:100	-21
$CaCl_2 \cdot 6H_2O$	100:100	-29
$CaCl_2 \cdot 6H_2O$	143:100	-55

In organic labs, the most commonly used cooling medium is the mixture of crushed ice and sodium chloride, which can maintain temperature in the range of -5 ℃ to -20 ℃. Still lower temperatures are possible using combinations of organic liquids (ethanol, diethyl ether or acetone) and either dry ice (solid carbon dioxide) or liquid nitrogen.

2.3.3 Stirring Methods and Equipment

Heterogeneous reaction mixtures must be stirred to distribute the reactants uniformly and facilitate the chemical reactions. Stirring is most effectively achieved using mechanical or magnetic stirring devices, but sometimes swirling is sufficient.

(1) Swirling

If the reactions are made in a small scale, at an ambient or low temperature, and within a short time, the simplest means of mixing the contents of a flask is swirling. When a reaction mixture must be swirled, carefully loosen the clamps that support the flask and attached apparatus, and periodically swirl the contents with a circular motion during the course of the reaction. After each time swirling, re-clamp the flask and attached apparatus. If the entire apparatus is supported by clamps attached to a single ring stand, the clamps attached to the flask do not have to be loosened. Just make sure all the clamps are tight, pick up the ring stand, and gently move the entire assembly in a circular motion to swirl the contents of the flask.

(2) Magnetic stirring

A very convenient mode for mixing contents of a flask is magnetic stirring. The equipment consists of a magnetic stirrer and a stirbar. In the case of introducing a stirbar into a flask, you should not simply drop the stirbar in because it may crack or break the flask. Rather, tilt the flask and let the stirbar gently slide down the side. A flask containing a stirbar should be centered on the magnetic stirrer so that the stirbar rotates smoothly and does not wobble. The stirring rate is adjusted using the dial on the stirring motor, and excessive speed should be avoided because it often causes the stirbar to wobble.

(3) Mechanical stirring

Thick mixture and large volumes of fluids are most efficiently mixed using a mechanical stirrer. Figures 2.3-1a~c depict three types of set-ups for mechanical stirring. A variable-speed, explosion-proof, electric motor drives a stirring shaft and paddle that extend into the flask. The stirrer shaft is usually constructed of glass or Teflon with different shape paddles (Figure 2.3-2). The flask can be sealed either simply by a rubber tubing (Figures 2.3-1a and b) or by a liquid seal bearing, which has a cup filled with a few drops of silicon or mineral oil to lubricate the shaft and to provide an effective seal (Figure 2.3-1c). The shaft and the bearing must be exactly adapted. First fix the motor tightly, and then connect the stirrer shaft, which is already fitted with a bearing, to the motor with short heavy-walled rubber tubing. Subsequently, insert the shaft into the flask and leave 5 mm between the paddle and the bottom of the flask, and clamp the flask. The motor and shaft must be carefully aligned to avoid wearing on the glass surfaces of the shaft and bearing and to minimize vibration of the apparatus. Finally,

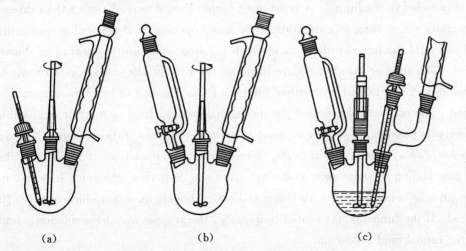

(a)   (b)   (c)

Figure 2.3-1   Mechanical stirring apparatus

Basic Techniques for Organic Experiments

equip a condenser, a dropping funnel or a
thermometer to the flask, and clamp the
condenser and the dropping funnel. The
whole apparatus should be fixed on the same
stand. After setup of the apparatus, manually rotate the shaft to see whether it can move
freely. At first, start the motor at a low
speed. If there is no friction between the
shaft and bearing, adjust the rate of stirring
to the desired speed.

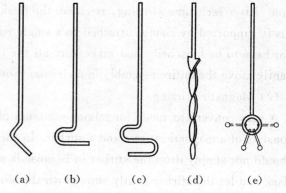

(a)   (b)   (c)   (d)   (e)

Figure 2.3-2   Mechanical stirrer shafts

2.4   Extraction

2.4.1   Liquid-Liquid Extraction

Solvent extraction and liquid washing are common techniques in the organic chemistry laboratory for isolating and purifying the products of a chemical reaction. They are based on the same
principle that substances have different solubility in two immiscible solvents.

Separatory funnels are commonly used for extracting the desired product from one immiscible
liquid phase into another and for "washing" organic layers to remove undesired substances such
as acids or bases from the desired organic compound. Make a leak proofness of the funnel with
water before use it. One of the two layers is usually an aqueous layer and the other is an organic
solvent.

The stopcock should be closed and a clean beaker should be placed under the funnel before
any liquid is added to the funnel. A separatory funnel should never be more than three-quarters
full, especially when doing an extraction. The upper opening of the funnel is then tightly stop-
pered. Then hold the funnel in both hands with the stopcock pointing upward as shown in Figure 2.4-1. The stopper should be placed against the base of the index finger of one hand and
the funnel should be grasped with other fingers of this hand, and hold the stopcock with the
other hand. The contents of a funnel should be shaken or swirled to mix the immiscible liquids
as intimately as possible. *The funnel must be vented from the stopcock every few seconds to
avoid the buildup of pressure within the funnel.* Venting is particularly important when using
volatile, low-boiling solvents such as diethyl ether and methylene chloride. It is also necessary
whenever an acid is neutralized with either sodium carbonate or sodium bicarbonate, since CO_2
is produced. If the funnel is not vented frequently, the stopper may be accidentally blown out,
or even the funnel might blow up.

At the end of shaking, the funnel is vented a final time, and then supported on an iron ring

Extraction

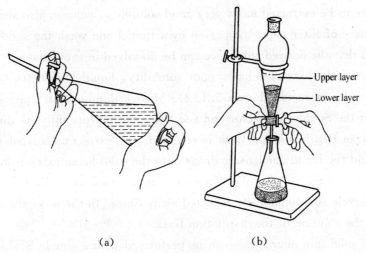

(a)   (b)

Figure 2.4-1   Operation of a separatory funnel

to allow the layers to separate. The iron ring should be covered with a length of rubber tubing or asbestos cord to prevent breakage. Sometimes an emulsion is formed after vigorously shaking. If you know that an emulsion might form, you should avoid shaking the funnel too vigorously; instead, swirl it gently to mix the layers. An emulsion has to be left unattended for an extended period of time to separate, or you can add a certain amount of a saturated solution of aqueous sodium chloride, commonly called brine, to the funnel and re-shake the contents gently. This increases the ionic strength of the water layer, which helps force the organic material into the organic layer.

When the layers are well separated with a clear demarcation line, remove the stopper and carefully drain the lower layer into a proper container through the stopcock, while the upper layer should be decant into another container. Both layers should always be saved until there is no doubt about the identity of each and the desired product has been isolated.

It will give a better effectiveness to use a certain amount of solvent for several times of extractions than to use all of it at one time.

Microscale liquid-liquid extraction can be made in a small tube. Bulb gas into the liquid of the tube with a Pasteur pipet to let the immiscible liquids well mixed. Allow the tube stand for a while to separate, and isolate the two layers with Pasteur pipet. Repeating these operations can attain the purpose of extraction.

2.4.2   Liquid-Solid Extraction

The simplest method for isolating a desired substance from a solid mixture is the liquid-solid extraction. Put the ground solid mixture to a container, add a certain amount of a proper solvent, vigorously swirl or stir the suspension, and then filter or decant the extract to remove the remaining solid.

Basic Techniques for Organic Experiments

If the substance to be extracted has a very good solubility, you can also simply put the solid mixture onto a piece of filter paper supported by a funnel and wash the solid with solvent for several times, so that the desired substance can be dissolved in the filtrate.

If the substance to be extracted has a poor solubility, liquid-solid extraction is better performed with a Soxhlet extractor (Figure 2.4-2). Make a thimble with a piece of filter paper in a size suitable for the Soxhlet extractor and add the solid mixture into the thimble. When the extraction solvent in the distillation flask is refluxed, the extraction-solvent vapor goes up to the condenser, and the liquid condensate drops onto the solid being extracted. When the liquid level reaches the top of the siphon tube, the extract is returned to the flask as a result of siphoning action. The cycle is automatically repeated many times. In the way, the desired substance is extracted into the solution of the distillation flask.

Extraction of a solid in a micro-scale can be performed with a simple Soxhlet extractor or a micro-scale apparatus for distillation (Figure 2.4-3). Put the solid into the Hickman stillhead and add solvent to the stillhead and to the distillation flask. When the extraction solvent in the distillation flask is refluxed, the extraction-solvent vapor is condensed into the stillhead, and then the extract overflows back to the distillation flask. The desired substance is then concentrated in the flask.

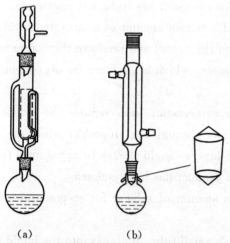

(a)　　　　　　　　(b)

Figure 2.4-2　A Soxhlet extractor

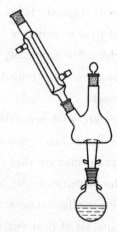

Figure 2.4-3　Microscale liquid-solid
extraction apparatus

2.5　Drying and Drying Agents

2.5.1　Drying Organic Liquids

Drying reagents, solvents or products will be encountered at some stage of nearly every reaction performed in the organic chemistry laboratory. In order to dry the organic liquid, drying agents, sometimes called desiccants, are used.

(1) Types of drying agents

Some commonly used drying agents are listed in Table 2.5-1. They can be divided into three types: ① Drying agents interact reversibly with water by simple adsorption, such as molecular sieves, silicon gel, etc.; ② Drying agents combine with water reversibly by formation of hydrates, such as calcium chloride, magnesium sulfate, sodium sulfate, etc.; ③ Drying agents react irreversibly with water by serving as acids or bases, such as phosphorus pentoxide, calcium oxide, etc.

Table 2.5-1   Commonly used drying agents

organic compound	drying agents
hydrocarbon 碳氢化合物	$CaCl_2$, Na, molecular sieves
halohydrocarbon 卤代烷烃	$CaCl_2$, $MgSO_4$, Na_2SO_4
alcohol 醇	K_2CO_3, $MgSO_4$, Na_2SO_4, CaO
ether 醚	$MgSO_4$, Na_2SO_4, Na
aldehyde 醛	$MgSO_4$, Na_2SO_4
ketone 酮	K_2CO_3, $CaCl_2$
ester 酯	$MgSO_4$, Na_2SO_4, K_2CO_3
nitro compound 硝基化合物	$CaCl_2$, $MgSO_4$, Na_2SO_4
organic acid and phenol 有机酸和酚	$MgSO_4$, Na_2SO_4
amine 胺	NaOH, KOH, K_2CO_3

(2) Selection of drying agents

When you choose a drying agent, you should first consider the chemical properties of the drying agent and the organic substance to be dried. There are two general requirements for a drying agent: ① neither it nor its hydrolysis product may react chemically with the organic liquid being dried, and ② it should not be dissolved in the organic liquid and can be completely and easily removed from the dry liquid. In addition, the capacity, drying speed and efficiency of a drying agent as well as the cost of a drying agent should be considered. Several mostly used drying agents are introduced in the following part.

Anhydrous calcium chloride is a widely used drying agent in the organic laboratory. It is a neutral agent and has a high capacity and a somewhat slow action of water uptake with reasonable efficiency. It is one of the cheapest drying agents. Hydrate $CaCl_2 \cdot 6H_2O$ is formed at the temperature below 30 ℃. Because drying agent $CaCl_2$ normally contains a small amount of $Ca(OH)_2$, it cannot be used to dry acids and other acidic compounds. In addition, it cannot be used to dry alcohols, amines, phenols, amides and esters because calcium chloride can form complexes with these organic compounds.

Anhydrous magnesium sulfate is a neutral agent. It is an inexpensive and excellent preliminary drying agent. It has a good capacity and a rapid action of water uptake with moderate efficiency. Anhydrous magnesium sulfate can be used to dry functional organic compounds such as alcohols, aldehydes, esters, acids and phenol, which cannot be dried by calcium chloride.

Anhydrous sodium sulfate is also a neutral agent. It is an inexpensive and a widely used preliminary drying agent. It has a high capacity but relatively slow action of water uptake with low efficiency. Anhydrous sodium sulfate is often used to dry organic liquid containing a considerable amount of water, and the preliminarily dried liquid are usually dried further with other drying agent of high efficiency. Hydrate $Na_2SO_4 \cdot 10H_2O$ is formed at the temperature below 32.4 ℃. If the temperature is higher than 32.4 ℃, $Na_2SO_4 \cdot 10H_2O$ is decomposed to lose water. Therefore anhydrous sodium sulfate cannot be used as drying agent at the temperature higher than 32.4 ℃.

Potassium carbonate has a low capacity of water uptake. Hydrate $K_2CO_3 \cdot 2H_2O$ is formed during drying process. It can be used to dry nitriles, ketones, esters, etc., but cannot be used to dry acids, phenols and other acidic compounds.

Sodium hydroxide and potassium hydroxide are effective drying agents for amines. Because sodium hydroxide and potassium hydroxide readily react with many organic compounds, such as acids, phenol, esters, and amides, etc., and can be dissolved in some liquid organic compounds, their uses as drying agents are limited.

Calcium oxide has a high efficiency but slow action for water uptake. It is commonly used to dry alcohols, and the dried solution can be distilled from this drying agent if desired. As calcium oxide is a basic agent, it cannot be used to dry acidic compounds and esters.

Sodium metal is used to dry ethers, alkanes and arenes, and cannot be used to dry compounds sensitive to alkali metals or bases. Preliminary drying with other drying agents to remove most of water from the liquid is required before using sodium metal to dry the liquid. Sodium metal should be cut into thin pieces or pressed to thread by a sodium press to increase the contact surface of the sodium drying agent with the liquid. *Caution: Care must be exercised in destroying excess sodium metal and hydrogen gas is evolved with this drying agent.*

Molecular sieves (4A and 5A, these numbers refer to the nominal pore size, in Angström units, of the sieve) are rapid and highly efficient for water uptake. It can be used to neutral organic compounds and the dried solution can be distilled from this drying agent if desired. Hydratedsieves can be reactivated by heating at 300~320 ℃ under vacuum or at 400~450 ℃ at atmospheric pressure.

(3) Operations

Place the organic liquid to be dried in an Erlenmeyer flask of suitable size so that it will be no more than half-filled with liquid. Then add a small spatula-tip full of drying agent to the solution or organic liquid and swirl the flask gently for a few minutes. If the drying agent 'clumps' or if liquid still appears cloudy after the drying agent has settled to the bottom of the flask, add more drying agent and swirl again. Repeat this process until the liquid appears clear and some of the drying agent flows freely upon swirling the mixture. If there is a considerable amount of water in the liquid and an insufficient amount of drying agent is added, the drying agent might be dissolved in the absorbed water. In this case, remove the water phase and re-add the drying agent. Do not use an unnecessarily large quantity of drying agent when drying a liquid, since the desiccant may absorb the desired organic product along with water. The granules of drying agent should be in a proper size. Large granules of drying agent reduce the contact surface and apparently slow down the water uptake action, while a drying agent powder may form slurry during the drying process, which is difficult to separate. After drying is complete, remove the drying agent either by gravity filtration or by decantation. If necessary, rinse the drying agent once or twice with a small volume of the dried organic solvent and transfer the rinse solvent to the organic solution.

2.5.2　Drying Solids

(1) Air dry

The most convenient and economical way to dry a solid is to allow it air-dry at room temperature, provided it is not hygroscopic. Spread the solid on a piece of filter paper or on a clean watchglass and allow it to stand overnight or longer.

(2) Oven dry

If a sample is hygroscopic or if it has been isolated from water or a high-boiling solvent, it must be dried in an oven operating at a temperature below the melting or decomposition point of the sample. Place the solid on a watchglass or an evaporating dish, and gently heat it with a hot-water-bath, under an infrared lamp or in an oven.

(3) Vacuum dry

Easily decomposed or sublimed solid should be dried in a desiccator or a vacuum desiccator. Air-sensitive solids must be dried either in an inert atmosphere, such as in nitrogen or helium or under reduced pressure.

2.6　Gas Traps

In organic laboratories, sometimes irritant and toxic gases, such as chlorine, hydrochloride, hydrobromide, sulfur trioxide and phosgene, etc., have to be used as reactants and some organic reactions release noxious gases as side-products. The gases should not escape into the laboratory atmosphere. The most convenient and effective method is to absorb them with a gas trap containing an absorber.

(1) Absorbers

Noxious gases can be absorbed either by physical method to dissolve the gas in an absorber, or by chemical method to let the gas react with an absorber. For the physical method, the ab-

Basic Techniques for Organic Experiments

sorber used depends on the solubility of the gas to be trapped. Organic solvents are used for absorbing organic gases and water is often used for absorbing inorganic gases. For the chemical method, the absorber used depends on the chemical property of the gas to be trapped. Acidic gases such as hydrochloride, sulfur dioxide and thiols, etc. , are effectively absorbed by aqueous basic solutions of sodium hydroxide and sodium carbonate, and so on, while aqueous hydrochloride solution can be used to absorb basic gases such as ammonia and amine.

(2) Apparatus

Gas trap apparatus are shown in Figure 2. 6−1. A stemmed funnel is placed upside down with its rim just above or resting on the surface of the water or other absorber. Don't immerse the whole rim of the funnel in the water to avoid backflow of the absorber to the flask.

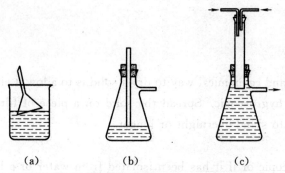

(a)　　　　　　(b)　　　　　　(c)

Figure 2. 6−1　Gas trap apparatus

2. 7　Separating and Purifying Liquid Compounds

2.7.1　Simple Distillation

(1) Principle

Simple distillation is a useful method for isolating a pure liquid compound from other substances that are not volatile. Organic chemists frequently use this technique to separate a desired product from the solvents used for the reaction or work-up. Simple distillation allows isolation of the various components of the mixture in acceptable purity if the difference between the boiling points of each pure substance is greater than 40 ℃.

A pure organic compound boils at a constant temperature under a certain pressure, while most mixtures of liquids boil over a fairly wide range. Therefore, simple distillation can be used as one convenient means to approximately determine the boiling point and purity of the compound being distilled. Some organic compounds can form binary or ternary azeotropes with other substances. An azeotrope also has a fixed boiling point, called azeotropic point. According-

Separating and Purifying Liquid Compounds

ly, we cannot say that liquids that can give constant boiling points during distillation are all pure compounds, sometimes they are azeotrope mixtures.

(2) Simple distillation apparatus

Typical examples of laboratory apparatus for performing simple mini-scale distillations are shown in Figure 2.7—1a. The apparatus is mainly comprised of a stillpot, also called the distillation flask, a water-or air-cooled condenser and a receiver. The size of the stillpot depends on the volume of the liquid to be distilled. The stillpot should be filled with liquid in 1/3 to 1/2 of its total volume. If the stillpot is over charged with liquid, the hot solution may burst from the stillpot when the liquid mixture is heated to boil, or the small drops of hot liquid are carried by the vapor to the receiver. And if too less liquid is added to the stillpot, a considerable amount of liquid will remain in the stillpot when distillation is complete.

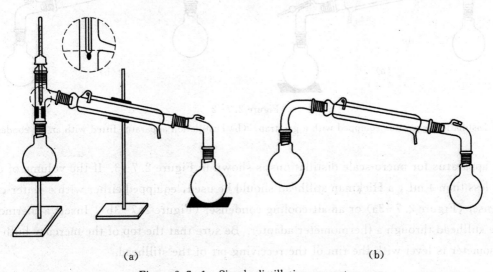

Figure 2.7—1   Simple distillation apparatus
(a) with a thermometer   (b) without a thermometer

Start assembling the apparatus according to the "bottom-to-top" and "left-to-right" principle. First, place a stirbar or 2~3 pieces of boiling chips alone with the liquid to be distilled to the stillpot, and clamp it on an iron stand. The stillpot should be 15 cm or so above the bench to allow placement of a suitable heat source. Equip the stillhead on the stillpot. Align and fit the sidearm outlet of the stillhead with the condenser, which is clamped on the other iron stand. Put the vacuum adapter at the end of the condenser, and then install a receiver. Finally, fit a thermometer to the stillhead through a thermometer adapter. Be sure that the top of the mercury bulb of the thermometer is level with the bottom of the sidearm of the stillhead. All joints must fit exactly so that flammable vapors do not leak from the apparatus into the laboratory.

For removal of volatile solvent(s) from a product, just connect the stillpot and the condenser with an adaptor of a 75° bent-angle as shown in Figure 2.7—1b.

Basic Techniques for Organic Experiments

A drying tube containing calcium chloride should be equipped to the distillation adaptor if the liquid being distilled is sensitive to moisture. When some flammable or poisonous gas is released during distillation, a gas trap should be connected to the distillation adaptor (Figure 2.7-2a).

When the boiling point of the compound to be distilled is higher than 140 ℃, an air-cooling condenser should be used (Figure 2.7-2b).

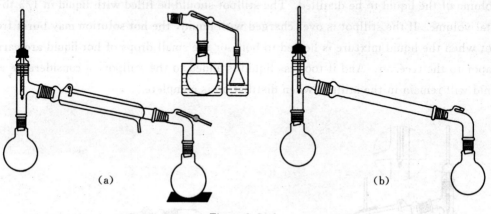

(a)   (b)

Figure 2.7-2

(a) Distillation apparatus equipped with a gas trap   (b) Distillation apparatus fitted with an air condenser

An apparatus for micro-scale distillations is shown in Figure 2.7-3. If the volume of distillate is less than 4 mL, a Hickman stillhead should be used, equipped either with a water-cooling condenser (Figure 2.7-3a) or an air-cooling condenser (Figure 2.7-3b). Insert a thermometer to the stillhead through a thermometer adapter. Be sure that the top of the mercury bulb of the thermometer is level with the rim of the receiving pit of the stillhead.

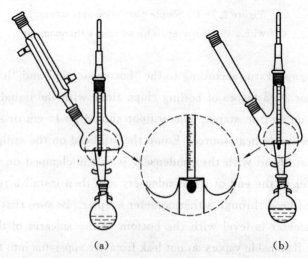

(a)   (b)

Figure 2.7-3   Microscale distillation apparatus

(a) with an air-cooling condenser   (b) with a water-cooling condenser

Separating and Purifying Liquid Compounds

(3) Simple distillation procedure

The heating device should be chosen according to the boiling point, viscosity, and flammability of the liquid to be distilled. When distilling a substance of low boiling point such as diethyl ether, it is strictly forbidden to use a flame as a heating source. There should be no flame in the near area.

If a water-cooling condenser is used, connect the "water-in" and "water-out" hoses to the condenser. Note that the "water-in" hose is always attached to the lower point, and the "water-out" hose is always connected to the upper point. Adjust the water flow through the condenser to a modest flow rate.

After make sure that a stirbar or boiling chips have been put into the stillpot and all connections in the apparatus are tight, begin heating the stillpot. As soon as the liquid begins to boil and the condensing vapors have reached the thermometer bulb, regulate the heat supply so that distillation continues steadily at a rate of 2~4 drops per second. To ensure an accurate temperature reading, a drop of condensate must adhere to the bottom of the mercury bulb. The temperature read on the thermometer is termed as the head temperature and the temperature of the boiling liquid in the stillpot is called the pot temperature. Record the head temperature for the first drop distilled into the receiver. As soon as the distillation rate is adjusted and the head temperature is constant, change for a clean and weighed receiver, and record the head temperature. Change for another receiver if necessary. Record the range of the head temperature and the total weight for each receiver. Discontinue heating when no distillates come out at the desired temperature and the temperature decreased suddenly. Remove the heating source, stop the cooling water, and disassemble the apparatus following the "right-to-left" and "top-to-bottom" principle.

2.7.2 Fractional Distillation

(1) Principle

The technique of fractional distillation is a more effective method than simple distillation for isolating the individual pure liquid components from a mixture containing two or more volatile substances. The difference in boiling points between the two pure components of a mixture should be no less than 20 ℃ for a fractional distillation in order to get a satisfactory purity of the substance. The principal difference between an apparatus for fractional and simple distillation is the presence of a fractional distillation column between the stillpot and stillhead.

During a fractional distillation, the vapor from the stillpot rises up the column and some of it condenses in the column and returns to the stillpot. If the lower part of the column is maintained at a higher temperature than the upper part of the column, the condensate will be partially revaporized as it flows down the column. The uncondensed vapor, together with that produced by revaporization of the condensate in the column, rises higher and higher in the column and undergoes a repeated series of condensations and revaporizations. This repetitive process is

Basic Techniques for Organic Experiments

equivalent to performing several successive simple distillations. Within the column, the vapor phase produced in each step becomes increasingly richer in the more volatile component and the condensate that flows down the column correspondingly becomes richer in the less volatile component, so that the more volatile component is selectively carried to the top of the column and then into the receiver through a condenser, while the higher boiling-point components remain in the stillpot.

(2) Apparatus and working procedure

Two types of commonly used columns are shown in Figure 2.7－4. The Hempel column is normally more efficient, which is packed with some column packings. Common packings include glass tubing sections, glass beads, glass helices or metal helices.

An apparatus for fractional distillation at an atmospheric pressure is shown in Figure 2.7－5. Assemble the apparatus for fractional distillation using the general guidelines for simple distillation apparatus. Start by adding the liquid to be distilled, along with a stirbar or 2～3 pieces of boiling chips, into the stillpot, then clamp the flask in place. Do not fill the stillpot more than half-full. Attach the distillation column and make sure that it is vertical. Install a stillhead, condenser, vacuum adaptor and re-

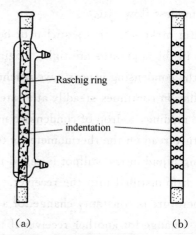

Figure 2.7－4　Mini-scale fraction columns
(a) Hempel column filled with packing material
(b) Vigreux column

ceiver step by step. Finally, fit a thermometer to the stillhead through a thermometer adapter. After carefully check the tightness of all connections in the apparatus, the stirbar or boiling chips in the stillpot and the running water in the condenser, you can begin the distillation. The following points should be noticed while making a fractional distillation:

(a) Choose a proper heating source according to the boilingpoint range of the liquid to be distilled. Do not heat the stillpot on the asbestos pad with a flame. It is better to heat the stillpot with a water or oil bath so that the temperature of the liquid in the stillpot can rise gently and evenly.

(b) As soon as the liquid begins to boil and the vapor rises up the column, regulate the heat supply so that the vapor goes up slowly along the column. If the room temperature is low or the boiling point of the component is relatively high, the outside of the fractional column should be wrapped with asbestos cord, glasswool or other thermal insulation materials for heat preservation.

(c) When the vapor reaches the top of the column, adjust the heating supply so that the distillation continues steadily at a rate of 1～3 drops per second. If the distillation rate is too fast, the purity of the distilled component will decrease; while slow distillation will result in fluctuation of the head temperature.

(d) According to the requirements of the experiment, collect different fractions, and record the temperature range and the weight of each fraction.

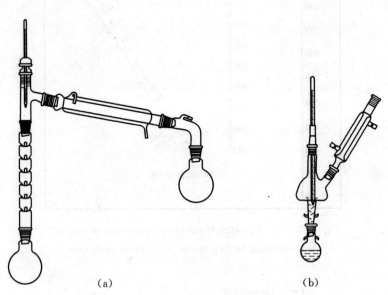

(a)   (b)

Figure 2.7−5   Fractional distillation apparatus

(a) For mini-scale experiment   (b) For micro-scale experiment

2.7.3   Vacuum Distillation

(1) Principle

Many organic compounds that have high boiling points or many functional groups may partially or entirely decompose at temperatures below their atmospheric boiling points. These problems can be circumvented if the distillation is conducted at a pressure less than one atmosphere. The technique involved in such distillation is termed as vacuum distillation. In general, reduction from atmospheric pressure to 2 666 Pa (20 mmHg) lowers the boiling point of a compound that boils at 250~300 ℃ at atmospheric pressure by about 100~120 ℃. As we know the boiling temperature of a compound closely depends on the pressure. We can make estimates of the effect of pressure upon the boiling point of a liquid by using a pressure-temperature alignment nomograph shown in Figure 2.7−6. For example, the boiling point of ethyl salicylate is 234 ℃ at atmospheric pressure. To determine the boiling point of it at 2 666 Pa (20 mmHg), connect the point for 234 ℃ (column B) to the point for 20 mmHg (column C) with a line, and extend this line to column A. The intersection at column A represents the boiling point of ethyl salicylate at 20 mmHg, which is about 118 ℃.

(2) Apparatus for vacuum distillation

The simple apparatus for vacuum distillation is shown in Figure 2.7−7, which is mainly com-

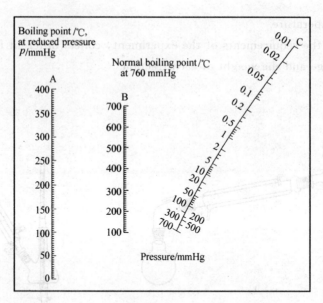

Figure 2.7-6　Pressure-temperature alignment monograph
for estimating boiling points at different pressures

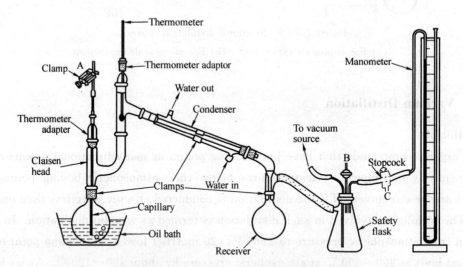

Figure 2.7-7　Vacuum distillation apparatus

prised of a stillpot, a condenser, a receiver, a Claisen head, a manometer, a heavy-walled filter flask as a safety trap and a vacuum source. An oil bath is commonly used for vacuum distillations. The Claisen head has two mouths. The side mouth of the Claisen head is normally fitted with a thermometer through an adaptor. The main mouth is commonly equipped with a capillary bubbler through a thermometer adaptor or a holed rubber stopper. The tip of the bubbler should be 1~2 mm above the bottom of the stillpot. Place a short rubber tube at the top of the bubbler and insert a very thin metal wire (about 1 mm diameter) to the rubber tube. Then clip the rubber tube with a screw clamp. During vacuum distillation, air comes into the stillpot via the capillary bubbler to generate fine bubbles. Adjust the screw clamp, you can control the rate of bubbling and prevent the liquid from bumping. Another option is to add a stirbar or boiling chips to the stillpot to keep a gentle boiling of the liquid in vacuum distillation.

Round-bottom flasks and heavy-walled test tubes with a ground-glass joint are commonly used as receiver for vacuum distillation. Never use glassware with cracks, thin walls or flat bottoms, such as Erlenmeyer flasks, in vacuum distillation, because they may not be able to withstand the vacuum. If more than one fraction is to be collected, a swallowtail-shaped vacuum adaptor should be used (Figure 2.7–8), which can be connected to three flasks. The ground-glass joints of the vacuum adaptor and the condenser must be lubricated with vacuum grease for successively rotating the flasks into the receiving position.

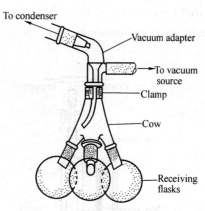

Figure 2.7–8   A swallowtail-shaped vacuum adaptor

The vacuum adaptor is normally linked to a heavy-walled filter flask with a heavy-walled vacuum tubing. This flask serves as a safety trap to prevent back-up of water or oil into the apparatus, which may occur if the vacuum source is suddenly decreased or stopped. The safety trap is covered with a three-holed rubber stopper and each hole has a glass tubing. These glass tubings are connected to a manometer, a stopcock release valve and a vacuum source, respectively. The other end of the glass tubing connected to the vacuum source should be close to the bottom of the safety flask.

Reduced pressures can be obtained by using a water aspirator pump, a cycle water pump or a mechanical vacuum pump. The vacuum produced by a water aspirator or a cycle water pump is limited by the vapor pressure of the water at the working temperature. Pressures as low as 1 066~1 333 Pa (8~10 mmHg) may be obtained from a water aspirator or a cycle water pump with cold water, but pressures in the range of 2 000~2 666 Pa (15~20 mmHg) are more common. A good mechanical pump can evacuate the apparatus to less than 1.3 Pa (0.01 mmHg), which should be used for distillations at pressures lower than 2 666 Pa (20 mmHg). It is important to maintain the mechanical vacuum pump and to change the oil periodically. To protect the pump from the vapors of organic substances, water, and acids, a cooling trap, two absorbing towers and a trap flask should be placed in the given order between the vacuum adaptor of the apparatus and the pump. The cooling trap is placed in a Dewar bottle and cooled with ice-salt or dry ice-alcohol coolants. One of the two absorbing towers is filled with granules of sodium hydroxide and the other with activated carbon or molecular sieves.

The pressure at which the distillation is being conducted in the apparatus is measured by a manometer, which is placed between the vacuum adaptor and the pump. The pressure should

Basic Techniques for Organic Experiments

be recorded together with the boiling point. Two types of U-shaped manometers are commonly used in the organic laboratory (Figure 2.7−9). The manometer may be broken if air suddenly comes into the evacuated manometer and the mercury in it may flow to the laboratory. It is suggested to close the two-way stopcock of the manometer when the pressure in the system is constant. Slowly open the stopcock of the manometer only when you want to read the accurate pressure of the system. Always slowly release the vacuum in the manometer.

If the volume of the liquid to be distilled is in the range of 1∼10 mL, the modified apparatus (Figure 2.7−10) can be used, in which the condenser is omitted to minimize the loss of the desired component. If the substance to be distilled is volatile, the receiver should be cooled with a cold water or ice-water bath.

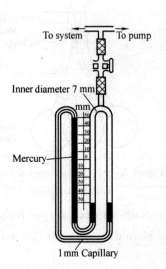

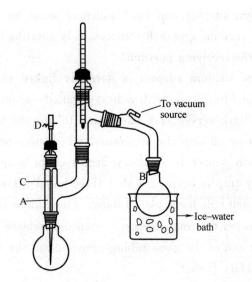

Figure 2.7−9   U-shaped manometers

Figure 2.7−10   Modified apparatus for mini-scale
shortpath vacuum distillation

If a micro-scale liquid is going to be distilled, the apparatus shown in Figure 2.7−11 can be used. In Figure 2.7−11a, a two-neck flask is used as the stillpot. The side arm of the flask is equipped with a capillary bubbler and the main mouth with a Hickman stillhead. The side arm of the Hickman stillhead is equipped with a cooling finger and the main mouth of the stillhead is fitted with a thermometer by a tight rubber tubing. If only solvent is going to be distilled, the thermometer is not required and the apparatus of Figure 2.7−11b with a stirbar in the stillpot can be used for the micro-scale distillation.

(3) Working procedure

Apparatus assembling: The apparatus shown in Figure 2.7−7 is assembled according to the same general guidelines that are for setting up the apparatus for simple distillation. Lubricate all ground-glass joints carefully with vacuum grease during assembly of the apparatus. Heavy-walled vacuum tubing must be used for all vacuum connections.

Air-tight test: After assembling the apparatus, connect the empty system to the vacuum

Separating and Purifying Liquid Compounds

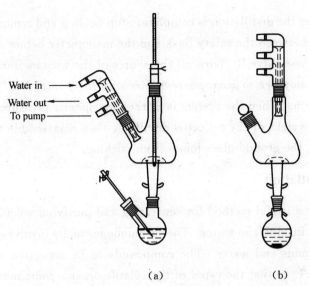

Water in
Water out
To pump

(a)   (b)

Figure 2.7-11   Apparatus for micro-scale vacuum distillation
(a) with a two-neck flask   (b) with a one-neck flask

source by opening the stopcock between the safety flask and the vacuum pump, and then close the stopcock until the pressure of the manometer keeps constant, to make sure that the complete apparatus is air-tight. Slowly vent the system by opening the stopcock of the safety flask.

Liquid addition: Using a funnel with a stem, add the liquid to be distilled to the flask, making certain that the flask is no more than half-filled.

Turning on the vacuum pump: Clip the screw clamp (A in Figure 2.7-7) if a capillary bubbler is used, or begin stirring the liquid. Keep the release valve on the safety flask open when turning on the vacuum, slowly close the release valve while watching the liquid in the flask. Be careful if the liquid contains small quantities of low-boiling solvents, foaming and bumping are likely to occur in the distillation flask. If this occurs, adjust the release valve until the foaming abates. This may have to be done several times until the low-boiling solvent has been removed completely. Reduce the pressure of the system gradually to the desired pressure by adjusting the clamp A and the stopcock B. To make the distillation system reach its maximum attainable vacuum, clip the clamp A tightly and close the stopcock B completely. The corresponding boiling point of the liquid at a special pressure can be found from the pressure-temperature alignment nomograph Figure 2.7-6.

Distillation: Two third of the flask should be immersed in the oil bath, and do not let the bottom of the flask sit on the bottom of the oil bath. Heat the oil bath gently and maintain the temperature of the bath, so that the distillate is collected at a rate of 3 to 4 drops per minutes. Do not begin heating the liquid until the pressure of the system is stable. Record the pressure, the temperatures of the vapor and oil bath and the rate of the distillation, and check these data occasionally. If it is necessary to use multiple receivers to collect fractions of different boiling ranges, a swallowtail-shaped vacuum adaptor should be used (Figure 2.7-8).

Disassembling: After the distillation is complete, stop heating and remove the heating source. Close the stopcock C between the safety flask and the manometer before slowly open the clamp A and the vacuum release valve B. Turn off the source of the vacuum immediately (*Always remember that open the stopcock to atmosphere before stop the pump !*). Then slowly open the stopcock C with caution. When the system is at the atmospheric pressure, remove the receiver (s) and calculate the weight of the collected distillate, then disassemble the apparatus as soon as possible to prevent the ground-glass joints from sticking.

2.7.4 Steam Distillation

Steam distillation is a useful method for separating and purifying volatile organic compounds that are immiscible or insoluble in water. The technique normally involves the codistillation of a mixture of organic liquids and water. The compounds to be separated should have a certain vapor pressure at 100 ℃ so that the vapor of the volatile organic compounds can be distilled out with steam at a temperature lower than 100 ℃.

(1) Principle

The total pressure of a mixture of immiscible, volatile compounds at a given temperature is equal to the sum of the partial pressure p_A of each compound, which is identical to the vapor pressure (p_A^0) of the pure compound at the same temperature and does not depend on the mole fraction of the compound in the mixture. Therefore, the total vapor pressure of the mixture at any temperature is always higher than the vapor pressure of even the most volatile component at that temperature, owing to the contributions of the vapor pressures of the other constituents in the mixture. The boiling point of a mixture of immiscible compounds must then be lower than that of the lowest-boiling component. Accordingly, the water immiscible, volatile compound can be distilled out with the steam below its normal boiling point.

The composition of the distillate from a steam distillation depends upon the molecular weights of the compounds being distilled and upon their respective vapor pressure at the temperature at which the mixture steam-distils. The weight ratio of the organic compound (m_A) distilled to water (m_{H_2O}) can be expressed by the following equation:

$$\frac{m_A}{m_{H_2O}} = \frac{M_A \times p_A}{M_{H_2O} \times p_{H_2O}}$$

Here p_A is the vapor pressure of the pure compound A, p_{H_2O} is the vapor pressure of water, M_A is the relative molecular weight of compound A and M_{H_2O} is the relative molecular weight of water.

For example, when the mixture of aniline (bp 184.4 ℃) and water is distilled, it boils at 98.4 ℃. At this temperature, the total pressure (101 325 Pa) of the mixture is equal to the sum of the vapor pressures of aniline (5 599.5 Pa) and water (95 725.5 Pa). The relative molecular weights of aniline and water are 93 g·mol^{-1} and 18 g·mol^{-1}, respectively, so the weight ratio of aniline and water in the distillate is:

$$\frac{93 \times 5\,599.\,5}{18 \times 95\,725.\,5} = \frac{1}{3.\,3}$$

Because aniline is slightly soluble in water, the calculated value is only an approximate value.

Steam distillation is often of great use for the following cases: a mixture containing large amounts of nonvolatile residues such as inorganic salts and not suitable for common distillation, filtration and extraction; a mixture containing tar-like substances and difficult to be purified by common distillation and extraction; and a high boiling-point and heat-sensitive organic compound which decomposes at its boiling point.

(2) Apparatus and working procedure for steam distillation

The glassware used for steam distillation mainly includes a steam generator, a round-bottom flask, a Claisen adapter, a stillhead, a condenser, a vacuum adapter and a receiver. For large scale distillation, pour the organic compound(s) to be distilled into a stillpot, which should be filled to no more than one-third of its capacity. Equip the flask with a Claisen adapter, a stillhead, a condenser, an adapter and a receiver, as depicted in Figure 2. 7-12. Because the turbulence associated with the boiling action tends to cause occasional violent splashing, the Claisen adapter is necessary to prevent the mixture from splattering into the condenser. A long condenser should be used with a sufficient flow rate of cooling water, to effectively cooling the vapor passing through the condenser.

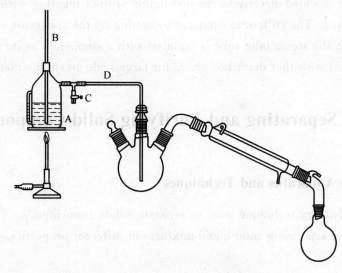

Figure 2. 7-12   Apparatus for steam distillation

A—steam generator   B—safety tube   C—screw clamp   D—steam inlet tube

The steam tube is replaced with a stopper if steam is generated by direct heating

Steam may be produced externally in a generator as shown in Figure 2. 7-12. The round-bottom flask is initially half-filled with water, and boiling chips are added before heating. The

Basic Techniques for Organic Experiments

safety tube relieves internal pressure if steam is generated at too high a rate or the outlet tube to the apparatus becomes clogged. The steam inlet tube is inserted through a screw adapter to the stillpot. The end of the tube should be close to the bottom of the stillpot so that the steam can bubble through and well contact with the organic phase. The outer diameter of the steam inlet tube should not be less than 7 mm to make sure that the steam can flow easily. Connect the outlet of the steam generator and the inlet of the stillpot with a T-tube, which bears a rubber tubing with a screw clamp on its side-arm. Keep the line from the steam generator to the still-pot as short as possible.

Before starting distillation, make sure that all connections are tight, the screw clamp on the T-tube is open, and the cooling water is running in the condenser. Heat the steam generator to boiling. When steam goes out of the T-tube, close the clamp. Adjust the heat source so that the distillation proceeds at a rate of 1 to 3 drops per second. Avoid applying excess heat to the stillpot to cause violent splattering. Occasionally watch the level of water in the safety tube to avoid over pressure or back-flow phenomenon. If some abnormal phenomena happen during the distillation, immediately open the screw clamp of the T-tube and remove the heating source. Check and fix the breakdown, and then re-start the distillation. When oil droplets are no longer observable and the distillate turns clear, open the clamp of the T-tube, and then stop heating. Allow the distillate to cool to room temperature and disassemble the apparatus.

For mini-scale steam distillation, a simplified method involving internal steam generation may be employed. Water is added directly to the distillation stillpot together with the organic compounds to be separated. The stillpot is equipped by setting up the apparatus as shown in Figure 2.7-12, except that the steam inlet tube is replaced with a stopper. The distillation procedure is essentially identical with that described above for large scale steam distillation.

2.8　Separating and Purifying Solid Compounds

2.8.1　Filtration Apparatus and Techniques

Filtration is the primary technique used to separate solids from liquids. There are different filtration methods for separating solid-liquid mixtures of different properties. Some of them are described below.

(1) Filtration media

Various types of materials are used in conjunction with funnels to produce the barrier that is the key to separating solids from liquids. The most commonly used medium is filter paper. Glasswool and cotton may serve as filters, but they are considerably more porous than paper and thus are used only when relatively large particles are to be separated from a liquid. Silica gel and Celite® are sometimes used with filter paper when the particles of the solid to be filtered

Separating and Purifying Solid Compounds

are so fine that they could clog the filter paper or cloth. These materials generally function by adsorption of solids and colloidal materials from the solution being filtered.

(2) Gravity filtration

A stemmed funnel, a piece of filter paper, a ring clamp and a receiver are needed for proceeding a gravity filtration. The filter paper must be folded to fit the funnel. Just fold the paper in half, and then in quarters. Fold edge 2 onto 3 to form edge 4, and then 1 onto 3 to form 5 as shown in Figure 2.8−1a. Now fold edge 2 onto 5 to form 6, and 1 onto 4 to form 7 (Figure 2.8−1b). Continue by folding edge 2 onto 4 to form 8, and 1 onto 5 to form 9 (Figure 2.8−1c). Do not crease the fold tightly at the center, because this might weaken the paper and cause it to tear during filtration. Then make folds in the opposite direction to produce the fan-like appearance shown in Figure 2.8−1d. Open the paper (Figure 2.8−1e) and fold each of the sections 1 and 2 in half with reverse folds to form paper that is ready to use (Figure 2.8−1f).

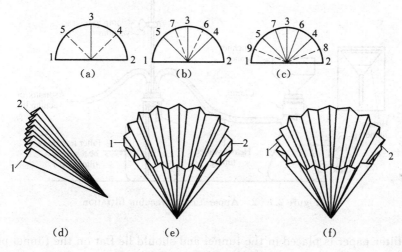

Figure 2.8−1   Folding filter paper

To perform a filtration, the folded paper is first placed in a funnel and wetted with a small amount of an appropriate solvent. The solution containing the solid is then poured onto the filter paper with the aid of a glass stirring rod to avoid dripping down the sides of the flask. The level of the solution on the funnel should be kept 1 cm lower than the rim of the filter paper. If only large particles such as drying agents are to be filtered, glasswool or cotton can be used to replace filter paper. If very fine or sticky solids are to be filtered, leave the solution standing for a while to deposit before filtration. Then carefully decant the upper clear solution onto the filter paper and finally pour the solids onto the funnel so that to ensure the filter rate.

If filtration is made in micro-scale, a Pasteur filter-tip pipet can be used. Just transfer the solution into the top of the filter-tip pipet. This method is also useful for micro-scale hot filtration.

(3) Vacuum filtration

A typical apparatus used for vacuum filtration is shown in Figure 2.8−2. Either a Büchner or

Basic Techniques for Organic Experiments

a Hirsch funnel is used, with the latter being better suited for isolating quantities of solid ranging from 100~500 mg. The funnel is fitted to a vacuum filter flask using a rubber adaptor or a rubber stopper with a hole. The oblique mouth of the funnel should face the sidearm of the filter flask, which is connected to an aspirator through a trap using heavy-walled rubber tubing. The trap, either a vacuum filter flask or a heavy-walled bottle, equipped with a two-way stopcock, prevents water from the aspirator from backing up into the filter flask when there is loss of water pressure. In the case of a sudden back-flow, immediately release the vacuum by opening the stopcock on the trap to atmosphere. The glass tube that extends to within approximately 2~3 cm of the bottom of the trap is connected to the water aspirator pump so that any water that collects in the trap can be evacuated back to the aspirator pump. Any filtrate that may overflow the filter flask will also be collected in the trap.

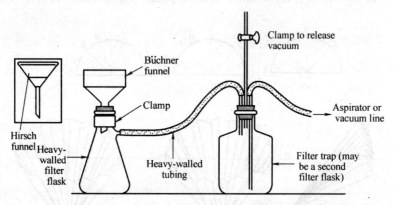

Figure 2.8-2   Apparatus for vacuum filtration

A piece of filter paper is placed in the funnel and should lie flat on the funnel plate, covering all the small holes in the funnel. It should not extend up the sides of the funnel. A vacuum is applied to the system, and the filter paper is wetted with a small amount of pure solvent in order to form a seal with the funnel. The solution to be filtered is then poured slowly to the funnel. A stirring rod or spatula may be used to aid the transfer. The last of the solids may be transferred to the funnel by washing them from the flask with some of the filtrate. The solids should be evenly dispersed on the funnel plate. When there is almost no solvent dropping from the funnel, the vacuum is released slowly by opening the screw clamp or the stopcock on the trap.

The solids are washed by adding pure solvent to the funnel to just cover the solids. Vacuum is reapplied until the washing solvent passes through the solids and drops from the funnel. The solids are pressed as dry as possible with a spatula or a cork while the funnel is under vacuum. Repeat this process for several times to completely remove the mother liquor. *Always remember that open the stopcock on the trap or remove the rubber tubing from the sidearm of the filter flask before stop the pump.*

If a strong acidic or basic solution is filtered, a piece of glass cloth or polyester cloth should be used to replace filter paper.

(4) Hot filtration

Sometimes hot filtration must be performed during purification of an organic solid by recrystallization. A hot filtration funnel (Figure 1.4−3d) or a short stemmed filter funnel should be used for hot filtration. The filter paper should be folded as shown in Figure 2.8−1. You'd better prewarm the funnel and flask to prevent solute from quick crystallization in the funnel. When the flask and funnel are hot, pour the hot solution onto the filter paper. The level of the solution on the funnel should be kept 1.5 cm lower than the rim of the filter paper. The funnel could be covered with a watchglass to reduce evaporation of solvent. Don't pour a large amount of the solution to the funnel, otherwise the solid will appear in the funnel or even clog the stem of the funnel when the solution turns cold. After all the hot solution has been poured onto the filter paper, several milliliters of hot solvent are added to the flask that contained the original recrystallization solution. The additional hot solvent is poured onto the filter paper to ensure the complete transfer of material to the flask containing the filtrate.

Sometimes it is necessary to make hot filtration under reduced pressure using a Büchner funnel. The funnel must be prewarmed in an oven or by a hot water bath to prevent solute from crystallization in the funnel.

2.8.2 Centrifugation and Decanting Solutions

Centrifugation is a useful technique to facilitate the separation of two immiscible phases, and it is sometimes more effective than filtration for removing suspended solid impurities in a liquid, especially when the particles are so fine they may pass through a filter paper. The procedure simply involves spinning a sample in one or more tubes at high speed in a bench-top centrifuge. It is important to balance the centrifuge before spinning to avoid vibrating the centrifuge during spinning. For example, if the sample to be centrifuged is placed in a single centrifuge tube, you should then fill a second tube with an equal volume of solvent and place this tube opposite the sample tube in the centrifuge. After the sample has been spun, the phases may be separated by decanting or removing the liquid phase with a Pasteur or filter-tip pipet.

If solids are easily deposited, they can be removed by simple decantation. To decant a liquid from a solid, the solid should first be allowed to settle to the bottom of the container. A loosely packed ball of glasswool can be put in the neck of the flask to keep the solid in the container. Then the container is carefully tilted, and the liquid is slowly poured into another container. Decantation is preferable to gravity filtration when working with very volatile organic liquids.

2.8.3 Evaporating Solvents

For many experiments and laboratory operations, it is necessary to remove the excess solvents to recover the product. The simplest way is to automatically evaporate the solvent by

Basic Techniques for Organic Experiments

leaving an Erlenmeyer flask or beaker containing the solution in a hood for a long time. A variety of techniques may be used to speed the process.

The common method for removing solvent is simple distillation. Discontinue heating when only a small amount of solvent remains, and do not overheat the stillpot as the product may decompose if heated too strongly. The stillpot should be cooled to room temperature, and change simple distillation to vacuum distillation by setting up the apparatus as shown in Figure 2.7-7 to remove the last trace of solvent.

A rotary evaporator (Figure 2.8-3) is especially designed for the rapid evaporation of solvents without bumping. A variable speed motor is used to rotate the flask containing the solvent being evaporated. While the flask is being rotated, a vacuum is applied and the flask is heated. The rate of evaporation may be controlled by adjusting the vacuum, the temperature of the water bath and the rate of rotation of the flask.

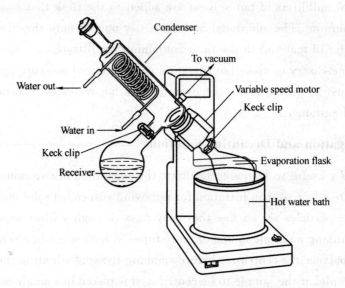

Figure 2.8-3 A rotary evaporator

2.8.4 Decolorizing Carbon

The color of the product caused by colored impurities can be removed by adding activated decolorizing carbon to the solution and then removing the carbon by filtration; sometimes heating is required. Polar, colored impurities bind preferentially to the surface of decolorizing carbon, but some of the desired products may also be adsorbed, so excessive quantities of decolorizing carbon should not be used.

In a typical mini-scale procedure, a small amount of decolorizing carbon is added to the solution contained in an Erlenmeyer flask. The suspension is gently heated to a temperature 10~20 ℃ below the boiling point of the solution while being continuously stirred or swirled.

There are no firm rules concerning the amount of decolorizing carbon that should be used, but a good first approximation is to add about 0.5 g to 1 g per 100 mL of solution. If the solution is not completely decolorized (Suppose the product is colorless), carefully re-add the decolorizing carbon in small portions. Don't add the decolorizing carbon at the boiling point of the solution because it will cause sudden vigorous boiling and the liquid may froth over the top of the flask or even the top of the condenser. The decolorizing carbon is then removed by gravity filtration or hot filtration. The suspension should be carefully poured onto the filter paper so that none of the small black specks of carbon runs down the side of the funnel. A filter-aid such as Celite® will facilitate complete removal of all of the carbon.

2.8.5 Recrystallization

(1) Selection of solvent

The solid products obtained from reactions may be contaminated by some impurities. Solution recrystallization is one of the most useful and effective methods for purification of solids. The choice of solvent is perhaps the most critical step in the process of recrystallization since the correct solvent must be selected to form a product of high purity and in good recovery or yield. The process of solvent selection can be aided by consideration of some generalizations about solubility characteristics for classes of solutes. Polar compounds are normally soluble in polar solvents and insoluble in nonpolar solvents, whereas nonpolar compounds are more soluble in nonpolar solvents. Such characteristics are summarized as "like dissolves like".

Consequently a solvent should satisfy certain criteria for use in recrystallization: ① The solvent should not react chemically with the substance being purified; ② The desired compound should be reasonably soluble in the hot solvent, and insoluble or nearly insoluble in the cold solvent; ③ Conversely, the impurities should either be insoluble in the solvent at all temperatures or must remain at least moderately soluble in the cold solvent; ④ The boiling point of the solvent should be low enough so that it can readily be removed from the crystals. ⑤ The boiling point of the solvent should generally be lower than the melting point of the solid being purified. In addition, some other factors, such as toxicity, flammability, price as well as the recovery possibility of the solvent, should also be considered.

The solvents commonly used in recrystallization and their boiling points are listed in Table 2.8-1.

Table 2.8-1 common solvents for recrystallization

solvent	boiling point/℃	solvent	boiling point/℃	solvent	boiling point/℃
water	100	ethyl acetate 乙酸乙酯	77	chloroform 氯仿	62
methanol 甲醇	65	tetrahydrofuran 四氢呋喃（THF）	65	dichloromethane 二氯甲烷	41

Basic Techniques for Organic Experiments

Continued

solvent	boiling point/℃	solvent	boiling point/℃	solvent	boiling point/℃
ethanol 乙醇	78	acetone 丙酮	56	cyclohexane 环己烷	81
diethyl ether 乙醚	35	petroleum ether 石油醚	60-150	toluene 甲苯	111

The chemical literature is a valuable source of information about solvents suitable for recrystallizing known compounds. If the compound has not been prepared before, it is necessary to resort to trial-and-error techniques to find an appropriate solvent for recrystallization. The experimental procedure is as follows. Prepare several clean test tubes, and place 0.2 g of substance to be recrystallized to each tube. Add different solvents (0.5~1 mL) to the tubes and heat the solution to completely dissolve the solute. The solvent which can give the product in high recovery upon cooling is the appropriate solvent for recrystallization of this substance. If the solid cannot be completely dissolved in 3 mL of hot solvent, this solvent is not suitable for recrystallization of the substance. If the solid can be dissolved in a hot solvent but cannot be crystallized from the solution upon cooling, rub the inside surface of the test tube at the air/solution interface by using a glass rod to facilitate the crystallization. If there is still no crystal appearing in the tube, the solvent is not appropriate for recrystallization of the substance because the solute has a large solubility in this solvent. Occasionally a mixture of solvents is required for satisfactory recrystallization of a solute. The mixture is usually comprised of only two miscible solvents. One of these dissolves the solute even when cold and the other one does not. The commonly used two-component mixtures of solvents are ethanol/water, toluene/petroleum ether, acetone/diethyl ether, and so on.

(2) Procedures for recrystallization

The process of recrystallization involves the following steps: ① dissolution of the solid in an appropriate solvent at an elevated temperature; ② hot filtration to remove the insoluble impurities and decolorizing carbon; ③ the re-formation of the crystals upon cooling so that soluble impurities remain in solution; ④ vacuum filtration to separate the crystals from the mother liquor; ⑤ washing the crystals to remove the mother liquor on the surface of the crystals, and finally ⑥ drying the crystals.

The solid to be purified is weighed and placed in an Erlenmeyer flask of appropriate size. A magnetic stirring bar or 2~3 boiling chips should be added to the flask to prevent bumping of the solution while boiling. A few milliliters of solvent are added to the flask, and the mixture is then heated to the boiling point with a water or oil bath. To avoid inhaling the vapors of solvent, equip a condenser on the flask or perform the operations in a hood. More solvent is added from the top of the condenser to the flask in small portions until the solid just dissolves. It is important to let boiling resume after each addition so that a minimum amount of solvent is used to effect dissolution. If adding solvent fails to dissolve any more solid, it is likely that insoluble impurities are present. Using excessive amount of solvent decreases the recovery of the solute. If it is necessary to perform a hot filtration, it is prudent to add an additional $2\% \sim 5\%$ of solvent to prevent premature crystallization during this operation.

If there are some colored impurities in the solid, the decolorizing carbon is added to remove the impurities as described in section 2.8.4.

The hot solution is allowed to cool slowly to room temperature, and crystallization should occur. Rapid cooling of the solution is undesirable because the crystals formed tend to be very small, and their resulting large surface area may foster adsorption of impurities from solution. Generally, the solution should not be disturbed as it cools, since this also leads to production of small crystals. Failure of crystallization to occur after the solution has cooled somewhat usually means that either too much solvent has been used or that the solution is supersaturated. A supersaturated solution can usually be made to produce crystals by seeding. A crystal of the original solid is added to the solution to induce crystallization. Alternatively, crystallization can often be induced by using a glass rod to rub the inside surface of the crystallization vessel at or just above the air/solution interface. After the solution is cooled to room temperature, the flask can be further cooled by immersing it in an ice-water bath to completely crystallize the solute from the solution.

The crystals are isolated by vacuum filtration using a Büchner funnel and a clean, dry filter flask. The crystals are commonly washed using a small amount of pure, cold solvent, with the vacuum off. The vacuum is reapplied to remove as much solvent as possible from the filter cake. The crystals are then transfered from the filter paper of the Büchner funnel to a watch-glass or vial for air-or oven-drying.

The organic solvents used should be poured into a recovery container.

2.8.6   Sublimation

If the vapor pressure of a solid is greater than the ambient pressure at its melting point, the solid undergoes a direct phase transition to the gas phase without first passing through the liquid state. This process is called sublimation. Sublimation is thus generally a property of relatively nonpolar substances having fairly symmetrical structures. In order to purify a compound by sublimation, it must have a relatively high vapor pressure, and the impurities must have vapor pressures significantly lower than the compound being purified. Since few organic solids exhibit vapor pressures high enough to sublime at atmospheric pressure, sublimation is normally performed at reduced pressure. The solid must be completely dried before sublimation. The product obtained by sublimation has high purity but low yield.

A ground-glass cold-finger and test tube (Figure 2.8-4a) are often used for vacuum sublimation of a small amount of a solid compound. The test tube is evacuated using a water aspirator or vacuum pump and the cold-finger is cooled by running water. The cold-finger provides a surface upon which the sublimed crystals may form. A simple sublimation apparatus can be assem-

Basic Techniques for Organic Experiments

bled inexpensively from two test tubes. One of them should have a sidearm (Figure 2.8–4b). A small vacuum filtration flask may also be used (Figure 2.8–4c) in place of the test tube with a sidearm. The cold-finger is cooled either with running water or with ice chips.

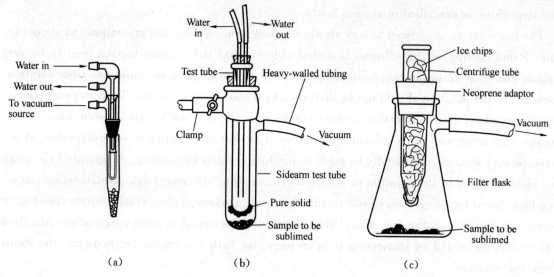

Figure 2.8–4   Sublimation apparatus
(a) Cold-finger sublimator   (b) Test tube sublimator   (c) Filter-flask sublimator

In order to purify an impure substance by sublimation, first place the sample at the bottom of the sublimation chamber. This is then heated under reduced pressure to a temperature below the melting point of the sample. The solid will be vaporized and transferred via the vapor phase to the surface of the cold-finger, where it condenses directly as a pure material to the solid state. After the sublimation is complete, the pressure must be released carefully to avoid dislodging the crystals from the cold-finger with a surge of air. For similar reason, care must be exercised when removing the cold-finger from the sublimation apparatus. The pure crystals are scraped from the cold-finger with a spatula.

2.9　Chromatography

The word chromatography was first used to describe the colored bands observed when a solution containing plant pigments is passed through a glass column filled with an adsorbent packing material. The term now encompasses a variety of separation techniques that are widely used for analytical and preparative purposes. Because of the high efficiency, sensitivity and accuracy, the chromatographic methods have been widely used in scientific researches on organic chemistry, biochemistry, the chemical industry and other related fields to identify and separate components of a mixture, which could be a gas and liquid sample or a solid sample dissolved in a proper solvent. Nowadays, a pair of enantiomers can also be identified and even separated by the chromatographic method with a chiral column.

All methods of chromatography operate on the principle that the components of a mixture will distribute unequally between two immiscible phases. The **mobile phase** is generally a liquid such as an organic solvent or an inert gas that flows continuously over the fixed **stationary phase**, which may be a solid adsorbent or a liquid coated on a solid support. The individual components of the mixture have different affinities for the mobile and stationary phases, so a dynamic equilibrium is established, in which each component is selectively, but temporarily, removed from the mobile phase by binding to the stationary phase. The component that interacts with or binds more strongly to the stationary phase moves more slowly in the direction of the flow of the mobile phase. The attractive forces that are involved in this selective adsorption are electrostatic and dipole-dipole interactions, hydrogen bonding, complication and van der Waals forces.

According to the nature of the mobile and stationary phases used, the chromatographic methods can be divided into the following categories: ① column chromatography; ② thin-layer chromatography (TLC); ③ paper chromatography; ④ gas chromatography (GC); ⑤ high-pressure (or high-performance) liquid chromatography (HPLC).

2.9.1 Column Chromatography

Column chromatography, a form of solid-liquid adsorption chromatography, is a powerful technique for separation of a multi-component mixture in synthetic organic chemistry. Column chromatography can be used to separate a multi-component mixture in different quantities from a few milligrams to several grams. The diameters of columns commonly used in laboratory are 0.5~10 cm. The height-to-diameter ratio for the packed column is between 1:10 to 1:4. An active and finely divided solid adsorbent filled in a column is used as the stationary phase (Figure 2.9-1). A multi-component mixture dissolved in a small amount of an appropriate solvent is carefully poured to the top of the packed column. The individual components of the mixture, which were initially adsorbed on the stationary phase at the top of the column, begin to move downward with the eluting solvent. The components move at different rates depending on their relative affinities for the packing material; a more weakly adsorbed

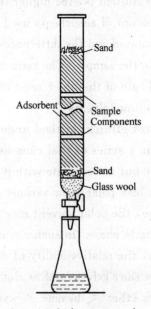

Sand
Adsorbent
Sample Components
Sand
Glass wool

Figure 2.9-1 A chromatography column

Basic Techniques for Organic Experiments

compound is eluted faster from the column than a more strongly adsorbed compound. As the individual components exit from the bottom of the column in bands, they are collected in separate receivers. The solvent is then removed from each fraction by evaporation to provide the pure components.

When all of the components of a mixture are colored, their bands are easily observed. If organic compounds are colorless, special methods are required for detecting the bands as they elute from the column. For those organic compounds that absorb ultraviolet light, an ultraviolet lamp is used to locate the bands of the individual components exiting the column. The most effective technique for separation of colorless organic compounds is to collect fractions of equal amount in a series of tared flasks followed by evaporating the solvent, and then to reweigh the flasks. The fractions containing different bands may then be easily identified by the relative amounts of solute in each flask. One may also use TLC to monitor the separation.

(1) Adsorbents

The adsorbents most commonly used to separate organic compounds are alumina (Al_2O_3) and silica gel ($SiO_2 \cdot H_2O$). Alumina is a highly active and strongly adsorbing polar substance that is commercially available in three forms: neutral, acidic and basic. Acidic and basic alumina are sometimes used to separate basic and acidic compounds, respectively, and neutral alumina is frequently the packing of choice. Commercially silica gel is slightly acidic. The particle size of the adsorbents used for column chromatography is about 100 μm. The moving rate of eluents will increase and therefore the separation efficiency will decrease if larger particles of adsorbents are used. On the contrary, smaller particles of adsorbents lead to relatively slow moving rate of eluents and broad bands. The activity of adsorbents is related to the content of water. The less the water content is, the higher the activity of adsorbents will be.

The amount of adsorbents used to prepare the column depends on the quantity of the sample to be separated and the differences in partition coefficients and polarities of the individual components in the sample. The ratio of adsorbent to sample varies in a range of 10 : 1 to 200 : 1. As a general rule of thumb, a ratio of about 25 : 1 is a convenient starting point.

(2) Eluting solvents

The most efficient method to determine the optimal solvent(s) for column chromatography is to perform a series of trial runs using TLC. An effective eluting solvent must readily dissolve the solute but not compete with it for binding sites on the stationary phase, and it must be significantly less polar than various components of the mixture to obtain an effective separate. Otherwise, the polar solvent may bind strongly to the adsorbent and force the solute to remain in the mobile phase. In such circumstances, the components will move rapidly on the column. As a rule, the relative ability of different solvents to move a given substance down a column of alumina or silica gel, termed as eluting power, is generally found to follow the order shown below:

petroleum ether < hexane < cyclohexane < toluene < dichloromethane < chloroform < cyclohexane/ethyl acetate (80 : 20, V/V) < dichloromethane/diethyl ether (80 : 20, V/V) <

dichloromethane/diethyl ether (60 : 40, V/V) < cyclohexane/ethyl acetate (20 : 80, V/V) < diethyl ether < diethyl ether/methanol (99 : 1) < ethyl acetate < acetone < 1-propanol < ethanol < methanol < water. In general, polar solvents are effective to elute polar compounds down a column and nonpolar solvents are effective to move nonpolar compounds down. A mixed eluent of two or three solvents is often used to separate the components of the mixture having similar polarities.

(3) Column packing

Proper packing of the column is one of the key points to determine the efficiency of separation. Fix the column vertically on an iron stand and close the stopcock of the column. A plug of cotton or glasswool is first inserted into the small end of the column and a layer of white sand, approximately 1 cm thick, is then added to provide an even bed for the adsorbent (Figure 2.9-1). There are two methods to pack the column with adsorbents. One is the dry packing method. The dry adsorbent is slowly added through a funnel to the column half-filled with the solvent that will serve as eluent. The other technique is the wet pack method, in which a slurry of the adsorbent in the eluting solvent is added to the column 1/4-filled with the eluting solvent. With both methods, the column is constantly tapped as the solid settles through the liquid to ensure even and firm packing of the adsorbent and to remove any trapped air bubbles. Some solvent may be slowly dropped from the column into an Erlenmeyer flask during this operation, but the liquid level in the column should never be allowed to fall below the top of the adsorbent. If this occurs, the air bubbles in the column will allow the formation of some channels, which results in poor efficiency of separation. Finally, a layer of sand (ca. 1 cm thick) is normally placed on the top of adsorbent to prevent disruption of the packing material as eluting solvent is added.

(4) Dissolving and loading samples

Dissolve the sample to be separated in a minimal volume of a solvent, and then transfer the solution to the top of the column. It is important to distribute the sample evenly on the surface of the adsorbent and to use as little solvent as possible in loading the column. The initial band will be broad and poor resolution of the components may result if too much solvent is used to dissolve the sample.

(5) Elution

The simple elution technique, in which a single solvent is used for chromatography, works well for separation of mixtures containing only two or three compounds having similar polarities. However, a stepwise or fractional elution technique is mostly used in column chromatography. In this technique, a series of increasingly more polar solvents is used so that individual bands remaining on the column are separated and not coeluted. As the polarity of the solvent increases, those components of the mixture that are more tightly adsorbed on the adsorbent will begin to move.

(6) Experiment for separation of methyl orange and methylene blue

Basic Techniques for Organic Experiments

A buret or a thin column with its stopcock ungreased is used in the experiment. The buret is packed with 4 grams of dry neutral alumina according to the procedures described above. In a small test tube, dissolve the mixture of 10 mg of methyl orange and 20 mg of ethylene blue in a minimum amount of 95% ethanol. The solution should be evenly loaded to the top of the buret. Open the stopcock when the liquid level is at the top of the alumina and add a small amount of 95% ethanol. A blue band of methylene blue is eluted down, while methyl orange remains on the top of the column. Elute the column with enough ethanol to completely separate methylene blue. When the elutant from the column is colorless, change the eluting solvent to water to wash down the methyl orange.

2.9.2　Thin-Layer Chromatography (TLC)

TLC is another form of solid-liquid adsorption chromatography and involves the same fundamental principle as column chromatography (Section 2.9.1). It is a quick, efficient and convenient method for analysis of the mixture of organic compounds using a micro-scale of samples. TLC is frequently used for determining the optimal combinations of solvent and adsorbent for preparative column chromatographic separations and for monitoring the progress of a reaction. It can also be used for separating compounds on a scale between milligrams to grams, by drawing a line with a capillary on the surface of a preparative TLC plate about 1 cm from the end of the plate. Note that TLC method is limited to relatively nonvolatile compounds that have boiling points higher than 150 ℃, especially for those compounds that are easily decomposed at high temperature and not suitable for GC analysis.

(1) Adsorbents and eluting solvents

The properties of the adsorbents and the relative eluting abilities of the solvents given for column chromatography also apply to TLC. For TLC, the adsorbent, usually alumina or silica gel with a particle size of 260 mesh or above, is mixed with a small quantity of a binder, such as starch or calcium sulfate, and spread as a layer approximately 0.25 mm thick on a glass plate. Unlike column chromatography where the mobile phase moves down the column, the mobile phase in TLC moves up the plate. The components of the mixture are carried up by the eluent at different rates due to their different affinities for the thin-layer adsorbent so as to separate the components of the mixture.

(2) General procedure for TLC experiment

The presence of water molecules on the surface of the adsorbent decreases its activity and effectiveness in separating the components of the mixture, so TLC plates are usually dried in an oven for an hour or more at 110 ℃ prior to use to remove any adsorbed moisture. Obtain a proper sized strip of pre-coated TLC plate, and then lightly and briefly apply a small drop of a solution of a mixture near one end of the plate (about 1 cm from the edge, Figure 2.9−2a) using a capillary tube; as the sample is applied, you may blow gently on the strip to dry the spot quickly. The diameter of the spot of the sample on the plate should not be larger than 1∼

2 mm. The spotting process can be performed several times, allowing the solvent of each drop to evaporate before adding the next. Place a 0. 8 cm layer of the eluent on the bottom of the developing chamber and saturate the chamber with vapors of the eluting solvent by shaking. The eluting solvent is either a pure solvent or a mixture of two or more solvents. When the spot has thoroughly dried, place the strip with its spotted end down in a closed developing chamber (Figure 2. 9-3). Note that the level of the eluent should be just below that of the spot. As the solvent moves up the strip, the components of the mixture are carried along at different rates to produce a series of spots on the strip as depicted in Figure 2. 9-2b). When the solvent front is about 2~3 mm to the top of the strip, remove the strip from the developing chamber. Mark the solvent front with a pencil, and allow the strip to air-dry.

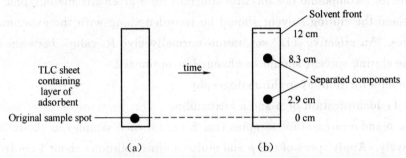

Figure 2. 9-2   Thin-layer chromatography
(a) Original plate   (b) Developed chromatogram

(3) Visualization techniques

If colored compounds are separated, the spots of the separated substances can be seen easily. Many organic compounds are colorless, however, a variety of indirect visualization techniques have been developed to detect their presence on the plate:

(a) The spots for compounds that fluoresce can be located by putting the plate under an ultraviolet (UV) lamp. All spots must be circled with a pencil since the spots cannot be seen when the UV light is removed;

(b) Commercially available TLC plates containing a fluorescent material as part of their coating can be used for compounds that do not fluoresce but absorb UV

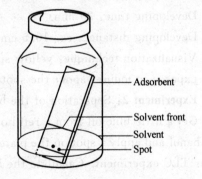

Figure 2. 9-3   TLC developing chamber

light. These compounds appear as dark spots under the UV light, and the positions of the spots should be marked with a pencil;

(c) The other method is to expose the TLC plate to an iodine vapor by placing it in a closed chamber containing several crystals of iodine. As the iodine vapor reacts with various organic compounds to form complexes, which appear as the brown spots on a white or tan background.

Basic Techniques for Organic Experiments

Since the reaction is reversible, the spot must be circled with a pencil immediately after the plate is removed from the chamber;

(d) In addition, the TLC plate may be sprayed with a variety of reagents, or dipped in a visualizing solution containing some special reagents. These reagents can react with the separated compounds to produce colored or dark spots.

(4) Calculation of the retention factor (R_f)

The retention factor (R_f) of each separated component can be calculated as shown below.

$$R_f = \frac{\text{distance traveled by substance}}{\text{distance traveled by solvent}}$$

The R_f value for a compound is a physical constant for a given chromatographic condition, so the adsorbent and the eluting solvent should be recorded along with the experimentally determined R_f values. An effective TLC separation normally give R_f values between 0.15 ~ 0.75, otherwise, the eluting solvent should be changed or optimized.

(5) Experiments for thin-layer chromatography

Experiment 1: Identification of p-and o-nitroaniline

Dissolve the p-and o-nitroaniline samples (ca. 5 mg for each sample) in about 0.5 mL of ethanol, respectively. Apply spots of the p-and o-nitroaniline solutions about 1 cm from one end of the plate using capillary tubes. The two spots should be 1 cm apart and at the same distance from the bottom of the plate. Then make the experiment as described above. Calculate the R_f values for p-nitroaniline and o-nitroaniline.

Adsorbent: a properly sized strip of the TLC plate pre-coated with silica gel G.

Developing solvent: toluene: ethyl acetate = 4:1 (V/V).

Developing time: 20 min.

Developing distance: ca. 10.5 cm.

Visualization technique: yellow spots on the white background. If the chromatographic plate is exposed to iodine vapor, the spots turn yellow-brown.

Experiment 2: Separation of the blue oil from a refill of a ball-point pen

Get a little blue oil from a refill of a ball-point pen. Dissolve the oil with a small amount of ethanol and apply a spot on the plate. Make the separation as described in the general procedure for TLC experiment. Calculate the R_f values for three spots.

Adsorbent: a properly sized strip of the TLC plate pre-coated with silica gel G.

Developing solvent: 1-butanol: ethanol: water = 9:3:1 (V/V/V).

Developing time: 35 min.

Developing distance: ca. 4.5 cm.

Separation results: Three spots can be seen on the plate, that is, a sky-blue spot (basic bright-blue) with the largest R_f value, a purple spot (basic purple) and a blue spot (copper phthalocyanine) with the smallest R_f value.

2.9.3 Gas Chromatography (GC)

（1）Principle

Gas chromatography is an analytical tool, developed in the 50's of the 20th century, to separate and identify the components of a mixture of volatile compounds. In gas chromatography, the mobile phase is a flowing inert gas, which is called the carrier gas, and a stationary phase is a solid substance or a finely divided solid support coated with a viscous, high-boiling liquid. Depending on the stationary phase, the former is termed as gas-solid chromatography (GSC) and the latter is termed as gas-liquid chromatography (GLC). Gas chromatography operates on the principle of partitioning the components of a mixture between a mobile phase and a stationary phase. A sample injected into a GC instrument is immediately vaporized and carried through a column by a mobile phase, and its components are continuously partitioned between the two phases. The separation occurs as the components that show a weaker affinity for the stationary phase move through the column more quickly, whereas those with a stronger attraction to the stationary phase migrate more slowly.

（2）Columns, stationary phases and carrier gases

There are two general types of columns, packed columns made from stainless steel tubes and capillary columns made from fused silica tubes. Packed columns have an internal diameter of 2 mm to 6 mm and are 1 m to 3 m long, and capillary columns have an internal diameter of 0.15 mm to 1 mm and are 10 m to 100 m long. Both of these columns contain stationary phases. The choice of a stationary liquid phase is a crucial factor for the separation efficiency. The general principle is to choose a stationary liquid phase that features some similar structures and properties, such as functional groups and polarity, etc., with the substances to be separated. Nonpolar stationary liquid phases are usually used for separation of nonpolar substances, whereas polar samples are most effectively separated by using a polar liquid phase. In the former circumstance, compounds to be separated exit from the column in the order of their boiling points, while in the latter case, compounds come out of the column in the order of their polarities. Nitrogen is commonly used as a carrier gas, and the other gas such as helium, argon, hydrogen or carbon dioxide can also be used as carrier gases. The choice of carrier is mainly determined by the detector and the property of the substances to be separated.

（3）Flowchart and instruments of gas chromatography

Figure 2.9-4 schematically illustrates the flowchart of a GC instrument, which is generally composed of carrier gas system (parts a～e), separation system (parts f～h), detection system (part i) and data storage and processing system (part j).

Carrier gas system includes a steel bottle of a carrier gas, a pressure-reducing valve, a desiccant column to remove traces of water and other impurities, a flow regulator to control the flow rate (generally 30～120 mL·min^{-1}) of the carrier gas.

Separation system includes a heated injection port, a chromatographic column, an oven and

Basic Techniques for Organic Experiments

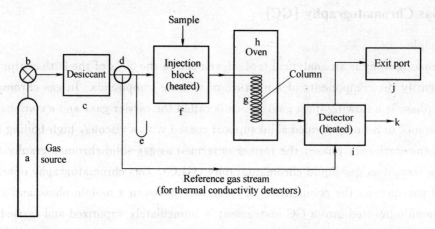

Figure 2.9-4 A schematic diagram of apparatus for gas chromatography

a—Carrier gas supply b—Pressure-reducing valve c—Desiccant d—Fine-control valve

e—Flowmeter f—Heated injection port g—Column h—Oven i—Detector

j—Data system k—Exit port

electric control units. The sample is injected using a gas-tight syringe through a septum into the injection port (f), an individually heated chamber in which the sample is immediately vaporized. The sample then enters the flowing stream of carrier gas and is swept into and through the column (g), which is located in an oven (h). In the column, the individual components separate into bands that ultimately pass through a detector (i).

Detection system includes a detector that produces signals of voltages proportional to the amount of material. Two types of detectors are commonly used for GC instruments. A thermal conductivity detector (TCD) operates on the basis of differences in the thermal conductivity of the mobile phase as a function of its composition. A flame ionization detector (FID) is much more sensitive and operates by detecting the number of ions produced by passing the mobile phase through a hydrogen flame.

Data storage and processing system includes a computer installed with a special GC working station. The computer records the changes in voltage measured by the detector as a function of time to give the gas chromatogram, which can be plotted by a printer.

(4) Gas chromatographic analysis

Water, inorganic acids and bases must be removed from the sample to prevent the instrument, especially the column, from damaging. Carefully read the manual of operating rules and regulations for gas chromatograph before beginning GC analysis and operate the instrument following the regulations.

Qualitative analysis: The time taken for a particular compound to travel through the column to the detector is known as its **retention time**. For a pure compound, it is constant under the same experimental conditions, including the column, temperature and flow rate. Therefore, the retention time can be used as a first step to identify an unknown compound or the individual components in a mixture. In an experiment, first measure the retention time(s) of the unknown compound(s) or the component(s), and then measure the retention time(s) of the known sample(s) under the same condition. Comparison of the retention times of the known samples with those of the unknown compounds allows a preliminary identification of the unknown compounds. A convenient way to confirm that the retention times of a known sample and the unknown are the same involves injecting a sample prepared by combining equal amounts of both known and unknown samples. However, observation of the same retention time for a known and an unknown substance is a necessary but not sufficient evidence to confirm their identity, because it is possible for two different compounds to have the same retention time. Further confirmation of the unknown compound by spectral or other means is imperative.

Quantitative analysis: The voltage output of the detector is related to the mole fraction of the material being detected in the vapor, so there is a correlation between the relative area of the peak in the chromatogram and the relative amount of each component in the mixture. Although the peak areas are related to the mole fraction of the component in the mobile phase, they are not quantitatively related, since detector response varies with the class of compounds. Thus it is necessary to correct the measured areas in the chromatogram using the appropriate **correction factor** to attain accurate results from quantitative analysis of the mixture. Correction factors for different compounds can be determined experimentally using a known sample, or found in monographs on gas chromatography. The relative correction factor (f') is widely used in quantitative analysis, which can be calculated by the following equation:

$$f' = \frac{f_i}{f_s} = \frac{A_s m_i}{A_i m_s}$$

Where, m_i and m_s are the masses of compound **i** and internal standard **s**;

A_i and A_s are the peak areas of compound **i** and internal standard **s**;

f_i and f_s are the absolute correction factors of compound **i** and internal standard **s**.

The percentage composition of a mixture may be calculated by normalization method, external standard method (to compare with an external standard substance) or internal standard method (to add a certain amount of a standard substance to the mixture to be analyzed). For normalization method, first, determine the f'_i, and then measure the peak area of each component in a mixture. The weight percentage (P_i) of a compound **i** in a mixture is calculated according to the following equation, and the total area of the mixture is considered as 100%.

$$P_i = \frac{f'_i A_i}{f'_1 A_1 + f'_2 A_2 + f'_3 A_3 + \cdots} \times 100\%$$

The prerequisite of application of normalization method is that all components of the mixture must come out of the column and display corresponding peaks.

2.9.4　High-Performance Liquid Chromatography (HPLC)

(1) Principle

High-performance liquid chromatography (or high pressure liquid chromatography, HPLC) is one of the powerful tools to separate, identify and quantify compounds of a mixture. Most theories and technologies of GC are applicable to HPLC. The main differences between HPLC and GC are the mobile phase and operation conditions. The mobile phase for GC is an inert gas. The separation efficiency mainly depends on the interaction between the molecules of components in a mixture and the stationary phase. GC analysis is operated at the temperature close to the boiling points of the components to be separated. Therefore GC is generally used for separation and analysis of substances that have boiling points lower than 500 ℃. In HPLC, the mobile phase is a solvent, which is pumped under high pressure through a column. The stationary phase is a finely divided solid held inside the column. There is a certain affinity between the mobile phase of HPLC and the components of a mixture. Therefore the separation efficiency of HPLC depends not only on the properties of the components in a mixture and the stationary phase, but also closely on the property of solvent(s) used as mobile phase. HPLC is generally operated at room temperature, so it is especially useful for separation and analysis of substances with high boiling points (> 500 ℃), low volatility and poor thermostability. The advantages of HPLC are high efficiency, high sensitivity, convenient operation, fast analysis as well as using a small amount of sample.

Different components of the sample are carried forward at different rates by the moving liquid phase, due to their different interactions with the stationary and mobile phases. Therefore different compounds have different retention times. For a particular compound, the retention time will vary depending on the following factors:

(a) the pressure used (because that affects the flow rate of the solvent);

(b) the nature of the stationary phase (not only what material it is made of, but also the particle size);

(c) the composition of the eluent;

(d) the temperature of the column.

Manipulation of these parameters can alter the retention time of a compound. This means that conditions have to be carefully controlled if you are using retention times as a way to identify compounds.

(2) Instruments

The instrument of HPLC is composed of solvent reservoirs, a high-pressure pump, an injector, a column, a detector and a data processing system. A flowchart for HPLC is shown in Figure 2.9-5. The solvents used as mobile phase for HPLC must be degassed before HPLC analysis. The solvent is pumped into the injector where it mixes with the sample and the mixture flows into a column. The individual components of a mixture separated in a column go to the detector. The detected results are sent to a chromatography data system in a computer, where the results are processed and displayed as a series of peaks. The individual components of the sample can be recovered at the outlet of the instrument.

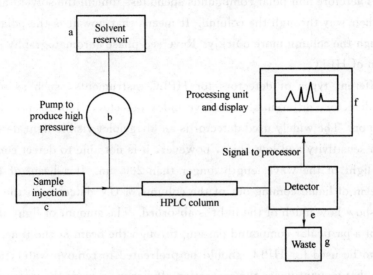

Figure 2.9-5   A schematic diagram of high performance liquid chromatography
a—Solvent reservoir   b—Pump   c—Injector   d—Column
e—Detector   f—Data system   g—Waste Collector

The column is the most important factor for the separation efficiency. It holds chromatographic packing material (stationary phase). The choice of the column depends on the properties of compounds to be analyzed. For HPLC, the average diameter (d_p) of the particles packed into narrow columns is in the range of 30 μm to 75 μm. The separation of the components of a mixture is more efficient if small particles are used as stationary phase, however, the liquid will pass slowly through the column. Therefore, a shorter column is used in HPLC and a high-pressure pump is used to force the liquid through the column. Pressure may reach as high as 40 MPa or about 400 atmospheres and typical flow rates of a mobile phase are in the range of 0.5 mL·min^{-1} to 5 mL·min^{-1} for analytical HPLC.

There are two types of columns for HPLC, normal phase and reversed-phase chromatographic columns. In a **normal phase chromatography**, the column is filled with tiny silica particles and the solvent is a non-polar compound such as n-hexane and n-heptane. Polar compounds in the mixture being passed through the column will stick longer to the polar silica than non-polar compounds will. The non-polar ones will therefore pass more quickly through the column. While in a **reversed-phase chromatography**, the silica of the column is modified to make it non-polar by attaching long hydrocarbon chains to its surface, typically with either 8 or 18 carbon atom hydrocarbons. A polar solvent such as methanol, acetonitrile, water and their mixed solvents in different ratios are usually adopted as mobile phase. In this case, there will be a strong attraction between the polar solvent and polar molecules in the mixture being passed through the column, while non-polar compounds in the mixture will tend to form attractions with the hydrocarbon groups attached to the silica (the stationary phase) because of van der Waals dispersion forces. Therefore non-polar compounds spend less time in the solvent and this will slow them down on their way through the column. It means that now it is the polar molecules that will travel through the column more quickly. Reversed-phase chromatography is the most commonly used form of HPLC.

There are different types of detectors for HPLC instruments, such as ultraviolet-visible (UV-vis) light detector, differential refractive index detector, fluorescence detector, ampere detector, and so on. The widely used detector is an ultraviolet-visible light detector. It has advantages of high-sensitivity and low noise, however, it is not able to detect compounds that do not absorb UV light of the wave length longer than 200 nm. If a beam of UV light shines through the stream of liquid coming out of the column, a UV detector on the opposite side of the stream can show how much of the light is absorbed. The amount of light absorbed depends on the amount of a particular compound passing through the beam at the time.

The samples to be used for HPLC should be pretreated to remove water, acids, bases and other impurities that may influence the separation efficiency or erode the instrument. The liquid samples can be directly measured by HPLC, and the solid samples must be pre-dissolved in a proper concentration. The commonly used solvents are alkanes, haloalkanes, methanol, acetonitrile, tetrahydrofuran (THF), and so on. Solvents must be purified before used for HPLC.

2.10　Measuring Physical Constants of Organic Compounds

The most frequently measured physical properties of organic compounds are melting point (mp), boiling point (bp), index of refraction (n), density (d), specific rotation ($[\alpha]$) and solubility. These properties are useful in the identification and characterization of substances, which are previously known. Comparison of the difference between a found value of a physical property for a sample and a standard datum for a pure compound can help us to estimate the purity of the sample. The values of one or two of the common physical properties may be identical for more than one compound, but it is most unlikely that values of several such properties will be the same for two different compounds. Consequently, a list of physical constants is a highly useful way to characterize a substance. Different organic compounds can be separated and purified according to their different physical constants such as melting points, boiling points, solubility, and so on.

2.10.1　Melting Point

(1) Principle

Measuring Physical Constants of Organic Compounds

The melting point of a substance is defined as the temperature at which the liquid and solid phases existing in equilibrium with one another without change of temperature. The melting point is expressed as the temperature range over which the solid starts to melt and then is completely converted to liquid. Consequently, rather than a melting point of a single temperature, a melting range is actually measured. A pure substance has a constant melting point and melts over a temperature range no more than 1 ℃. The presence of impurities will apparently broaden the melting point range of the substance and decrease its melting point. Accordingly, the measured melting point of a sample is useful in identification of the substance and in estimating the purify of the sample.

(2) Melting point methods

Determination of the melting point of a compound simply involves heating a small amount of a solid and observing the temperature at which it melts. Many different types of heating devices can be used, but the technique using the capillary-tube melting-point procedure is the one used most commonly in the student laboratory. Prior to making a measurement of a melting point, the sample should be finely ground and completely dried in a desiccator or an oven.

Thiele tube method: The first step is loading the sample into the capillary tube, which has one sealed end and is commercially available. Place a small amount of the solid sample on a clean watchglass and press the open end of the capillary tube into the solid to force a small amount of solid into the capillary tube (Figure 2.10−1a). Hold the capillary tube vertically with open-mouth up and slightly drop it from about 5 cm height to the bench top to make sample go to the sealed end of the tube. Repeat these sample loading operations to transfer enough sample to the capillary tube. Then take 40 cm to 50 cm of tubing with a diameter of 6∼8 mm, hold it vertically on a hard surface such as the bench top or floor, and with the sealed end down (Figure 2.10−1b), drop the capillary tube down the long tubing several times, so that the solid sample is packed evenly and tightly at the sealed end of the capillary tube. The height of a sample should be about 2∼3 mm.

Thiele tube is shaped such that the heat applied to a heating liquid in the sidearm by a burner is distributed evenly to all parts of the vessel by convection currents. Temperature control is accomplished by adjusting the flame of the burner. Fix the capillary tube to the thermometer at the position indicated in Figure 2.10−2b using a rubber band, and then support the thermometer and the attached capillary tube containing the sample in the apparatus with a cork. Since the fluid will expand on heating, make sure that the height of the heating fluid is approximately at the level indicated in Figure 2.10−2a.

The maximum temperature to which the apparatus can be heated is dictated by the nature of the heating fluid. The commonly used heating fluids are sulfuric acid, glycerol, liquid paraffin, and so on. The choice of heating fluid depends on the melting point of the substance to be measured. If the required temperature is lower than 140 ℃, liquid paraffin or glycerol can be used as a proper heating fluid. Medical liquid paraffin can be heated to 220 ℃ without apparent-

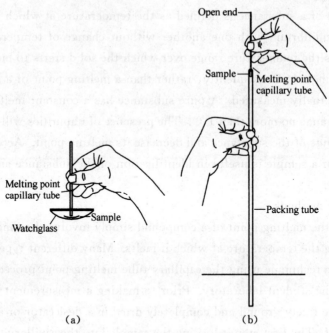

Figure 2.10-1

(a) Filling a capillary melting point tube

(b) Packing the sample at the bottom of the capillary tube

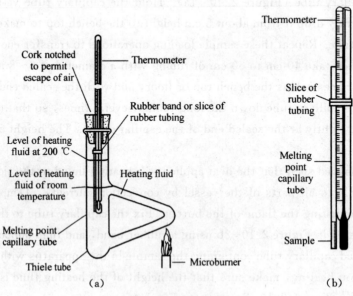

Figure 2.10-2

(a) Thiele melting point apparatus

(b) Arrangement of sample and thermometer for determining melting point

ly changing its color. Sulfuric acid is used as heating fluid when the required temperature is higher than 140 ℃. When sulfuric acid is used, take great care and bear a protecting glasses

Measuring Physical Constants of Organic Compounds

during the measurement. When sulfuric acid is heated to the temperature higher than 250 ℃, a white smoke will generated, and it will be difficult to read the datum of a thermometer. In this case, a potassium sulfate saturated solution of sulfuric acid is used as heating fluid.

For each sample, the melting point should be measured at least twice. In the first time, the temperature can be increased at the rate of 5 ℃·min^{-1}, to get an approximate melting point of the sample. Then let the heating bath cool down, change the capillary tube used for a new one containing the sample (Each capillary tube containing a sample can be used only for once), and make the measurement for the second time. In the beginning of the second time measurement, temperature can be increased at a rate of 10 ℃·min^{-1}, and then slow down the increasing rate to 5 ℃·min^{-1}. To get the most reproducible and accurate results, the sample should be heated at a rate of about 1 ℃·min^{-1}, when the temperature is about 10 ℃ to the melting point of the sample. Carefully observe the changes of the sample in the capillary tube and note down both the temperature at which the first tiny drop of liquid appears and the one at which the solid has just completely melted. The range between these temperature points is termed as the melting point range. The purer the sample is, the smaller the range will be. If the temperature is increased too quickly, the melting point range obtained may be broadened.

Electric melting point apparatus: The Thiele tube has been replaced in many laboratories by various electric melting point devices, which are more convenient to manipulate. One common type of electric melting point apparatus is a microscopic melting point unit. In this apparatus, the finely ground sample ($<$ 0.1 mg) is placed between two pieces of glass sheet, which is put on a heated metal block. A thermometer is inserted into a hole bored into the block and it gives the temperature of the metal block and the sample. Heating is accomplished by controlling the voltage applied to the heating element contained within the metal block. The melting process of the sample can be observed using a microscope. Record the melting point range as described above. Carefully operate the instrument according to the rules and regulations indicated in the operation instructions when you use such a melting point apparatus.

Calibration of a thermometer: The accuracy of any type of temperature measurement ultimately depends on the quality and calibration of the thermometer. The melting point measured by the methods above may be different from the authentic melting point of the compound by a degree or two, because of the error of the thermometer. A calibrated thermometer should be used for melting point measurement. For calibration of a thermometer, the melting points of pure organic compounds are commonly used as calibration standards. Choose a series of pure organic compounds as standard substances for the measurement of the temperature in the range of the thermometer. Plot a curve with the melting points observed as a horizontal coordinate and the differences between the observed and the true temperatures as a vertical coordinate. The curve provides a correction that can be applied to the observed readings at the temperature within the range of the thermometer. Calibration over the range of temperature encompassed by the thermometer is necessary because the error is likely to vary at different temperatures.

Basic Techniques for Organic Experiments

A list of suitable standards for thermometer calibration is provided in Table 2.10-1.

Table 2.10-1 Standard compounds for thermometer calibration

compound	melting point/℃	compound	melting point/℃
ice-water	0	urea 尿素	132
p-dichlorobenzene 对二氯苯	53	salicylic acid 水杨酸	159
phenyl benzoate 苯甲酸苯酯	70	2,4-dinitrobenzoic acid 2,4-二硝基苯甲酸	183
naphthalene 萘	80	3,5-dinitrobenzoic acid 3,5-二硝基苯甲酸	205
m-dinitrobenzene 间二硝基苯	90	anthracene 蒽	216
acetanilide 乙酰苯胺	114	p-nitrobenzoic acid 对硝基苯甲酸	242
benzoic acid 苯甲酸	122	anthraquinone 蒽醌	286

The zero point of a thermometer is better calibrated using a mixture of distilled water and pure ice. Pour 20 mL of distilled water into a 15 cm × 2.5 cm test-tube and cool the tube in a brine-ice bath. When the distilled water in the tube is partially frozen, stir the ice-water mixture with a glass rod. After remove the brine-ice bath, put the thermometer to the tube and gently stir the mixture. When the temperature keeps constant (after 2~3 min), note down the readings of the temperature.

2.10.2 Boiling Point

(1) Principle

Boiling point is defined as the temperature at which the total vapor pressure of the liquid is equal to the external pressure. At boiling point, the rate of evaporation increases dramatically and bubbles form in the liquid. Since the boiling point is dependent upon the total pressure, that pressure must be specified when boiling points are reported. The normal boiling point of a liquid is measured at 760 Torr (1 atm). A pure liquid generally boils at a constant temperature or over a narrow temperature range, provided the total pressure in the system remains constant. However, the boiling point of a liquid is affected by the presence of both nonvolatile and volatile impurities, and most mixtures of liquids boil over a fairly wide range.

(2) Boiling point methods

When multi-gram quantity of the sample is available, the boiling point of a liquid is commonly determined by reading the thermometer during a simple distillation. However, for small

Measuring Physical Constants of Organic Compounds

amounts of liquid, a micro boiling point apparatus is used for measurement.

(3) Micro-scale method

First, prepare a capillary ebullition tube by taking a standard melting point capillary tube, which is already sealed at one end, and make a seal in it about 1 cm from the open end. Second, seal a piece of a glass tubing of 4~6 mm internal diameter at one end and cut it to a length about 1 cm longer than the capillary ebullition tube.

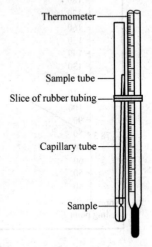

Thermometer

Sample tube

Slice of rubber tubing

Capillary tube

Sample

Figure 2. 10-3   Micro boiling point apparatus

Attach the 4~6 mm tube to a thermometer with a rubber ring near the top of the tube. The bottom of the tube should be even with the mercury bulb of the thermometer. Put the capillary ebullition tube into the larger glass tube, and with a Pasteur pipet add the liquid to be measured until the level of the liquid is about 2 mm above the seal of the capillary tube (Figure 2. 10-3).

Immerse the thermometer and the attached tubes in a heating bath. Heat the oil bath at a rate of about 5 ℃•min^{-1} until a rapid and continuous stream of bubbles comes out of the capillary ebullition tube. However, this is not the boiling point! Remove the heating source and allow the bath to cool slowly. As the liquid start to rise into the capillary tube, note the temperature measured by the thermometer. This is the boiling point of the liquid. At this temperature, the vapor pressure of the liquid becomes equal to the external pressure.

Remove the capillary ebullition tube and expel the liquid from the small end by gently shaking the tube. Replace it in the sample tube and repeat the determination of the boiling point by heating the oil bath at a rate of 1~2 ℃•min^{-1} when the temperature is within 10~15 ℃ of the approximate boiling point as determined in the previous experiment. Note the accurate boiling point of the liquid and the barometric pressure.

(4) Calibration of boiling points

The boiling point of a compound varies under different pressures. In general, the boiling point of a compound will decrease by ca. 0. 35 ℃ from the standard boiling point under 760 mmHg when the external pressure is 10 mmHg lower than the standard atmospheric pressure (760 mmHg). The measured boiling points under different pressures can be calibrated to standard boiling points by using Figure 2. 10-4.

2. 10. 3   Refractive Index

(1) Principle

Refractive index is one of the important physical constants of organic compound. It is useful for identification of a liquid compound and for determination of its purity.

Basic Techniques for Organic Experiments

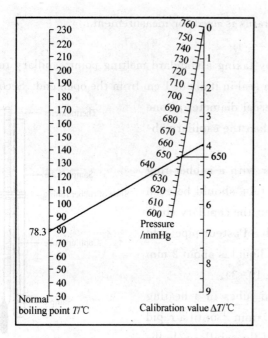

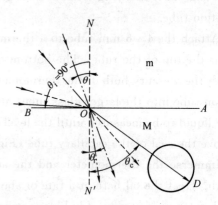

Figure 2.10-4   Nomograph for calibrating boiling points   Figure 2.10-5   Diagram for light refraction

When a beam of light goes into the medium M from another medium m, the speed and the direction of light will change (Unless the beam of light is perpendicular to the interface of two mediums, Figure 2.10-5). This phenomenon is called light refraction. The change in the direction of light is expressed by using an incident angle (θ_i) and refraction angel (θ_r).

According to the law of light refraction, the ratio of the velocity of light in vacuum to its velocity in a given substance can be expressed as following equation. The ratio of v_m/v_M is termed as the refraction index (n) of medium M (vs medium m).

$$n = \frac{v_m}{v_M} = \frac{\sin\theta_i}{\sin\theta_r}$$

When m represents a vacuum circumstance, $v_m = c$ (the velocity of light in vacuum):

$$n = \frac{c}{v_M} = \frac{\sin\theta_i}{\sin\theta_r}$$

Measurement of the refractive index of a liquid is commonly made with light going from air into a liquid medium. Therefore, the equation can be expressed as follows:

$$\frac{c}{v_{air}} = 1.000\ 27 \text{ (refractive index of air)}$$

Thus, in practice, the refractive indexes measured in air are used as the refractive indexes of liquid compounds.

$$n = \frac{v_{air}}{v_{liquid}} = \frac{\sin\theta_i}{\sin\theta_r}$$

Measuring Physical Constants of Organic Compounds

Refractive indexes are influenced by the wavelength of the incident light and the temperature of the liquid. A refraction index is therefore expressed as n_λ^t. For example, n_D^{20} expresses that the refractive index n was measured at 20 ℃ and with the sodium D line ($\lambda = 589$ nm) as the source of illumination. When the wavelength of the incident light and the temperature of the liquid compound are fixed, the refractive index of the compound is a constant.

Because the velocity of light in air is close to that in vacuum, while the velocity of light in any liquid medium is always slower than that in vacuum, therefore, all refractive indexes of liquid compounds are larger than 1. That means θ_i is larger than θ_r in the above equations.

When $\theta_i = 90°$, the θ_r reaches its maximum value, which is called the critical angel (θ_c).

If the θ_i values of incident monochromatic lights vary from 0° to 90°, the refractive light can be observed in the range of $\theta_r = 0°$ to $\theta_r = \theta_c$. So the $N'OD$ region in Figure 2. 10-5 is bright, and the DOA region is dark; OD is a critical boundary between the bright and dark regions. The θ_c can be determined based on the position of the critical boundary. If $\theta_i = 90°$, $\theta_r = \theta_c$; so long as the θ_c is determined, the refractive index of the compound can be obtained according to the following equation.

$$n = \frac{\sin 90°}{\sin \theta_c} = \frac{1}{\sin \theta_c}$$

(2) Instrument

The Abbe refractometer is commonly used to measure the refractive index in the laboratory of organic chemistry. A common type of Abbe refractometer is shown in Figure 2. 10-6. The refractive index can be directly read from the graduate disc of the Abbe refractometer. Since an antichromatic dispersion prism is installed in the instrument, we can directly use white light as a light source, and the obtained refractive index is just the same as that measured with the sodium D line.

(3) Measuring procedure using an Abbe refractometer

First connect the refractometer to a constant temperature bath. Start the circulation water and let the temperature keep at 20 ℃ during the measurement. Carefully open the two prisms. Rinse the surfaces of the prisms with a small amount of acetone, ethanol or diethyl ether, and then gently wipe the surfaces in one direction with lens paper. Wait until the surfaces are completely air-dried, then adjust the surface of the bottom prism in a level state and place a

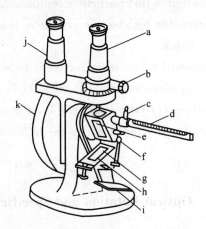

Figure 2. 10-6   Abbe refractometer

a—Eyepiece with lens   b—Chromatic adjustment collar
c—Water exit   d—Thermometer   e~g—Hinged prism
h—Groove for sample   i—Reflector   j—Lens to view
index of refraction scale   k—Index of refraction scale

drop of distilled water on the surface. Take a special care not to touch the surface of the prism! Close the two prisms and gently fasten the shift knob. Turn on the light, look into the eyepiece, and adjust the refraction mirror to make the light shine through the window onto the sample area. Now rotate the prism until a sharp critical boundary between the bright and the dark regions can be clearly seen in the field observable from the eyepiece. If the boundary is in color or somewhat diffused, adjust antichromatic dispersion prism until the boundary becomes clear and sharp, and then rotate the prism to make the boundary positioned exactly through the intersection of the cross lines. At last, adjust the eyepiece of the microscope to focus the image. Note down the reading and the temperature. Repeat the measurement several times by moving the boundary out from the cross lines and recentering it to get a second reading. Take the average value of the readings. The calibration value of the instrument can be obtained by comparing the observed refractive index of pure water with its standard value ($n_D^{20} = 1.332\,99$). Then measure the refractive index of the liquid sample using the same operation procedure. Normally, the calibration value of the instrument is quite small. If the difference between the observed and standard refractive indexes is large, the instrument should be regulated by your instructor.

When using the Abbe refractometer, be careful not to touch the surfaces of the prisms with any hard material and not to scratch the surfaces. Do not use liquids that may erode the parts or dissolve the adhesive between the parts. After measurement, immediately clean the refractometer prism surfaces with lens paper moistened with ethanol or diethyl ether.

It should be noticed that the refractive index has additive property. Even the measured refractive index is identical with that of a compound, we cannot confirm that the sample have been measured is that particular compound. It is possible that the sample is a mixture of two or more compounds because the refractive index of a mixture may also display the same value of refractive index.

The standard values of refractive indexes of compounds, given in handbooks and textbooks, are generally measured at 20 ℃ with the D line of a sodium lamp. If the measurement is made at a temperature (t) rather than 20 ℃, the observed refractive index n_{obs}^t can be corrected to the standard refractive index n_D^{20} by the following equation:

$$n_D^{20} = n_{obs}^t + 0.000\,45(t/℃ - 20)$$

2.10.4 Optical Rotation and Specific Rotation

(1) Principle

Chiral compounds can rotate the plane of polarized light, and the rotation angel is expressed by α. Therefore, chiral compounds are also termed as optically active compounds. Most alkaloids and organic compounds existing in organisms are optically active compounds. When the observer views through the sample toward the source of the plane-polarized light, a clockwise

Measuring Physical Constants of Organic Compounds

rotation of the plane of polarized light is called dextrorotatory, and a counterclockwise rotation is called levorotatory. The direction of rotation is specified by the $(+)$ or $(-)$ sign of the rotation: Dextrorotatory rotations are expressed by $(+)$ sign and levorotatory rotations by $(-)$ sign; the racemate is expressed by $(\pm)$ or (d, l).

In addition of the optical activity of the compound, the rotation (α) also depends on the concentration of the sample solution, the length of the cell, the wavelength of light, the temperature of measurement as well as the property of the solvent. To use the rotation of polarized light as a characteristic property of a compound, the specific rotation $([\alpha])$ is defined as the rotation found using a 10 cm sample cell and a concentration of $1 \text{ g} \cdot \text{mL}^{-1}$ of the sample. With the same wavelength of light and at an identical temperature, the specific rotation of an individual compound is a constant. It is a useful physical property for characterization of chiral compounds and determination of their optical purity in asymmetric synthesis and catalysis studies.

$$[\alpha]_\lambda^t = \frac{\alpha(\text{observed})}{c \cdot l}$$

Where

$\alpha(\text{observed})$ = observed rotation (degrees)

c = concentration $(\text{g} \cdot \text{mL}^{-1})$ of solution

l = path length of cell (decimeters, dm)

λ = wavelength of the light source (nanometers, nm), generally the sodium D line

t = temperature (℃) at which the measurement is made

The solvent used for measurement of the specific rotation should be given together with the $[\alpha]$ value.

The optical purity (op) of a mixture of chiral compounds can be calculated by specific rotations. The optical purity of a mixture is defined as the ratio of its rotation to the rotation of a pure enantiomer measured under the same condition.

$$\text{op} = \frac{[\alpha]_\lambda^t (\text{observed rotation})}{[\alpha]_\lambda^t (\text{rotation of a pure enantiomer})} \times 100\%$$

The enantiomeric excess(ee) is a similar method for expressing the relative amounts of enantiomers in a mixture. For a chemically pure compound, the calculation of enantiomeric excess generally gives the same result as the calculation of optical purity.

(2) Polarimeter

There are different types of polarimeters with varied scales and reading forms. Before using a polarimeter, read the manual of operating rules and regulations for the instrument and understand all points for attention. The modern polarimeters are capable of automatic adjustment and display, and the operation is quite convenient. Figure 2. 10−7 shows a schematic diagram of a polarimeter. When the light passes through a polarizing filter and the cell, an optically active solution can rotate the plane of polarized light. Another polarizing filter is used as an analyzing filter equipped with a protractor. It is turned until a maximum amount of light is observed, and

Basic Techniques for Organic Experiments

the rotation is read from the protractor.

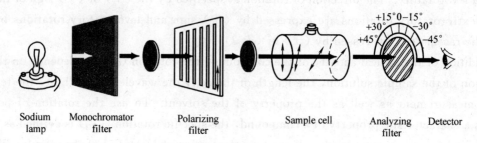

Figure 2. 10−7　Schematic diagram of a polarimeter

(3) Measuring procedure

(a) First, prepare the sample solution. Accurately weigh 0. 1~0. 5 g sample and place it to a 25 mL volumetric flask, then add a certain amount of solvent such as water, ethanol or chloroform to the flask.

(b) Connect the instrument to a 220 V AC power source and turn on the power. Pre-warm and stabilize the instrument for 5 min. Consequently, the sodium lamp lightens.

(c) Turn on the reading switch and regulate the rotation value to the zero point.

(d) Fill the cell with distilled water or a blank solvent. Place the cell into the sample chamber and cover the chamber. The cell should be full of liquid and not have air bubbles. Gently wipe up the mist droplets on the surfaces of the two end of the cell with a soft cloth. If the cap is screwed too tightly, the data observed may be not accurate because of a small stress generated in the cell. Finally, check whether the zero point is in the original position.

(e) Full fill a clean cell with a sample liquid as described in (d). Turn the scale disc to obtain the optical rotation value of the sample.

(f) Reset the instrument and repeat the readings for three times. Take the average value as the final result.

(g) During measurement, the temperature should be kept at (20 ± 2) ℃. The rotation of most optically active compounds will decrease approximately by 0. 3% as the temperature increases by 1 ℃.

2. 10. 5　Relative Density

Relative density is one of the important physical constants for characterization of liquid compounds. It is useful for distinguishing the compounds that have the similar composition but different densities, especially for the liquid samples that cannot be converted to proper solid derivatives. For example, liquid alkanes are usually identified by measurement of their boiling points, densities, refractive indexes and other physical constants. In micro-scale experiment, the volumes of liquid reagents are often calculated on the basis of their densities.

The mass of a substance per unit volume is defined as the density of that compound. The value of density is commonly expressed by d_4^{20}, also called relative density. The value of d_4^{20} represents the mass ratio of the substance at 20 ℃ to water at 4 ℃ in the same volume. Because the density of water at 4 ℃ is 1. 000 00 $g \cdot mL^{-1}$, the d_4^{20} represents the density of a substance when $g \cdot mL^{-1}$ is used as a unit. In general, the density of a substance is influenced by the circumstance conditions such as temperature and pressure. As for solid and liquid substances, the influence of pressure on density can be neglected.

2. 11   Spectroscopic Identification of Organic Compounds

Infrared (IR), nuclear magnetic resonance (NMR) and ultra-violet-visible (UV – Vis) spectroscopy are the most important spectral methods for determining the exact structures of organic compounds. The basic principles and procedures of these spectroscopic techniques are briefly introduced in this chapter.

2. 11. 1   Infrared (IR) Spectroscopy

(1) Principle

Infrared (IR) spectroscopy provides a simple and rapid instrumental technique for determining the presence of various functional groups in the molecules of organic compounds, and therefore it is used widely in chemical studies and productions. When a molecule is irradiated with infrared radiation, energy is absorbed when the frequency of the radiation matches the frequency of the vibrational motion of the molecule. Since each frequency absorbed by a molecule corresponds to a specific molecular motion that involves the specific arrangement of bonded atoms, absorption of IR energy by an organic molecule will occur in a manner characteristic of the types of bonds and atoms present in the specific functional groups of that molecule. According to the positions of the absorption bands in the IR spectrum, we can find out what kinds of bonds and functional groups are present in the molecule. The molecular structure of a compound may be deduced by combining IR spectroscopy with other chemical and instrumental methods.

Common IR spectrometers operate in the region of wavelengths between 2. 5 $\times$ 10^{-4} cm and 25 $\times$ 10^{-4} cm, corresponding to frequencies of 4 000 cm^{-1} to 400 cm^{-1}. The frequency, expressed in wavenumbers (σ) with units of cm^{-1}, is the reciprocal of the wavelength in centimeters. In practice, peak intensities are roughly expressed in terms of strong (s), medium (m) and weak (w) peaks.

(2) Assignments of absorption bands in IR spectra

In general, vibrations of bonds with dipole moments will result in IR absorption and are said to be IR active, while vibrations that produce no change in the dipole moment cannot cause absorption in the IR spectrum and are said to be IR inactive. Short, strong bonds vibrate at a

Basic Techniques for Organic Experiments

higher energy and frequency than long, weak bonds do. Thus, triple bonds absorb at a higher frequency than double bonds, which in turn absorb higher frequency than single bonds. Furthermore, C—H, O—H and N—H bonds vibrate at a higher frequency than bonds between heavier C, O and N atoms.

An IR absorption spectrum can be divided into several regions:

(a) The region from 4 000 cm^{-1} to 2 500 cm^{-1} corresponds to absorptions caused by N—H, O—H and C—H single-bond stretching motions.

(b) The region from 2 500 cm^{-1} to 2 000 cm^{-1} corresponds to absorptions caused by triple-bond (C=C, C≡N) stretching and accumulated double-bond (C=C=C, C=C=O and —N=C=O) antisymmetric stretching motions.

(c) The region from 2 000 cm^{-1} to 1 500 cm^{-1} is where all kinds of double bonds (C=O, C=N and C=C) absorb. Carbonyl groups generally absorb in the range 1 670～1 780 cm^{-1}, and carbon-carbon double-bond stretching normally occurs in the narrow range 1 640 cm^{-1} ～ 1 680 cm^{-1}. Since the absorptions in the region from 4 000 cm^{-1} to 1 500 cm^{-1} are all caused by the motions of functional groups of organic compounds, this region is also called functional group region.

(d) The region from 1 500 cm^{-1} to 600 cm^{-1} is the so-called fingerprint region, including C—C, C—O, C—N and C—X (X=F, Cl, Br, I) stretching as well as C—C and C—O skeleton vibration absorptions.

Table 2.11−1 lists the characteristic IR bands of some common groups.

Table 2. 11−1　Characteristic IR absorptions of some common groups

group	frequency range/cm^{-1}	group	frequency range/cm^{-1}
1. —OH	3 580～3 670	4. ＼C=O／	1 630～1 780
—OH (H−bonded)	3 200～3 400		
2. ＼NH／	3 300～3 500	esters	1 720～1 760
		aldehydes	1 690～1 740
		acyl anhydrides	1 750～1 800
＼NH／ (H−bonded)	3 200～3 400	ketones	1 680～1 750
3. C—H		carboxylic acids	1 710～1 780
		amides	1 630～1 690
≡CH	3 200～3 310	(i) RCO—NH$_2$	$\nu_{C=O}$ 1 650～1 690
=CH—	3 080 ± 10		δ_{N-H} 1 620～1 630
Ar—H	3 000～3 090	(ii) RCO～NHR	$\nu_{C=O}$ 1 640～1 680
—CH$_3$	ν_{as} 2 960 ± 5		δ_{N-H} 1 530～1 570
		(iii) RCO—NR′R″	$\nu_{C=O}$ 1 650
	ν_s 2 870 ± 10	5. C≡C	2 150～2 250
—CH$_2$—	ν_{as} 2 930 ± 5	6. C=C	1 600～1 650
		7. skeleton of benzene ring	1 600, 1 580
	ν_s 2 850 ± 10		1 500, 1 450

Continued

group	frequency range/cm^{-1}	group	frequency range/cm^{-1}
8. C≡N	2 240～2 260	10. NO$_2$	
9. S=O		(i) aliphatic C—NO$_2$	ν_{as} 1 550
(i) sulfoxides RR'SO	1 040～1 060		ν_s 1 370 ± 10
(ii) sulfones RSO$_2$R'	ν_{as} 1 310～1 350	(ii) aromatic C—NO$_2$	ν_{as} 1 525 ± 15
	ν_s 1 120～1 160		ν_s 1 345 ± 10

(3) Measuring procedure

An IR spectrometer operates by passing a beam of infrared radiation through a sample and comparing the radiation transmitted through the sample with that transmitted in the absence of the sample. Any frequencies absorbed by the sample will be apparent by the difference. The spectrometer plots the results as a graph showing transmittance (%) versus frequency (cm^{-1}).

Infrared spectra can be measured using solid, liquid or gaseous samples. For determining the structure of a compound by IR spectroscopy, a pure sample must be used. A solid sample may be measured in three ways: ① to grind the solid with KBr and press the mixture into a disk; ② to grind the solid into a pasty mull with paraffin oil and place the mull between two salt plates made of NaCl (4 000～600 cm^{-1}) or KBr (4 000～400 cm^{-1}); ③ to dissolve the solid in common solvents such as CH$_2$Cl$_2$, CCl$_4$ or CS$_2$ that do not have absorption in the areas of interest. The measurement of a liquid sample is made by simply placing a drop of liquid as a thin film between two salt plates. A gaseous sample is inlet into a longer cell (about 10 cm) with polished salt windows. The KBr, paraffin oil and solvents for IR measurement must be completely dried prior to use and the salt plates must be kept dry and stored in a desiccator.

(4) Examples for interpretation of IR spectra

When interpreting an IR spectrum of a substance, you'd better know the procedure by which it has been prepared. If the melting point, boiling point, refractive index, relative formula weight, solubility and elemental analysis of the substance have been measured by simple physical and chemical methods, these data may help the resolution of the IR spectrum for the substance. The absorptions useful for identifying specific functional groups are usually found in the region from 1 500 cm^{-1} to 3 300 cm^{-1}. Pay particular attention to the carbonyl region (1 670～1 780 cm^{-1}), the aromatic region (1 660～2 000 cm^{-1}), the triple-bond region (2 000～2 500 cm^{-1}) and the C—H region (2 500～3 500 cm^{-1}).

Example 1: Figure 2.11-1 shows the IR spectra of toluene and hexane. The characteristic frequencies for the aromatic compound and aliphatic compound can be clearly seen from the IR spectra of toluene and hexane.

Basic Techniques for Organic Experiments

The co-existence of the aromatic C—H stretching vibration band at 3 030 cm^{-1} and the C=C vibration bands of the benzene skeleton at 1 500 cm^{-1} and 1 600 cm^{-1} in Figure 2. 11−1a provide strong evidence for the presence of an aromatic ring. The aromatic C—H out-of-plane bending bands at 650~900 cm^{-1} give useful information for determining the number and position(s) of the substituents on the benzene ring. The two bands at 690 cm^{-1} and 750 cm^{-1} in Figure 2. 11−1a are the characteristic bands for the monosubstituted derivative of benzene.

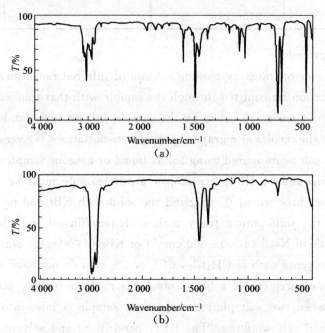

Figure 2. 11−1 IR spectra of (a) toluene and (b) hexane

In Figure 2. 11−1b, there is neither the band at 3 030 cm^{-1} nor bands at 1 500 cm^{-1} and 1 600 cm^{-1}, indicating that this compound is not an aromatic compound.

The C—H stretching vibration bands of alkanes are especially useful for distinguishing saturated hydrocarbons from unsaturated ones. When strong absorption bands appear under 3 000 cm^{-1}, at ca. 2 860 cm^{-1} and 2 930 cm^{-1}, it can be attributed to the absorptions of the saturated C—H bond. If a molecule consists of an alkenyl group (=CH$_2$), in the IR spectrum, the absorption band will appear near 3 100 cm^{-1}, which is higher than the aromatic C—H stretching vibration frequency. For terminal alkynes, the frequency of the ≡C—H absorption band is commonly displayed near 3 300 cm^{-1}.

The strong bands between 2 800 cm^{-1} and 3 000 cm^{-1} in Figure 2. 11−1b result from C—H stretching vibration and there is no band observed in the region higher than 3 000 cm^{-1}. In addition, the band at 1 460 cm^{-1} results from a scissoring vibration of the —CH$_2$— groups and the absorption at 1 380 cm^{-1} results from the rocking of —CH$_3$. The band at 720 cm^{-1} is a characteristic band due to the in-plane rocking of a long chain —(CH$_2$)$_n$—($n \geqslant 4$). On the analysis of Figure 2.11−1b, we could be fairly certain that there is no functional group in the compound. The spectrum suggests that it is an alkane with a C_6 or longer than C_6 chain in the molecule.

Example 2: Figure 2.11−2 compares the IR spectra of butanone, butyraldehyde, and methyl butyrate. All three spectra show intense absorptions in the carbonyl region, at 1 715 cm^{-1}, 1 725 cm^{-1} and 1 735 cm^{-1} in Figure 2.11−2a−c, respectively. We cannot simply designate Figure 2.11−1a−c to butanone, butanal and methyl butyrate only according to the C=O stretching vibrations. The other characteristic bands must be considered.

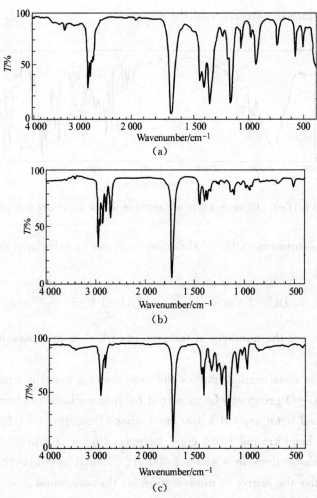

Figure 2.11−2   IR spectra of (a) butanone, (b) butyraldehyde
and (c) methyl butyrate

In addition to the strong C=O stretching absorption, an aldehyde displays two characteristic bands around 2 700 cm^{-1} and 2 800 cm^{-1} arising from the C—H stretching frequencies of the O=C—H group. Neither a ketone nor an ester shows these absorptions. Figure 2.11 − 2b

Basic Techniques for Organic Experiments

shows two characteristic bands at 2 720 cm^{-1} and 2 820 cm^{-1}, so this spectrum can be designate to butyraldehyde.

In addition to the strong C=O stretching absorption, an ester also displays typical band(s) between 1 050 cm^{-1} to 1 300 cm^{-1} due to the symmetric and antisymmetric stretching vibration of C—O—C bonds. The antisymmetric stretching vibration band in the fingerprint region of 1 160~1 210 cm^{-1} is usually strong and broad, and sometimes splits into two bands. We can observe an intense absorption at about 1 200 cm^{-1} in Figure 2. 11-2c. So it can be ascribed to methyl butyrate.

Example 3: Figure 2. 11-3 shows an IR spectrum of a compound with a molecular formula C$_9$H$_{10}$O. Try to deduce the structure of the compound.

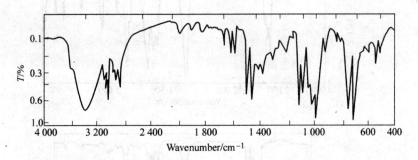

Figure 2. 11-3   IR spectrum of a compound with a molecular formula C$_9$H$_{10}$O

The degree of unsaturation (DU) of the compound can be calculated according to the following equation:

$$DU = 1 + n_4 + \frac{n_3 - n_1}{2} \qquad DU = 1 + 9 + \frac{0 - 10}{2} = 5$$

Where n_4, n_3 and n_1 are the numbers of tetravalent, trivalent and univalent atoms, respectively, in the molecule.

The high degree of unsaturation implies the presence of a benzene ring in the molecule.

The presence of C=O group can be ruled out because no band is observed near 1 700 cm^{-1}. The strong and broad band around 3 400 cm^{-1} arises from the stretching vibration of O—H group. The strong band around 1 050 cm^{-1} suggests that it is a primary alcohol. A series of weak and medium absorptions in 1 450~1 600 cm^{-1} found in Figure 2. 11-3 are typical for benzene ring. Because the degree of unsaturation for the compound is 5, there should be another C=C bond, which may conjugate with the benzene ring. Furthermore, the absorption bands at 700 cm^{-1} and 750 cm^{-1} indicate that the benzene ring is monosubstituted. On the basis of these analyses, the compound might be 3-phenyl-2-propen-1-ol.

The structure of the sample must be further verified. If the sample is a known compound, look up the standard IR spectrum of that compound from an IR atlas such as Sadtler IR atlas, and compare the standard spectrum of that compound with that of the sample. If the positions, shapes and relative intensities of the characteristic bands are all identical in the two spectra, the structure of the sample can be confirmed. In another way, you can record the IR spectrum of the pure compound that is proposed for the sample to be verified under the same condition, and see whether the spectra of the pure compound and the sample are identical. If the sample is an unknown compound, the structure of a new compound cannot be convincingly determined using only the IR spectrum. Other advanced techniques such as elemental analysis, MS, NMR, UV−Vis spectroscopy and even single crystal X−ray diffraction should be utilized, and sometimes other chemical analysis are helpful for confirming the structures of complicated molecules.

2.11.2   Nuclear Magnetic Resonance (NMR) Spectroscopy

(1) Principle

Nuclear magnetic resonance spectroscopy (NMR) is the most powerful spectroscopic method available for determining the structures of organic compounds. This technique depends on the property of nuclear spin that is exhibited by certain nuclei when they are placed in a magnetic field. The nuclei of ^1H, ^2H, ^{19}F, ^{13}C, ^{15}N and ^{31}P have this property. For organic chemists, proton (^1H) and carbon−13 (^{13}C) NMR are the most useful because hydrogen and carbon are major components of organic compounds. When one places a compound containing ^1H or ^{13}C atoms in a very strong magnetic field and simultaneously irradiates it with electromagnetic energy, the nuclei of the compound may absorb energy through a process called magnetic resonance. This absorption of energy is quantized and gives a characteristic spectrum for the compound.

Instruments known as NMR spectrometers allow chemists to measure the absorption of energy by ^1H or ^{13}C nucleus and by some other nuclei. Like IR spectroscopy, NMR spectra can be measured with a very small amount of sample, and it does not destroy the sample. The variations in the positions of NMR absorptions are called chemical shift with units of parts per million (δ, ppm). The chemical shift of tetramethylsilane (TMS) is set as the zero point. Therefore, the chemical shift in a ^1H—NMR spectrum is defined as the difference between the resonance frequency of the proton being observed and that of TMS. Similarly, the chemical shift in a ^{13}C—NMR spectrum is defined as the difference between the resonance frequency of the carbon−13 being observed and that of TMS. The NMR spectrum is printed with absorption intensity on the y axis and the chemical shifts on the x axis.

(2) Structural information from ^1H—NMR spectra

Most of ^1H—NMR signals of organic compounds occur 0~10 ppm downfield from the proton signal of TMS. The absorptions of more shielded protons and carbons appear upfield, toward the right of the spectrum, and less shielded protons and carbons appear down field, toward the left. Figure 2.11−4 gives the regions of the chemical shifts of protons with various chemical environments.

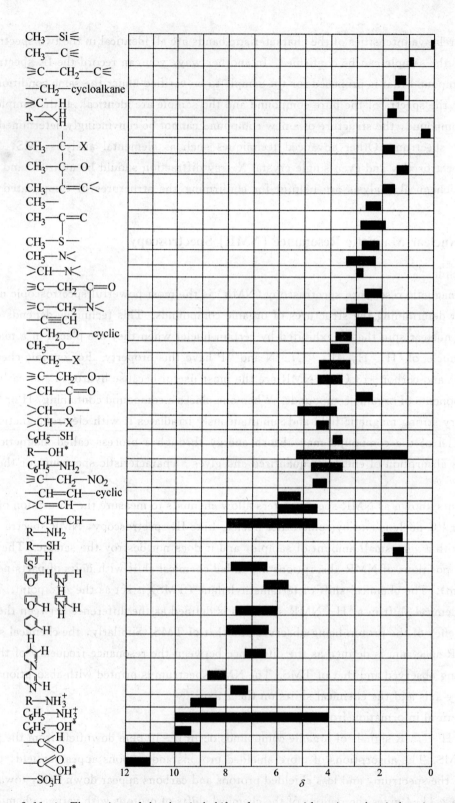

Figure 2.11-4   The regions of the chemical shifts of protons with various chemical environments

Spectroscopic Identification of Organic Compounds

We can get important information in three aspects from a ^{1}H—NMR spectrum:

(a) The position of the absorption (the chemical shift) of a proton depends on its chemical environment, that is, the property of the atom or group bonded with the proton. According to the number of the signals, we can determine how many types of protons are present in the molecule being detected.

(b) The area under a signal, either singlet or multiplet, is proportional to the number of hydrogen atoms contributing to that signal. The relative areas of signals are integrated by the integral trace. Thus the height of the integral trace is proportional to the number of hydrogen atoms contributing to that signal. The ratio of the heights of integral traces for all signals reflects the ratio of different types of relative protons in the molecule. Figure 2.11−5 shows the integrated spectrum of ethyl 2−phenylacetate. The ratio of the integral trace heights from left to right is 60 : 24 : 24 : 36. That equals to 5 : 2 : 2 : 3, representing the ratio of these four different types of protons.

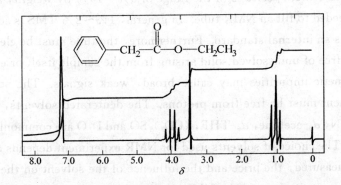

Figure 2.11−5 ^{1}H—NMR spectrum of ethyl 2−phenylacetate

(c) When two different types of protons are close enough, their signals will be split into multiplets because the interaction or coupling, of the spins of nearby nuclei. Chemically equivalent protons do not show this kind of spin-spin splitting. In general, the multiplicity of a signal is given by the "$n+1$" rule, that is, if a signal is split by n equivalent neighboring protons it is split into $n+1$ peaks with a coupling constant (J). Therefore, according to the splitting pattern of a signal for a specific proton and the coupling constant, we can deduce the number of its neighboring protons and the spatial relationship of the protons in a molecule.

Figure 2.11−6 shows the ^{1}H—NMR spectrum of chloroethane. Let us analyse the splitting of the signals for the ethyl group in chloroethane. The signal of the methyl ($-CH_3$) protons is split into a triplet of areas 1 : 2 : 1 by two adjacent protons of $-CH_2-$, and the signal of the methylene ($-CH_2-$) protons is split into a quartet of areas 1 : 3 : 3 : 1 by three protons of $-CH_3$. Two groups (a and b) of protons coupled to each other have the same coupling constant, $J_{ab} = J_{ba}$.

(3) Measuring procedure

Basic Techniques for Organic Experiments

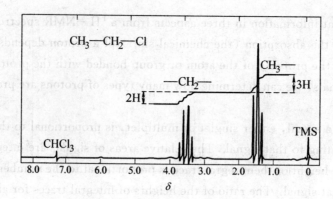

Figure 2.11-6 ^{1}H—NMR spectrum of chloroethane

Liquid samples are commonly used for measurement of NMR spectra. The liquid or solid sample is generally dissolved in an appropriate solvent. The proper concentration of the solutions to obtain satisfied NMR spectra is in the range of 5%~15% by weight, and about 0.5~ 1 mL of solution is needed to fill an NMR tube. In general, 1%~2% TMS is added to the solution to be measured as an internal standard. Furthermore, the tube must be clean and dry, and the solution must be free of undissolved solid arising from the sample itself or even dust. Trace amounts of ferromagnetic impurities may cause broad, weak signals. The solvents used for ^{1}H—NMR measurement must be free from protons. The deuterated solvents, such as $CDCl_3$, CD_2Cl_2, C_6D_6, CD_3CN, d_6-acetone, d_6-THF, $(CD_3)_2SO$ and D_2O are commonly used for ^{1}H—NMR measurement. The choice of solvents used for NMR experiment depends on the solubility of the sample to be measured, the price and the influence of the solvent on the spectrum.

(4) Examples for interpretation of ^{1}H—NMR spectra

Example 1:   Figure 2.11-7 shows the ^{1}H—NMR spectrum of 2-phenylpropane. The signal at δ 1.25 ppm is attributed to the two —CH_3 groups, which is split into a doublet by the adjacent proton of the methine $\left(\overset{|}{-CH-}\right)$ group. Accordingly, the heptet at δ 2.90 ppm belongs to the $\overset{|}{-CH-}$ group, which is coupled with the six equivalent adjacent protons of two —CH_3 groups. The same coupling constant of these two sets of signals further proves that the —CH_3 and $\overset{|}{-CH-}$ groups are adjacent to each other. The five protons of the benzene ring appear as a singlet at δ 7.25 ppm. According to the analysis, the structure of 2-phenylpropane can be confirmed.

Example 2:   An unknown liquid has a molecular formula of $C_8H_{14}O_4$ and a boiling point of 218 ℃. Its IR spectrum shows the presence of a carbonyl group and the absence of the aromatic ring in the molecule. The ^{1}H—NMR spectrum of this unknown liquid is given in Figure 2.11-8. Please deduce the structure of the unknown compound.

First, the unknown compound has 14 hydrogen atoms but displays only three ^{1}H—NMR sig-

Spectroscopic Identification of Organic Compounds

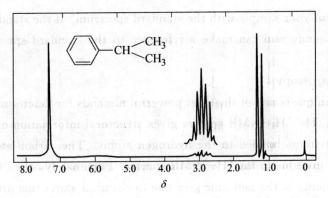

Figure 2. 11-7 ^{1}H—NMR spectrum of 2-phenylpropane

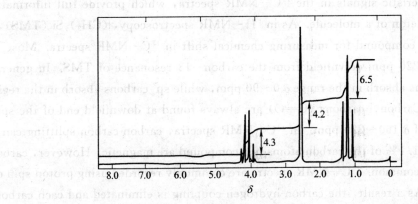

Figure 2. 11-8 ^{1}H—NMR spectrum of an unknown liquid

nals. This indicates that the compound might possess a symmetric molecular structure. Second, there is no signal in the region of $\delta > 6$ ppm, showing that the benzene ring and the =CH group are absent in the unknown compound. The triplet at δ 1.3 ppm (6H) is ascribed to the two —CH$_3$ groups, which is coupled with the two adjacent protons of —CH$_2$— group. Accordingly, the —CH$_2$— resonance appears as a quartet at δ 4.1 ppm (2H), resulting from coupling with a —CH$_3$ group. The downfield chemical shift of the —CH$_2$— group implies that the protons are apparently deshielded by connection of the —CH$_2$— group to an element with strong electronegativity. In the present compound, it should be an oxygen atom. The structure of —COOCH$_2$CH$_3$ is assumed to be the possible unit of the molecule. The singlet at δ 2.5 ppm (4H) is attributed to the two —CH$_2$— groups, that is, —CO—CH$_2$CH$_2$—CO—, in which the four protons are equivalent (Equivalent protons do not coupling with each other). The structure of the unknown compound can be drawn as follows on the basis of the above deduction.

$$CH_3CH_2—O—CO—CH_2CH_2—CO—OCH_2CH_3$$

If the prepared compounds are known compounds, you can look up the Sadtler NMR atlas or find the standard spectrum of that compound from the spectroscopic data bases on Internet, and

Basic Techniques for Organic Experiments

compare the spectrum of your sample with the standard spectrum. If the standard spectrum of a compound cannot be found, you can make a reference to the standard spectrum of a similar compound.

(5) ^{13}C—NMR spectroscopy

The ^{13}C—NMR technique is one of the most powerful methods for determining the structures of organic compounds. The ^{1}H—NMR spectra gives structural information of hydrogen atoms and the related carbon atoms bonded to the hydrogen atoms. The carbon atom that does not bond with hydrogen is invisible in the ^{1}H—NMR spectra. Fortunately, the ^{13}C nuclei in different electronic environments in the molecule give rise to chemical shifts that are characteristic of the magnetic environments of various types of carbon atoms. All types of carbon atoms, including primary, secondary, tertiary carbon atoms, the C=O, C≡N and other quarternary carbons, exhibit characteristic signals in the ^{13}C—NMR spectra, which provide full information about the carbon skeleton of a molecule. As in ^{1}H—NMR spectroscopy, $(CH_3)_4Si$ (TMS), is used as the reference compound for measuring chemical shift in ^{13}C—NMR spectra. Most ^{13}C resonances occur $1\sim220$ ppm downfield from the carbon−13 resonance of TMS. In general, sp^3−hybridized carbons absorb in the range $\delta\ 0\sim90$ ppm, while sp^2 carbons absorb in the region of $\delta\ 110\sim220$ ppm. Carbonyl carbons (C=O) are always found at downfield end of the spectrum, in the region of $\delta\ 160\sim220$ ppm. In ^{13}C—NMR spectra, carbon-carbon splitting can be ignored because only 1.1% of the carbon atoms in a compound are magnetic. However, carbon-hydrogen coupling is common. ^{13}C—NMR spectra are commonly recorded using proton spin decoupling technique. As a result, the carbon-hydrogen coupling is eliminated and each carbon−13 signal appears as a singlet.

The proton signals in ^{1}H—NMR spectrum of nicotine, as shown in Figure 2. 11−9a are apparently overlapped with each other and difficult to interpret, while in its ^{13}C—NMR spectrum (Figure 2. 11−9b), each carbon−13 atom of nicotine exhibits a singlet. The carbon−13 signals of the sp^3−hybridized carbon atoms ($-CH_3$, C−2′, C−3′, C−4′ and C−5′) appear in the high field of the spectrum and the signals of the aromatic ring (C−2, C−3, C−4, C−5 and C−6) appear in the downfield. Because ^{13}C—NMR spectroscopy has the above-mentioned advantages, it is one of the indispensable methods to verify and determine the structures of organic compounds, especially the compounds with complicated structures. In practical application, combination of ^{1}H and ^{13}C—NMR spectra is usually necessary for structure determination. These two methods can complement each other.

2.11.3 Ultra-Violet-Visible (UV-Vis) Spectroscopy

(1) Principle

Ultraviolet spectroscopy detects the electronic transitions of conjugated systems and provides information about the length and structure of the conjugated system of a molecule. The spectrometers often extend into the visible region and are called UV-Vis spectrometers, which com-

Spectroscopic Identification of Organic Compounds

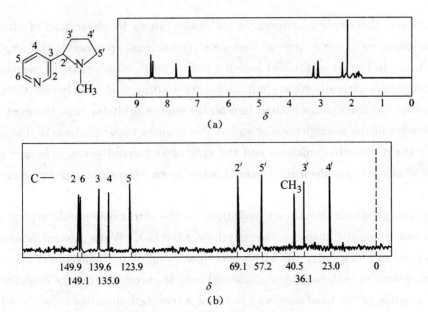

Figure 2. 11−9   Nicotine in d_6-acetone

(a) ^{1}H—NMR spectrum   (b) ^{13}C—NMR proton spin decoupling spectrum

monly operate in the range of 200 nm to 800 nm (nanometers, 10^{-9} m). When a compound containing multiple bonds is irradiated by ultraviolet-visible light, a portion of the radiation is absorbed by the compound. The absorbed UV-Vis energies correspond to the energies needed to excite electrons from molecular orbitals of lower energy to the ones of higher energy. The wavelengths of ultraviolet-visible light absorbed by a molecule are determined by the electronic energy differences between involved orbitals in the molecule.

The absorbance, A, of the sample at a particular wavelength is governed by the Beer-Lambert law.

$$A = \lg\left(\frac{I_r}{I_s}\right) = \varepsilon c l$$

Where

c = sample concentration in moles per liter;

l = path length of light through the cell in centimeters;

ε = the molar absorptivity (or molar extinction coefficient) of the sample.

The molar absorptivity, ε, being a characteristic physical constant of a conjugated organic compound, is a measure of how strongly the sample absorbs light at that wavelength. The wavelength of maximum absorbance is called λ_{max} and the maximum molar extinction coefficient at λ_{max} is termed as ε_{max}. An UV−Vis spectrum is a plot of the absorbance of the sample as a function of the wavelength. The spectral information is given as a list of the values of λ_{max} together with the corresponding values of ε_{max}.

The values of λ_{max} and ε_{max} for molecules depend on the exact nature of the conjugated system

Basic Techniques for Organic Experiments

and its substituents. Electronic transitions in molecules caused by absorption of ultraviolet or visible light include $n \to \pi^*$, $\pi \to \pi^*$, $n \to \sigma^*$ and $\sigma \to \sigma^*$ transitions. In general, the $\sigma \to \sigma^*$ and $n \to \sigma^*$ transitions occur in the far-ultraviolet region (< 200 nm), which must be measured under vacuum, therefore these transitions are not useful for routine analysis. In contrast, π bonds have electrons that are more easily excited into higher energy orbitals, thus the $\pi \to \pi^*$ and $n \to \pi^*$ transitions occur in the near-ultraviolet and visible regions ($200 \sim 800$ nm). They are most useful for both the quantitative analysis and the structural determination. The $\pi \to \pi^*$ transitions generally display strong absorption bands, while $n \to \pi^*$ transitions give rise to weak absorption bands.

Unsaturated groups which can absorb radiations in the ultraviolet-visible region are called chromophore, and it usually displays characteristic band(s). When several non-conjugated chromophores exist in a molecule, the ultraviolet absorption of the molecule is the supraposition of the absorptions of each individual chromophore; If chromophores are conjugated in the molecule, the position of the band moves to the long-wavelength direction, also called red shift or bathochromic shift, and the molar extinction coefficient of the compound will increase. Groups containing p electrons such as $-NR_2$, $-OR$, $-SR$, and $-X$ (X = F, Cl, Br, I) do not absorb radiation in the ultraviolet-visible region by themselves, but when they are connected with a chromophore to form a $\pi-p$ conjugated system, they can cause the absorptive maximum to shift to a longer wavelength. These functional groups are termed as auxochromes. The auxochromic effect of an auxochrome is constant.

(2) Application of UV-Vis spectroscopy

UV-Vis spectroscopy is used for both the structural characterization and the quantitative analysis of conjugated organic compounds. Because UV-Vis spectra usually display broad bands overlapped with each other, and most of simple functional groups have only weak absorption(s) or no absorption for the radiation in the ultraviolet-visible region, it is difficult to confirm the structure of a compound only by its UV-Vis spectrum. It must be combined with other instrumental and chemical methods. However, the detection sensitivity of the UV-Vis spectroscopy is very high. It can detect compounds in the concentration of 10^{-4} to 10^{-5} or even 10^{-6} to 10^{-7} mol$\cdot$L^{-1}. Thus, it is important technique for quantitative analysis of organic compounds.

There are two ways for the structure elucidation of organic compounds using UV-Vis spectra to indicate whether conjugation is present in a given sample. When the sample is a known compound, just compare the measured spectrum of the sample with the standard spectrum of the supposed compound from an atlas such as Sadtler Standard Spectra (Ultraviolet). If the two UV-Vis spectra are identical, we can make sure that the sample and the reference compound have the same structure of chromophore. The other method is to calculate the maximum absorption wavelengths (λ_{max}) by empirical rules, and compare the measured values with calculated ones. To do so, you should first look up the characteristic λ_{max} values of chromophores and the substituent corrections of auxochromes in the molecule, and then calculate the λ_{max} values of the measured compound according to the Woodward and Scott rules. The former rule is mainly used for conjugated polyenes and the latter for aromatic compounds. At last, compare the measured values with calculated values for structural determination.

A more widespread use of UV-Vis spectroscopy, however, is to determine the concentration of an unknown sample. The relationship $A = \varepsilon cl$ indicates that with a fixed path length (l) of the light beam, the amount of absorption by a sample at a certain wavelength is dependent on its concentration. This relationship is usually linear over a range of concentrations suitable for analysis. To determine the unknown concentration of a sample, a graph of absorbance versus concentration is made for a set of standards of known concentrations. The wavelength used for analysis is usually the λ_{max} of the sample. The concentration of the sample is obtained by measuring its absorbance and finding the corresponding value of concentration from the graph of known concentrations of the sample.

(3) Measurement of UV-Vis spectra

To measure the UV-Vis spectrum of a compound, the sample should be well dissolved in a solvent that does not absorb above 200 nm. Because UV-Vis spectroscopy is highly sensitive, samples and solvents for UV-Vis spectroscopy must be extremely pure. A minute impurity with a large absorptivity can easily obscure the spectrum of the desired compound. The sample solution is placed in a quartz cell, and some of the solvent is placed in a reference cell. The concentration of the sample solution is commonly 10^{-4} mol·L^{-1} to 10^{-6} mol·L^{-1}. An ultraviolet spectrometer operates by comparing the amount of light transmitted through the sample (the sample beam, I_s) with the amount of light in the reference beam (I_r). The reference beam passes through the reference cell to compensate for any absorption of light by the cell and the solvent. The measurement of UV-Vis spectra is normally made at room temperature.

2.12   Manipulation Techniques for Air-Sensitive Compounds

2.12.1   General Introduction

Some organic compounds, especially organometallic compounds, are air-sensitive and tend to decompose if they are exposed to air. Therefore, when handling air-sensitive compounds, all manipulations must be made under protection of inert gas such as nitrogen, argon and helium. For carrying out experiments with exclusion of air, the following techniques are employed:

(a) vacuum line technique;

(b) Schlenk technique;

(c) glove-box technique.

Depending on the objectives and air sensitivity of the compounds handled, one technique or a combination of techniques are used. In general, techniques using vacuum line and Schlenk

Basic Techniques for Organic Experiments

glassware are sufficient and convenient for most purposes of handling air-sensitive compounds. For example, vacuum line and Schlenk technique must be used for preparation of Grignard reagents, lithium alkylides and other air-sensitive compounds in an organic laboratory.

2. 12. 2 Basic Techniques for Handling Air-Sensitive Compounds

For handling air-sensitive compounds, all glassware and apparatus must be completely dried before use. Clean glassware should be dried in an oven at 120 ℃ for more than 2 hours, and then place the dried glassware in a desiccator for cooling. Reagents and solvents must be distilled over proper drying agents and stored under inert gas. All air-sensitive materials, either reagents, intermediates or products, should be stored under protection of inert gas.

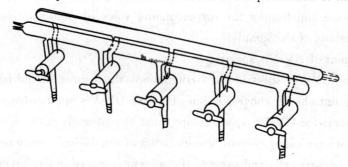

Figure 2. 12−1   A double bank manifold used for handling air-sensitive compounds

A useful apparatus is the double bank manifold (Figure 2. 12−1), which can conveniently switch between vacuum and inert gas. The common Schlenk tube is shown in Figure 2. 12−2. With the Schlenk tube connecting to a double bank manifold, we can transfer a solid or liquid in an atmosphere of an inert gas that is introduced from the stopcock A and escapes from the outlet B. The opening mouth B has a standard ground-glass joint. The Schlenk tube is stopped and evacuated by pumping through D. The inert gas can be introduced to the Schlenk tube through A by switching the stopcock on the manifold. The usual operation is to repeat the evacuation and the inert gas filling cycle a few times.

The transfer of a small amount of liquid can be performed by using a syringe with a long needle. The apparatus shown in Figure 2. 12−3 can be used for transfer of a liquid sample and filtration. A U-shape glass tube (A) is used as a siphon for transferring a liquid sample by applying a moderate pressure of inert gas through the side arm via stopcock B. If a glass-frit (C) is fused onto the

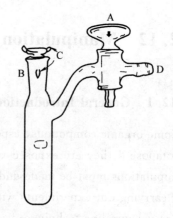

Figure 2. 12−2   A Schlenk tube used for handling air-sensitive compounds

transfer tube, a sample can be filtered and the filtrate is purged into a second Schlenk tube. This filtration method is convenient for a small amount of sample.

Manipulation Techniques for Air-Sensitive Compounds

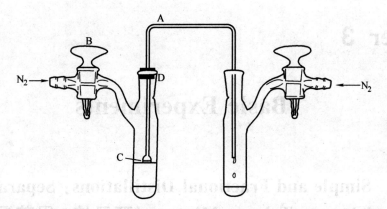

Figure 2.12−3   Filtration apparatus with a U-shape glass tube bridge equipped with a glass frit

Chapter 3

Basic Experiments

3.1   Simple and Fractional Distillations: Separation of a Cyclohexane-Toluene Mixture (环己烷－甲苯混合物)

Fundamental Knowledge

Simple and fractional distillations are fundamental techniques for separation and purification of liquid organic mixture. Whether simple or fractional distillation should be adopted for separating a liquid mixture mainly depends on two factors: (1) the difference of the boiling points among the components of the liquid mixture to be separated; (2) the purity requirements for the separated compounds. Simple distillation allows isolation of the various components of the mixture in acceptable purity if the difference between the boiling points of each pure substance is greater than 40~50 ℃. If this is not the case, the technique of fractional distillation is normally used to obtain each volatile component of a mixture in pure form.

For fundamental knowledge on simple and fractional distillations, please also see Section 2.7.1and 2.7.2.

Purposes and Requirements

(1) Understand the principles for simple and fractional distillations (Review the contents of Section 2.7.1 and 2.7.2).

(2) Master the manipulations of simple distillation and fractional distillation.

(3) Learn the method for determination of the percentage contents of the components in a liquid organic mixture by GC analysis.

Principle

The boiling points of pure cyclohexane and toluene are 81 ℃ and 110 ℃ (0.1 MPa, 760 mmHg), respectively. The difference of the boiling points of these two compounds is 29 ℃, so the cyclohexane-toluene mixture cannot be satisfactorily separated by simple distillation, and the fractional distillation will give a much better result.

Apparatus

A 50 mL round-bottom flask, simple distillation apparatus, fractional distillation apparatus, 50 mL graduated cylinder, six 25 mL Erlenmeyer flasks labeled with a series of No. 1 to No. 6.

Reagents

Cyclohexane (环己烷)	30 mL
Toluene (甲苯)	30 mL

Time   5 h

Safety Alert

(1) Cyclohexane and toluene are highly flammable, so it is better to use flameless heating.

(2) Examine your glassware for cracks and other weaknesses before assembling the distillation apparatus to prevent the glassware from breaking upon heating.

(3) Proper assemble of glassware is important in order to avoid possible breakage and spillage and to avoid the release of distillate vapors into the room.

(4) Be certain that the water hoses are securely fastened to the condenser and that the cooling water is running in the condenser before beginning the distillation.

(5) Never heat a closed system because the pressure buildup may cause the apparatus to explode.

(6) Avoid excessive inhalation of organic vapors at all times.

Procedure for Simple Distillation

(1) **Setting Up**   Pour 15 mL of cyclohexane and 15 mL of toluene into a 50 mL round-bottom flask. Add 2 pieces of boiling chips to the flask [1], and assemble a simple distillation apparatus as shown in Figure 2.7−1a according to the "bottom-to-top" and left-to-right" principle. Fit a thermometer to the stillhead through a thermometer adaptor. Make sure that the top of the mercury bulb of the thermometer is level with the bottom of the sidearm of the stillhead. Use a 10 mL graduated cylinder as a receiver. Finally, turn on the cooling water and let it go through the condenser from the lower entering nipple to the upper exit. Make sure that all connections in the apparatus are tight before beginning the distillation.

(2) **Simple Distillation**   Heat slowly the solution using the heating method specified by your instructor, and as soon as the liquid begins to boil and the condenser vapors have reached the thermometer bulb, regulate the heat supply so that distillation continues steadily at a rate of 1～2 drops per second. Record the temperature of the first-drop distillate[2]. Continue the distillation and record the head temperature whenever 1 mL of the distillate is collected in the graduated cylinder. Pour the distillate with the boiling point lower than 84 ℃ into the No. 1 Erlenmeyer flask. After the head temperature remains at 81 ℃ for a period of time, it will either

Basic Experiments

rise or drop slightly. As soon as the temperature deviates from 81 ℃ by more than ±3 ℃, in-crease the amount of heat supplied to the distillation flask. The temperature will start to rise again, and more liquid will distil. Record the head temperature and the volume of the distilled liquid more frequently as the temperature rises from 81 ℃ to 110 ℃. Pour the distillate between 84～107 ℃ into the No. 2 Erlenmeyer flask and the distillate with the boiling point higher than 107 ℃ into the No. 3 flask. Discontinue heating when only 2～3 mL of the liquid remains in the distillation flask[3]. Record the volumes of the distillates in No. 1, No. 2 and No. 3 Erlenmeyer flasks, and also note down the volume of the residue left in the stillpot.

Procedure for Fractional Distillation

(1) **Setting Up**   Pour 15 mL of cyclohexane and 15 mL of toluene into a 50 mL round-bottom flask. Add 2 pieces of boiling chips to the flask[1], and assemble a fractional distillation appara-tus as shown in Figure 2. 7-5a. Insulate the fractioning column by wrapping it with aluminum foil or glasswool[4]. The other setting-up operations are just the same as those described for simple distillation.

(2) **Fractional Distillation**   Heat the solution as described for simple distillation[5], and regu-late the heat so that distillation continues steadily at a rate no faster than 1 drop of distillate every 1 to 2 second; if a drop of liquid cannot be seen suspended from the end of the thermome-ter, the rate of distillation is too fast. The following operations are the same as those described for simple distillation. Pour the distillates that are collected below 84 ℃, between 84～107 ℃ and above 107 ℃ into No. 4, No. 5 and No. 6 Erlenmeyer flasks, respectively. Record the vol-umes of the distillates in the three flasks and also note down the volume of the residue left in the stillpot.

Notes

[1] Addition of boiling chips can prevent the solution from bumping. Do not add boiling chips to a hot solution, it may cause a bumping and vigorous boiling.

[2] If there is a fore-run, the head temperature of the first few drops could be somewhat lower than 81 ℃. Otherwise the head temperature at this moment should be the boiling point of cyclohexane.

[3] For safety, never distil liquids to dryness.

[4] This insulation measure can be omitted.

[5] It is important to make the vapor (the ring of condensates) rise slowly to the top of the fractionating column.

Finishing Touches

Decant the distillation flask residue into a container for waste organic solvents. Pour the dis-tillates into a designated container for the recovered cyclohexane and toluene.

Analysis and Data Processing

(1) If a GC instrument is available, analyze the percentage contents of the components in the six distillate samples obtained from the two distillation methods.

(2) Draw plots of simple distillation and fractional distillation on a piece of coordinate paper with the distilling temperature (℃) as ordinate and the volume of the distillate (mL) as abscissa. Compare the separation efficiency of simple distillation and fractional distillation.

(3) Fill in the following table and calculate the volume percentages of the components in each collected distillate and in the residue.

separation method	item	<84 ℃	84~107 ℃	>107 ℃	residue	loss	total
simple distillation	volume/mL						30
	volume percentage/%						100
fractional distillation	volume/mL						30
	volume percentage/%						100

Physical Property of Cyclohexane and Toluene

Cyclohexene: bp 81 ℃, n_D^{20} 1.425 2, d_4^{20} 0.779 0. Toluene: bp 110 ℃, n_D^{20} 1.496 8, d_4^{20} 0.865 0.

Questions

(1) Compare the two distillation methods on the basis of the purity and the recovery of cyclohexane and toluene. Compare the separation efficiency of two distillation methods by means of the separation plots or the data of GC analysis.

(2) Explain why the column of a fractional distillation apparatus should be aligned as near to the vertical as possible.

(3) The top of the mercury bulb of the thermometer placed at the head of a distillation apparatus should be adjacent to the exit opening to the condenser. Explain the effect on the observed temperature reading if the bulb is placed (a) below the opening to the condenser or (b) above the opening.

(4) In the distillation of the cyclohexane-toluene mixture, the first few drops of distillate may be cloudy. Explain.

(5) What effect does the reduction of atmospheric pressure have on the boiling point? Can cyclohexane and toluene be separated if the external pressure is 350 mmHg (0.046 MPa) instead of 760 mmHg (0.1 MPa)?

3.2   Intramolecular Dehydration of Alcohols: Preparation of Cyclohexene (环己烯)

Fundamental Knowledge

Dehydration of alcohols is one of the practical methods to prepare alkenes, especially in laboratory. The reaction is catalyzed by strong acids, such as sulfuric acid and phosphoric acid. An acidic catalyst can protonate the hydroxyl group of the alcohols and convert it to a good leaving group (H_2O). The alkene is generated by loss of water from a protonated alcohol to form a carbocation, followed by loss of a proton from the adjacent carbon of the carbocation. As acid-catalyzed dehydration undergoes by E1 elimination, tertiary and secondary alcohols give good to high yields of alkenes, while poor yields are common with primary alcohols. Rearrangements of the primary and secondary carbocations may take place, if it is possible, to give isomeric alkenes. The more highly substituted alkene is the major product, in accordance to the Zaitsev's rule.

cyclohexanol   oxonium ion   carbocation   cyclohexene

Purposes and Requirements

(1) Review the acid-catalyzed dehydration of alcohols, e.g., the mechanism and regionselectivity of the reaction as well as the stability and rearrangement of carbocations.

(2) Master the techniques of fractional distillation and simple distillation.

(3) Master the operation method of a separatory funnel.

(4) Understand the function of a fractionating column.

Principle

In the present experiment, cyclohexene is prepared by dehydration of cyclohexanol using phosphoric acid as catalyst.

cyclohexanol   cyclohexene

Apparatus

A 50 mL round-bottom flask, 25 mL and 50 mL Erlenmeyer flask, thermometer, separatory funnel and fractional distillation apparatus with a short fractionating column.

Reagents

Cyclohexanol (环己醇)	10 mL (9.6 g, ca. 0.1 mol)
85% Phosphoric acid (磷酸)	5 mL
Sodium chloride (氯化钠)	
5% Aqueous sodium carbonate solution (碳酸钠水溶液)	
Anhydrous calcium chloride (无水氯化钙)	

Time   4 h

Safety Alert

(1) The product cyclohexene is highly flammable, make sure that all joints in the apparatus are tightly mated and always use an asbestos pad if a flame has to be used in the reaction and distillation steps. If possible, flameless heating is preferred.

(2) Wear latex gloves when handling the strongly acidic catalysts during the work-up and washing steps in which a separatory funnel is used. If acidic solutions accidentally come in contact with your skin, immediately flood the affected area with excess water, and then wash it with 5% sodium bicarbonate solution.

Procedure for Mini-scale Preparation

(1) **Setting Up**   Pour 10 mL (9.6 g, ca. 0.1 mol) of cyclohexanol and 5 mL of 85% phosphoric acid into a 50 mL round-bottom flask, and mix them thoroughly by gently swirling the flask. Add 2~3 boiling chips to the flask. Assemble a fractional distillation apparatus as shown in Figure 2.7-5a but modified by use of a short fractionating column and a 50 mL Erlenmeyer flask as a receiver, which should be immersed in an ice-water cooling bath [1].

(2) **Reaction**   Heat slowly the reaction solution to boil on an asbestos pad using a Bunsen burner [2] Note that the temperature of the distilling vapor should not exceed 73 ℃ [3]. The distillate is a turbid liquid of the mixture of cyclohexene and water. When there is no distillate coming out, continue distillation with a somewhat stronger flame. Stop heating when the temperature of the distilling vapor reaches 85 ℃, and allow the solution to cool down before further proceeding.

(3) **Work-Up**   Add 1 g of sodium chloride to the collected distillate in the receiver until the water layer is saturated [4], and then add 3~4 mL of 5% aqueous sodium carbonate solution to neutralize the small amount of acid [5]. Pour the distillate into a separatory funnel. Shake and vent the funnel alternatively, and let it stand for a while to allow the layers to separate. Drain

the water layer from the two-way cock of the funnel, and then decant the organic layer from the top of the funnel into a dry Erlenmeyer flask. Add 2～3 g of anhydrous calcium chloride to the Erlenmeyer flask, and shake it occasionally to dry the product thoroughly. A clear liquid of cyclohexene is obtained.

(4) **Isolation**   Dry completely all glassware used for distillation in an oven[6]. Assemble the fractional distillation apparatus again. Decant the crude product into a round-bottom flask through a stemless funnel plugged with a bit of cotton to remove the drying agent. Add 2～3 boiling chips to the flask, and distil fractionally the crude product with a water bath. The weighted receiver, a 25 mL Erlenmeyer flask, should be submerged up to its neck in an ice-water bath to avoid evaporation loss of the product. Collect the fraction of 82～85 ℃. Weigh the distillate and calculate the yield of cyclohexene in grams and in percentage. Yield: 4～5 g.

(5) **Identification**   Identify the product with a standard sample if a GC instrument is available and determine the purity of the product by GC analysis. Polyglycol or dinonyl phthalate can be used as a stationary liquid.

Notes

[1] Since dehydration is reversible, cyclohexene and water are removed by fractional distillation from the reaction mixture as they formed, to drive the equilibrium to completion.

[2] It is better to use an oil bath, which can heat the mixture evenly.

[3] Cyclohexene co-distils with water at 70.8 ℃, and the distillate contains 10% of water in mass percent. Cyclohexanol also co-distils with water at 97.8 ℃. Therefore, the reaction solution should be heated carefully. The temperature of the distilling vapor should not exceed 73 ℃, to avoid distilling cyclohexanol from the reaction mixture.

[4] The solubility of cyclohexene in the aqueous layer can be decreased by dissolved salt.

[5] As a small amount of phosphoric acid is distilled out with the azeotrope of cyclohexene and water, the distillate must be washed with an aqueous sodium carbonate solution to remove the acid.

[6] The azeotrope is a mixture of cyclohexene and water that distils below the boiling point of either pure compound. This makes it vital that crude product and all glassware be dried thoroughly prior to simple distillation.

Procedure for Micro-scale Preparation

(1) **Setting Up**   Weigh 500 mg (5 mmol) of cyclohexanol[1] in a 5 mL round-bottom flask, and add one drop of 85% phosphoric acid with a Pasteur pipet. Mix them thoroughly by gently swirling the flask. Add a piece of boiling chip to the flask. Assemble an apparatus for micro-scale fractional distillation as shown in Figure 2.7-5b and equip a 150 ℃ thermometer on the top of the Hickman fractionating head. The flask is immersed in a sand bath.

(2) **Reaction**   Heat slowly the reaction solution to boil with a sand bath [2] using a Bunsen

burner. Control the temperature at the thermometer and do not let the temperature exceed
73 ℃[2]. Stop heating when white smog appears in the flask and the solution turns black[3].

(3) **Work-Up**   Transfer the fraction from the port of the stillhead to a test tube, and add
several pieces of NaCl to the test tube to get a NaCl saturated solution. Remove the water layer
with a Pasteur pipet and wash the organic layer once more with an equal volume of NaCl saturated aqueous solution. Add several pieces of anhydrous CaCl₂ to dry the organic layer. When
the organic layer is well dried (a clear solution), move it to a 5 mL round-bottom flask. Assemble the distillation apparatus as shown in Figure 2. 7－3a and collect the fraction of 82～
85 ℃[4]. Weigh the distillate and calculate the yield of cyclohexene in grams and in percentage.
Yield: ca. 100 mg[5].

Notes

[1] The small amount of cyclohexanol cannot be measured in volume because of its large viscosity.

[2] With slowly heating, the temperature will not exceed 71 ℃.

[3] The temperature at the thermometer begins to drop at this moment. It indicates the end of
   the reaction.

[4] The fraction of 60～80 ℃ is often collected in the experiment since the amount of the distilled liquid is very small.

[5] The percentage yield of cyclohexanol is only 25% with 100% purity determined by GC
   analysis.

Finishing Touches

Combine the residue in the distillation flask and the washes, dilute the solution with water,
neutralize it with sodium carbonate, and flush it down the drain with large quantities of water.
Evaporate the solvents from the calcium chloride used as drying agent in the hood, and place it
in a container for nonhazardous solid.

Physical Property of Cyclohexene

Cyclohexene is a clear and colorless liquid if thoroughly dried. If it is cloudy, add an additional anhydrous calcium chloride (0. 5 g) to dry the product again. bp 83 ℃, n_D^{20} 1. 446 5,
d_4^{20} 0. 810 2.

¹H—NMR Spectrum of Cyclohexene in CDCl₃

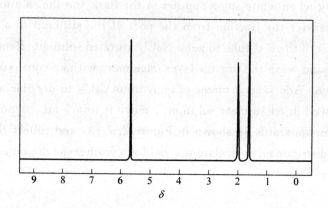

IR Spectrum of Cyclohexene Using Liquid Film

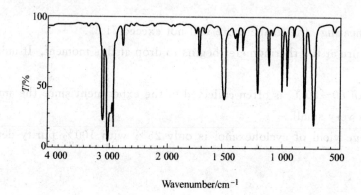

Wavenumber/cm⁻¹

Questions

(1) What is the advantage with H_3PO_4 as catalyst in comparison to H_2SO_4?

(2) Why must any acid be neutralized before the final distillation of cyclohexene?

(3) If you get a low yield of the product, consider that the loss of the product may result from which manipulation(s).

(4) Assign all signals in the ¹H—NMR spectrum of cyclohexene.

(5) In the IR spectrum of cyclohexene, specify the absorption bands associated with the carbon-carbon double bond and with the carbon-hydrogen bonds of cyclohexene.

3. 3   Intermolecular Dehydration of Alcohols:
Preparation of Dibutyl Ether（正丁醚）

Fundamental Knowledge

There are two important and practical methods for the preparation of ethers, that is, the Williamson ether synthesis and the acid-catalyzed bimolecular dehydration.

The former method is the most reliable and versatile ether synthesis method. It is especially useful for the preparation of unsymmetrical ethers. This method involves the S_N2 attack of an alkoxide ion on an unhindered primary alkyl halide or tosylate. Secondary alkyl halides and tosylates are occasionally used in the Williamson ether synthesis, but E2 elimination competes, and the yields of ethers are often poor. If the starting compound is a tertiary alkyl halide or tosylate, E2 elimination to an alkene is the exclusive result.

The Williamson ether synthesis:

$$R—\ddot{O}\!:^- \ +\ R—\ddot{X}\!: \longrightarrow R—\ddot{O}—R \ +\ :\!\ddot{X}\!:^-$$

alkoxide   alkyl   ether   halide
ion   halide   ion

The acid-catalyzed bimolecular dehydration of alcohols is the least expensive and an industrially used method for preparing simple symmetrical ethers. The starting compounds for this method are limited to unhindered primary alcohols. Attempts to synthesize ethers with secondary alkyl groups by intermolecular dehydration of secondary alcohols are usually unsuccessful because alkenes form too easily. Attempts to make ethers with tertiary alkyl groups by this method lead exclusively to the alkenes. Although this method is not useful for the preparation of unsymmetrical ethers from primary alcohols because the reaction leads to a mixture of products, it can be used to prepare unsymmetrical ethers in which one alkyl group is a *tert*-butyl group and the other group is primary. This synthesis can be accomplished by adding *tert*-butyl alcohol to a mixture of the primary alcohol and sulfuric acid at room temperature. In the acid-catalyzed dehydration, first, protonation of the alcohol converts the hydroxyl group from a poor leaving group (—OH) to a good leaving group (H_2O). This protonated alcohol is then attacked by the second molecule of the alcohol to form a protonated ether. Proton transfer from a protonated ether to a molecule of water or to another molecule of the alcohol gives the final product. All the three steps are reversible. The equilibrium will shift to right if the ether or water is continuously removed from the reaction system.

Acid-catalyzed bimolecular dehydration of alcohols:

Basic Experiments

Step 1: Protonation of alcohol

$$R\!-\!\ddot{O}H \;+\; H^+ \;\rightleftharpoons\; R\!-\!\overset{+}{\underset{}{O}}\overset{H}{\underset{H}{{}}}$$

alcohol   protonated
                           alcohol

Step 2: Nucleophilic substitution (S_N2 reaction)

$$R\!-\!\ddot{O}H \;+\; R\!-\!\overset{+}{O}\!\!\overset{H}{\underset{H}{{}}} \;\rightleftharpoons\; R\!-\!\overset{H}{\underset{}{\overset{+}{O}}}\!\!-\!R \;+\; :\!\ddot{O}\!-\!H$$

protonated
ether

Step 3: Deprotonation of the oxonium ion of ether

$$R\!-\!\overset{H}{\underset{}{\overset{+}{O}}}\!\!-\!R \;+\; :\!\ddot{O}\!-\!H \;\rightleftharpoons\; R\!-\!\ddot{O}\!-\!R \;+\; H\!-\!\overset{H}{\underset{}{\overset{+}{O}}}\!\!-\!H$$

ether   hydronium
                           ion

Purposes and Requirements

(1) Review reactions and mechanisms for the preparation of ethers, and summarize the advantages and the limits for each synthetic method.

(2) Learn the operation method of a water segregator.

(3) Review the manipulations of reflux and simple distillation.

Principle

Dibutyl ether is prepared by intermolecular dehydration of n-butanol in the presence of a catalytic amount of concentrated sulfuric acid. The water formed in the reaction is continuously removed by azeotropic distillation using a water segregator to drive the reaction to completion.

$$2CH_3CH_2CH_2CH_2OH \xrightarrow[135\ ℃]{conc.\ H_2SO_4} (CH_3CH_2CH_2CH_2)_2O + H_2O$$

The temperature of the reaction mixture should be carefully controlled. If the temperature is higher than 140 ℃, the intramolecular dehydration of n-butanol would take place to form butenes as by-products.

$$CH_3CH_2CH_2CH_2OH \xrightarrow[>140\ ℃]{conc.\ H_2SO_4} CH_3CH_2CH=CH_2 + CH_3CH=CHCH_3 + H_2O$$

Apparatus

A 100 mL two-neck round-bottom flask, 30 mL round-bottom flask, 200 ℃ thermometer, water segregator, reflux condenser, apparatus for simple distillation, separatory funnel,

100 mL Erlenmeyer flask.

Reagents

n-Butanol（正丁醇）	31 mL (25 g, 0.34 mol)
Concentrated sulfuric acid（浓硫酸）	5 mL
50% Cold sulfuric acid	
Anhydrous calcium chloride（无水氯化钙）	

Time   6 h

Safety Alert

(1) Concentrated sulfuric acid is very corrosive. Wear latex gloves when handling it. If it accidentally comes in contact with your skin, immediately wash it off with large amounts of water, and then with dilute sodium bicarbonate solution.

(2) Both n-butanol and dibutyl ether are flammable, be certain that all joints in the apparatus are tightly mated and do not heat the flask containing n-butanol and dibutyl ether directly on a flame in the reaction and distillation steps.

Procedure

(1) **Setting Up**   Pour 31 mL (25 g, 0.34 mol) of n-butanol into a 100 mL two-neck round-bottom flask, and then slowly add 5 mL of concentrated sulfuric acid to the flask with swirling. After well mixing the catalyst with the reactant, add 2 boiling chips to the flask. Equip the flask with a water segregator and a 200 ℃ thermometer as shown in Figure 1.4-9a, and fit a reflux condenser on the top of the water segregator. Pour a certain amount of water into the segregator and keep the level of the water slightly lower than the branch of the segregator[1].

(2) **Reaction**   Heat slowly the mixture on an asbestos pad and keep the solution gentle refluxing for 1 h. During the reaction process, the water layer collected in the segregator continuously increases and the temperature of the reaction mixture gradually rises. Occasionally drain the water from the two-way cock of the segregator and always keep the level of the water slightly lower than the branch of the segregator. Stop heating when the amount of the separated water reaches 4.5~5 mL[2] and the temperature of the reaction mixture reaches 140 ℃ or so. The solution would turn black and a large amount of by-product (butenes) would be formed[3] if the heating time is too long. Allow the mixture to cool down before proceeding.

(3) **Work-Up**   Demount the reaction apparatus and set up an apparatus for simple distillation as shown in Figure 2.7-1b. Add 2 boiling chips to the flask and distill the mixture until no distillate comes out[4]. Pour the distillate into the separatory funnel and separate the water layer. Sequentially wash the organic layer twice with 50% cold sulfuric acid (15 mL×2)[5] and then twice with water (15 mL×2). Dry the crude product over 1~2 g of anhydrous calcium chloride.

(4) **Isolation** Decant the dried crude product, without the drying agent, into a dry 30 mL round-bottom flask and add 2 boiling chips to the flask. Assemble an apparatus for simple distillation as shown in Figure 2. 7−2b. Distil the crude product on an asbestos pad and collect the fraction of 140～144 ℃. Weigh the product and calculate the percentage yield of the dibutyl ether obtained. Yield: 7～8 g.

(5) **Identification** Determine the purity of the product obtained by GC analysis if it is available.

Notes

[1] The water formed in the dehydration is continuously removed from the flask as azeotropes in the present experiment. n−Butanol, dibutyl ether and water can form different azeotropes, the azeotropic points of which are given in the following table.

	azeotrope	azeotropic point/℃	mass percent of the components/%		
			dibutyl ether	n−butanol	water
binary azeotrope	dibutyl ether−water	94. 1	66. 6		33. 4
	n−Butanol−water	93. 0		55. 5	44. 5
ternary azeotrope	dibutyl ether−n−butanol	117. 6	17. 5	82. 5	
	dibutyl ether− n−butanol−water	90. 6	35. 5	34. 6	29. 9

The azeotropes separate to two layers at room temperature. The upper layer mainly contains dibutyl ether and n−butanol, and the lower layer is an aqueous layer. During the reaction process, the distilled organic layer in the water segregator overflows into the reaction flask from the branch of the segregator.

[2] The theoretical amount of water generated in the reaction is ca. 3 g. The amount of water practically separated from the reaction should be somewhat larger than the calculated amount. Otherwise the yield of the product will be relatively low.

[3] Intermolecular dehydration to ether usually takes place at a lower temperature than intramolecular dehydration to the alkene, so the reaction temperature must be carefully controlled.

[4] This distillation step may be left out. Just pour the cold reaction mixture into a separatory funnel containing 50 mL of water, and then make the following work-up in the same way. In this case, it may be difficult to get a clear separation of two layers when washing the organic layer because some impurities exist in the crude product.

[5] The 50% aqueous sulfuric acid is made by mixing 20 mL of concentrated sulfuric acid with 34 mL of water. n−Butanol can be dissolved in a 50% aqueous sulfuric acid, while dibutyl ether has a poor solubility in such an acidic aqueous solution.

Finishing Touches

The aqueous solution should be neutralized before flushing it down the drain with excess water. Decant the residue from the stillpot into a container for waste organic solvents. Place the calcium chloride used as drying agent in a container for nonhazardous solid.

Physical Property of Dibutyl Ether

Pure dibutyl ether is a colorless liquid. bp 142 ℃, n_D^{20} 1.399 2, d_4^{20} 0.769 4.

^{1}H—NMR Spectrum of Dibutyl Ether in CDCl$_3$

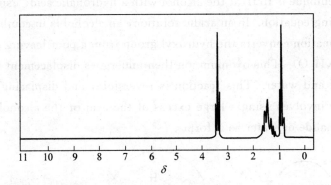

IR Spectrum of Dibutyl Ether Using Liquid Film

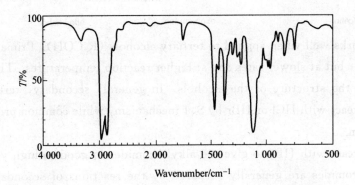

Questions

(1) Calculate the theoretical amount of water generated in the reaction. Try to explain why the amount of water practically separated from the reaction is larger than the calculated amount.

(2) Whether the n-butanol can be removed from the product by fraction distillation if it is left in the dried crude product? What is the influence on the experimental result if the unreacted n-butanol is removed in the final distillation step?

(3) In the IR spectrum of dibutyl ether, specify the absorptions associated with the carbon-

oxygen and carbon-hydrogen bonds of dibutyl ether.

(4) Assign all signals in the ^{1}H—NMR spectrum of dibutyl ether.

3.4   The S$_N$2 Reaction: Preparation of 1−Bromobutane (1−溴丁烷)

Fundamental Knowledge

One of the most important methods for preparing alkyl halides is to make them from alcohols. A common technique is to treat the alcohol with a hydrohalic acid, usually HCl or HBr as shown in the following equation. In an acidic solution, an alcohol is in equilibrium with its protonated form. Protonation converts the hydroxyl group from a poor leaving group (—OH) to a good leaving group (H$_2$O). This oxonium ion then undergoes displacement by the halide ion to form an alkyl halide and water. This reaction is reversible, and displacing the equilibrium to completion normally involves using a large excess of the acid or the alcohol in experiment, or removing the alkyl halide or water as it forms.

$$R—\overset{..}{\underset{..}{O}}H + H^+ \rightleftharpoons R—\overset{+}{\underset{..}{O}}\overset{H}{\underset{H}{<}} \quad X:^- \rightleftharpoons R—X + H_2O$$

where X = Cl, Br

alcohol   oxonium ion   alkyl halide

The reaction works well when applied to tertiary alcohols (R$_3$COH). Primary and secondary alcohols also react, but at slower rates and at higher reaction temperatures. The reaction mechanism depends on the structure of the alcohols. In general, secondary, tertiary, allylic and benzylic alcohols react with HCl or HBr by S$_N$1 mechanism, while common primary alcohols by the S$_N$2 mechanism.

Many alcohols react with HBr to give the alkyl bromides in good to high yields. However, secondary alkyl bromides are generally prepared by the reactions of secondary alcohols with phosphorus tribromide (PBr$_3$) to decrease the by-products from elimination of secondary alcohols and rearrangement of carbocation intermediates. Hydrochloric acid reacts with tertiary alcohols to give the corresponding tertiary alkyl chlorides in high yields, while an additional Lewis acid, zinc chloride (ZnCl$_2$), is usually necessary to promote the reaction of HCl with primary and secondary alcohols. Even with ZnCl$_2$ added, poor yields of alkyl chlorides from primary and secondary alcohols are generally obtained. Primary and secondary alcohols are best converted into alkyl chlorides by treatment with thionyl chloride (SOCl$_2$) or phosphorus chlorides (PCl$_3$ or PCl$_5$), and SOCl$_2$ generally gives better yields than PCl$_3$ and PCl$_5$. The reactions of alcohols with HI cannot give acceptable yields of alkyl iodides. A phosphorus and iodine combination

The S_N2 Reaction: Preparation of 1-Bromobutane (1-溴丁烷)

(P/I_2) is one of the best reagents for converting a primary and secondary alcohol to the alkyl iodide.

Purposes and Requirements

(1) Summarize the methods you have learnt for preparation of alkyl halides from alcohols and review the acid-catalyzed nucleophilic substitution of alcohols, e. g. , the mechanism of the reaction and the rearrangement of carbocations.

(2) Skillfully master the operation method of a separatory funnel and the technique of distillation.

(3) Know how to use a gas trap apparatus.

Principle

1-Bromobutane is prepared by heating 1-butanol with HBr in the presence of sulfuric acid. In the reaction, the sulfuric acid serves two important purposes: (1) it is a dehydrating agent that reduces the activity of water and shifts the position of equilibrium to the right, and (2) it provides an additional source of hydrogen ions to increase the concentration of the oxonium ion. The use of concentrated HBr also helps to establish a favorable equilibrium.

$$1-C_4H_9OH \ + \ HBr \overset{\triangle}{\rightleftharpoons} 1-C_4H_9Br + H_2O$$

1-butanol   hydrobromic   1-bromobutane
acid

Apparatus

A 25 mL and 50 mL round-bottom flask, separatory funnel, ice-water bath, condenser, thermometer, gas trap, magnetic stirrer, apparatus for simple distillation and two 50 mL Erlenmeyer flasks.

Reagents

1-Butanol (正丁醇)	6.2 mL (5.0 g, 0.068 mol)
Anhydrous sodium bromide (无水溴化钠)[1]	8.3 g (0.08 mol)
Concentrated sulfuric acid (浓硫酸)	10 mL (d=1.84, 0.18 mol)
10% Aqueous sodium carbonate solution (碳酸钠水溶液)	
Anhydrous calcium chloride (无水氯化钙)	

Time   6 h

Safety Alert

(1) Examine your glassware for cracks and chips. This experiment involves heating concentrated acids. If defective glassware breaks under these conditions, hot corrosive chemicals

would spill on you and those working around you.

(2) Concentrated sulfuric acid and water mix with the evolution of substantial quantities of heat. Always add the acid slowly to the water with swirling to ensure thorough mixing and to disperse the heat through warming of the water.

(3) If possible, wear latex gloves in this experiment. Be very careful when handling concentrated sulfuric acid. If it accidentally comes in contact with your skin, wash it off immediately with large amounts of water and then with dilute sodium bicarbonate solution.

Procedure for Mini-scale Preparation

(1) **Preparation**   Pour 10 mL of water into a 50 mL Erlenmeyer flask and cool it with a cold water bath. Slowly add 10 mL of concentrated sulfuric acid to the Erlenmeyer flask with continuous swirling.

(2) **Setting Up**   Add 8.3 g (0.08 mol) of well-ground anhydrous sodium bromide, 6.2 mL (5.0 g, 0.068 mol) of 1−butanol and 2 boiling chips to a 50 mL round-bottom flask. Equip the flask with a reflux condenser. Pour the diluted sulfuric acid solution to the flask from the top of the condenser in 4 portions. After addition of each portion, mix the contents in the flask thoroughly by swirling. Connect the condenser to a gas trap made with an inverted funnel in a beaker (Figure 2.6−1a), which contains an aqueous sodium hydroxide solution.

(3) **Reaction**   Slowly heat the reaction solution under gentle reflux on an asbestos pad using a Bunsen burner, and continue heating under reflux for 30 min. Allow the mixture to cool down before beginning the work-up procedure.

(4) **Work-Up**   Demount the reflux condenser and the gas trap, and re-add 2 boiling clips to the flask. Assemble a simple distillation apparatus as shown in Figure 2.7−1b. Distil the mixture and collect the distillate, which contains water and 1−bromobutane. Continue distilling until the distillate is clear[2]. Transfer the distillate to a separatory funnel and allow the layers to separate. Drain the lower organic layer from the two-way cock of the funnel into a dry Erlenmeyer flask[3]. Add 3 mL of concentrated sulfuric acid to the Erlenmeyer flask in two portions with continuous swirling[4]. Cool the Erlenmeyer flask with a cold water bath if it becomes warm. Pour the mixture to a separatory funnel. When the mixture is separated clearly into two layers, drain the lower aqueous sulfuric acid solution. Wash the organic layer sequentially with 10 mL of water[5], 5 mL of 10% aqueous sodium carbonate solution and 10 mL of water. Check the pH of the water layer. It should be about 7. If not, repeat the water wash. Save the organic layer in a dry Erlenmeyer flask (Be clear which layer contains 1−bromobutane!). Dry the crude product over 1∼2 g of anhydrous calcium chloride. Swirl the flask occasionally until the liquid is clear.

(5) **Isolation**   Decant the crude 1−bromobutane, without the drying agent, into a dry 25 mL round-bottom flask and add 2 boiling chips to the flask. Assemble a simple distillation apparatus as shown in Figure 2.7−1a without connection to vacuum. Carefully distil the product on an

asbestos pad using a Bunsen burner, and collect the fraction of $99 \sim 102$ ℃. Determine the weight of the 1−bromobutane obtained and calculate the percentage yield. Yield: $5.5 \sim 6.5$ g.

(6) **Identification**   If a GC instrument is available, analyze the purity of the product with di-nonyl phthalate as a stationary phase[6].

Notes

[1] In case of sodium bromide hydrate ($NaBr \cdot 2H_2O$) being used, add 11.2 g (0.08 mol) $NaBr \cdot 2H_2O$, and reduce the adding amount of water accordingly.

[2] Collect a few drops of distillate with a test tube containing 0.5 mL of water and observe whether there are drops of oil in the surface of the water layer, to judge whether distillation of 1−bromobutane has finished. The estimated amount of crude 1−bromobutane is about 7 mL.

[3] At room temperature, the distillate separates into two layers. The lower layer is normally the oil layer of 1−bromobutane, and the upper layer is the water layer. If there is a large amount of unreacted 1−butanol or HBr in the distillate, the relative densities of the layers may change and the oil layer becomes the upper layer. In this case, add water to deposit the oil layer.

[4] Washing the oil layer with concentrated sulfuric acid can remove the unreacted 1−butanol, the by-product dibutyl ether, as well as 1−and 2−butene. 1−Butanol cannot be removed from the crude 1−bromobutane by distillation because it forms an azeotrope with 1−bro-mobutane.

[5] If the oil layer turns red-brown, the product is contaminated with free bromine. Wash the oil layer with the aqueous sodium bisulfite ($NaHSO_3$) solution to remove bromine.

[6] The GC analysis shows that the isolated 1−bromobutane contains $1\% \sim 2\%$ of 2−bromobu-tane. The content of 2−bromobutane will increase with a long period of reflux.

Procedure for Micro-scale Preparation

(1) **Setting Up**   Add 400 mg (3.8 mmol) of well-ground anhydrous sodium bromide, 0.3 mL (3.2 mmol) of 1−butanol and 0.48 mL water to a 5 mL round-bottom flask. Mix them well by gently swirling the flask. Then add 0.48 mL of concentrated sulfuric acid and a piece of boiling chip to the flask. Equip the flask with a reflux condenser[1].

(2) **Reaction and Work-Up**   Slowly heat the reaction solution under gentle reflux with a sand bath for 30 min. Allow the mixture to cool down before disassemble the condenser. Re-add a piece of boiling clip to the flask and assemble an apparatus for micro-scale distillation as shown in Figure 2.7−3a. Distil the mixture and collect the distillate until the distillate is clear. Care-fully transfer the organic layer in the port of the stillhead to a 3 mL test tube. Add 0.1 mL of concentrated sulfuric acid to the test tube and mix the liquids thoroughly by bubbling the layer of sulfuric acid with a Pasteur pipet. The mixture is separated into two layers after standing for

Basic Experiments

a while. Remove the layer of sulfuric acid. The organic layer is washed successively with an equal volume of water, 10% Na_2CO_3 solution and water. Add a piece of anhydrous $CaCl_2$ to dry the crude product.

(3) **Isolation**   Transfer the crude 1 − bromobutane, without the drying agent, into a dry 5 mL round-bottom flask with a Pasteur pipet and add a piece of boiling chip. Assemble an apparatus for microscale distillation as shown in Figure 2. 7−3a. Carefully distil the product with a sand bath, and collect the fraction of 1−bromobutane[2]. Determine the weight of the 1−bromobutane obtained and calculate the percentage yield. Yield: ca. 100 mg[3].

Notes

[1] Only a small amount of HBr will be released from the micro-scale experiment. The gas trap can be omitted.

[2] The fraction of 55~100 ℃ is collected in the experiment since the amount of the distilled liquid is very small.

[3] The percentage yield of 1−bromobutane is 30% with 98. 3% purity determined by GC analysis.

Finishing Touches

Carefully dilute the residue remaining in the reaction flask with water and then combine this slowly with the aqueous solution and the sodium carbonate washes. Neutralize the combined aqueous mixture with sodium carbonate, and flush the solution down the drain with excess water. Place the residue remaining in the stillpot into the container for halogenated liquids. The calcium chloride used as the drying agent is contaminated with product, so place it in the container for halogenated solids.

Physical Property of 1−Bromobutane

Pure 1−bromobutane is a clear and colorless liquid. bp 102 ℃, n_D^{20} 1. 440 1, d_4^{20} 1. 275 8.

¹H—NMR Spectrum of 1−Bromobutane in CDCl₃

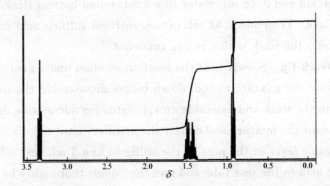

IR Spectrum of 1-Bromobutane Using Liquid Film

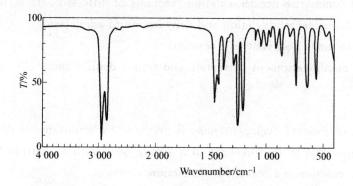

Questions

(1) Some water was added to the initial reaction mixture in the procedure. What product(s) would be favored if the water was not added? And how might the yield of product be affected by adding twice as much water as is specified, while keeping the quantities of the other reagents the same?

(2) Why must the crude 1-bromobutane be dried carefully with anhydrous calcium chloride prior to the final distillation?

(3) Explain the role of each washing step in the work-up procedure. Why must the organic layer be washed with water before washing with 10% NaOH.

(4) The alkyl bromide is dried with anhydrous calcium chloride in this procedure. Could solid sodium hydroxide or potassium hydroxide be used for this purpose? Explain.

(5) What side-reactions may occur and how to depress the side-reactions?

(6) Suggest reasonable mechanisms for the formation of all possible by-products.

(7) Assign all signals in the ^{1}H—NMR spectrum of 1-bromobutane.

3. 5   Decarboxylation of Dicarboxylic Acids: Preparation of Cyclopentanone (环戊酮)

Fundamental Knowledge

Adipic acid (hexanedioic acid) loses water and carbon dioxide to form cyclopentanone when it is heated with a strong base. This reaction can be used as one of the methods for preparation of five-membered ketones. Although in the presence of a strong base, pimelic acid (heptanedioic acid) undergoes an essentially identical reaction like adipic acid, cyclohexanone is usually prepared by oxidation of cyclohexanol both in laboratory and in the chemical industry.

Purposes and Requirements

(1) Review and summarize decarboxylation reactions of different carboxylic acids. To demonstrate a simultaneous decarboxylation and dehydration of adipic acid.

(2) Learn how to make a solvent-free reaction.

(3) Review the manipulations of extraction and simple distillation.

Principle

In the present experiment, cyclopentanone is prepared by simultaneous decarboxylation and dehydration of adipic acid in the presence of a strong base such as barium hydroxide at high temperature. This reaction is a solvent-free reaction.

$$\begin{array}{c} CH_2CH_2COOH \\ | \\ CH_2CH_2COOH \end{array} \xrightarrow[285\sim290\,^\circ C]{Ba(OH)_2} \bigcirc\!\!=\!\!O + CO_2 + H_2O$$

Apparatus

A 50 mL pear-shaped flask, 50 mL Erlenmeyer flask, apparatus for simple distillation, 360 ℃ thermometer, mortar, separatory funnel.

Reagents

Adipic acid (hexanedioic acid, 己二酸)	20 g (0.14 mol)
Barium hydroxide (氢氧化钡)[1]	1 g
Anhydrous potassium carbonate (无水碳酸钾)	

Time   4 h

Safety Alert

(1) Barium hydroxide is a corrosive agent. Do not allow it to come in contact with your skin when grinding it.

(2) The product cyclopentanone is flammable, so be certain that all joints in the apparatus are tightly mated and do not heat the organic solution directly on a flame in the reaction and distillation steps.

Procedure

(1) **Setting Up**   Finely grind 20 g (0.14 mol) of adipic acid and 1 g of barium hydroxide in a mortar. Transfer the ground solid mixture to a 50 mL pear-shaped flask, and assemble an apparatus for simple distillation as shown in Figure 3.5-1. Fit a 360 ℃ thermometer from the top of the still head, and the mercury head of the thermometer should be about 0.5 cm to the bottom of the flask.

Decarboxylation of Dicarboxylic Acids: Preparation of Cyclopentanone (环戊酮)

(2) **Reaction**   Heat carefully the solid mixture on an asbestos pad and shake the flask occasionally to mix well the barium hydroxide with the fused adipic acid. When all solids are fused, heat quickly the mixture to 285 ℃. Keep the temperature between 285~290 ℃[2], and distil the cyclopentanone and water as they form until no more cyclopentanone comes out. This procedure needs 1. 5~2 h. There is only a little dry residue left in the flask[3].

(3) **Work-Up and Isolation**   Add solid potassium carbonate to the distillate until it is saturated with potassium carbonate[4]. Decant the solution into a separatory funnel. After drain the water layer, pour the organic layer into a 50 mL Erlenmeyer flask and dry it over an-

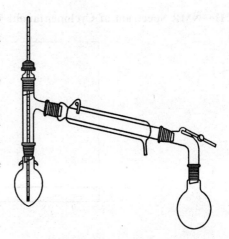

Figure 3. 5-1   Apparatus for preparation of cyclopentanone.

hydrous potassium carbonate. Distil the dried crude product on an asbestos pad and collect the fraction of 128~131 ℃. Weigh the product and calculate the percentage yield of the cyclopentanone obtained. Yield: 6~7 g.

(4) **Identification**   If an IR instrument is available, record the IR spectrum of the product and compare the spectrum with that of the authentic sample.

Notes

[1] An equal quantity of potassium fluoride can be used to replace barium hydroxide.

[2] The boiling point of adipic acid is 256 ℃/1 333 Pa. If the temperature of the reaction mixture exceeds 300 ℃, the reactant, adipic acid, would be distilled out.

[3] It is difficult to wash away the solid residue in the flask. Add several pellets of sodium hydroxide and a certain amount of ethanol to the flask, and let it stand overnight before washing it.

[4] The small amount of the unreacted adipic acid in the distillate is neutralized by potassium carbonate to form adipate salt that is soluble in water. This dissolved salt can play a salting-out role to reduce the content of the cyclopentanone in the aqueous layer.

Finishing Touches

All aqueous solutions should be diluted with water and neutralized before flushing down the drain. Decant the residue remaining in the stillpot into a container for waste organic liquids. Place the potassium carbonate used as drying agent in a container for nonhazardous solid.

Physical Property of Cyclopentanone

Pure cyclopentanone is a colorless liquid. bp 131 ℃, n_D^{20} 1.436 6, d_4^{20} 0.951 0.

^{1}H—NMR Spectrum of Cyclopentanone in CDCl$_3$

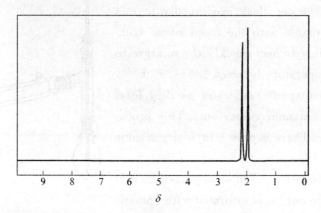

IR Spectrum of Cyclopentanone Using Liquid Film

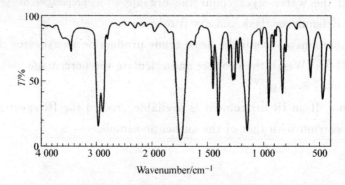

Questions

(1) Why a pear-shaped flask is used in this experiment?

(2) What is the major product when a mixture of sodium adipate (hexanedioate) and caustic lime is heated to fuse?

(3) What is the major product if glutaric acid (pentanedioic acid) is heated with acetic anhydride?

(4) In the IR spectrum of cyclopentanone, specify the absorption associated with the carbon-oxygen double bond of the ketone.

(5) Assign all signals in the ^{1}H—NMR spectrum of cyclopentanone.

3.6　Oxidation of Secondary Alcohols to Ketones: Preparation of Cyclohexanone (环己酮)

Fundamental Knowledge

One of the efficient methods for preparing aldehydes and ketones is oxidation of primary and secondary alcohols. The choice of oxidant depends on factors such as reaction scale, cost, toxicity and the stability of the alcohols. Oxidation of a primary alcohol to an aldehyde requires a moderate oxidant to avoid overoxidation to a carboxylic acid. In general, oxidation of primary alcohols with pyridinium chlorochromate (PCC, $C_5H_6NCrO_3Cl$) as an oxidant provides good yields of aldehydes without overoxidation. Secondary alcohols are readily oxidized to ketones by chromic acid (H_2CrO_4), or potassium permanganate ($KMnO_4$). These oxidants are excellent oxidizing agents, but they are derived from heavy metals, a class of elements that are commonly toxic and therefore environmentally hazardous. Environmentally benign alternatives to chromate and permanganate ions for oxidizing alcohols are sodium hypochlorite (NaOCl), known as household bleach and calcium hypochlorite ($Ca(OCl)_2$).

The plausible mechanism by which hypohalites oxidize secondary alcohols involves initial formation of an alkyl hypohalite. This product arises from reaction of the alcohol with the hypohalous acid, which is in equilibrium with hypohalite ion in the aqueous solution. Base-promoted E2 elimination of the elements of H^+ and X^- from the alkyl hypoalite leads directly to a ketone.

$$XO:^- + H-OH \rightleftharpoons X-OH + {}^-OH$$

hypohalite ion   hypohalous acid

$$R-\underset{\underset{H}{|}}{\overset{\overset{R'}{|}}{C}}-OH + X-OH \rightleftharpoons[-H_2O] R-\underset{\underset{H}{|}}{\overset{\overset{R'}{|}}{C}}-O \xrightarrow[{}^-OH]{} \underset{R}{\overset{R'}{>}}C=O + X^-$$

alcohol   hypohalous acid   alkyl hypohalite   ketone   halide ion

Purposes and Requirements

(1) Summarize the methods you have learnt for preparation of ketones and review the contents on oxidation of alcohols.

(2) Master skillfully the techniques of mechanical stirring, extraction and distillation.

(3) Understand the function of salting-out agents used in layer separation.

Principle

Cyclohexanone is an important feed stock for production of polycaprolactam (Nylon−6). In the present experiment, cyclohexanone is prepared by the oxidation of cyclohexanol in acetic acid using sodium hypochlorite as an oxidizing agent. Cyclohexanone cannot be further oxidized by sodium hypochlorite, while potassium permanganate and nitric acid readily oxidize it to adipic acid (hexanedioic acid), which is one of the raw materials for manufacture of Nylon−66.

Basic Experiments

Apparatus

A 250 mL three-neck round-bottom flask, reflux condenser, pressure-equalized dropping funnel, mechanical stirrer, drying tube, separatory funnel, Erlenmeyer flask and apparatus for simple distillation.

Reagents

Cyclohexanol（环己醇）	10.4 mL (10.0 g, 0.1 mol)
Aqueous sodium hypochlorite solution（次氯酸钠水溶液）	80 mL (0.15 mol, 1.8 mol·L^{-1})
Glacial acetic acid（冰醋酸）	25 mL
Methyl t-butyl ether（甲基叔丁基醚）	25 mL
Saturated sodium bisulfite solution（饱和亚硫酸氢钠溶液）	
KI-starch test paper（KI-淀粉试纸）	
Sodium bicarbonate（碳酸氢钠）	
Anhydrous sodium carbonate（无水碳酸钠）	
Anhydrous magnesium sulfate（无水硫酸镁）	

Time　4 h

Safety Alert

Sodium hypochlorite is a bleaching agent. Do not allow the solution of sodium hypochlorite to come in contact with your skin or eyes. If it does, flush the affected area immediately with large amounts of water.

Procedure

(1) **Setting Up**　Add 10.4 mL (10.0 g, 0.1 mol) of cyclohexanol and 25 mL of glacial acetic acid to a 250 mL three-neck round-bottom flask equipped with a mechanical stirrer, a dropping funnel, a reflux condenser and a thermometer as shown in Figure 2.3－1c. The condenser is connected to a drying tube filled with granular sodium bicarbonate[1]. Decant the sodium hypochlorite solution into the dropping funnel[2].

(2) **Reaction**　With stirring, drop the sodium hypochlorite solution into the flask at a speed that maintains the temperature between 30~35 ℃. After addition of 75 mL of the sodium hypochlorite solution, the reaction mixture turns yellow-green in color. Continue stirring for another 5 min, and test the aqueous layer with KI-starch test paper[3]. If the KI-starch test paper

does not turn deep blue (a negative result), continue dropping the sodium hypochlorite solution (ca. 5 mL) until a positive test for excess sodium hypochlorite is observed. The resulting solution is stirred for another 15 min, and the saturated sodium bisulfite solution is added dropwise to the reaction mixture until the aqueous layer of the solution gives a negative KI-starch test.

(3) **Work-Up**   Demount the reaction apparatus, and add 60 mL of water and 2 boiling chips to the flask. Assemble a simple distillation apparatus, distil the mixture[4] and collect the distillate below 100 ℃ (ca. 50 mL) [5]. Add anhydrous sodium carbonate in small portions to the distillate with stirring until the evolution of carbon dioxide ceases (ca. 6.5~7 g anhydrous sodium carbonate). Then add 10 g of sodium chloride to the mixture and stir it for 15 min to let the water layer saturated with sodium chloride[6]. Pour the mixture into a separatory funnel and save the organic layer in a 50 mL Erlenmeyer flask. Wash the water layer with 25 mL of methyl t-butyl ether, and combine the ethereal layer with the crude cyclohexanone. Dry the organic layer over anhydrous magnesium sulfate. Swirl the Erlenmeyer flask occasionally for a period of 15~20 min to facilitate drying.

(4) **Isolation**   Decant the dried liquid, without the drying agent, into a dry 50 mL round-bottom flask and add 2 boiling chips to the flask. Assemble a simple distillation apparatus. First, remove the methyl t-butyl ether by simple distillation with a water bath, and then distil the cyclohexanone on an asbestos pad. Collect the fraction of 150~155 ℃. Determine the weight of the cyclohexanone obtained and calculate the percentage yield of the product. Yield: 7~8 g.

(5) **Identification**   If a GC instrument is available, analyze the purity of the product and identify the product with a standard sample. Record the IR spectrum of the product if an IR instrument is available, and compare the spectrum with that of the authentic sample.

Notes

[1] Sodium bicarbonate ($NaHCO_3$) can absorb the chlorine gas possibly released from the reaction.

[2] The sodium hypochlorite solution should be handled in a well-ventilated area.

[3] Put a drop on the KI-starch test paper. If the paper turns blue immediately, there exists an excess of sodium hypochlorite in the reaction mixture (a positive test).

[4] Addition of aluminum chloride can prevent the solution from foaming in distillation.

[5] Cyclohexanone co-distils with water at 95 ℃. The fraction below 100 ℃ mainly contains cyclohexanone, water and a small amount of acetic acid.

[6] Saturating the aqueous layer with sodium chloride will decrease the solubility of cyclohexanone in water, therefore improving the separation of the organic and water layers.

Finishing Touches

Flush all aqueous solution down the drain with excess water. Decant the methyl t-butyl .

Basic Experiments

ether collected by distillation into the container for recovered methyl t-butyl ether. The sodium bicarbonate in the drying tube may be contaminated with chlorine, so place it in the container for halogenated solids. Evaporate the solvents from the magnesium sulfate used as drying agent in the hood, and place it in a container for nonhazardous solid.

Physical Property of Cyclohexanone

Pure cyclohexanone is a clear and colorless liquid. bp 156 ℃, n_D^{20} 1.450 7, d_4^{20} 0.947 8.

^{1}H—NMR Spectrum of Cyclohexanone in CDCl$_3$

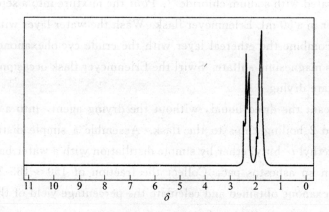

IR Spectrum of Cyclohexanone Using Liquid Film

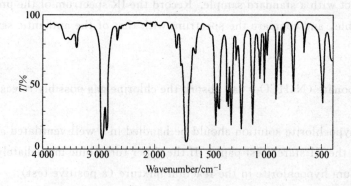

Questions

(1) In addition to sodium bicarbonate solid, are there any other methods to absorb chlorine?

(2) Why must the saturated sodium bisulfite solution be added to the mixture after reaction?

(3) What is the role of anhydrous sodium carbonate in the isolating procedure of cyclohexanone?

(4) The Swern oxidation is another efficient method to convert alcohols to ketones and aldehydes. Do you know the oxidant used for the Swern oxidation?

(5) In the functional group region of the IR spectrum of cyclohexanone, specify the absorption associated with the carbon-oxygen double bond of the ketone.

(6) Assign all signals in the ^{1}H—NMR spectrum of cyclohexanone.

3.7 Oxidation of Primary Alcohols to Aldehydes: Preparation of Benzaldehyde (苯甲醛)

Fundamental Knowledge

There are many ways of preparing aldehydes in laboratory, such as oxidation of primary alcohols, reduction of acyl chlorides, ozonolysis of alkenes and hydroboration-oxidation of terminal alkynes. Among these synthetic methods, oxidation of primary alcohols is a practical way of preparing aldehydes because of the commercial availability of various alcohols and convenient manipulations of the experiment. Oxidation of a primary alcohol to an aldehyde requires careful selection of an oxidizing agent because aldehydes are easily oxidized to carboxylic acids. A conventional oxidizing agent used for selective oxidation of primary alcohols is pyridinium chlorochromate (PCC, $C_5H_6NCrO_3Cl$), a complex of chromium trioxide with pyridine and HCl. PCC is not an environmentally benign agent even though it provides good yields of aldehydes without overoxidation. In recent years, many green synthetic methods have been reported for oxidation of primary alcohols to aldehydes. For examples, in the presence of a catalyst $Na_2WO_4 \cdot 2H_2O$ and a phase-transfer catalyst $(C_4H_9)_4NHSO_4$, primary alcohols can be selectively oxidized to their corresponding aldehydes in an aqueous solution using 30% hydrogen peroxide (H_2O_2) as an oxidizing agent.

Aliphatic aldehydes are usually prepared by oxidation-dehydrogenation of primary alcohols at high temperature in the presence of metal catalysts such as silver and cupper, or by hydroformation of terminal alkenes catalyzed by metal carbonyl complexes in chemical industry. Aryl aldehydes such as benzaldehyde are usually prepared by Gatterman-Koch synthesis, in which the formylation of an arene is accomplished by using a high-pressure mixture of carbon monoxide and HCl together with a catalyst consisting of a mixture of cuprous chloride (CuCl) and aluminum chloride (AlCl$_3$).

For fundamental knowledge about phase-transfer catalysis, please see Section 3.17.

Purposes and Requirements

(1) Review and summarize the reactions you have learnt for preparation of aldehydes, and compare the advantages and disadvantages of these synthetic methods.

(2) Learn the basic knowledge on phase-transfer catalysis.

(3) Master the manipulation of vacuum distillation.

(4) Review extraction and simple distillation procedures.

Principle

In the present experiment, benzaldehyde is prepared by oxidation of benzyl alcohol using hydrogen peroxide as an oxidizing agent. The oxidation reaction is catalyzed by $Na_2WO_4 \cdot 2H_2O$ and a phase-transfer catalyst $(C_4H_9)_4NHSO_4$ in benzyl alcohol/water two phase medium.

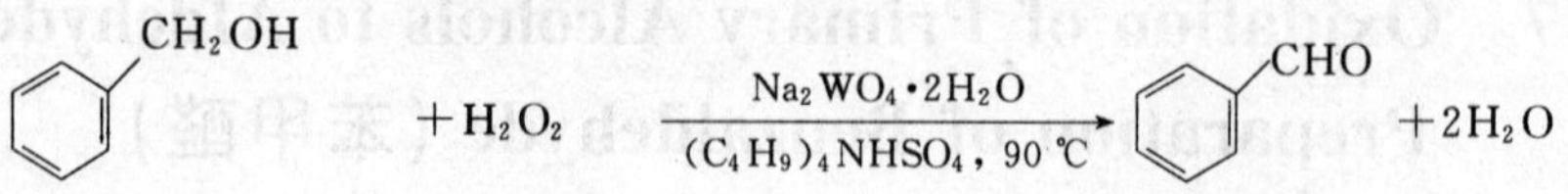

$$\underset{\text{benzyl alcohol}}{\text{CH}_2\text{OH}} + \underset{\text{hydrogen peroxide}}{H_2O_2} \xrightarrow[\text{(C}_4\text{H}_9)_4\text{NHSO}_4,\ 90\ \text{℃}]{\text{Na}_2\text{WO}_4 \cdot 2\text{H}_2\text{O}} \underset{\text{benzaldehyde}}{\text{CHO}} + 2H_2O$$

Apparatus

A 50 mL two-neck round-bottom flask, 100 mL Erlenmeyer flask, dropping funnel, condenser, Hickman stillhead, 150 ℃ thermometer, magnetic stirrer, separatory funnel, apparatus for vacuum distillation.

Reagents

Benzyl alcohol (苯甲醇)	6.2 mL (6.5 g, 0.06 mol)
30% Hydrogen peroxide (过氧化氢)	7.5 mL (0.07 mol)
Tetrabutylammonium bisulfate ($(C_4H_9)_4NHSO_4$, 四正丁基硫酸氢铵)	0.2 g
Sodium wolframate hydrate ($Na_2WO_4 \cdot 2H_2O$, 钨酸钠水合物)	0.2 g
Saturated aqueous sodium thiosulfate (饱和硫代硫酸钠溶液)	
Methyl t-butyl ether (甲基叔丁基醚)	20 mL
Anhydrous magnesium sulfate (无水硫酸镁)	

Time 4 h

Safety Alert

(1) The 30% hydrogen peroxide used is a strong oxidant and may blister the skin on contacting. If you accidentally spill some on your skin, wash the affected area with copious amounts of water.

(2) The product and organic reagents used in the experiment are flammable, heat with a water bath for the reaction and for distillation of methyl t-butyl ether. If possible, flameless heating is preferred.

Procedure

(1) **Setting Up and Reaction** To a 50 mL two-neck round-bottom flask successively add 0.2 g of tetrabutylammonium hydrogen sulfate, 0.2 g of sodium wolframate hydrate, 7.5 mL of 30% hydrogen peroxide and 10 mL of water. Assemble an apparatus for reflux as shown in Figure 1-4-8a. Turn on the magnetic stirrer. After 5 min, add 6.2 mL (6.5 g, 0.06 mol) of

benzyl alcohol. Heat the mixture with a water bath and keep the temperature of the vapor at 90 ℃ for 3 h.

(2) **Work-Up and Isolation**   Allow the reaction mixture to cool down to room temperature, and separate the organic layer. Extract the aqueous layer twice with methyl *t* − butyl ether (10 mL×2)[1]. Combine the ethereal extracts with the organic layer, wash the combined liquid with 10 mL of saturated sodium thiosulfate[2], and dry it over anhydrous magnesium sulfate. Set up an apparatus for vacuum distillation after distill methyl *t* − butyl ether from the crude product. Distil the product and collect the fraction of 59~61 ℃ under the pressure of 1. 33 kPa (10 mmHg). Weigh the benzaldehyde obtained and calculate the percentage yield. Yield: ca. 0. 5 g.

(3) **Identification**   Record the IR spectrum of the product if an IR instrument is available, and compare the spectrum with that of the authentic sample.

Notes

[1] The crude product can also be isolated by steam distillation. Cool down the flask after the mixture reacts at 90 ℃ for 3 h, and decant 10 mL of saturated aqueous sodium thiosulfate into the flask. Set up an apparatus for steam distillation, and distil the mixture of benzaldehyde and water. Stop distillation when the temperature of the vapor reaches 100 ℃.

[2] The hydrogen peroxide left in the reaction solution is removed by sodium thiosulfate.

Finishing Touches

Pour the methyl *t*-butyl ether distillate into a special container for the recovered methyl *t*-butyl ether. Pour the residue remaining in the stillpot into a container for waste organic liquids. Dilute the aqueous solution and flush it down the drain with excess water. Evaporate the solvents from the magnesium sulfate used as drying agent in the hood, and place it in a container for nonhazardous solid.

Physical Property of Benzaldehyde

Pure benzaldehyde is a clear and colorless liquid. bp 178 ℃, n_D^{20} 1. 546 3, d_4^{20} 1. 046 0.

¹H—NMR Spectrum of Benzaldehyde in CDCl₃

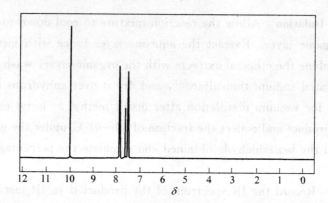

IR Spectrum of Benzaldehyde Using Liquid Film

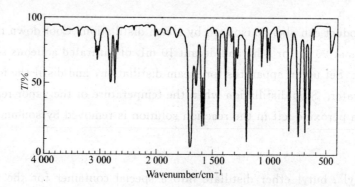

Questions

(1) What other phase-transfer catalysts can be used in this experiment?

(2) How is the unreacted benzyl alcohol removed from the crude product?

(3) Specify the absorption associated with the carbon-oxygen double bond of the aromatic aldehyde in the IR spectrum of benzaldehyde.

(4) Assign all signals in the ¹H—NMR spectrum of benzaldehyde, and notice the chemical shift of the aldehyde hydrogen nuclei.

3.8　Fischer Esterification of Carboxylic Acids:
n-Butyl Acetate (乙酸正丁酯)

Fundamental Knowledge

One of the practical methods to prepare esters is the Fischer Esterification of a carboxylic acid with an alcohol in the presence of a catalytic amount of strong acid such as sulfuric acid, hydrogen chloride and toluene sulfonic acid. The Fischer Esterification reaction is an acid-catalyzed nucleophilic acyl substitution reaction. The process of the reaction can be considered as two stages: ① acid-catalyzed addition of the alcohol to the carbonyl group and ② acid-catalyzed dehydration of the ester hydrate intermediate. Carboxylic acids are not reactive enough to be attacked by neutral alcohols, but protonation of the carbonyl oxygen atom by a strong acid makes them much more reactive toward nucleophilic attack by alcohols. The addition of the alcohol to the carbonyl group is followed by transferring of a proton from one oxygen atom to another. Subsequent loss of water and deprotonation gives the ester.

Step 1: acid-catalyzed addition of the alcohol to the carbonyl group

Step 2: acid-catalyzed dehydration of the ester hydrate intermediate

All steps of the reaction are reversible and typical equilibrium constants for esterification are not very large. The equilibrium may be driven to the right by using an excess of one of the reactants or by removing one of the products. Continuous removal of water from the reaction system by azeotropic distillation or by addition of a dehydrating agent is a practical measure to drive an esterification to completion.

The rate of esterification is affected significantly by the structures of the alcohol and the acid, and steric factors play an important role. Increasing the steric hindrance, whether in the alcohol or the acid, slows the reaction markedly. Therefore acid-catalyzed esterification is limited for the preparation of esters of primary and secondary alcohols with sterically unhindered carboxylic acids. Tertiary alcohols react very slowly in acid-catalyzed esterification that they usually undergo elimination instead. Because of the rate problem and the side-reaction, sterically hindered esters should be prepared by methods other than direct esterification, that is, by alcoholysis of acid chlorides, acid anhydrides and nitriles, or by reaction of a salt of the carboxylic acid with an alkyl halide in the presence of a secondary amine as catalyst.

Purposes and Requirements

(1) Review and summarize the reactions you have learnt for preparation of esters, and compare the advantages and limits of these synthetic methods. Review the mechanism of the acid-catalyzed esterification.

(2) Master the operation method of water segregator.

(3) Consolidate the technical know-how for distillation and separation of organic liquids.

Principle

n-Butyl acetate is prepared by the Fischer esterification of acetic acid with an equivalent of n-butanol in the presence of a catalytic amount of sulfuric acid. The water is removed as it forms by azeotropic distillation using a water segregator to drive the reaction to completion.

$$CH_3C\overset{O}{\underset{OH}{}} + n\text{-}C_4H_9OH \underset{}{\overset{H_2SO_4}{\rightleftharpoons}} CH_3C\overset{O}{\underset{OC_4H_9\text{-}n}{}} + H_2O$$

acetic acid n-butanol n-butyl acetate

Apparatus

A 50 mL round-bottom flask, reflux condenser, water segregator, separatory funnel, 50 mL Erlenmeyer flask and apparatus for simple distillation.

Reagents

n-Butanol（正丁醇）	11.5 mL (9.3 g, 0.125 mol)
Glacial acetic acid（冰醋酸）	7.2 mL (7.5 g, 0.125 mol)
Concentrated sulfuric acid（浓硫酸）	
10% Aqueous sodium carbonate solution（10%碳酸钠水溶液）	
Anhydrous magnesium sulfate（无水硫酸镁）	

Time   4 h

Safety Alert

Be very careful when handling concentrated sulfuric acid. If any of it comes in contact with your skin, immediately wash it off with large amounts of water and then with dilute sodium bicarbonate solution.

Procedure for Mini-scale Preparation

(1) **Setting Up**   To a 50 mL round-bottom flask first add 11.5 mL (9.3 g, 0.125 mol) of n-butanol, 7.2 mL (7.5 g, 0.125 mol) of glacial acetic acid and 2 boiling chips, and then add 3~4 drops (ca. 0.5 mL) of concentrated sulfuric acid to the flask with swirling[1,2]. Equip the

flask with a water segregator and a reflux condenser as shown in Figure 1.4−9b. Pour water into the water segregator and keep the level of the water slightly lower than the branch of the water segregator.

(2) **Reaction**　Heat slowly the reaction solution under reflux on an asbestos pad using a Bunsen burner. Drain the water occasionally from the water segregator, and always keep the level of the water slightly lower than the branch of the water segregator[3] during the reaction process. Stop heating when no water comes out[4], and note down the amount of water collected[5]. Allow the mixture to cool down before beginning the work-up procedure.

(3) **Work-Up**　Demount the condenser and the water segregator. Decant both the aqueous solution in the water segregator and the reaction mixture in the flask into a separatory funnel, and drain the water layer. Wash the organic layer first with 10 mL of water and then with 10 mL of 10% aqueous sodium carbonate solution[6]. Test the pH of the water layer. Go ahead if the pH is about 7. Otherwise, wash the organic layer again with 10% sodium carbonate solution. Remove the water layer and wash the organic layer with 10 mL of water. Transfer the crude product to a 50 mL Erlenmeyer flask and dry it over a small amount of anhydrous magnesium sulfate.

(4) **Isolation**　Decant the dried liquid, without the drying agent, into a dry 30 mL stillpot. Add 2 boiling chips to the stillpot and assemble a simple distillation apparatus. Distil the *n*−butyl acetate on an asbestos pad and collect the fraction of 124∼126 ℃. Determine the weight of the *n* − butyl acetate obtained and calculate the percentage yield of the product. Yield: 10∼11 g.

(5) **Identification**　Analyze the purity of the product with dinonyl phthalate as a stationary phase if a GC instrument is available. GC conditions: the temperature of the column and detector 100 ℃, the temperature of the injector 150 ℃, a thermal conductivity detector, H_2 as a carrier gas, the flow-rate of the carrier gas 45 mL·min^{-1}.

Notes

[1] Sulfuric acid is used as a catalyst, thus only a catalytic amount of sulfuric acid is needed for the reaction.

[2] Sulfuric acid should be added dropwise with continuous swirling to avoid carbonization of the reactants, caused by the high concentration of the sulfuric acid ($d_4^{20} = 1.841$) in the bottom of the flask.

[3] In the present experiment, the water formed in the esterification is continuously removed from the flask as azeotropes. *n*−Butanol, *n*−butyl acetate and water form different azeotropes. The azeotropes separate to two layers at room temperature. The upper layer contains *n*−butyl acetate, *n*−butanol and a small amount of water, and the lower layer is an aqueous layer.

Basic Experiments

azeotrope		azeotropic point/℃	mass percent of the components/%		
			n−butyl acetate	n−butanol	water
binary azeotrope	n−butyl acetate−water	90.7	72.9		27.1
	n−butanol−water	93.0		55.5	44.5
	n−butyl acetate−n−butanol	117.6	32.8	67.2	
ternary azeotrope	n−butyl acetate−n−butanol−water	90.7	63.0	8.0	29.0

[4] The reaction takes about 40 min to complete.

[5] The extent of the esterification can be approximately estimated by comparing the amount of the separated water (Deduct the pre-added water in the segregator) with the theoretical amount of the water that could be produced from the reaction.

[6] Vent the separatory funnel occasionally to avoid a high pressure in the funnel caused by the released carbon dioxide when washing the mixture with the basic solution.

Procedure for Micro-scale Preparation

(1) **Setting Up**　To a dry 5 mL round-bottom flask first add 2.76 mL (2.27 g, 0.03 mol) of n−butanol, 1.68 mL (1.8 g, 0.03 mol) of glacial acetic acid and a piece of boiling chip, and then add 1 drop of concentrated sulfuric acid with a Pasteur pipet. Mix well these compounds with swirling. Equip the flask with a Hickman stillhead as a water segregator. Add a proper amount of water to its collecting port (Figure 1.4−9), and keep the level of the water slightly lower than the rim of the port.

(2) **Reaction**　Heat slowly the reaction solution under reflux with a sand bath for 30 ∼ 40 min. When no water comes out (No water drop is contained in the condensed liquid flowing down from the condenser), stop heating and allow the solution to cool down. If the water in the port of the stillhead is overflowing to the flask during reflux, remove the water from the port using a syringe through the side neck to ensure that the water in the port cannot overflow to the flask. Allow the mixture to cool down before beginning the work-up procedure.

(3) **Work-Up**　Transfer both the reaction mixture in the flask and the aqueous solution in the port of the stillhead into a small separatory funnel, and drain the water layer. Wash the organic layer successively with an equal volume of water, 10% aqueous sodium carbonate solution, and then with water again. Transfer the organic layer to a dry 10 mL Erlenmeyer flask and dry it over a small amount of anhydrous magnesium sulfate.

(4) **Isolation**　Decant the dried liquid, without the drying agent, into a dry 5 mL stillpot. Add a piece of boiling chip to the stillpot and assemble an apparatus for micro-scale simple distillation (Figure 2.7−3a). Distil the mixture on an asbestos pad and collect the distilate of 124∼126 ℃. Determine the weight of the n−butyl acetate obtained and calculate the percentage yield of the product. Yield: ca. 2.3 g[1].

Notes

[1] If several pieces of molecular sieve are added to the flask to absorb the water formed during the reaction, the amount of reagents used can be reduced in proportion. In this case, the microscale reaction can be made without a Hickman stillhead.

Finishing Touches

Neutralize the aqueous solution before flushing it down the drain with excess water. Decant the organic waste into the container for used organic solvents. Place the magnesium sulfate used as drying agent in a container for nonhazardous solid.

Physical Property of n-Butyl Acetate

Pure n-butyl acetate is a clear and colorless liquid. bp 127 ℃, n_D^{20} 1.394 1, d_4^{20} 0.882 0.

^{1}H—NMR Spectrum of n-Butyl Acetate in CDCl$_3$

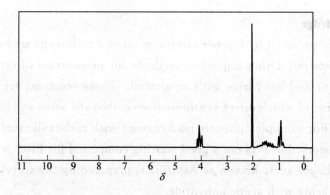

IR Spectrum of n-Butyl Acetate Using Liquid Film

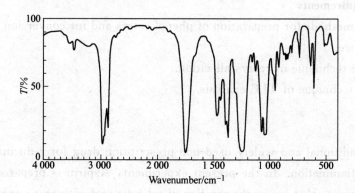

Questions

(1) Calculate the theoretical amount of the water that will be produced from the reaction.

(2) In the present experiment, what principles and methods are adopted to improve the yield of the *n*-butyl acetate?

(3) What impurities are removed by washing the crude product with an aqueous sodium carbonate solution? Can the sodium carbonate solution be replaced by the sodium bicarbonate solution?

(4) Calculate the percentage contents of the impurities in your product based on the GC analysis results.

(5) In the functional group region of the IR spectrum of *n*-butyl acetate, specify the absorptions associated with the carbon-oxygen single and double bonds.

(6) Assign all signals in the ^{1}H—NMR spectrum of *n*-butyl acetate.

3.9   Acetylation of Salicylic Acid:
Preparation of Acetylsalicylic Acid (乙酰水杨酸)

Fundamental Knowledge

Esters are usually prepared by Fischer esterification of a carboxylic acid with an alcohol using a mineral acid as catalyst. Other important methods for preparation of esters are the reactions of an acid chloride or acid anhydride with an alcohol. These reactions are especially useful for preparation of esters, of which direct synthesis from carboxylic acids and alcohols gives difficulties or low yields. For example, phenols readily react with carboxylic acid anhydrides and acid chlorides to form esters, but it is not a good starting compound for Fischer esterification. Commercially, acetylsalicylic acid, known as Aspirin, is prepared by the acetylation of salicylic acid (*o*-hydroxybenzoic acid) with acetic anhydride.

Purposes and Requirements

(1) Learn the methods for preparation of phenol esters and for conversion of acid anhydrides to esters in practice.

(2) Master the technique of recrystallization.

(3) Learn the technique of TLC analysis.

Principle

Aspirin is a traditional and widely used non-prescription drug for reducing fevers, relieving pains and anti-inflammation. In the present experiment, Aspirin is prepared according to the commercial procedure, that is, by the reaction of salicylic acid with acetic anhydride in the presence of a catalytic amount of sulfuric acid.

Acetylation of Salicylic Acid: Preparation of Acetylsalicylic Acid（乙酰水杨酸）

$$\text{o-hydroxybenzoic acid} + \text{acetic anhydride} \xrightarrow[85\sim90\ ℃]{H_2SO_4} \text{acetylsalicylic acid (Aspirin)} + CH_3COOH$$

o-hydroxybenzoic acid   acetic anhydride   acetylsalicylic acid（Aspirin）   acetic acid

Apparatus

A 100 mL Erlenmeyer flask, 200 mL beaker, Büchner funnel, filter flask and watchglass.

Reagents

Salicylic acid（水杨酸）	3.2 g（0.023 mol）
Acetic anhydride（乙酸酐）	5.0 mL（5.4 g, 0.05 mol）
Concentrated sulfuric acid（98%，浓硫酸）	5 drops
Saturated aqueous sodium bicarbonate（饱和碳酸氢钠水溶液）	35 mL
95% Ethanol（乙醇）	
1% Ferric chloride（三氯化铁）	

Time   4 h

Safety Alert

（1）The starting acetic anhydride is an irritant, so handle it with care.

（2）It is better to carry out the reaction in a hood because an irritant by-product, acetic acid, will be released from the reaction when the mixture is heated.

（3）Concentrated sulfuric acid is very corrosive. If it accidentally comes in contact with your skin, wash it off immediately with large amounts of water and then with dilute sodium bicarbonate solution.

Procedure

（1）**Setting Up and Reaction**   Place 3.2 g（0.023 mol）of salicylic acid and 5.0 mL（5.4 g, 0.05 mol）of acetic anhydride in a 100 mL Erlenmeyer flask. Swirl the flask to make the solid dissolved. Continue swirling and carefully add 5 drops of concentrated sulfuric acid. Heat the mixture with a water bath, keep the temperature of the water bath between 85~90 ℃[1], and swirl the solution occasionally. After 15 min, stop heating and allow the reaction solution to cool down to room temperature.

（2）**Work-Up and Isolation**   Pour slowly the solution into a 200 mL beaker containing 50 mL of ice-water [2], and cool the beaker in an ice-water bath to crystallize the product completely.

Transfer all crystals into a Büchner funnel and make a vacuum filtration. Rinse the flask several times until there is no solid left in it and wash the crystals twice with ice-water (8 mL × 2). Press the crystals as dry as possible on the Büchner funnel.

(1) **Recrystallization**   Transfer the crude product into a 200 mL beaker. With stirring, pour 35 mL of saturated aqueous sodium bicarbonate into the beaker. Continue stirring for several minutes until no bubble (CO_2) comes out. Remove the undissolved by-products by vacuum filtration and wash the funnel with 6~10 mL of water. Decant the filtrate into a 200 mL beaker containing a solution of 5~6 mL of concentrated hydrochloric acid and 10 mL of water. Cool the beaker in an ice-water bath, and then repeat vacuum filtration as above-described. Air-dry the crystals on a watchglass[3]. The product may be further purified by recrystallization from a mixed solvent of ethanol and water. Weigh the product and calculate the percentage yield of the acetylsalicylic acid obtained. Yield: 2.5~3 g.

(2) **Identification**   Measure the melting point of the acetylsalicylic acid obtained. Determine the purity of the product obtained by TLC analysis with pentane/ethyl acetate (8 : 2, v/v) as eluent. If an IR instrument is available, record the IR spectrum of the product and compare the spectrum with that of the authentic sample.

Notes

[1] Salicylic acid is a bifunctional compound. The reaction temperature should be controlled to reduce the unwanted side-reactions.

[2] The unreacted acetic anhydride is decomposed by water. The acetylsalicylic acid will crystallize from ice-cold water.

[3] The following procedures can be used to test whether salicylic acid exists in the product obtained: Place a small amount of the aspirin sample and 5 mL of distilled water in a test tube and shake the tube to dissolve the crystals; Add several drops of 1% aqueous ferric chloride to the tube; Observe the color change of the aqueous solution. If the solution turns purple, it can be deduced that the sample is contaminated with salicylic acid.

Finishing Touches

Dilute and neutralize the aqueous solution before flushing it down the drain with water.

Physical Property of Acetylsalicylic Acid

Pure acetylsalicylic acid is a colorless needle crystal. mp 138~140 ℃.

¹H—NMR Spectrum of Acetylsalicylic Acid in CDCl₃

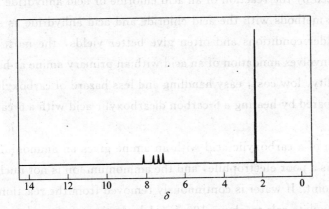

IR Spectrum of Acetylsalicylic Acid Using KBr Disc

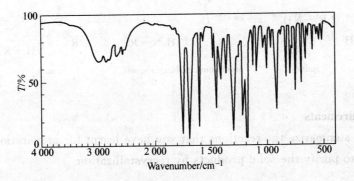

Questions

(1) What are the possible by-products formed in the reaction?

(2) What is the purpose to add the concentrated sulfuric acid in preparation of Aspirin?

(3) Why the hydroxyl (—OH) group of salicylic acid, instead of the carboxyl (—COOH) group, reacts with acetic anhydride?

(4) Specify the absorptions associated with the carbon-oxygen double bonds of the ester and the carboxyl group in the IR spectrum of acetylsalicylic acid.

(5) Assign all signals in the ¹H—NMR spectrum of acetylsalicylic acid.

3.10   Amidation of Carboxylic Acids:
Preparation of Acetanilide（乙酰苯胺）

Fundamental Knowledge

Amides can be prepared in a variety of ways from acyl chlorides, acid anhydrides, carboxylic

Basic Experiments

acids and esters. The partial hydrolysis of nitriles also gives amides. In the laboratory, amides are usually synthesized by the reaction of an acid chloride or acid anhydride with an amine. Although the synthetic methods with the acid chloride and acid anhydride as starting compounds take place under milder conditions and often give better yields, the most common industrial synthesis of amides involves amidation of an acid with an primary amine at high temperature because of the availability, low cost, easy handling and less hazard of carboxylic acids. For example, Nylon-66 is prepared by heating a 6-carbon dicarboxylic acid with a 6-carbon diamine in the chemical industry.

The initial reaction of a carboxylic acid with an amine gives an ammonium carboxylate salt. The carboxylate ion is a poor electrophile, and the ammonium ion is not nucleophilic, so the reaction stops at this point. If water is continuously removed from the reaction system by heating the ammonium carboxylate salt to above 100 ℃, dehydration of the salt occurs readily to give an amide.

acid   amine   ammonium carboxylate salt   amide

Purposes and Requirements

(1) Review and summarize the reactions that you have learnt for preparation of amides.

(2) Learn how to purify the solid products by recrystallization.

Principle

Acetanilide is prepared by acetylation of aniline with an excess of acetic acid in the present experiment. The water is removed as it forms by distillation to get a high yield of acetanilide. The acetyl group is often used as a protective group for aniline when the basic and nucleophilic amino group may cause problems in a synthesis. The acetyl group can be removed from the nitrogen atom by hydrolysis of acetanilide derivatives in either an aqueous acidic or aqueous basic solution.

aniline   acetic acid   acetanilide

Apparatus

A 25 mL Erlenmeyer flask, fractionating column, thermometer, graduated cylinder, distillation adapter, beaker, Büchner funnel, filter flask and watchglass.

Reagents

Aniline（苯胺）	5.0 mL (5.1 g, 0.055 mol)
Glacial acetic acid（冰醋酸）	7.4 mL (7.8 g, 0.13 mol)
Zinc powder（锌粉）	0.1 g
Activated carbon（活性炭）	0.5 g

Time   6 h

Safety Alert

Aniline is toxic and irritant. Avoid inhaling the vapor from aniline and do not allow it to contact your skin.

Procedure for Mini-scale Preparation

(1) **Setting Up**   To a 25 mL Erlenmeyer flask add 5.0 mL (5.1 g, 0.055 mol) of the freshly distilled aniline[1], 7.4 mL (7.8 g, 0.13 mol) of glacial acetic acid and 0.1 g of zinc powder[2]. Assemble the flask with a fractional column, and fit a thermometer on the top of the column as shown in Figure 3.10−1. Use a graduated cylinder as a receiver.

(2) **Reaction**   Heat slowly the reaction solution under gentle reflux on an asbestos pad using a Bunsen burner. Control the flame to keep the temperature of the distilling vapor at about 105 ℃. The water formed in the reaction could be distilled completely (containing a small amount of acetic acid) in 40~60 min. When the temperature of the distilling vapor fluctuates[3], the reaction has ended, then stop heating.

(3) **Work-Up and Isolation**   The hot solution is slowly poured into a beaker containing 100 mL of cold water with stirring. Cool the aqueous solution with vigorous stirring to make the acetanilide completely precipitate as fine crystals. Collect the crude product in a Büchner funnel by vacuum filtration, and wash the product with 5~10 mL of ice-water to remove the remaining acetic acid.

(4) **Recrystallization**   Re-dissolve the crude product in 150 mL of hot water and heat the aqueous solution to boil. If there are undissolved oil drops [4], add some additional hot water until all oil drops dissolve in the solution[5]. Cool the solution for a while, and then add 0.5 g of activated carbon[6]. Stir the mixture with a glass rod and heat it to boil for 1~2 min. Filter the mixture when it is hot with a pre-warmed Büchner funnel or with a thermos funnel[7].

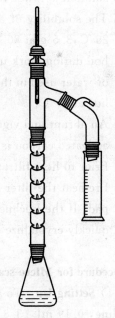

Figure 3.10−1

Apparatus for
preparation of acetanilide

The acetanilide precipitates as colorless flake crystals when the solution is cooled down. Collect the product by vacuum filtration, and press the crystalline solid as dry as possible. After air-dry the product on a watchglass, weigh the product and calculate the percentage yield of the acetanilide obtained. Yield: 4~5 g.

(5) **Identification**　Measure the melting point of the acetanilide obtained. Record the IR spectrum of the product if an IR instrument is available, and compare the spectrum with that of the authentic sample.

Notes

[1] Aniline turns red-brown after stored for a long time. This may influence the quality of the product acetanilide.

[2] Zinc powder is added to prevent the aniline from being oxidized during reaction. Do not add too much zinc powder, otherwise the water-insoluble zinc hydroxide would appear in the procedure of work-up.

[3] Sometimes white smog appears in the flask.

[4] These oil drops are the melted water-containing acetanilide (at 83 ℃, with 13% of water). The undissolved acetanilide exists as solids in the aqueous solution if the temperature of the solution is lower than 83 ℃.

[5] The solubility of acetanilide in water at different temperatures is as follows: 0.563 g at 25 ℃, 3.5 g at 80 ℃ and 5.2 g at 100 ℃. Some water will evaporate when it is heated to boil during work-up, so add some hot water occasionally to the flask. The proper amount of water used in the recrystallization is to make the aqueous solution saturated with acetanilide at 80 ℃.

[6] An abrupt and vigorous boiling may occur and the mixture may rush out of the flask if the activated carbon is added to the hot solution.

[7] Prior to heat filtration, fix an inverted Büchner funnel and heat it thoroughly with steam. Pre-heat the filter flask in a hot water bath. Do not heat the flask directly on the asbestos pad! If the Büchner funnel and the filter flask are not well warmed, the acetanilide would quickly crystallize in the Büchner funnel, resulting in the great loss of the product.

Procedure for Micro-scale Preparation

(1) **Setting Up**　To a 5 mL Erlenmeyer flask add 0.13 mL (1.4 mmol) of the freshly distilled aniline, 0.19 mL (3.3 mmol) of glacial acetic acid and 3 mg of zinc powder. Assemble the flask with a Hickman fractionating head, and fit the still head with a thermometer and a condenser as shown in Figure 2.7−5b.

(2) **Reaction**　Heat slowly the reaction solution to gentle reflux with a sand bath. Completely distill the water formed in the reaction[1]. Stop heating when the temperature at the thermometer begins to decrease and white smog appears in the flask.

(3) **Work-Up and Isolation**   The hot solution is slowly poured into a beaker containing 3 mL of cold water with stirring. Cool the aqueous solution with stirring to make the acetanilide completely precipitate as fine crystals. Collect the crude product in a Büchner funnel by vacuum filtration, and wash the product with 0. 05 mL of ice-water.

(4) **Recrystallization**   Re-dissolve the crude product in 4 mL of hot water and heat the aqueous solution to boil. If there are undissolved oil drops, add some additional hot water until all oil drops dissolve in the solution[2]. The acetanilide precipitates as colorless crystals when the solution is cooled down. Collect the product by vacuum filtration and air-dry the product on a watchglass. Weigh the product and calculate the percentage yield of the acetanilide obtained. Yield: ca. 50 mg.

(5) **Identification**   Measure the melting point of the acetanilide obtained.

Notes

[1] Because only a small amount of water is formed in a micro-scale experiment, the temperature at the thermometer cannot reach 100 ℃. Normally, it is between 70～80 ℃.

[2] Since a very small amount of product is obtained, decolorizing with activated carbon is not proceeded.

Finishing Touches

All aqueous solutions should be diluted with water and neutralized before flushing down the drain with a large excess of water.

Physical Property of acetanilide

Pure acetanilide is a colorless flake crystal. mp 113～115 ℃.

¹H —NMR Spectrum of Acetanilide in CDCl₃

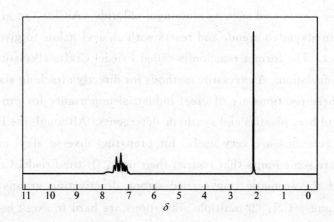

Basic Experiments

IR Spectrum of Acetanilide Using KBr Disc

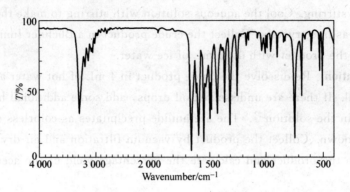

Questions

(1) Do you know any other methods for preparing acetanilide from aniline?

(2) To improve the yield of acetanilide, which operations should be paid special attention to in the procedure of recrystallization?

(3) Calculate the amount of the acetanilide left in the mother solution after recrystallization.

(4) What is the white smog in the flask?

(5) Specify the absorptions associated with the carbon-oxygen double bond of the amide and with the benzene ring in the IR spectrum of acetanilide.

(6) Assign all signals in the ^{1}H—NMR spectrum of acetanilide to the hydrogen nuclei responsible for them.

3.11 Friedel-Crafts Reaction:
Preparation of Acetophenone (苯乙酮)

Fundamental Knowledge

In the presence of a Lewis acid such as aluminum chloride ($AlCl_3$), an arene reacts with an alkyl halide to give an alkylated arene, and reacts with an acyl halide to give an acylated arene (an alkyl aryl ketone). The former reaction is called Friedel-Crafts alkylation and the latter is called Friedel-Crafts acylation. As versatile methods for directly attaching alkyl and acyl groups to aromatic rings, these reactions are of great industrial importance for producing high-octane gasoline, synthetic rubber, plastics and synthetic detergents. Although the Friedel-Crafts alkylation and acylation reactions are very useful for preparing diverse alkyl aromatics and alkyl aryl ketones, there are some limits that restrict their uses: ① the Friedel-Crafts alkylation and acylation both fail if the aromatic ring carried strong deactivating groups, such as —NO_2, —R_3N^+, —C(O)R and —CN; ② multiple alkylations are hard to avoid because alkyl groups are activating substituents; and ③ the Friedel-Crafts alkylation is susceptible to carbocation rearrangements. As a result, mixtures of isomeric products may be formed in the alkylation. In contrast, the acylation stops after mono-acylation because an acyl group is a strong deactivating group, and no rearrangement occurs in the acylation. The other important difference between the Friedel-Crafts alkylation and acylation reaction is that the former process needs only a catalytic amount of aluminum chloride, while the latter requires use of a stoichiometric amount of aluminum chloride because the carbonyl group of the acylated product forms a one-to-one complex with aluminum chloride.

The Friedel-Crafts alkylation and acylation reaction are classic examples of electrophilic aromatic substitution. The generally accepted mechanism for Friedel-Crafts acylation is illustrated in the following equations. In the Friedel-Crafts alkylation, the role of aluminum chloride, a strong Lewis acid, is to convert the alkyl halide into a reactive electrophilic intermediate, in the form of a carbocation for secondary and tertiary alkyl halides or a highly polarized carbon-halogen bond for primary alkyl halides. This electrophile then undergoes attack by an arene, which functions as a Lewis base, resulting in a positively charged and resonance-stabilized sigma complex, also termed as arenium ion. This is a rate-determining step. Finally, a halide ion from $XAlCl_3^-$ deprotonates this sigma complex to give HX and form product complex. The mechanism of Friedel-Crafts acylation resembles that for alkylation, except an acylium ion is formed in the first-step reaction of an acyl halide with aluminum chloride. The acylium ion is a strong electrophile. It reacts with benzene or an activated benzene derivative to form an aluminum chloride complex of the acylbenzene. Addition of water hydrolyzes this complex, giving the free acylbenzene.

The mechanism of Friedel-Crafts acylation:

Step 1: Formation of an acylium ion

Step 2: Electrophilic attack

Step 3: Deprotonation and complexation

σ complex   acylbenzene   product complex

Purposes and Requirements

(1) Review and summarize the electrophilic aromatic substitution reactions and mechanisms, such as Friedel-Crafts alkylation and acylation, bromination, nitration and sulfonation.

(2) Learn Friedel-Crafts acylation reaction in practice.

(3) Master the technique for distilling organic liquids of high boiling points.

(4) Review the manipulations of extraction and simple distillation.

Principle

Acetophenone is prepared by Friedel-Crafts acylation of benzene with acetic anhydride in the presence of an excess amount of aluminum chloride. Benzene is used as both a reagent and a solvent in the reaction. Two equiv of anhydrous aluminum chloride is used relative to the acetic anhydride because two equiv of aluminum chloride will be consumed in the reaction. The acyl group of the product acetophenone forms a complex ($C_6H_5COCH_3 \cdot AlCl_3$) with an equiv of aluminum chloride and the acetic acid generated in the reaction can also react with an equiv of aluminum chloride to form a carboxylate compound ($CH_3COOAlCl_2$). Hydrolysis of these complexes gives the free acylbenzene and the acetic acid.

benzene   acetic anhydride   product complex   acetate   free acylbenzene   acetic acid

Apparatus

A 100 mL three-neck round-bottom flask, mechanical stirrer fitted with a liquid-seal tube, dropping funnel, reflux condenser, drying tube, gas trap, 300 mL beaker, 125 mL Erlenmeyer flask, separatory funnel, air condenser, thermometer, apparatus for simple distillation, 10 mL and 100 mL round-bottom flask.

Friedel-Crafts Reaction: Preparation of Acetophenone (苯乙酮)

Reagents

Benzene (苯) [1]	25 mL (22 g, 0.28 mol)
Acetic anhydride (乙酐)	4.7 mL (5.1 g, 0.05 mol)
Anhydrous aluminum chloride (无水三氯化铝)	16 g (0.12 mol)
Concentrated sulfuric acid (浓硫酸)	
Concentrated hydrochloric acid (浓盐酸)	
5% Aqueous sodium hydroxide solution (氢氧化钠水溶液)	

Time   8 h

Safety Alert

(1) Anhydrous aluminum chloride is extremely hygroscopic and reacts rapidly with water, even the moisture on your hands, producing fumes of hydrogen chloride, which are highly corrosive. Do not allow aluminum chloride to come in contact with your skin. If it does, flush the affected area with large amounts of water. Minimize exposure of aluminum chloride to the atmosphere!

(2) Benzene is flammable and toxic. Assemble the apparatus carefully and be sure that all joints are tightly mated. If possible, flameless heating is preferred for heating the reaction mixture and for distilling benzene.

Procedure

(1) **Setting Up**   Equip the side mouths of a 100 mL three-neck round-bottom flask with a dropping funnel and a reflux condenser, respectively[2]. The middle mouth of the flask is equipped with a mechanical stirrer fitted with a liquid-seal tube. Add concentrated sulfuric acid to the liquid-seal tube. Fit a drying tube containing anhydrous calcium chloride on the top of the condenser, then link the drying tube to a gas trap for removing fumes of hydrogen chloride (See Figure 1.4-7c). Weigh quickly the aluminum chloride powder in a dry vial or test tube in the hood and immediately transfer it to the reaction flask[3], and then decant 20 mL of benzene into the flask. Place 4.7 mL (5.1 g, 0.05 mol) of freshly distilled acetic anhydride and 5 mL of benzene in the dropping funnel, and gently swirl the funnel.

(2) **Reaction**   Drop slowly the benzene solution of acetic anhydride to the flask with stirring. The start of the reaction can be observed by evolution of bubbles of hydrogen chloride. The temperature of the reaction mixture rises spontaneously. Drop the acetic anhydride over a period of 10 min to keep the benzene solution refluxing gently. After addition of acetic anhydride, turn off the two-way cock of the dropping funnel, and heat the reaction solution under gentle reflux on an asbestos pad for 1 h[4]. Be sure to cool the solution to room temperature before proceeding.

(3) **Work-Up**   Working in the hood, slowly pour the cold reaction mixture into 50 g of ice

Basic Experiments

and stir the mixture vigorously. With continuous stirring, slowly add 30 mL of concentrated hydrochloric acid to dissolve aluminum hydroxide. If there is still some solid in the solution, add an additional concentrated hydrochloric acid until all aluminum hydroxide disappears. Pour the mixture into a separatory funnel, separate the benzene layer, and extract the water layer twice with benzene (10 mL×2). Combine all of the benzene solutions, and wash the organic layer sequentially with 15 mL of 5% sodium hydroxide solution and then with water. Save benzene layer in an Erlenmeyer flask.

(4) **Isolation**   Equip the stillpot with a dropping funnel. Assembly an apparatus for simple distillation as shown in Figure 2.7−1a, and change the gas trap to a long rubber tube leading to a sink. Decant the benzene solution into the dropping funnel, and draw about 10 mL of the benzene solution into the stillpot. Distil benzene with a boiling water bath, and gradually drop the benzene solution remaining in the funnel into the distillation flask at the same time. Heat the solution until no benzene can be distilled from the pot[5]. Change the dropping funnel on the stillpot to a 250 ℃ thermometer. Remove the benzene left in the stillpot by distillation on an asbestos pad. When the temperature of the vapors reaches 140 ℃, stop heating. Allow the solution to cool for a while, then change the water-cooled condenser to an air-cooled condenser and change the receiver. Continue distilling and collect the fraction of 195～202 ℃[6]. Weigh the product and calculate the percentage yield of the acetophenone obtained. Yield: 3.5～4 g.

(5) **Identification**   If an IR instrument is available, record the IR spectrum of the product obtained and compare it with the authentic spectrum of acetophenone.

Notes

[1] It is better to use thiophene-free benzene in this experiment. To remove thiophene from benzene, just wash it with concentrated sulfuric acid until no thiophene can be detected in benzene. The proper amount of concentrated sulfuric acid used in each time is about 15% of the volume of benzene. The method for testing thiophene in benzene is as follows: Add 2 mL of 0.1% isatin solution in sulfuric acid to 1 mL of the sample contained in a test tube, shake the tube for several minutes. If there is thiophene in benzene, the acid layer will turn light blue-green.

[2] All the glassware to be used before hydrolysis in this experiment must be thoroughly dried and the reagents must be absolutely anhydrous. Otherwise, the result of the experiment would be significantly influenced.

[3] When handling aluminum chloride, be aware that aluminum chloride is very susceptible to moisture. When exposed to humid air, it is quickly hydrolyzed.

[4] Extending the refluxing period can improve the yield of the product.

[5] The small amount of water in the benzene solution is distilled with benzene as an azeotrope.

[6] It is better to make a vacuum distillation for product and collect the fraction of 86～90 ℃/ 1.6 kPa (12 mmHg). The boiling points of acetophenone at different pressures are given in

Friedel-Crafts Reaction: Preparation of Acetophenone (苯乙酮)

the following table.

pressure/kPa	26.7	20	8.0	6.7	5.3	4.0	3.3	1.6
pressure/mmHg	200	150	60	50	40	30	25	12
boiling point/ ℃	155	146	120	115.5	110	102	98	88

Finishing Touches

Pour the benzene distillate into a designated container for recovered benzene. Flush the aqueous solution containing aluminum salts down the drain with excess water.

Physical Property of Acetophenone

Pure acetophenone is a clear and colorless oily liquid. mp $19 \sim 20$ ℃, bp 202 ℃, n_D^{20} 1.5370, d_4^{20} 1.0280.

^{1}H—NMR Spectrum of Acetophenone in CDCl$_3$

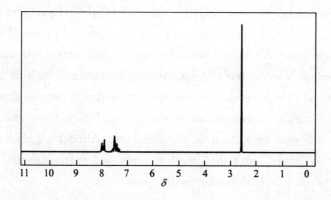

IR Spectrum of Acetophenone Using Liquid Film

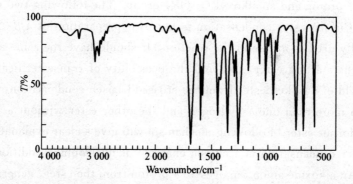

Questions

(1) Why it is important that the glassware and reagents used for the Friedel-Crafts reaction should be thoroughly dry?

(2) Why should the acetic acid be added dropwise?

(3) Why should hydrochloric acid be added after decomposition of the reaction mixture in ice-water?

(4) Which reagent can replace acetic anhydride in preparation of acetophenone?

(5) Explain why a catalytic amount of aluminum chloride is insufficient to promote the Friedel-Crafts acylation of benzene and acetic anhydride.

(6) In the functional group region of the IR spectrum of acetophenone, specify the absorptions associated with the ketone carbonyl group and the aromatic rings.

(7) Assign all signals in the ^{1}H—NMR spectrum of acetophenone.

3.12   The Claisen Ester Condensation:
Preparation of Ethyl Acetoacetate (乙酰乙酸乙酯)

Fundamental Knowledge

Carbonyl condensations are the reactions between two carbonyl partners via nucleophilic attack of an enolate ion, derived from one partner, on the carbonyl group of the second partner. In the reaction, the carbonyl compound behaves both as an electrophile and as a nucleophile, and a new carbon-carbon bond is built. Carbonyl condensations, such as aldol condensation, Claisen condensation and Perkin condensation, are very useful in organic synthesis because they enable larger, more complex organic molecules to be assembled from smaller, simpler ones. These reactions are also very important in biochemistry. Almost all classes of biomolecules, such as carbohydrates, lipids, proteins, nucleic acids and many others, are biosynthesized through routes that involve carbonyl condensation reactions.

The Claisen ester condensation occurs between two ester molecules via nucleophilic acyl substitution by an enolate ion. The overall reaction combines two ester molecules to give a β-ketoester by loss of a proton and an alkoxyl (—OR) group. The following two matters should be noticed when the Claisen ester condensation is used for preparation of a β-ketoester. ① An alkoxide is normally used as a base in the reaction. It should have the same alkyl group as the alkoxyl group of the starting ester, to avoid the possibility of transesterification of the ester; ② To get high yield of a β-ketoester from the crossed Claisen condensation, it is important to use one ester with more than one α hydrogen and the other ester without α hydrogen such as benzoic ester and formic ester. Following mechanism will give a clear explanation for this limit.

The Claisen ester condensation is a classic example of nucleophilic addition-elimination at a carbonyl group. An alkoxide anion removes an α proton from the ester, generating a resonance-stabilized enolate anion. The nucleophilic enolate anion attacks the carbonyl carbon of the other ester molecule, followed by expelling an alkoxide anion to form a β-ketoester. Although the equilibriums for the formation of an enolate anion and for the nucleophilic addition-elimination are both unfavorable, the following step to remove an α proton from the newly formed β-ketoester by an alkoxide anion is highly favorable because a resonance stabilized β-ketoester anion is formed. This step is of critical importance for the success of the reaction, which draws the overall equilibrium toward the final product. If the ethanol formed in the reaction is continuously distilled from the reaction mixture, the equilibrium can be further drawn toward the desired product. An acid should be added to protonate the β-ketoester anion after reaction and neutralize the alkoxide base.

Step 1: Formation of an enolate anion

ester   alkoxide   a resonance-stabilized enolate anion
               anion

Step 2: Nucleophilic addition-elimination

ester   enolate anion β-ketoester   alkoxide
                                                                               anion

Step 3: Formation of a β-ketoester anion

β-ketoester   alkoxide β-ketoester anion   ethanol
                           anion

Step 4: Acidification

β-ketoester anion β-ketoester

Purposes and Requirements

(1) Learn more theoretical and practical knowledge on the Claisen ester condensation from this experiment.

(2) Master the technique of vacuum distillation.

Principle

Ethyl acetoacetate (ethyl 3-oxobutanoate) is prepared by the self Claisen ester condensation

Basic Experiments

of ethyl acetate. Because commercial ethyl acetate contains a small amount of ethanol (ca. 2%), sodium is directly added to the ethyl acetate to generate ethoxide ions *in situ*. After reaction the mixture is neutralized by dilute acetic acid to get the final product.

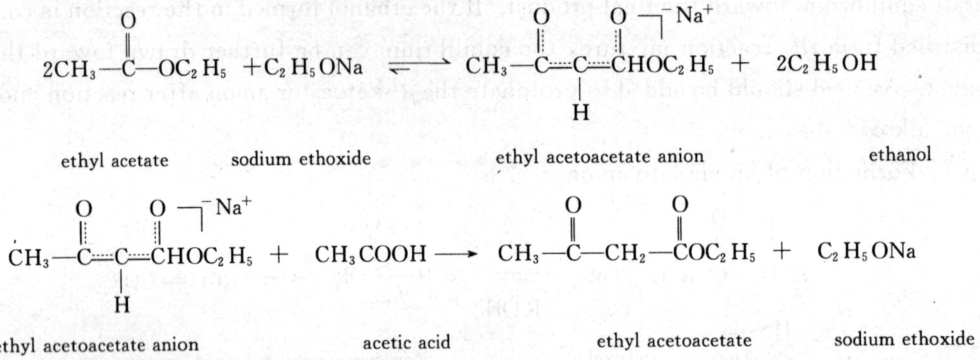

$$2CH_3-\overset{O}{\overset{\|}{C}}-OC_2H_5 + C_2H_5ONa \rightleftharpoons CH_3-\overset{O}{\overset{\|}{C}}-\overset{O}{\underset{H}{\overset{\|}{C}}}-CHOC_2H_5^- Na^+ + 2C_2H_5OH$$

　ethyl acetate　　　sodium ethoxide　　　　ethyl acetoacetate anion　　　　　ethanol

$$CH_3-\overset{O}{\overset{\|}{C}}-\overset{O}{\underset{H}{\overset{\|}{C}}}-CHOC_2H_5^- Na^+ + CH_3COOH \longrightarrow CH_3-\overset{O}{\overset{\|}{C}}-CH_2-\overset{O}{\overset{\|}{C}}OC_2H_5 + C_2H_5ONa$$

ethyl acetoacetate anion　　　　　acetic acid　　　　ethyl acetoacetate　　　sodium ethoxide

Apparatus

A 125 mL round-bottom flask, reflux condenser, drying tube, 250 mL Erlenmeyer flask, separatory funnel, thermometer, apparatus for simple distillation and apparatus for vacuum distillation.

Reagents

Ethyl acetate (乙酸乙酯)　　　　　　　　　　　48.9 mL (44.0 g, 0.5 mol)

Sodium (金属钠)　　　　　　　　　　　　　　　5.0 g (0.22 mol)

Dilute acetic acid (稀醋酸)

5% Aqueous sodium carbonate solution (碳酸钠溶液)

Anhydrous potassium carbonate (无水碳酸钾)

Saturated sodium chloride solution (饱和食盐水)

Saturated calcium chloride solution (饱和氯化钙)

Anhydrous magnesium sulfate (无水硫酸镁)

Time　8 h

Safety Alert

Sodium metal is very susceptible toward water and moisture. All glassware used in the reaction before acidification must be thoroughly dried. Place the paper used for cleaning and weighing the sodium in a beaker containing a small amount of ethanol before throw it into an ash can.

Procedure for Mini-scale Preparation

(1) **Setting Up**   To a dry 250 mL round-bottom flask[1], add 48.9 mL (44.0 g, 0.5 mol) of anhydrous ethyl acetate[2] and 5.0 g (0.22 mol) of sodium in small pieces[3]. Equip the flask quickly with a reflux condenser and fit a drying tube containing anhydrous calcium chloride on the top of the condenser as shown in Figure 1.4-7b.

(2) **Reaction**   Heat the mixture with a water bath to promote the start of the reaction. If the reaction is too vigorous, immerse the flask in a cold water bath until the reaction undergoes smoothly. Heat the mixture continuously under gentle reflux with a water bath. Stop heating when the pieces of sodium completely disappear[4]. The solution is clear red with green fluorescence [5].

(3) **Work-Up**   Allow the resulting solution cool to room temperature and remove the condenser. Cool the solution further in an ice-water bath. With swirling, drop slowly the dilute acetic acid (20%~30%) [6] into the reaction mixture until the solution is slightly acid to blue litmus paper (pH = 5~6) and all solid in the solution disappears. Separate the red ester layer using a separatory funnel, extract the water layer with 20 mL of ethyl acetate, and then combine the ester layers. Wash the organic layer first with 5% sodium carbonate solution until it is neutral to pH paper, then with an equal volume of saturated aqueous sodium chloride solution. Allow the mixture to stand for a while to separate. Save ester layer in an Erlenmeyer flask and dry it over anhydrous potassium carbonate or anhydrous magnesium sulfate.

(4) **Isolation**   Decant the dried crude product into a stillpot and set up an apparatus for simple distillation. Distil the ethyl acetate from the crude product with a water bath. Assemble an apparatus for vacuum distillation, and distil the ethyl acetoacetate under reduced pressure. The boiling point of the collected fraction depends on the pressure of the distillation system[7]. Weigh the product and calculate the percentage yield of the ethyl acetoacetate obtained. Yield: 8.5~9.5 g.

(5) **Identification**   The tautomerization of ethyl acetoacetate can be verified by the simple testing method: Add 2~3 drops of ethyl acetoacetate to 2 mL of water in a test tube, then add a drop of 1% ferric chloride solution, and observe the change of the color. Quickly drop bromine until the color of the solution fades. Allow the solution to stand for a while. When the color re-appears, drop the bromine again. Repeat this test for several times.

If IR and NMR instruments are available, record the IR and ^{1}H—NMR spectra of the product obtained and compare the recorded spectra with the standard spectra of the authentic sample.

Notes

[1] All the glassware used before acidification in this experiment must be dried thoroughly and the reagents must be absolutely anhydrous. Otherwise, the result of the experiment would be significantly influenced.

[2] The ethyl acetate used in the experiment should be free of water. Ethyl acetate can be purified by the following method: Wash the commercial ethyl acetate with saturated calcium chloride solution for several times, and dry it over fused anhydrous potassium carbonate.

Basic Experiments

Then distil the dried ethyl acetate with a water bath and collect the fraction of 76~77 °C.

[3] Clean the protective oil on the sodium with filter paper and cut off the oxidized surface of the sodium. Weigh it quickly, cut it into small pieces in the cold anhydrous diethyl ether, and immediately place the sodium in the flask containing anhydrous ethyl acetate.

[4] The time needed for disappearance of the sodium depends on the size of the sodium pieces. It takes 1.5~3 h in general.

[5] A light yellow precipitate may sometimes appear.

[6] The dilute acetic acid should be added slowly and carefully. It will react with the acetic acid vigorously if there is a small amount of sodium left in the reaction mixture. Do not add an excess of acetic acid in the acidification step. The solubility of the ester will increase in the aqueous layer with an excess of acetic acid, and result in decrease of the yield.

[7] The boiling points of ethyl acetoacetate at different pressure are given in the following table.

pressure/kPa	1.6	1.9	2.4	2.7	4.0	5.3	8.0	10.7	101.3
pressure/mmHg	12	14	18	20	30	40	60	80	760
boiling point/ °C	71	74	78	82	88	92	97	100	181

Procedure for Micro-scale Preparation

(1) **Setting Up**   To a dry 10 mL round-bottom flask, add 0.9 mL of anhydrous ethyl acetate and 0.09 g of sodium in small pieces. Equip the flask quickly with a reflux condenser and fit a drying tube containing anhydrous calcium chloride on the top of the condenser as shown in Figure 1.4−7b.

(2) **Reaction**   Heat the mixture continuously under gentle reflux with a sand bath. Stop heating when the pieces of sodium completely disappear. The solution is clear red with green fluorescence and a light yellow precipitate may sometimes appear.

(3) **Work-Up**   Allow the resulting solution to cool to room temperature, and then with swirling, drop slowly the dilute acetic acid (20%~30%) into the reaction mixture until the solution is slightly acidic to blue litmus paper (pH = 5~6). Separate the red ester layer using a separatory funnel, extract the water layer with 2 mL of ethyl acetate, and combine the ester layers. Wash the organic layer first with an equal volume of 5% sodium carbonate solution, then with an equal volume of saturated aqueous sodium chloride solution. Save ester layer in an Erlenmeyer flask and dry it over anhydrous potassium carbonate.

(4) **Isolation**   Filter the dried crude product to a 5 mL round-bottom flask and add a piece of boiling chip. Recover the ethyl acetate from the crude product by simple distillation (Figure 2.7−3a), and then distil the ethyl acetoacetate under reduced pressure (Figure 2.7−11a). Collect the fraction of 77~81 °C at the pressure of 2.4 kPa (18 mmHg). Weigh the product and calculate the percentage yield of the ethyl acetoacetate obtained. Yield: ca. 80 mg[1].

Notes

[1] The purity of ethyl acetoacetate obtained is 98. 2% according to GC analysis.

Finishing Touches

Pour the residue remaining in the stillpot into a container for waste organic liquids. Neutralize the aqueous solution and flush it down the drain with excess water. Evaporate the solvents from the magnesium sulfate used as drying agent in the hood, and place it in a container for nonhazardous solid.

Physical Property of Ethyl Acetoacetate

Pure ethyl acetoacetate is a clear and colorless oily liquid. bp 181 ℃, n_D^{20} 1. 419 0, d_4^{20} 1. 027 0.

^{1}H—NMR Spectrum of Ethyl Acetoacetate in CDCl$_3$

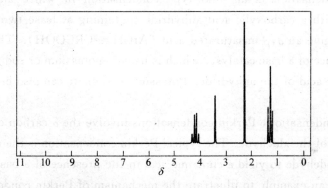

IR Spectrum of Ethyl Acetoacetate Using Liquid Film

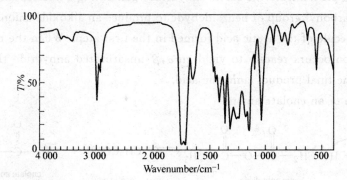

Questions

(1) What is the influence of water and moisture on this reaction?

(2) Why should the ethyl acetoacetate be isolated by vacuum distillation?

(3) Why should the acetic acid be added to the reaction mixture after reaction?

(4) Why is saturated sodium chloride solution used in the work-up procedure?

(5) Write the tautomerization process of β−ketoester using curved arrows to show the flow of

Basic Experiments

electrons?

(6) When a crossed Claisen condensation is made with two esters, one with two *a* hydrogen atoms and the other without *a* hydrogen, which ester should be gradually dropped into the basic solution contained in a flask?

(7) Specify the absorptions associated with the carbonyl groups and the carbon-oxygen single bond in the functional group region of the IR spectrum of ethyl acetoacetate.

(8) Assign all signals in the ^{1}H—NMR spectrum of ethyl acetoacetate.

3.13   Perkin Condensation: Preparation of Cinnamic Acid (肉桂酸)

Fundamental Knowledge

The Perkin condensation is an aldol-type condensation in which an aromatic aldehyde (ArCHO) reacts with a carboxylic acid anhydride containing at lease two α hydrogen atoms, (RCH$_2$CO)$_2$O, to give an α,β-unsaturated acid (ArCH =CRCOOH). The two reactants are heated in the presence of a base catalyst, which is usually potassium or sodium salt of the corresponding carboxylic acid of the anhydride. Potassium carbonate can also be used as catalyst for the reaction.

Like the aldol condensation, Perkin condensations involve the α carbon of the anhydride and the carbonyl group of the aldehyde. The typical Perkin condensation is the reaction of acetic anhydride with benzaldehyde to yield a cinnamic acid in the presence of a base catalyst. Here we use this reaction as an example to illustrate the mechanism of Perkin condensation. An acetate anion removes an α proton from the acetic anhydride, generating a nucleophilic enolate anion. It then attacks the carbonyl group of benzaldehyde to produce an alkoxide anion, which removes a proton from a molecule of the acetic acid formed in the first step. When the reaction solution is heated, dehydration occurs readily to yield an α,β-unsaturated anhydride that undergoes hydrolysis to form the final product cinnamic acid.

Step 1: Formation of an enolate anion

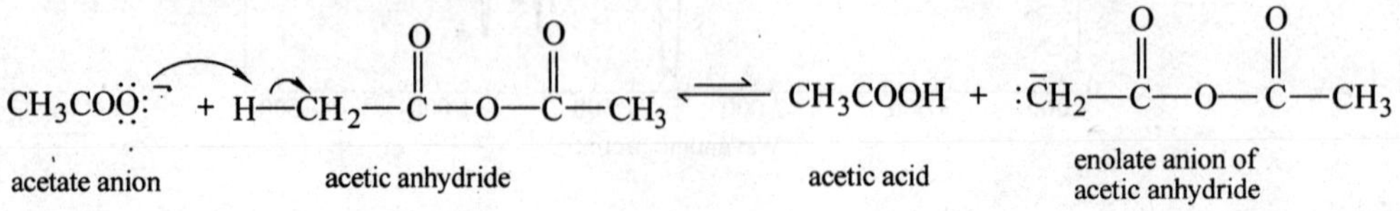

Step 2: Nucleophilic addition

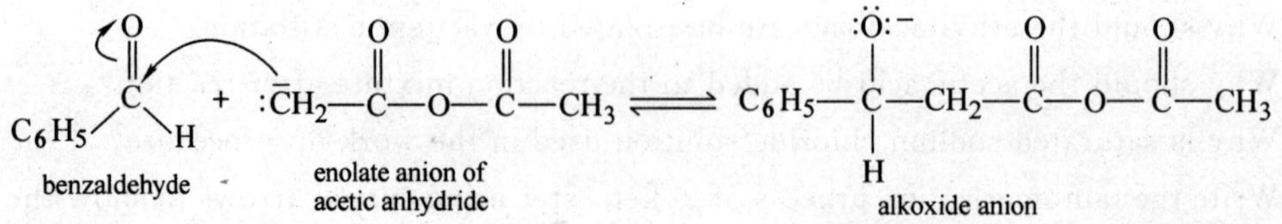

Perkin Condensation: Preparation of Cinnamic Acid（肉桂酸）

$$CH_3COO-H + C_6H_5-\underset{H}{\overset{\overset{:\ddot{O}:^-}{|}}{C}}-CH_2-\overset{\overset{O}{\|}}{C}-O-\overset{\overset{O}{\|}}{C}-CH_3 \rightleftharpoons CH_3CO\ddot{O}:^- + C_6H_5-\underset{H}{\overset{\overset{OH}{|}}{C}}-CH_2-\overset{\overset{O}{\|}}{C}-O-\overset{\overset{O}{\|}}{C}-CH_3$$

acetic acid   alkoxide anion   acetate anion   β-hydroxy anhydride

Step 3: Dehydration

$$C_6H_5-\underset{H}{\overset{\overset{OH}{|}}{C}}-CH_2-\overset{\overset{O}{\|}}{C}-O-\overset{\overset{O}{\|}}{C}-CH_3 \rightleftharpoons C_6H_5-\underset{H}{\overset{}{C}}=CH-\overset{\overset{O}{\|}}{C}-O-\overset{\overset{O}{\|}}{C}-CH_3 + H_2O$$

β-hydroxy anhydride   α, β-unsaturated anhydride

Step 4: Hydrolysis

$$C_6H_5-\underset{H}{\overset{}{C}}=CH-\overset{\overset{O}{\|}}{C}-O-\overset{\overset{O}{\|}}{C}-CH_3 + H_2O \longrightarrow C_6H_5-\underset{H}{\overset{}{C}}=CH-\overset{\overset{O}{\|}}{C}-OH + CH_3COOH$$

α, β-unsaturated anhydride   cinnamic acid   acetic acid

Purposes and Requirements

(1) Learn more theoretical and practical knowledge on the Perkin condensation from this experiment.

(2) Understand the principle of steam distillation and master the technique of steam distillation.

(3) Review the manipulation of recrystallization.

Principle

Cinnamic acid is prepared by the Perkin condensation of benzaldehyde with acetic anhydride in the presence of anhydrous potassium acetate. An excess of acetic anhydride is used in the experiment to improve the conversion of benzaldehyde. After reaction, the α,β-unsaturated anhydride is hydrolyzed to get the final product. Cinnamic acid has *cis* and *trans* isomers. The product prepared by the Perkin condensation is usually a *trans* isomer.

$$\underset{C_6H_5}{\overset{\overset{O}{\|}}{C}}{\overset{}{\diagdown}}H + CH_3-\overset{\overset{O}{\|}}{C}-O-\overset{\overset{O}{\|}}{C}-CH_3 \xrightarrow[150\sim170\,℃]{CH_3COOK} \underset{C_6H_5}{\overset{H}{\diagup}}C=C\underset{H}{\overset{C-OH}{\diagup}} + CH_3COOH$$

benzaldehyde   acetic anhydride   cinnamic acid   acetic acid

Basic Experiments

Apparatus

A 50 mL pear-shaped flask, 250 mL round-bottom flask, Claisen adaptor, air-cooled condenser, 250 ℃ thermometer, apparatus for steam distillation, Büchner funnel, filter flask and watchglass.

Reagents

Benzaldehyde（苯甲醛）	3.0 mL (3.2 g, 0.03 mol)
Acetic anhydride（乙酐）	5.5 mL (6.0 g, 0.06 mol)
Anhydrous potassium acetate（无水醋酸钾）	3.0 g (0.03 mol)
Saturated sodium carbonate solution（饱和碳酸钠溶液）	
Concentrated hydrochloric acid（浓盐酸）	
Activated carbon（活性炭）	

Time   6 h

Safety Alert

(1) Benzaldehyde is an irritant. Acetic anhydride and hydrochloric acid are corrosive liquids. Do not allow them to come in contact with your skin and avoid breathing the vapor from all these compounds.

(2) Do not heat the flask containing benzaldehyde and acetic anhydride directly on a flame.

Procedure for Mini-scale Preparation

(1) **Setting Up**   To a dry 50 mL pear-shaped flask[1], add 3.0 g (0.03 mol) of freshly fused and finely grinded anhydrous potassium acetate[2], 3.0 mL (3.2 g, 0.03 mol) of benzaldehyde[3] and 5.5 mL (6.0 g, 0.06 mol) of acetic anhydride[4]. Benzaldehyde and acetic anhydride should be redistilled before use. Swirl the flask to mix well the reactants. Equip the flask with an air-cooled condenser and a 250 ℃ thermometer by using a Claisen adaptor (Figure 3.13−1). Immerse the mercury head of the thermometer in the solution but do not allow it to touch the bottom of the flask. Fit a drying tube containing anhydrous calcium chloride on the top of the condenser as shown in Figure 1.4−7b.

(2) **Reaction**   Heat the mixture under reflux on an asbestos pad for 1 h. The temperature of the reaction mixture should be kept in the range of 150～170 ℃. Decant the hot reaction mixture (ca. 100 ℃) into 25 mL of water in a 250 mL round-bottom flask. Rinse the reaction flask twice with hot water (20 mL× 2) and pour the washes into the flask containing the hydrolyzed mixture.

(3) **Work-Up**   Add slowly saturated aqueous sodium carbonate so-

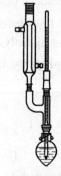

Figure 3.13−1   Apparatus for preparation of cinnamic acid

lution[5] to the flask with vigorous shaking until the mixture becomes weakly basic. Check the basicity of the mixture with litmus red test paper until it turns blue. Assemble an apparatus for steam distillation as shown in Figure 2.7−12, and then distil the unreacted benzaldehyde from the flask until the distillate is clear. Allow the solution to cool for a while and add a small amount of activated carbon to the flask[6]. After heat the solution under reflux for about 10 min, filter the hot solution to a 250 mL beaker. Allow the filtrate to cool down to room temperature and acidify it by slow addition of concentrated hydrochloric acid with strong stirring until the evolution of carbon dioxide ceases.

(4) **Isolation**   Cool the solution in a cold water bath to allow the cinnamic acid to crystallize completely. Collect the product by vacuum filtration, wash it with a small amount of cold water, drain the water off thoroughly, and air-dry the crude product on a watchglass. It can be recrystallized from hot water or from the mixture of water and ethanol in a ratio of 3 : 1 (V/V)[7]. Weigh the product and calculate the percentage yield. Yield: 2～2.5 g.

(5) **Identification**   Measure the melting point of the cinnamic acid obtained. Record the IR spectrum of the product obtained if IR instrument is available, and compare the recorded spectrum with the standard spectrum of the authentic sample.

Notes

[1] All the glassware used before hydrolysis in this experiment must be thoroughly dried and the reagents must be absolutely anhydrous because fused potassium or sodium carboxylate salts are used as catalyst to induce the reaction.

[2] Fused potassium acetate should be freshly prepared. It can be replaced by anhydrous sodium acetate or anhydrous potassium carbonate.

[3] If benzaldehyde is stored for a long time, it may contain a small amount of benzoic acid, which is formed by automatic oxidation of benzaldehyde. Therefore, benzaldehyde should be redistilled prior to use and the fraction of 170～177 ℃ should be collected and used immediately. The existence of benzoic acid would influence the reaction and it is difficult to remove benzoic acid from the product.

[4] Acetic anhydride may be converted to acetic acid by hydrolysis when it is exposed to moisture for a long time, so it should be redistilled before use as well.

[5] Aqueous sodium carbonate solution cannot be replaced by sodium hydroxide solution in the reaction.

[6] If the activated carbon is added to the hot solution, an abrupt and vigorous boiling may occur and the mixture may rush out of the flask.

[7] The cinnamic acid can be recrystallized from other organic solvents. Consider the solubility of cinnamic acid given in the following table.

Basic Experiments

temperature/ ℃	solubility of cinnamic acid		
	10^{-2} g/g of water	10^{-2} g/g of anhydrous ethanol	10^{-2} g/g of furaldehyde
0			0.6
25	0.06	22.03	4.1
40			10.9

Procedure for Micro-scale Preparation

(1) **Setting Up**   To a dry 5 mL pear-shaped flask add 0.15 g of freshly fused and finely grinded anhydrous potassium acetate, 0.15 mL of freshly distilled benzaldehyde and 0.3 mL of freshly distilled acetic anhydride. Swirl the flask to mix well the reactants. Equip the flask with an air-cooled condenser and a 250 ℃ thermometer by using a Claisen adaptor (Figure 3.13−1). Immerse the mercury head of the thermometer in the solution but do not allow it to touch the bottom of the flask. Fit a drying tube containing anhydrous calcium chloride on the top of the condenser as shown in Figure 1.4−7b.

(2) **Reaction**   Heat the mixture under reflux with a sand bath for 20~30 min. The temperature of the reaction mixture should be kept within the range of 150~170 ℃. Decant the hot reaction mixture into 1.5 mL of water in a 10 mL round-bottom flask. Rinse the reaction flask twice with hot water (0.5 mL×2) and pour the washes into the flask containing the hydrolyzed mixture.

(3) **Work-Up**   Slowly add saturated aqueous sodium carbonate solution to the flask with shaking until the mixture becomes weakly basic. Add 2 mL of water to the stillpot and assemble an apparatus for micro-scale steam distillation as shown in Figure 2.7−3a, and then distill the unreacted benzaldehyde from the flask with a sand bath. Stop heating when the temperature of the thermometer reaches 100 ℃. Allow the solution to cool for a while and add a small amount of activated carbon to the flask. After heat the solution under reflux for several minutes, filter the hot mixture with a Hirsh funnel and a small Büchner flask under a reduced pressure. Add concentrated hydrochloric acid to the filtrate until it is apparently acidic. Cool the solution in a cold water bath to allow the cinnamic acid to crystallize. Collect the product by vacuum filtration and wash it with a small amount of cold water, and then dry the product at the temperature below 100 ℃. Finally, weigh the product and calculate the percentage yield. Yield: ca. 90 mg.

Finishing Touches

Pour the distillate into a container for waste organic liquids. Neutralize the aqueous solution and flush it down the drain with large amounts of water. Place the used activated carbon in a container for nonhazardous solid.

Perkin Condensation: Preparation of Cinnamic Acid (肉桂酸)

Physical Property of Cinnamic Acid

Pure cinnamic acid is a colorless crystal. mp 135~136 ℃.

^{1}H—NMR Spectrum of Cinnamic Acid in CDCl$_3$

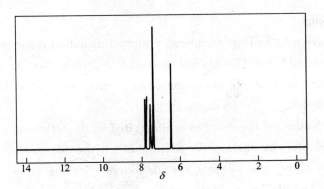

IR Spectrum of Cinnamic Acid in KBr Disc

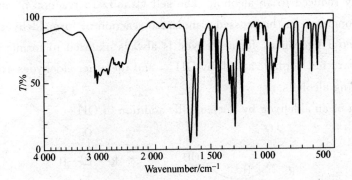

Questions

(1) What kind of aldehyde can be used as starting compound for the Perkin condensation?

(2) Why cannot the aqueous sodium carbonate solution be replaced by a sodium hydroxide solution to neutralize the aqueous solution?

(3) What component is removed from the crude product by steam distillation? Can the crude product be purified by other methods instead of steam distillation?

(4) Specify all the important absorptions associated with the functional groups in the functional group region of the IR spectrum of cinnamic acid.

(5) Assign all signals in the ^{1}H—NMR spectrum of cinnamic acid.

3.14　Cannizzaro Reaction：Preparation of Benzyl Alcohol (苯甲醇) and Benzoic Acid (苯甲酸)

Fundamental Knowledge

Aldehydes that have no α hydrogen undergo a mutual oxidation-reduction in the presence of an excess of concentrated base. This kind of reaction is called the Cannizzaro reaction. This reaction has few practical applications and is limited to aromatic aldehydes, formaldehyde and trisubstituted acetaldehydes.

The accepted mechanism of the reaction is illustrated in the following equations. The Cannizzaro reaction takes place by nucleophilic addition of a hydroxide anion to an aldehyde to give a tetrahedral intermediate, which expels hydride ion as a leaving group. A second aldehyde molecule accepts the hydride ion in another nucleophilic addition step, resulting in a simultaneous oxidation and reduction. One molecule of aldehyde undergoes a substitution of H^- by OH^- and is thereby oxidized to an acid, while a second molecule of aldehyde undergoes an addition of H^- and is thereby reduced to an alcohol. The self Cannizzaro reaction of an aldehyde is also called disproportionation. In the crossed Cannizzaro reaction of formaldehyde with other aldehydes that have no α hydrogen, formaldehyde is always oxidized to formic acid because it is more reactive toward nucleophilic attach by OH^-, and the other aldehydes are usually oxidized to the corresponding alcohols.

Step 1：Oxidation of an aldehyde by nucleophilic addition of OH^-

Step 2：Reduction of an aldehyde by nucleophilic addition of H^-

Step 3：Proton transfer to form a carboxylate salt

Purposes and Requirements

(1) Learn more theoretical and practical knowledge about the Cannizzaro reaction from this experiment.

(2) Master the general method for isolation of solid carboxylic acids.

(3) Master the manipulation for distilling organic liquids of high boiling points.

Principle

In the present experiment, benzaldehyde is used as the starting compound for the Cannizzaro reaction. It is converted to a 1 : 1 mixture of benzyl alcohol and sodium benzoate when treated with an excess of sodium hydroxide in an aqueous solution. Sodium benzoate yields benzoic acid upon acidification of the reaction mixture.

$$2C_6H_5CHO + NaOH \longrightarrow C_6H_5COONa + C_6H_5CH_2OH$$
$$C_6H_5COONa + HCl \longrightarrow C_6H_5COOH + NaCl$$

Apparatus

A 100 mL Erlenmeyer flask, separatory funnel, 50 mL round-bottom flask, air-cooled condenser, 250 ℃ thermometer, apparatus for simple distillation, Büchner funnel, filter flask and watchglass.

Reagents

Benzaldehyde (苯甲醛)	12.6 mL (13.2 g, 0.125 mol)
Sodium hydroxide (氢氧化钠)	11.0 g (0.275 mol)
Methyl t-butyl ether (甲基叔丁基醚)	
10% Aqueous sodium carbonate solution (碳酸钠水溶液)	
Concentrated hydrochloric acid (浓盐酸)	
Saturated sodium bisulfite solution (饱和亚硫酸氢钠溶液)	
Anhydrous magnesium sulfate (无水硫酸镁)	

Time   7 h

Safety Alert

(1) The concentrated solution of sodium hydroxide is highly caustic. Do not allow it to come in contact with your skin. Should it do so, flush the affected area immediately with excess water and then thoroughly rinse it with 1% acetic acid. Wear latex gloves when handling solution of concentrated sodium hydroxide.

(2) Do not distill flammable organic solvents directly on the asbestos pad.

Procedure

(1) **Setting Up and Reaction**　Place 11. 0 g (0. 275 mol) of sodium hydroxide and 11 mL of water[1] in a 100 mL Erlenmeyer flask. Swirl the mixture until all sodium hydroxide pellets are dissolved in water. Allow the solution to cool to room temperature, and add 12. 6 mL (13. 2 g, 0. 125 mol) of freshly distilled benzaldehyde in four portions to the flask with shaking. After addition of each portion (ca. 3 mL), cork the flask tightly and shake it vigorously. If the temperature of the solution is too high, cool the Erlenmeyer flask in a cold water bath. The mixture becomes a wax-like solution in the end of the reaction. Cork the flask tightly and let it stand overnight[2].

(2) **Work-Up and Isolation of Benzyl Alcohol**　Decant 40～50 mL of water into the reaction mixture, and heat gently the aqueous solution until all solid is dissolved in water. After the solution is cooled to room temperature, decant it into a separatory funnel. Extract the solution three times with methyl t-butyl ether (10 mL×3). Save the aqueous layer for the next work-up step! Combine the extracts of methyl t-butyl ether and wash sequentially the ethereal layer with 5 mL of saturated sodium bisulfite solution, 10 mL of 10% sodium carbonate solution, and then 10 mL of cold water. Save the ethereal layer in an Erlenmeyer flask and dry it over anhydrous magnesium sulfate or anhydrous potassium carbonate. Decant the dried ethereal solution into a 50 mL stillpot. After distilling the methyl t-butyl ether out of the crude product by heating the solution with a hot water bath, change the water-cooled condenser to an air-cooled condenser. Distil the benzyl alcohol on an asbestos pad and collect the fraction of 200～208 ℃. Weigh the product and calculate the percentage yield. Yield: 4～4.5 g.

(3) **Work-Up and Isolation of Benzoic Acid**　Slowly pour the aqueous solution saved from the last work-up step, with continuous stirring, into a mixture of 40 mL of concentrated hydrochloric acid, 40 mL of water and about 25 g of crushed ice. Cool the resulting mixture with an ice bath and allow the benzoic acid to deposit completely. Collect the crystalline product by vacuum filtration, wash the solid with a small amount of cold water, drain thoroughly the water off, and air-dry the crude product. The crude benzoic acid can be recrystallized from water. Weigh the product and calculate the percentage yield. Yield: 6～7 g.

(4) **Identification**　Measure the melting point of the benzoic acid obtained. If IR instrument is available, record the IR spectra of the products obtained and compare the recorded spectra with the standard spectra of benzyl alcohol and benzoic acid.

Notes

[1] Potassium hydroxide (11. 5 g) solution in 10 mL water can be used as strong base in the reaction instead of sodium hydroxide.

[2] The reaction can also be made by using less sodium hydroxide and heating under reflux: Dissolve 7. 5 g of sodium hydroxide in 30 mL of water in a 100 mL round-bottom flask. After allow the solution to cool to room temperature, add 10 mL of freshly distilled benzalde-

hyde and 2 boiling chips to the flask. Equip the flask with a water-cooled condenser, then heat the mixture under reflux on an asbestos pad for 1 h and shake the flask occasionally. The reaction terminates when the oil layer of benzaldehyde disappears and the solution turns clear. After the reaction mixture is cooled down, extract the solution three times with benzene (13 mL×3). Combine the extracts and distil the benzene with a boiling water bath. The following operations are the same as those described above for isolation of benzyl alcohol and benzoic acid.

Finishing Touches

Pour the methyl *t*-butyl ether distillate into a designated container for recovered methyl *t*-butyl ether. Pour the residue remaining in the stillpot into a container for waste organic liquids. Neutralize the aqueous solution and flush it down a drain with large amounts of water. Evaporate the solvents from the magnesium sulfate used as drying agent in a hood, and place it in a container for nonhazardous solid.

Physical Property of Benzyl Alcohol and Benzoic Acid

Pure benzyl alcohol is a clear and colorless liquid. bp 205 ℃, n_D^{20} 1.5403, d_4^{20} 1.0450. Benzoic acid is a colorless needle crystal. mp 121~123 ℃.

IR Spectrum of Benzyl Alcohol Using Liquid Film

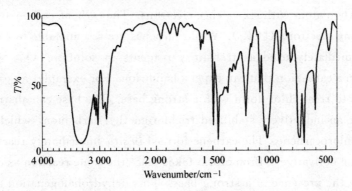

IR Spectrum of Benzoic Acid Using KBr Disc

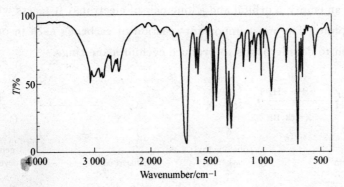

Questions

(1) What kind of aldehyde can undergo Cannizzaro reaction?

(2) Why should the benzaldehyde be freshly distilled prior to use? What impurity may exist in benzaldehyde if it is stored for a long time? How does this impurity influence the reaction if it is not removed from the benzaldehyde?

(3) Why should the methyl *t*-butyl ether solution be washed with a saturated sodium bisulfite solution after extraction? Should the water layer be washed with a saturated sodium bisulfite solution as well? Why?

(4) In the functional group region of the IR spectra of benzyl alcohol and benzoic acid, specify all the important absorptions associated with the hydroxyl group of benzyl alcohol and the carboxyl group of benzoic acid.

3.15 Carbene Additions with Phase-Transfer Catalysis: Preparation of 7,7-Dichlorobicyclo[4.1.0]heptane (7,7-二氯双环[4.1.0]庚烷)

Fundamental knowledge

(1) **Carbene generation and reactions** Carbenes are uncharged reactive intermediates containing a divalent carbon atom with six valence electrons. The carbene carbon atom has two bonds and two nonbonding electrons ($:CR_2$). While carbenes are too unstable to isolate, they can be generated and immediately used as transitory reagents in solution. One way of generating carbenes is to form a carbanion that can expel a halide ion. For example, an easy way to prepare dichlorocarbene is to treat chloroform with a strong base. The base can abstract a proton from chloroform to give an inductively stabilized trichloromethyl carbanion, which ejects a chloride ion to produce dichlorocarbene. The carbene formed *in situ* immediately reacts with alkenes to afford cyclopropane derivatives. Bromoform takes place the same reaction as chloroform to give dibromocarbene in the presence of a strong base. This dehydrohalogenation is called an alpha-elimination because the hydrogen and the halogen are lost from the same carbon atom. Because a carbene has both an empty *p* orbital and a lone pair of electrons, it reacts with either a nucleophile or an electrophile. The most important reaction of carbenes used in organic synthesis is the carbene addition to double bonds to produce cyclopropane rings.

haloform   trihalomethyl carbanion   dihalocarbene   geminal dihalocyclopropane

(2) **Phase-transfer catalysis**   In some bimolecular reactions, organic reactants, such as alkenes and haloalkanes, dissolve only in organic solvents, while inorganic reagents dissolve in water. There is little chance for the reactants segregated in two immiscible solutions to meet each other, still less to react. As an example, imagine an experiment in which cyclohexene is dissolved in chloroform and treated with aqueous NaOH. Since the organic layer and the water layer are immiscible, the base in the aqueous phase does not come into contact with chloroform in the organic phase, and there is no reaction. A convenient solution to these experimental difficulties entails the addition of a catalytic amount of a quaternary ammonium salt to the heterogeneous mixture of the aqueous base and the alkene. The tetraalkyl ammonium salt partitions between the aqueous and organic phases because of the amphoteric nature of the catalyst: It is lipophilic due to the alkyl groups and hydrophilic due to the ionic ammonium function, respectively. Therefore, the tetraalkyl ammonium salt can exist in both organic and aqueous phases and easily transfer from one phase to the other. When the catalyst is in the basic aqueous phase, it can exchange its chloride ion for a hydroxide ion. On transfer back to the organic phase the hydroxide is carried along as a tight ion pair to preserve charge neutrality. In the organic phase the hydroxide ion reacts with the chloroform to produce dichlorocarbene, which preferentially reacts with the high local concentration of alkene present. The chloride ion and water formed in the organic phase are transferred to the aqueous phase along with the catalyst, where the chloride ion is exchanged for another hydroxide ion. The phase-transfer catalysis of carbene addition between dichlorocarbene and alkene is shown in the following figure (Figure 3.15−1). Commonly used phase-transfer catalysts include benzyltriethylammonium chloride, tetrabutylammonium bisulfate and methyltrioctylammonium chloride (Aliquat 336®). Many other kinds of organic reactions, including oxidations, reductions, carbonyl-group alkylations and S_N2 reactions, are subject to phase-transfer catalysis, often with considerable improvements in reaction rates and yields.

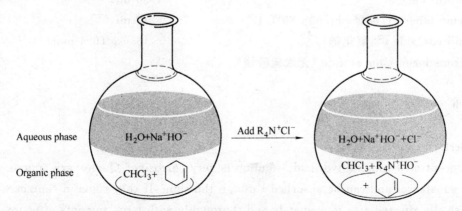

Figure 3.15−1   A scheme for phase-transfer catalysis of carbene addition between
dichlorocarbene and alkene

Purposes and Requirements

(1) Review and summarize the contents in the textbook on carbene generation and reactions.

(2) Understand the principle of phase-transfer catalysis and its application in organic synthesis.

(3) Demonstrate formation of the dichlorocarbene from the reaction of chloroform and NaOH.

(4) Review the techniques of extraction and vacuum distillation.

Principle

7,7-Dichlorobicyclo[4.1.0]heptane is prepared by addition of dichlorocarbene to the double bond of cyclohexene. The dichlorocarbene is freshly generated from the reaction of chloroform and NaOH using tetraethylammonium bromide (TEAB) as phase-transfer catalyst, and reacts *in situ* with cyclohexene.

cyclohexene   chloroform   7,7-dichlorobicyclo[4.1.0]heptane

Apparatus

A 25 and 100 mL round-bottom flask, 100 mL three-neck round-bottom flask, separatory funnel, 125 mL Erlenmeyer flask, apparatus equipped with a mechanical stirrer, a thermometer and a reflux condenser.

Reagents

Cyclohexene (环己烯)	10.1 mL (8.2 g, 0.1 mol)
Tetraethylammonium bromide (TEAB, 四乙基溴化铵)	0.4 g
Chloroform (氯仿)	30 mL
Petroleum ether (石油醚, bp 60~80 ℃)	30 mL
Sodium hydroxide (氢氧化钠)	16.0 g (0.4 mol)
Anhydrous magnesium sulfate (无水硫酸镁)	

Time 8 h

Safety Alert

(1) Concentrated sodium hydroxide solution is very corrosive. Quaternary ammonium salts are toxic substances and can be absorbed through the skin. If they come in contact with your skin, wash the affected area immediately and thoroughly with large amounts of water.

(2) Chloroform is a cancer suspect agent and should be used in a well-ventilated area.

(3) The product and all organic reagents used in the reaction are highly flammable, be cer-

tain that all joints in the apparatus are tightly mated and do not heat the flask containing flammable organic liquids directly on a flame. If possible, flameless heating is preferred.

Procedure

(1) **Preparation**   Place 16.0 g (0.4 mol) of sodium hydroxide pellets in a 125 mL Erlenmeyer flask and add 16.0 mL of cold water. Swirl the flask to dissolve the base. Considerable heat develops as the sodium hydroxide dissolves and the solution should be cooled to room temperature.

(2) **Setting-Up**   Equip a 100 mL three-neck round-bottom flask with a mechanical stirrer, a reflux condenser, and a thermometer. Add 0.4 g of tetraethylammonium bromide[1], 10.1 mL (8.2 g, 0.1 mol) of cyclohexene and 24.0 mL (36.0 g, 0.3 mol) of chloroform to the flask[2].

(3) **Reaction**   Add the prepared aqueous base from the top of the condenser in 3~4 portions over a period of 5 min with rapid stirring[3]. The reaction is apparently exothermic upon addition of the base. The reaction mixture becomes an emulsion in 10 min. The temperature of the solution rises gradually to 50~55 ℃[4]. Keep the reaction at this temperature for 1 h[5]. The solution turns yellow-brown and some solids appear in the flask. Continue stirring the reaction mixture for another 1 h at room temperature.

(4) **Work-Up**   Add 40 mL of ice-water to the reaction flask. Decant the mixture to a separatory funnel, rinse the flask with 6 mL of chloroform and add the rinse to the funnel. Shake the funnel thoroughly and allow the layers to separate. Drain the lower organic layer from the two-way cock of the funnel into a 125 mL Erlenmeyer flask. Sequentially extract the aqueous layer with two 15 mL portions of petroleum ether. Combine the petroleum ether extract with the chloroform solution in the Erlenmeyer flask. Wash the organic layer with 25 mL of HCl (2 mol·L^{-1}), and then wash it twice with water (25 mL×2)[6]. Dry the organic layer over anhydrous magnesium sulfate with occasional swirling for at lease 0.5 h.

(5) **Isolation**   Decant the dried organic layer, without the drying agent, into a 100 mL round-bottom flask, and add 2 boiling chips. Slowly distill the petroleum ether and the chloroform with a water bath, and then vacuum-distill the product and collect the fraction of 79~80 ℃ under the pressure of 2 kPa (15 mmHg). Weigh the product and calculate the percentage yield. Yield: 9~10 g.

(6) **Identification**   Identify the product spectroscopically if IR and NMR instruments are available, and compare the recorded spectra with the standard spectra of the authentic sample.

Notes

[1] Other phase-transfer catalysts such as tetraethylammonium chloride, methyltrioctylammonium chloride and benzyltriethylammonium chloride can also be used for the reaction.

[2] Alcohol-free chloroform should be used. In general, a small amount of alcohol is added to the commercial chloroform to prevent it from decomposition to very toxic phosgene. The

Basic Experiments

alcohol must be removed from the chloroform by the following method: Wash the chloro-form 2～3 times with an equal volume of water, and then dry the chloroform with anhy-drous calcium chloride for several hours before distillation, or dry the chloroform with 4 Å molecular sieves overnight.

[3] One factor that determines the overall rate of a reaction involving phase-transfer catalysis is the efficiency of the partitioning of the reagents and reactants between the two phases. This is a function of the total surface area at the interface of the phases. To increase the re-action rate, the mixture must be vigorously stirred to promote the formation of tiny drop-lets of the immiscible layers.

[4] If the temperature of the reaction mixture cannot reach 50～55 ℃ spontaneously, heat gen-tly the mixture with a water bath and keep the temperature of the mixture at 55～60 ℃ for 1 h.

[5] Extending the reaction period can enhance the yield of the product.

[6] Wash the separatory funnel immediately after use, to prevent the cock of the funnel from corrosion by the basic residue.

Finishing Touches

Carefully combine the washes and the residue remaining in the stillpot, neutralize the aque-ous solution before flushing it down the drain with large amounts of water. Evaporate the sol-vents from the sodium sulfate used as drying agent in a hood, and place it in a container for nonhazardous solid. Pour the organic waste, a mixture of the used chloroform and petroleum ether, in a container for halogenated organic solvents.

Physical Property of 7,7-Dichlorobicyclo[4.1.0]heptane

7,7-Dichlorobicyclo[4.1.0]heptane is a clear and colorless liquid. bp $197 \sim 198$ ℃, n_D^{20} 1.502 2, d_4^{20} 1.213 0.

^{13}C—NMR Spectrum of 7,7-Dichlorobicyclo[4.1.0]heptane

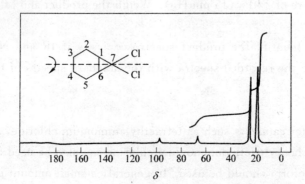

Questions

(1) Describe how the benzyltriethylammonium chloride catalyzes the dichlorocarbene formation and cyclopropanation reaction?

(2) What product would be formed by reaction of dichlorocarbene with phenanthrene?

(3) Why should the alcohol-free chloroform be used in the reaction?

(4) Try to assign all signals in the ^{13}C—NMR spectrum of 7,7-Dichlorobicyclo[4.1.0]heptane to the carbon nuclei responsible for them.

3.16   Nitration Reaction: Preparation of *p*-Nitroaniline (对硝基苯胺)

Fundamental Knowledge

In general, nitro-substituted aromatic compounds are prepared by nitration of the corresponding aromatic compounds. A mixture of nitric acid and sulfuric acid, called mixed acid, is usually used as nitrating agent.

$$ArH + HNO_3 \xrightarrow{H_2SO_4} ArNO_2 + H_2O$$

On the basis of the structures of reactants to be nitrated, different concentrations of the mixed acid and reaction temperature should be used in the nitration. Toluene reacts faster than benzene for nitration under the same conditions, while nitration of nitrobenzene is more difficult than benzene. Nitration is an irreversible reaction. The concentrated sulfuric acid acts as a catalyst, allowing nitration to take place more rapidly and at lower temperature. Addition of sulfuric acid benefits the formation of the nitronium ion ($^+NO_2$), which is a powerful electrophile. Increase of the concentration of the $^+NO_2$ ion can raise the rate of nitration reaction.

The nitric acid is a strong oxidizer. Aromatic amines are easily oxidized, and therefore they cannot be directly nitrated by the mixed acid. The amino group should be protected by formation of an acetylamino group before nitration of an aromatic amine.

Nitration is a strong exothermic reaction. It is important to strictly control the reaction temperature and the addition rate of the reactants when we are making a nitration reaction, and the mixture must be well stirred or fully swirled.

Purposes and Requirements

(1) Learn the nitration reaction and understand its application.

(2) Learn the protective group for amines used in organic synthesis.

(3) Master the technique for thin-layer chromatography (TLC) analysis.

(4) Review the manipulation of crystallization.

Principle

In this experiment, *p*-nitroaniline is prepared from aniline. We should first protect the amino group of aniline by introducing an acetyl group to the N atom (Here you can directly use acetanilide obtained from experiment 3.10), and then make nitration reaction. Nitration of acetanilide with the mixed acid at low temperature gives *p*-nitroacetanilide as major product while with the increase of temperature, the amount of *o*-nitroacetanilide will go up.

$$\text{\char"2B21—NHCOCH}_3 + HONO_2 \xrightarrow{H_2SO_4} O_2N\text{—\char"2B21—NHCOCH}_3 + H_2O$$

$$O_2N\text{—\char"2B21—NHCOCH}_3 + H_2O \xrightarrow{H_2SO_4} O_2N\text{—\char"2B21—NH}_2 + CH_3COOH$$

The possible side-reactions:

$$\text{\char"2B21—NHCOCH}_3 + H_2O \xrightarrow{H_2SO_4} \text{\char"2B21—NH}_2 + CH_3COOH$$

$$\text{\char"2B21—NHCOCH}_3 + HONO_2 \xrightarrow{H_2SO_4} \text{\char"2B21(NO}_2)\text{—NHCOCH}_3 + H_2O$$

Apparatus

A 100 mL Erlenmeyer flask, a 10 mL graduated cylinder, a 250 mL beaker, a 50 mL round flask, a reflux condenser, a set of Büchner flask and funnel.

Reagents

Acetanilide (乙酰苯胺)	5.0 g (0.037 mol)
Glacial acetic acid (冰醋酸)	5.0 mL
Concentrated sulfuric acid (浓硫酸)	23 mL
Concentrated nitric acid (浓硝酸, $d=1.40$)	2.2 mL
20% Aqueous NaOH solution (氢氧化钠水溶液)	
Ethanol (95%, 乙醇)	

Time 6~8 h

Safety Alert

Concentrated sulfuric acid and nitric acid are very corrosive liquids. Wear latex gloves when handling these acids. Do not allow the acids to come in contact with your skin, and wash it off immediately with large amounts of water if the acid accidentally comes in contact with your skin, and then with dilute sodium bicarbonate solution.

Nitration Reaction: Preparation of *p*-Nitroaniline (对硝基苯胺)

Procedure

(1) **Preparation of *p*-Nitroacetanilide**   To a 100 mL Erlenmeyer flask, add 5 g (0.037 mol) of acetanilide and 5 mL glacial acetic acid[1]. Cool the flask with a cold-water bath and add 10 mL of concentrated sulfuric acid slowly to it with continuous swirling. After acetanilide is dissolved, cool the solution with a brine-ice bath to 0~2 ℃. Drop cold mixed acid of concentrated nitric acid (2.2 mL) and sulfuric acid (1.4 mL) with a Pasteur pipet slowly to the Erlenmeyer flask with continuous swirling and keep the reaction temperature below 5 ℃[2]. Remove the brine-ice bath and place the flask at room temperature for 30 min with occasional shaking. When the resulting solution is poured slowly to the mixture of water (20 mL) and crushed ice (20 g), *p*-nitroacetanilide will precipitate instantly from the solution. Let this suspension stand for 10 min, and then make a vacuum filtration. Transfer all solid to a Büchner funnel and rinse the flask several times with cold water until there is no solid left in it. Press the acidic solution out of the crude product as much as possible and wash the solids 3 times with ice-water (10 mL ×3). Weigh 0.2 g of the crude product (sample A) and air-dry it. Recrystallize the left product[3] with 95% ethanol[4]. Filter the crystallized *p*-nitroacetanilide in vacuum, wash it with a small amount of cold ethanol, and press the crystals as dry as possible. Finally, air-dry the product (sample B). Yield: ca. 4 g. Evaporate the mother alcoholic solution to 2/3 of its original volume with a hot-water bath. Filter the precipitate if there is and keep the mother solution as sample C.

(2) **Thin-Layer Chromatography Analysis of Sample A, B, and C**   (see 2.9.2) The experimental conditions and results are as follows:

Developing solvents: toluene : ethyl acetate = 4 : 1 (v/v)

Absorbent: TLC plates pre-coated with silica gel G (produced in Qingdao)

Developing distance: 10 cm

Developing time: 20 min

Visualization technique: Air-dry the TLC plates and then expose it to an iodine vapor by placing it in a closed chamber containing several crystals of iodine. Circle the spot with a pencil immediately after the plate is removed from the chamber.

	R_f	
	p-nitroacetanilide	*o*-nitroacetanilide
sample A	0.23	0.64
sample B	0.23	—
sample C	0.23 (trace)	0.64

(3) **Preparation of *p*-Nitroaniline**   To a 50 mL round-bottom flask, add 4 g of *p*-nitroacetanilide and 20 mL of 70% sulfuric acid[5]. Place 2~3 pieces of boiling chips to the flask and equip it with a reflux condenser. Heat the solution to reflux on an asbestos pad for 10~20 min[6].

Pour the clear hot solution to 100 mL cold water, and then precipitate *p*-nitroaniline by adding an excess of 20% aqueous NaOH solution. Make a vacuum filtration after the mixture cools down and wash the solid with cold water to remove the base. The product is further purified by recrystallization from water[7]. Yield: ca. 2.5 g.

(4) **Identification** Measure the melting point of the *p*-nitroaniline obtained. If an IR instrument is available, record the IR spectrum of the product and compare the spectrum with that of the authentic sample.

Notes

[1] Acetanilide dissolves slowly in concentrated sulfuric acid at low temperature. Addition of glacial acetic acid can make it quickly dissolved in the acidic solution.

[2] The nitration of acetanilide with the mixed acid at 5 ℃ gives *p*-nitroacetanilide as major product, while at 40 ℃, about 25% of *o*-nitroacetanilide will be formed.

[3] The *o*-nitroacetanilide can also be removed from the crude product by the following method: Add the crude product to water (20 mL) in an Erlenmeyer flask. Sodium carbonate powder is added in portions to the flask with continuous stirring until the phenolphthalein test paper turns red with the solution. *p*-Nitroacetanilide will not be hydrolyzed when the mixture is heated to boil, while *o*-nitroacetanilide will be hydrolyzed to *o*-nitroaniline. Make a quick vacuum filtration when the mixture is cooled to 50 ℃. Press the solid to squeeze out the *o*-nitroaniline. Wash the product with water and press it as dry as possible, and finally air-dry it.

[4] *o*-Nitroacetanilide and *p*-nitroacetanilide have different solubilities in ethanol. Recrystallization of the crude product in ethanol can remove *o*-nitroacetanilide, which has a better solubility in ethanol.

[5] Preparation of 70% sulfuric acid: Carefully and slowly add 4 portion (volume) of concentrated sulfuric acid to 3 portion (volume) of cold water with continuous stirring.

[6] Add 1 mL of the reaction solution to 2~3 mL water. The hydrolysis has finished if the solution keeps clear.

[7] The solubility of *p*-nitroaniline in 100 mL water: 18.5 ℃, 0.08 g; 100 ℃, 2.2 g.

Finishing Touches

Pour all organic residues into a container for waste organic liquids. Neutralize the aqueous solution and flush it down the drain with excess water.

Physical Property of *p*-Nitroaniline

Pure *p*-nitroaniline is yellow needle crystals. mp 147.5 ℃.

¹H—NMR Spectrum of *p*-Nitroaniline in CDCl₃/DMSO-*d₆*

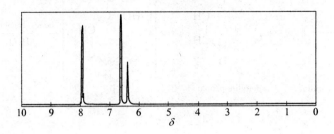

Questions

(1) Can *p*-nitroaniline be prepared by direct nitration of aniline? What are the possible side-reactions?

(2) How to remove *o*-nitroacetanilide from the *p*-nitroacetanilide crude product?

(3) *p*-Nitroacetanilide can be hydrolyzed either in acidic or basic medium. Please discuss advantages and disadvantages of each method.

(4) Assign all signals in the ¹H—NMR spectrum of *p*-nitroaniline.

3.17   Skraup Reaction: Preparation of Quinoline (喹啉)

Fundamental Knowledge

Quinoline is often prepared by the Skraup reaction, in which a mixture of aniline, anhydrous glycerol, concentrated sulfuric acid and nitrobenzene is heated in one flask. In the reaction, concentrated sulfuric acid acts as a dehydrating agent to make glycerol dehydrated to propenal. The nucleophilic addition of aniline to propenal gives *β*-anilinopropanal as an intermediate, which is dehydrated to form 1,2-dihydroquinoline. Nitrobenzene is used here as a weak oxidant to oxidize 1,2-dihydroquinoline to quinoline, and the nitrobenzene itself is reduced to aniline, which can take part in the reaction. Quinoline derivatives can also be prepared by the Skraup reaction. The corresponding nitroarenes should be adopted to avoid the complexity of the products if other arylamines are used as reactants in the reaction.

Step 1: Dehydration of glycerol

$$CH_2\text{—}CH\text{—}CH_2 \xrightarrow{\text{conc. } H_2SO_4} CH_2\text{=}CH\text{—}\overset{\displaystyle O}{\overset{\|}{C}}H + 2H_2O$$
$$\underset{\text{OH \quad OH \quad OH}}{}$$

glycerol   propenal

Step 2: Nucleophilic addition followed by cyclization

propenal   aniline   β-anilinopropanal   1,2-dihydroquinoline

Step 3: Oxidation

1,2-dihydroquinoline   nitrobenzene   quinoline   aniline

Purposes and Requirements

(1) Learn the Skraup reaction and understand its application.

(2) Master the technique for distilling organic compounds of high boiling points.

(3) Review the manipulation of steam distillation.

Principle

Quinoline is prepared by the Skraup reaction of aniline, nitrobenzene and anhydrous glycerol in the presence of concentrated sulfuric acid. In the reaction, the anhydrous glycerol is used in excess to improve the conversion of the aniline.

Apparatus

Two 250 mL round-bottom flasks, a reflux condenser, air-cooled condenser, separatory funnel, apparatus for steam distillation and apparatus for simple distillation.

Reagents

Aniline （苯胺）	6.9 mL (7.0 g, 0.075 mol)
Nitrobenzene （硝基苯）	4.4 mL (5.3 g, 0.043 mol)
Anhydrous glycerol （无水甘油）	22 mL (28 g, 0.304 mol)
Crystalline ferrous sulfate （结晶硫酸亚铁）	1.5 g
Benzene （苯）	40 mL

Skraup Reaction: Preparation of Quinoline (喹啉)

Concentrated sulfuric acid (浓硫酸)	12 mL
40% Aqueous sodium hydroxide solution (氢氧化钠溶液)	70 mL
10% Aqueous sodium nitrite (亚硝酸钠溶液)	20 mL
KI-starch test paper (KI-淀粉试纸)	

Time   12 h

Safety Alert

(1) Aniline and nitrobenzene are irritants. Avoid inhaling the vapors from these compounds.

(2) Concentrated sulfuric acid is a very corrosive liquid. Wear latex gloves when handling it. Do not allow it to come in contact with your skin, and wash it off immediately with large amounts of water if it accidentally comes in contact with your skin, and then with dilute sodium bicarbonate solution.

Procedure

(1) **Setting Up**   To a dry 250 mL round-bottom flask[1], add 1.5 g of finely grinded ferrous sulfate[2], 22 mL (28 g, 0.304 mol) of anhydrous glycerol[3], 6.9 mL (7.0 g, 0.075 mol) of aniline, 4.4 mL (5.3 g, 0.043 mol) of nitrobenzene and 2 boiling chips. Swirl the flask to mix the reactants well. Slowly add 12 mL of concentrated sulfuric acid dropwise with continuous swirling to facilitate the thorough dissolution of the aniline sulfate formed in the flask. Equip the flask with a reflux condenser.

(2) **Reaction**   Heat the mixture carefully on an asbestos pad. When there are small bubbles released and the solution begins to reflux gently, remove the flame immediately[4]. The heat released from the reaction can keep the reaction mixture refluxing for about 15 min. When the reaction undergoes smoothly, heat carefully the mixture again and keep it refluxing gently for 3 h. Stop heating and allow the mixture to cool to about 100 ℃.

(3) **Work-Up**   Pour 40 mL of water into the flask containing the reaction mixture. Assembly a steam distillation apparatus and distill the unreacted nitrobenzene until the distillate becomes clear and colorless. After the mixture remaining in the flask is cooled down, carefully add 35 mL of 40% sodium hydroxide to the flask to neutralize the sulfuric acid in the reaction mixture until the mixture turns basic. Rearrange a steam distillation apparatus to distill the quinoline and the unreacted aniline until the distillate becomes clear (using a 250 mL round-bottom flask as a receiver). Remove the unreacted aniline from the distillate by converting it to sodium phenolate via diazo-reaction and hydrolysis. The method is as follows: Acidify the distillate with concentrated sulfuric acid. Cool the mixture to the temperature below 5 ℃ with a brine-ice bath, and carefully drop 10% aqueous sodium nitrite solution (ca. 20 mL) until the reaction mixture gives a positive KI-starch test (deep blue)[5]. Heat the mixture with a water bath and shake the flask occasionally. When the release of nitrogen gas ceases, all the diazo salt has been

Basic Experiments

converted to phenol. Stop heating and allow the solution to cool to room temperature. Carefully add 40% sodium hydroxide solution (ca. 35 mL) until the mixture turns basic. Make a steam distillation again to collect an azeotrope of quinoline and water. The sodium phenolate is left in the flask.

(4) **Isolation**   Decant the distillate into a separatory funnel and allow the liquid to stand for a while. Separate the organic layer, and extract the aqueous layer twice with benzene (20 mL × 2). Combine the organic layer with benzene extracts. Pour the combined liquid into a stillpot and heat it with a water bath. After distilling benzene and a small amount of water from the crude product[6], change the water-cooled condenser to an air-cooled condenser. Collect the fraction of 233~239 ℃ (a light yellow oily liquid). It is better to make a vacuum distillation and collect the fraction of 118~120 ℃ (a colorless oily liquid) under the pressure of 2.66 kPa (20 mmHg). Weigh the product and calculate the percentage yield[7]. Yield: 6~7 g.

(5) **Identification**   If IR instrument is available, record the IR spectrum of the product obtained and compare the recorded spectrum with the standard spectrum of quinoline.

Notes

[1] All the glassware used before work-up in this experiment must be dried and the reagents must be anhydrous. Otherwise, the result of the experiment would be affected.

[2] Addition of ferrous sulfate is to control the reaction and to avoid an over-vigorous reaction. Ferrous sulfate must be added before the addition of concentrated sulfuric acid, otherwise, the reaction would be very fierce.

[3] The glycerol used in this reaction should be free of water. Anhydrous glycerol can be prepared by the following method: Place glycerol in an evaporating dish and heat it to 180 ℃ with a sand bath in a hood.

[4] This is an exothermic reaction. After the beginning of the reaction, the heat released from the reaction can keep the reaction mixture refluxing for about 15 min. The reaction would be too fierce and even the mixture would rush out of the flask if it is continuously heated in the initial stage of the reaction.

[5] After add several drops of 10% sodium nitrite solution to the mixture, wait for about 2 min before testing the solution with KI-starch test paper, because the diazo-reaction undergoes slowly.

[6] A small amount of water existing in the undried organic layer is distilled out with benzene as an azeotrope.

[7] The yield of quinoline is calculated based on the amount of aniline added. The small amount of aniline derived from nitrobenzene is neglected.

Finishing Touches

Pour the benzene distillate into the special container for recovered benzene. Pour all organic residues into a container for waste organic liquids. Neutralize the aqueous solution and flush it down the drain with excess water.

Physical Property of Quinoline

Pure quinoline is colorless oil. bp 238 ℃, n_D^{20} 1.626 8, d_4^{20} 1.095 0.

^{1}H—NMR Spectrum of Quinoline in CDCl$_3$

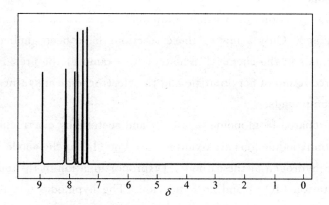

IR Spectrum of Quinoline Using Liquid Film

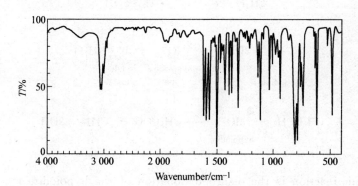

Questions

(1) What are the roles of nitrobenzene, glycerol, ferrous sulfate and concentrated sulfuric acid in the preparation of quinoline by the Skraup reaction?

(2) In the experiment, the steam distillation is made for three times. Explain the purpose of each steam distillation?

(3) Can the aniline and the product quinoline be distilled out in the first time steam distillation?

(4) Why should the mixture be adjusted to basic before the second and the third time steam distillation?

Basic Experiments

(5) In the functional group region of the IR spectrum of quinoline, specify all important absorptions associated with the fused aromatic rings of quinoline.

(6) Assign all signals in the ^{1}H—NMR spectrum of quinoline.

3.18   Electrochemical Synthesis: Preparation of Iodoform (碘仿)

Fundamental Knowledge

The electrochemical reactions of organic compounds such as Kolbe electrolysis were found more than a century ago. Only a few of these reactions have been applied for preparation of some organic compounds in the chemical industry, for example, the preparation of hexanedinitrile by electrolytic reduction of acrylonitrile and the electrochemical synthesis of some fluorine-containing organic compounds.

Iodoform can be prepared from iodide ions (I^-) and acetone by electrochemical synthesis. In the electrolytic reaction, iodide ions are oxidized to iodine (I_2) at the anode, while protons from water are reduced to hydrogen at the cathode. Disproportionation of the iodine in a basic medium gives a hypoiodite ion (IO^-) and an iodide ion. The hypoiodite ion is a strong oxidizing agent, which can oxidize acetone to form an acetate ion and iodoform.

$$2H_2O + 2e^- \xrightarrow{\text{cathode}} H_2 + 2OH^-$$

$$2I^- - 2e^- \xrightarrow{\text{anode}} I_2$$

$$\underset{\text{iodine}}{I_2} + 2OH^- \rightleftharpoons \underset{\substack{\text{hypoiodite} \\ \text{ion}}}{IO^-} + \underset{\substack{\text{iodide} \\ \text{ion}}}{I^-} + H_2O$$

$$\underset{\text{acetone}}{CH_3\overset{\overset{\textstyle O}{\|}}{C}CH_3} + \underset{\substack{\text{hypoiodite} \\ \text{ion}}}{3IO^-} \longrightarrow \underset{\text{acetate ion}}{CH_3COO^-} + \underset{\text{iodoform}}{CHI_3} + 2OH^-$$

The possible side-reaction is the disproportionation of the hypoiodite ion to an iodate ion (IO_3^-) and two iodide ions.

$$\underset{\substack{\text{hypoiodite} \\ \text{ion}}}{3IO^-} \longrightarrow \underset{\substack{\text{iodate} \\ \text{ion}}}{IO_3^-} + \underset{\substack{\text{iodide} \\ \text{ion}}}{2I^-}$$

Purposes and Requirements

(1) Understand the electrochemical synthesis.

(2) Learn the technique of electrolysis in practice.

(3) Review the manipulation of recrystallization.

Electrochemical Synthesis: Preparation of Iodoform (碘仿)

Principle

Iodoform is prepared by the electrochemical reaction of potassium iodide, acetone and water. The overall reaction of this electrolytic synthesis is given in the following equation.

$$3H_2O + 3I^- + CH_3\overset{\overset{\displaystyle O}{\|}}{C}CH_3 \xrightarrow{\text{electrolysis}} CH_3COO^- + CHI_3 + 2OH^- + 3H_2$$

Apparatus

A 150 mL beaker, four graphite electrodes[1], a Büchner funnel, filter flask, watchglass, magnetic stirrer and direct-current power source ($I \geqslant 1$ A, $V = 0 \sim 12$ V)[2].

Reagents

Potassium iodide (碘化钾)	6.0 g (0.036 mol)
Acetone (丙酮)	1.0 mL (0.8 g, 0.014 mol)
Ethanol (乙醇)	10 mL

Time 2 h

Safety Alert

Well fasten the graphite electrodes to avoid short-circuit.

Procedure

(1) **Setting Up**   Use a 150 mL beaker as an electrolytic bath, and four graphite rods as electrodes. Connect two graphite rods in parallel as an anode, and the other two graphite rods, also connected in parallel, as a cathode. Fasten well the graphite rods vertically on the wall of the beaker, or place a plate with four holes on the beaker and insert graphite rods in each hole. When fixing the graphite rods, do not let the graphite rods contact the bottom of the beaker, and leave enough room for the magnetic stirbar. Add 100 mL of distilled water and 6 g (0.036 mol) of potassium iodide to the beaker. After the potassium iodide is dissolved with stirring, decant 1 mL of acetone to the beaker and stir the solution to well mix the reactants.

(2) **Reaction**   Connect the electrodes to the direct-current power source and turn on the power. Adjust the intensity of current to 1 A and keep the current constant during the electrolysis. After 30 min, turn off the power and stop stirring.

(3) **Work-Up and Isolation**   Transfer all solids into a Büchner funnel and make a vacuum filtration. Save the filtrate in a beaker for recovery[3]. Rinse the electrodes and the beaker several times and combine the solid with the crude product, and then wash the crude product with water. Press the crystals as dry as possible on the Büchner funnel and air-dry the crude product[4].

(4) **Recrystallization**   The crude product may be recrystallized from ethanol to get pure crys-

tals. Weigh the product and calculate the percentage yield of the iodoform obtained. Yield: ca. 0. 6 g.

(5) **Identification**   Measure the melting point of the iodoform obtained.

Notes

[1] Use the graphite rods of waste batteries of size D as electrodes. The diameter of these graphite rods is 6 mm. Forty millimeters of the rods should be immersed in the reaction solution.

[2] The current of the power source used should not be smaller than 1 A and the voltage should be adjustable between $0 \sim 12$ V.

[3] The filtrate contains the large parts of the unreacted potassium iodide and the acetone, which can be reused in the identical experiment.

[4] The crude product is grey green when graphite rods are used as electrodes. If a platinum wire or a graphite rod coated with lead dioxide is used as an anodic electrode, the iodoform obtained will be bright yellow.

Finishing Touches

Decant the aqueous filtrate into the designated container for recovery. Pour the used ethanol from recrystallization into a container for halogenated liquids.

Physical Property of Iodoform

Pure iodoform is a bright yellow crystal. mp $119 \sim 121$ ℃.

Questions

(1) Calculate the conversions of the potassium iodide and the acetone in your experiment?

(2) During the electrolysis process, the pH of the reaction mixture increases gradually. Please try to explain this experimental phenomenon.

3. 19   Extraction: Isolation of Caffeine from Tea Leaves

Fundamental Knowledge

Caffeine, a nitrogen heterocycle of the molecular formula $C_8 H_{10} N_4 O_2$, belongs to a class of natural products called alkaloids. Its chemical name is 1,3,7-trimethyl-2,6-dioxopurine and the structure of caffeine is shown below. In 1895, caffeine was first synthesized by Fischer from dimethylurea and malonic acid.

Extraction: Isolation of Caffeine from Tea Leaves

$$H_3C-N \qquad O \qquad CH_3$$

caffeine

Purposes and Requirements

(1) Review the operations of solvent extraction and sublimation.

(2) Learn to extract caffeine from tea leaves by methods of simple extraction and traditional Soxhlet extraction.

Principle

Tea leaves contain $1\% \sim 4\%$ of caffeine. We will use ordinary tea bags as our source of raw material in this experiment. The caffeine will be extracted from tea leaves by two methods. One is simple extraction and the other is traditional Soxhlet extraction.

Apparatus

600 mL beaker, separatory funnel, flask, simple distillation apparatus, Soxhlet extraction apparatus, recrystallization apparatus, sublimation apparatus.

Reagents

Tea bags（袋装茶叶）	22 bags (about 2 g per bag)
Sodium carbonate（碳酸钠）	20 g
Dichloromethane（二氯甲烷）	200 mL
Anhydrous sodium sulfate（无水硫酸钠）	
Toluene（甲苯）	$5 \sim 7$ mL
Heptane（庚烷）	$7 \sim 10$ mL
Calcium oxide（CaO，生石灰）	4 g
Anhydrous ethanol（无水乙醇）	100 mL

Time   8 h

Safety Alert

Dichloromethane is an anesthetic if inhaled in large quantities. Use adequate ventilation and evaporate dichloromethane only in the fume hood.

Procedure

(1) **Simple Extraction**   In a 600 mL beaker, place 275 mL of distilled water, 20 g of sodium

carbonate and approximately 25 g of tea bags[1]. Bring the mixture to boil on a hot plate and boil for 20～30 minutes[2]. Remove the beaker from the heat and allow it to cool somewhat (around 50 ℃). Decant the dark aqueous layer from the tea bags into a 600 mL beaker[3]. Cool the aqueous solution to room temperature. Add 30 mL dichloromethane to the cooled beaker and slowly stir the mixture with a magnetic stirrer for 3～5 minutes[4]. Slowly transfer the mixture to a separatory funnel and remove the lower organic layer. Return the aqueous solution to the 600 mL beaker and repeat the extraction procedure four more times. Combine the organic layers and dry with anhydrous sodium sulfate. Decant the dichloromethane layer into a dry flask and remove the dichloromethane by simple distillation. As the final traces of solvent are removed, the caffeine will crystallize as an off-white or cream-colored solid.

The crude caffeine is recrystallized from a minimal amount of toluene-heptane to give small needles of a white crystallized solid. This material may be sublimed to give pure material of melting point 233 ℃ to 235 ℃.

(2) **Traditional Soxhlet Extraction**   Place approximately 10 g of tea bags into a porous thimble and put it into a Soxhlet extractor (Figure 2.4-2). Add 50 mL anhydrous ethanol and several boiling chips into a round-bottomed flask. Assemble an apparatus for Soxhlet extraction. Heat the flask with a water bath and keep the anhydrous ethanol reflux for about 3 h until the color of extracted liquid turns to be very light. Stop heating when the siphoning action commences and the extract is returned to the distillation flask.

Assemble a distillation apparatus and distill out most of the ethanol with a water bath. Put the concentrated residue into an evaporating dish. Wash the flask with small amounts of anhydrous ethanol and then transfer them also to the evaporating dish. Add about 4 g CaO into the evaporating dish and stir the mixture continuously. Then, put it on a boiling water bath and evaporate to dryness. Crush the solid to powder and sublime the caffeine twice[5]. Combine all the sublimed products. Calculate the yield and determine the melting point.

Notes

[1] Remove tags from tea bags before addition and don't tear the tea bags that can function as filter paper.

[2] Be careful not to heat too strongly, as bumping will occur.

[3] Be careful to obtain as much liquid as possible from the residue.

[4] If the extraction is performed with vigorous stirring, an emulsion that is very hard to break will form.

[5] The second sublimation should proceed after completely stirring.

Finishing Touches

Place your recovered materials in the labeled collection containers, as directed by your laboratory instructor. Clean your glassware with detergent. Wash your hands thoroughly with soap

Extraction: Isolation of Caffeine from Tea Leaves

or detergent before leaving the laboratory.

Physical Property

Pure caffeine is a white needle-shaped crystal. mp 233~235 ℃.

^{1}H—NMR Spectrum of Caffeine

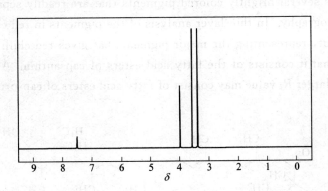

IR Spectrum of Caffeine

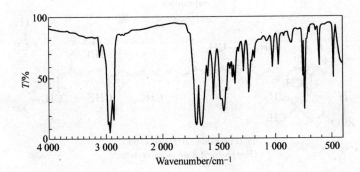

Questions

(1) What property of caffeine makes it sublime easily?

(2) Interpret the IR spectrum and ^{1}H—NMR spectrum of caffeine as completely as you can.

(3) Which is the key step for each extraction method?

(4) Compare the advantages and disadvantages of the two extraction methods mentioned in the procedure.

Basic Experiments

3. 20 Thin-Layer and Column Chromatography: Isolation of a Red Pigment from Red Chilli

Fundamental Knowledge

Red chilli contains several brightly colored pigments that are readily separated by thin-layer and column chromatography. In thin-layer analysis of the pigments in red chilli, we obtain one large, bright red spot, representing the major pigment that gives red chilli its deep red color. Evidence indicates that it consists of the fatty acid esters of capsanthin. A second, minor red spot with a slightly larger R_f value may consist of fatty acid esters of capsorubin. Red chilli also contains β–carotene.

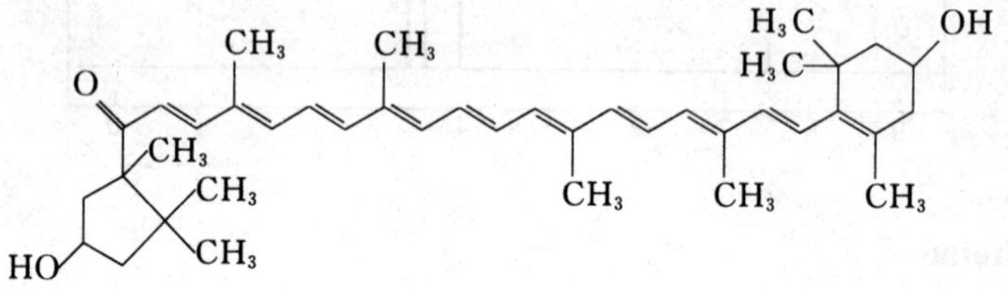

capsanthin

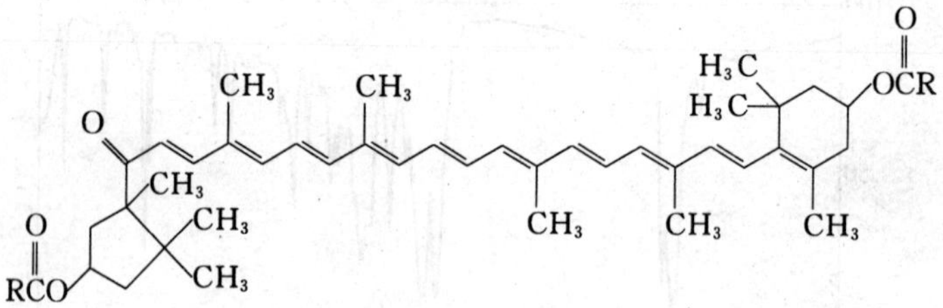

capsanthin fatty acid ester
(R=chain of 3 or more carbons)

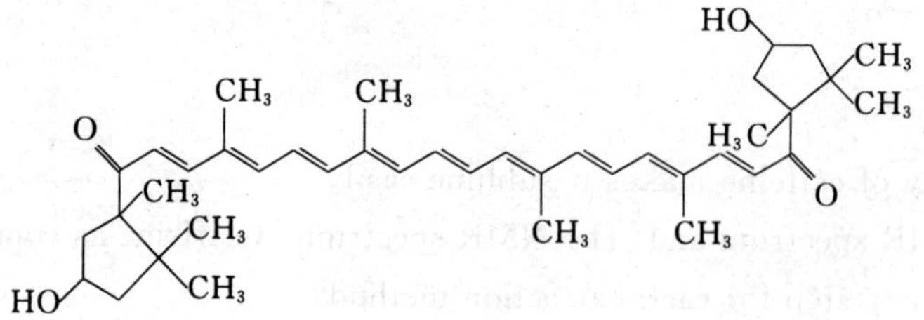

capsorubin

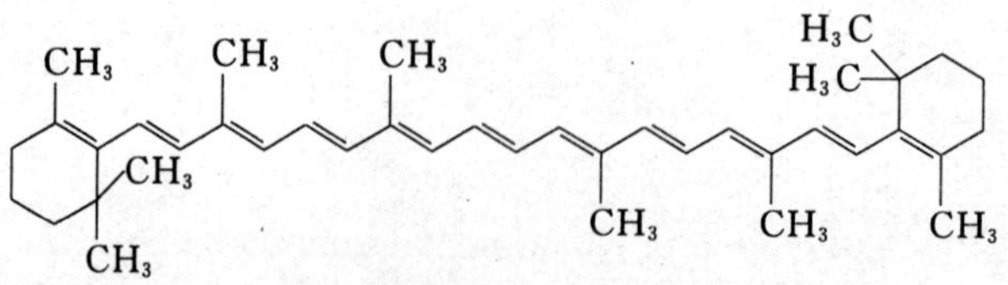

β–carotene

Thin-Layer and Column Chromatography: Isolation of a Red Pigment from Red Chilli

Purposes and Requirements

(1) Review the operations of thin-layer chromatography and column chromatography.

(2) Learn to analyze the red chilli pigment mixture by thin-layer chromatography.

(3) Learn to obtain a red pigment by means of column chromatography.

Principle

In this experiment, you will extract red chilli with dichloromethane to obtain a mixture of pigments, and then analyze the crude mixture by thin-layer chromatography. Finally the crude mixture of pigments is separated by column chromatography to obtain the red pigment (capsanthin fatty acid esters) in a reasonably pure form.

Apparatus

A 25 mL round-bottomed flask, reflux condenser, vacuum filtration apparatus, beaker, distillation apparatus, chromatography column, silica gel G plates, chromatographic tank and test tubes.

Reagents

Red chilli (干红辣椒)	1 g
Dichloromethane (二氯甲烷)	300 mL
Silica gel (60～200 mesh) (硅胶，60～200 目)	7.5 g

Time 8 h

Safety Alert

Dichloromethane is an anesthetic if inhaled in large quantities. Use adequate ventilation and evaporate dichloromethane only in the fume hood.

Procedure

(1) Place 1 g of red chilli and several boiling chips in a 25 mL round-bottomed flask. Add 10 mL of dichloromethane and reflux for 20 minutes. After reflux is complete, cool flask to room temperature and remove solid by vacuum filtration. Evaporate the filtrate to give a crude mixture of pigments.

(2) Prepare a chromatographic tank, using dichloromethane as an eluent. Scrape a tiny sample of the crude pigments into a beaker and dissolve in 5 drops of dichloromethane. Spot a 2 cm × 8 cm silica gel G plate. Run the chromatogram in the previously prepared chromatographic tank. Record color and calculate R_f value for each spot.

(3) Isolate the major red pigment with $R_f \approx 0.6$ by column chromatography. Pack a chromatographic column fitted with a glass or Teflon stopcock with 7.5 g of silica gel 60～200 mesh in

Basic Experiments

dichloromethane. After packing is complete, lower the level of dichloromethane eluent to the upper surface of the sand covering the silica pack. Dissolve the crude mixture of pigments in a minimum of dichloromethane (approximately 1. 0 mL) and place the solution on the surface of the column. After placing the pigment on the column, elute the pigment with dichloromethane by collecting 2 mL fractions in test tubes. Stop the column after the second yellow pigment is eluted. Monitor the column by thin-layer chromatography of the eluted samples, using 2 cm× 8 cm silica gel G. Identify the set of fractions that contain the red pigment. Combine each set of fractions that contain essentially one component[1]. Record the UV-Vis spectrum of the red pigment and compare your recorded spectrum with the standard UV-Vis spectrum of the red pigment.

Notes

[1] If a good separation is not obtained, chromatograph the combined fractions that contain the red pigment a second time by the same procedure.

Finishing Touches

Place your recovered materials in the labeled collection containers, as directed by your laboratory instructor. Clean your glassware with detergent.

UV-Vis Spectrum of the Pigments in Red Chilli

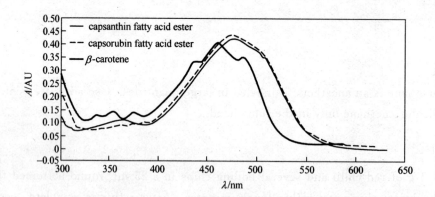

Questions

(1) Circle the separate isoprene units in capsanthin and β-carotene.

(2) Interpret your recorded UV-Vis spectrum of the red pigment as completely as you can.

Chapter 4

Comprehensive Experiments

4.1 Preparation of 5-*n*-Butylmalonyl Urea (5-*n*-Butylbarbituric Acid, 正丁基巴比妥酸)

Fundamental Knowledge

Barbituric acid results from the condensation of malonic acid and urea. It was first prepared in 1864 by Adolph von Baeyer, a young research assistant to Kekulé at the University of Ghent. As a derivative of barbituric acid, 5-*n*-butylbarbituric acid will be synthesized in this experiment by the following two steps. The first step is the alkylation of diethyl malonate with *n*-butyl bromide. The second step is a condensation reaction between urea and diethyl *n*-butylmalonate.

Purposes and Requirements

(1) Review the malonic ester synthesis reaction.

(2) To learn preparation of 5-*n*-butylbarbituric acid by way of a condensation reaction between urea and diethyl *n*-butylmalonate.

(3) Learn how to handle sodium metal and to gain experience in analyzing IR spectrum.

Principle

$$CH_2(COOCH_2CH_3)_2 + CH_3CH_2ONa \longrightarrow NaCH(COOCH_2CH_3)_2 + CH_3CH_2OH$$

diethyl malonate　　　sodium ethoxide　　　sodium diethyl malonate　　　ethanol

$$NaCH(COOCH_2CH_3)_2 + CH_3CH_2CH_2CH_2Br \longrightarrow CH_3CH_2CH_2CH_2CH(COOCH_2CH_3)_2 + NaBr$$

n-butyl bromide　　　　　　　diethyl *n*-butylmalonate

$$CH_3CH_2CH_2CH_2CH(COOCH_2CH_3)_2 + NH_2CONH_2 \longrightarrow CH_3CH_2CH_2CH_2CH \begin{array}{c} \overset{O}{\underset{\parallel}{C}} - \overset{H}{\underset{}{N}} \\ \diagdown \\ \underset{\parallel}{\underset{O}{C}} - \underset{H}{N} \end{array} C{=}O + 2CH_3CH_2OH$$

urea　　　　　　　　　　　　　　5-*n*-butylbarbituric acid

Comprehensive Experiments

Apparatus

A 100 mL 3-neck flask, drying tube, reflux condenser, mechanical stirrer, pressure equalizing addition funnel, separatory funnel, simple distillation apparatus, vacuum distillation apparatus, vacuum filtration apparatus.

Reagents

Diethyl malonate（丙二酸二乙酯）	7.5 mL
n-Butyl bromide（正溴丁烷）	5.5 mL
Sodium metal（金属钠）	1.9 g
Absolute ethanol（无水乙醇）	70 mL
Anhydrous potassium iodide（无水碘化钾）	0.7 g
Anhydrous magnesium sulfate（无水硫酸镁）	
Ethyl acetate（乙酸乙酯）	40 mL
Diethyl n-butylmalonate（正丁基丙二酸二乙酯）	4.3 g
Urea（尿素）	1.2 g
Concentrated hydrochloric acid（浓盐酸）	2 mL
Petroleum ether（bp 30～60 ℃）（石油醚 30～60 ℃）	
Calcium chloride（CaCl$_2$，氯化钙）	

Time   8 h

Safety Alert

Avoid skin contact with sodium metal. Sodium metal and water react very vigorously to produce hydrogen gas. Be careful not to allow sodium to come into contact with water. n-Butyl bromide is toxic in high concentrations. Avoid inhaling vapors.

Procedure

(1) **Synthesis of Diethyl n-Butylmalonate by the Malonic Ester Condensation**   Assemble a set-up involving a 100 mL 3-neck flask equipped with a stirrer, a pressure equalizing addition funnel, reflux condenser and a CaCl$_2$ drying tube[1]. Place 20 mL absolute ethanol in the 100 mL 3-neck flask. By lifting off the condenser, add 1.4 g sodium piece by piece to the absolute ethanol with gentle stirring [2]. As the sodium reacts with the alcohol, the ethanol solution will heat up substantially. When all the sodium has dissolved, cool the reaction mixture to room temperature [3]. Add 0.7 g anhydrous powdered potassium iodide to the flask [4]. With stirring and commence heating until the solution almost reaches reflux. Slowly add 7.5 mL diethyl malonate through the pressure equalizing addition funnel [5]. After the addition of the entire 7.5 mLdiethyl malonate, allow the reaction mixture to reflux for 10 minutes. Then, add 5.5 mL n-butyl bromide [6] dropwise through the pressure equalizing addition funnel and gently

reflux the reaction mixture for 40 minutes. During the reaction period, a yellow color, along with a white crystalline material will appear in the solution. After the reflux period is over, cool it to room temperature. Add 50 mL distilled water to the flask. Swirl the flask rigorously to decompose all the salts. After the hydrolysis of the salts, transfer the entire mixture to a separatory funnel, and extract the product with 20 mL×2 ethyl acetate. Combine the ester layers, and dry them over anhydrous $MgSO_4$. Distill off the ethyl acetate at atmospheric pressure, then distill it *in vacuo*, collecting the fraction coming over at 125~135 ℃ and 20 mm Hg (2.66 kPa) as product. Weigh the product and calculate its percent yield. The yield is about 8.0 g.

(2) **Synthesis of 5-n-Butylbarbituric Acid**   Assemble a set-up involving a 100 mL 3-neck flask equipped with a stirrer, a pressure equalizing addition funnel, reflux condenser and a $CaCl_2$ drying tube [1]. Place 44 mL absolute ethanol in the 100 mL 3-neck flask. By lifting off the condenser, add 0.5 g sodium piece by piece to the absolute ethanol with gentle stirring [2]. After all the sodium has dissolved [3], add 4.3 g diethyl n-butylmalonate dropwise through the pressure equalizing addition funnel with stirring. Then, add 1.2 g dry urea[7]. Swirl the mixture well and heat it under reflux for 1.5 h. During the reaction period, solid materials will appear. After the reflux period, cool the mixture to room temperature. Add 15 mL water to make the solid materials dissolved. Acidify the resulting solution with 2 mL of concentrated hydrochloric acid (pH = 2~3). Concentrate the solution to about 20 mL through simple distillation. Cool the solution in an ice bath and collect the crude product by vacuum filtration. Wash the crude product with a small amount of petroleum ether. Dry the product and recrystallize it from water. Weigh the product, determine the melting point and record the infrared spectrum. The purity of the 5-n-butylbarbituric acid can be checked using thin-layer chromatography. The yield is about 2.0 g.

Notes

[1] All apparatus must be thoroughly dried in a hot oven (>120 ℃) before use. The reaction must be carried out under strict anhydrous conditions.

[2] Place the sodium in a 100 mL beaker under inert solvents and cut it up carefully with a sharp blade.

[3] Make sure that all the sodium has completely reacted.

[4] The easiest way to do this is to remove the reflux condenser, fit a powder funnel in the neck of the flask, add KI through the powder funnel, and then re-equip the reflux condenser. Care should be taken not to allow any of the KI to contact the greased joint, as this will prevent a good fit between condenser and flask.

[5] Distill diethyl malonate before use.

[6] Dry n-butyl bromide over anhydrous $MgSO_4$ and distill it before use.

[7] Urea should be dried in the oven for more than 45 minutes at the temperature of 110 ℃. Then, put it in the desiccator for use.

Finishing Touches

Place your recovered materials in the labeled collection containers, as directed by your laboratory instructor. Clean your glassware with detergent.

Physical Property

Pure diethyl *n*-butylmalonate is a colorless liquid. bp 235~240 ℃. Pure 5-*n*-butylbarbituric acid is a colorless crystal. mp 209~210 ℃.

IR Spectrum of 5-*n*-Butylbarbituric Acid

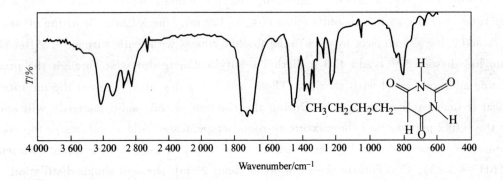

Questions

(1) Why is KI added in this experiment?

(2) Interpret your recorded IR spectrum of 5-*n*-butylbarbituric acid as completely as you can.

4.2 Diels-Alder Reaction: Microwave-Assisted Preparation of 9,10-Dihydroanthracene-9,10-α,β-Succinic Anhydride (9,10-二氢蒽-9,10-α,β-丁二酸酐)

Fundamental Knowledge

A Diels-Alder reaction is also known as a [4+2] cycloaddition. One component, the diene, contributes four atoms to the six-membered ring of the adduct; the other, the dienophile, contributes two atoms. The diene must be connected by two conjugated double bonds, and the dienophile must have a double or triple bond connecting the two carbon centers. The product of the Diels-Alder reaction is usually a structure that contains a cyclohexene ring system. A Diels-Alder reaction is sometimes carried out by simply mixing and heating the reactants. Since 1986, when microwave irradiation was first applied towards organic chemistry, microwave-assisted synthesis has become increasingly popular for modern chemical synthesis. Microwave-assisted synthesis is particularly interesting due to its high efficiency, leading to drastically reduced re-

Diels-Alder Reaction: Microwave-Assisted Preparation of
9,10-Dihydroanthracene-9,10-α,β-Succinic Anhydride (9,10-二氢蒽-9,10-α,β-丁二酸酐)

4.2   197

action time, higher yield and purer products.

Purposes and Requirements

(1) Review the Diels-Alder reaction.

(2) To learn microwave-assisted preparation of 9,10-dihydroanthracene-9,10-α,β-succinic anhydride by way of a Diels-Alder reaction between anthracene and maleic anhydride.

(3) To learn more about the operations of vacuum filtration, melting-point determination, microwave heating, recrystallization and thin-layer chromatography.

Principle

anthracene   maleic anhydride

9,10-dihydroanthracene-9,10-α,
β-succinic anhydride

Apparatus

A 50 mL beaker, mortar, watchglass, microwave oven, Büchner funnel.

Reagents

Anthracene (蒽)	1.8 g
Maleic anhydride (顺丁烯二酸酐)	0.98 g
Diglyme (二甘醇二甲醚)	5 mL
Ethyl ether (乙醚)	4 mL

Time 2 h

Safety Alert

Maleic anhydride is corrosive and toxic and can cause severe damage to the eyes, skin and upper respiratory tract. Wear gloves, avoid contacting with skin, eyes or clothing, and do not inhale the dust. If you must pulverize maleic anhydride briquettes, do it in a hood and wear protective clothing. Ethyl ether is extremely flammable and may be harmful if inhaled. Do not inhale the vapor, and keep the solvent away from flames and hot surfaces.

Procedure

Finely grind 1.8 g of anthracene and 0.98 g of maleic anhydride in a mortar[1]. Transfer the ground solid mixture to a 50 mL beaker, and add 5 mL diglyme, with swirling[2]. Cover the beaker with a watchglass, and put it into the microwave oven[3]. After irradiation for 3 minutes with medium heating temperature, the beaker is taken out and allowed to stand to enable complete crystallization of the product. The precipitated greenish product is filtered and washed with two 2 mL portions of ethyl ether[4]. Weigh the product, calculate the percent yield and determine the melting point. The purity of the product may be checked using thin-layer chromatography (TLC)[5]. The yield is about 1.9 g.

Notes

[1] High purity grade anthracene and maleic anhydride is recommended. The anthracene can be recrystallized from 95% ethanol. Maleic anhydride is purified by sublimation.

[2] The preferred reaction vessel is a beaker with a loose cover of much larger capacity than the volume of the reaction mixture.

[3] The maximum output power of the microwave oven is 700 W.

[4] If a purer product is desired, it can be recrystallized from xylene.

[5] Use silica gel H as adsorbent, mixture of petroleum ether and methyl t-butyl ether (volume ratio 1 : 1) as developing agent. The iodine method can be chosen for spot visualization.

Finishing Touches

Place your recovered materials in the labeled collection containers, as directed by your laboratory instructor. Clean your glassware with detergent.

Physical Property

Pure 9,10-dihydroanthracene-9,10-α,β-succinic anhydride is a crystal with melting point of 263~264 ℃.

Questions

(1) How to choose solvents used for microwave-assisted reactions?

(2) Recrystallizing the product of 9,10-dihydroanthracene-9,10-α,β-succinic anhydride from water or from an alcohol is rarely a good idea. Explain why.

(3) Compared with conventional heating techniques, what are the advantages of using microwave heating techniques?

(4) Why anthracene can form a Diels-Alder adduct with maleic anhydride?

4.3   Grignard Reaction: Preparation of Methyl Triphenylmethyl Ether (甲基三苯甲基醚)

Fundamental Knowledge

Victor Grignard (1871—1935), a professor at the Universities of Lyons and Nancy in France, was awarded the Nobel Prize in chemistry for his work with organomagnesium compounds. Organomagnesium halides, Grignard reagents, are among the most versatile synthetic intermediates for laboratory work. They are formed by simple, direct reaction of magnesium metal with alkyl or aryl halides (usually bromides) in the presence of a solvent such as ether or tetrahydrofuran. In this experiment, methyl triphenylmethyl ether will be prepared by the following three steps. The first step is the preparation of phenylmagnesium bromide from bromobenzene and magnesium turnings. The second step is the preparation of triphenylmethanol and the third step is to form methyl triphenylmethyl ether by reaction of triphenylmethanol with methanol.

Purposes and Requirements

(1) Learn to prepare Grignard reagent which is highly air-and moisture-sensitive material.

(2) To investigate the reaction of Grignard reagent with ester to form tertiary alcohol.

(3) Learn to prepare methyl triphenylmethyl ether by reaction of triphenyl methanol with methanol in the presence of concentrated sulfuric acid.

Principle

$$C_6H_5Br + Mg \xrightarrow{\text{ether}} C_6H_5MgBr$$
bromobenzene   phenylmagnesium bromide

$$C_6H_5COOC_2H_5 + 2C_6H_5MgBr \longrightarrow (C_6H_5)_3COMgBr \xrightarrow[H^+]{H_2O} (C_6H_5)_3COH$$
ethyl benzoate   triphenylmethanol

$$(C_6H_5)_3COH + CH_3OH \xrightarrow{H^+} (C_6H_5)_3COCH_3$$
methanol   methyl triphenylmethyl ether

Apparatus

A 250 mL round-bottomed flask, Claisen adaptor, reflux condenser, pressure equalizing addition funnel, a CaCl$_2$ drying tube, test tube, simple distillation apparatus, 50 mL Erlenmeyer flask, vacuum filtration apparatus.

Reagents

Bromobenzene (溴苯)	8.5 mL
Magnesium (镁)	1.5 g
Ethyl benzoate (苯甲酸乙酯)	3.8 g
Methyl *t*-butyl ether (甲基叔丁基醚)	40 mL
Methanol (甲醇)	6 mL
Concentrated sulfuric acid (浓硫酸)	1 mL
NH₄Cl (氯化铵)	7.5 g
Petroleum ether (bp 30~60 ℃) (石油醚 30~60 ℃)	70 mL
Iodine (碘)	a small piece

Time   10 h

Safety Alert

Bromobenzene fumes are toxic in high concentrations. Avoid inhaling vapors. Concentrated sulfuric acid is corrosive and can cause serious damage to skin.

Procedure

(1) **Preparation of Phenylmagnesium Bromide**   All apparatus used in the reaction must be thoroughly dried and the reagents must be anhydrous. Place 1.5 g magnesium, 10 mL anhydrous methyl *t*-butyl ether and a small piece of iodine in the 250 mL round-bottomed flask. Pour the mixture of 8.5 mL bromobenzene and 20 mL anhydrous methyl *t*-butyl ether into the pressure equalizing addition funnel and then drop approximately 5 mL of the mixture to the flask. Gently swirl the flask. If the reaction does not start, warm the flask gently in a bath of warm water. After the reaction has begun, stop warming, add the remainder of the bromo-benzene solution drop by drop to the flask to maintain a gentle reflux. After the addition of bromobenzene solution is complete, keep gentle reflux until magnesium completely disappears[1]. Cool it to room temperature and the Grignard reagent is now ready for further reaction[2].

(2) **Preparation of Triphenylmethanol**   Cool the reaction flask containing the Grignard reagent prepared before with cold water bath and place in the pressure equalizing addition funnel a solution of 3.8 g of pure ethyl benzoate in 5 mL anhydrous methyl *t*-butyl ether. Allow the ethyl benzoate solution to flow slowly into the Grignard reagent, with continuous swirling, and cool the flask from time to time to control the reaction. After all of the ethyl benzoate has been added, allow the mixture to gently reflux for 1 h. Cool the flask with an ice bath. Then, add slowly saturated salt solution containing 7.5 g NH₄Cl through addition funnel to the flask with continuous swirling[3]. Change to distillation apparatus, distill off the methyl *t*-butyl ether using a steam bath. Cool the flask and stir the residue with about 70 mL petroleum ether (bp 30~60 ℃). Collect the solid on a suction filter and wash it with water. The crude product can

Grignard Reaction: Preparation of Methyl Triphenylmethyl Ether (甲基三苯甲基醚)

be purified by recrystallization from ethanol. The yield is about 4.0 g.

(3) **Preparation of Methyl Triphenylmethyl Ether**   Weigh out 0.25 g of triphenylmethanol. Place it in a large test tube. Add 1 mL of concentrated sulfuric acid to the test tube. Stir until all the alcohol is dissolved. Add 5 mL of ice cold methanol to a 50 mL Erlenmeyer flask. Pour the alcohol formed before into the methanol. Use an additional 1 mL of ice cold methanol to rinse out the test tube and transfer to the 50 mL Erlenmeyer flask. Scratch the sides of the Erlenmeyer flask until crystallization occurs. Place in an ice bath for 5 minutes. Vacuum filter the crystals. Wash with 10 mL of ice cold water. Allow 30 minutes for drying. Then, determine the melting point and record.

Notes

[1] The reaction time is about 1 h. There will always be a small amount of magnesium left from forming a Grignard reagent. There is no need to concern it.

[2] Since the Grignard reagent decomposes when exposed to oxygen in air, it should be used for the next step in the same lab period.

[3] If $Mg(OH)_2$ precipitate does not completely dissolved, add small amount of dilute HCl.

Finishing Touches

Place your recovered materials in the labeled collection containers, as directed by your laboratory instructor. Clean your glassware with detergent.

Physical Property

Pure triphenylmethanol is a colorless crystal. mp 162~164 ℃. Pure methyl triphenylmethyl ether is a crystal with melting point of 81~83 ℃.

IR Spectrum of Triphenylmethanol Using Nujol Mull

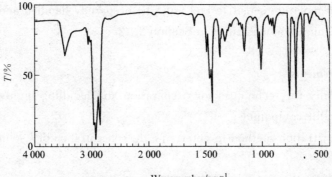

Comprehensive Experiments

IR Spectrum of Methyl triphenylmethyl Ether

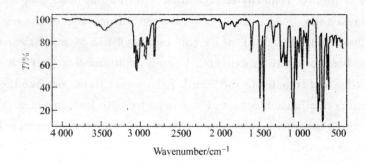

Wavenumber/cm^{-1}

Questions

(1) Why is ether, a relatively nonpolar solvent, essential to the preparation of Grignard reagent?

(2) Why is a small crystal of iodine added during preparation of phenylmagnesium bromide?

4. 4   Organometallic Chemistry: Preparation of *n*-Butyllithium (正丁基锂) and Titration of its Concentration

Fundamental Knowledge

Organometallic compounds are substances that contain carbon-metal bonds, such as organolithium, organomagnesium and organoaluminum. Alkyllithium and Grignard reagent (see Section 4. 3) are among the most important of all organometallic reagents used in organic synthesis. The polarization of the bond between the carbon atom and the electropositive metal in these reagents renders the carbon atom very electron-rich. Thus, one of the characteristic properties of these organometallic reagents is that the carbon atom directly bonded to the metal serves as a nucleophile in chemical reactions. Most organometallic reagents, especially alkyllithium compounds, are air- and moisture-sensitive and must be prepared, handled and stored under inert gas with special techniques as described in Section 2. 12.

Purposes and Requirements

(1) Master skillfully the techniques for preparation and handling highly air- and moisture-sensitive organometallic compounds.

(2) Learn double titration method to determine the concentration of a solution of alkyllithium.

Principle

Organolithium compounds are important reagents in organic synthesis and also catalysts for polymerization of dienes. *n*-Butyllithium is typically prepared by the reaction of *n*-butyl bromide orchloride with lithium metal in an anhydrous solvent of an ether or alkane. Normally lithium metal is used in excess in the preparation. The unreacted lithium metal and the formed lithium chloride salt are filtered after reaction.

$$CH_3CH_2CH_2CH_2Br + 2Li \xrightarrow[\text{dry ether}]{} CH_3CH_2CH_2CH_2Li + LiBr$$

$$\underset{n-\text{butyl bromide}}{} \qquad \underset{n-\text{butyllithium}}{}$$

The concentration of the *n*-butyllithium solution is determined by double titration method and the reagent in solution is directly used or stored under inert gas. The titration reactions are as follows:

First titration:

$$n-C_4H_9Li + (n-C_4H_9OLi + Li_2O + LiOH) + H_2O \longrightarrow n-C_4H_{10} + LiOH + (n-C_4H_9OH + LiOH)$$

$$LiOH + HCl \longrightarrow LiCl + H_2O$$

Second titration:

$$n-C_4H_9Li + (n-C_4H_9OLi + Li_2O + LiOH) \xrightarrow[\text{2) } H_2O]{\text{1) } C_6H_5CH_2Cl} C_6H_5CH_2CH_2C_6H_5 + n-C_4H_9CH_2C_6H_5$$

$$+ n-C_8H_{18} + LiCl + (n-C_4H_9OH + LiOH)$$

$$LiOH + HCl \longrightarrow LiCl + H_2O$$

Apparatus

A 250 mL three-neck round-bottom flask, reflux condenser, pressure-equalized dropping funnel, mechanical stirrer, T-tube, low temperature thermometer, graduated pipet and two 100 mL Erlenmeyer flasks.

Reagents

n-Butyl bromide（正溴丁烷）	16.2 mL (20.7 g, 0.15 mol)
Lithium metal（金属锂）	2.6 g (0.37 mol)
Methyl *t*-butyl ether（甲基叔丁基醚）	110 mL
Benzyl chloride（氯苄）	
Phenolphthalein indicator（酚酞指示剂）	
Pure nitrogen gas（高纯氮气）	

Time   4～6 h

Safety Alert

Lithium metal is highly sensitive toward water. All glassware used in preparation must be thoroughly dried. All ground-glass joints in the apparatus must be mated tightly to prevent the flask from moisture. Do not allow the solution of *n*-butyllithium to come in contact with your skin or eyes. If it does, flush the affected area immediately with large amounts of water.

Comprehensive Experiments

Procedure

(1) **Preparation**   Set up the reaction apparatus as shown in Figure 2−3−1c[1]. Purge the apparatus with pure nitrogen gas. A low temperature thermometer is installed and the top of the condenser is connected to a T-tube. Let nitrogen gas slowly flow through the T-tube during the reaction to prevent the apparatus from air. Add 50 mL of methyl t-butyl ether[2] and 2.6 g of lithium wires[3] to the flask. Cool it to −10 ℃ with the mixture of dry-ice and acetone and start the magnetic stirring. The solution of 16.2 mL n-butyl bromide[4] in 50 mL of methyl t-butyl ether is dropped to the flask during 30 min. The reaction solution turns turbid and the bright spots appear on lithium wires when the reaction starts. Remove the cooling bath and keep the mixture stirred for 3 h at room temperature. Filter the reaction mixture with an U-shape glass tube (See Figure 2−12−3) to a Schlenk tube, which is pre-purged with nitrogen gas. Tightly cover the Schlenk tube either with a lubricated ground-glass stopper or a rubber stopper.

(2) **Titration**   Quickly move 10 mL of the prepared n−butyllithium solution with a graduated pipet[5] from the Schlenk tube to an Erlenmeyer flask containing 10 mL of deionized water and add two drops of phenolphthalein indicator to the flask. Titrate the solution with the standard concentration of hydrochloric acid until the red color of the solution fades. The total concentration of bases in the solution is obtained by the first titration.

Move 10 mL of the prepared n-butyllithium solution with a graduated pipet to a dry Erlenmeyer flask[6] containing 1 mL of anhydrous benzyl chloride[7] and 10 mL of methyl t-butyl ether[2]. The solution turns yellow quickly and the reaction is endothermic. After the mixture stands for about 1 min, add 10 mL of deionized water and two drops of phenolphthalein indicator to the flask. Make the second titration with the standard concentration of hydrochloric acid until the red color of the solution fades.

The concentration of the n-butyllithium solution can be calculated by deduction of the result of the second titration from that of the first titration. Therefore, the yield of the product can be obtained.

Notes

[1] All glassware used in preparation must be thoroughly dried, and for manipulations please see Section 2.12.

[2] Methyl t-butyl ether should be dried over anhydrous magnesium sulfate and distilled prior to use.

[3] Clean the paraffin on the surface of lithium metal with methyl t-butyl ether. Then make the piece of lithium metal into a thin film and cut it to lithium wires and directly add them to the reaction flask.

[4] Dry n-butyl bromide with the same method described for methyl t-butyl ether.

[5] Purge the dry graduated pipet with nitrogen gas before use. Wash the pipet immediately with methyl t-butyl ether several times after the pipet is used each time.

[6] This Erlenmeyer flask must be dried and purged with nitrogen gas before use.

[7] Analytical pure benzyl chloride should be dried over P_2O_5 and distilled under reduced pressure.

Finishing Touches

Place the titration solution in the container for halogenated wastes. Give the *n*-butyllithium solution that you prepared to your instructor.

Questions

(1) How trace water in the solvent and reagents affect the formation of *n*-butyllithium?

(2) Why must a dry Erlenmeyer flask be used for the second titration?

Chapter 5

Self-Designing Experiments

5.1 Identification of Functional Compounds

Fundamental Knowledge

Identification of the molecular structure of organic compounds is one of the greatest challenges to the chemist. Perhaps the most important step in identifying an unknown substance is determining the functional group that may be present. There are two quite different approaches. One is the traditional method, which depends on chemical reactions. The other is spectrometric method, which is faster and capable of dealing with smaller amounts of compounds with more complex structures. Although the traditional method now is seldom used alone, the required techniques strongly reinforce fundamental chemical principles and expose the beginning student to the making of chemical judgments, an essential skill for productive research.

The traditional method involves performing a number of chemical tests on a substance, each of which is specific for a type of functional group. These tests can normally be done quickly and are designed so that the observation of a color change or the formation of a precipitate indicates the presence of a particular functional group. The following factors should be considered when performing qualitative classification tests for functional groups:

(1) A compound may contain more than one functional group, so the complete series of tests must be performed unless you have been told that the compound is monofunctional.

(2) Careful attention is required when the functional group tests are performed. Record all observations, such as the formation and color of any solid produced as a result of a test.

(3) It is of utmost importance to perform a qualitative test on both an unknown and a known compound that contains the group being tested. Some functional groups may appear to give only a slightly positive test, and it is helpful to determine how a compound known to contain a given functional group behaves under the conditions of the test being performed. It is most efficient and reliable to do the tests on standards at the same time as on the unknown.

In this experiment, you will use the traditional method to identify several unknown organic compounds (4 mL liquid or 400 mg solid).

Requirements:

(1) Give students 4~8 unknown organic compounds chosen by instructor.

(2) Read the corresponding references and design the experimental process.

(3) Certify the instruments and reagents, which will be used in your experiments.

(4) Perform experiments of the identification of unknown compounds.

(5) Write the experimental report (list the corresponding literatures).

References

[1] 袁履冰. 有机化学. 北京：高等教育出版社，2000.

[2] 周科衍，吕俊民. 有机化学实验. 2 版. 北京：高等教育出版社，1984.

[3] 苏州大学有机化学教研室. 有机化学演示实验. 北京：高等教育出版社，1992.

[4] Schoffstall A M, et al. Miniscale Organic Chemistry Laboratory Experiments. Boston：McGraw-Hill, 2000.

5.2   Microwave-Assisted Preparation of Acetaminophenol (醋氨酚)

Fundamental Knowledge

Acetaminophenol is mild analgesics (relieve pain) and antipyretics (reduce fever). The structure of acetaminophenol is as follows:

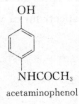

acetaminophenol

In this experiment, acetaminophenol will be prepared from *p*-aminophenol and acetic anhydride by microwave assistance.

¹H—NMR Spectrum of Acetaminophenol in DMSO-d_6

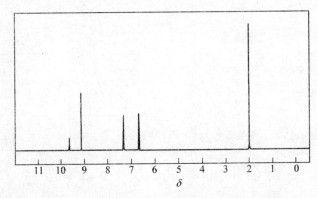

Self-Designing Experiments

IR Spectrum of Acetaminophenol Using Nujol Mull

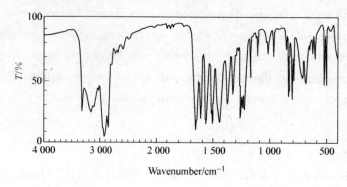

Wavenumber/cm^{-1}

Requirements:

(1) Acetaminophenol should be prepared by means of acylation reaction of p-aminophenol (the amount of p-aminophenol is 2.1 g) and acetic anhydride by microwave assistance.

(2) Before beginning this experiment, you should read the essay on the mechanism of the acylation formation of acetaminophenol.

(3) List the reagent table and draw the setup of apparatus for the reaction.

(4) Write the equations for the main reaction and the possible side reactions.

(5) Write the procedures and important notes in detail.

(6) Determine the melting point of the product.

(7) Record the IR and ^{1}H—NMR spectra of the acetaminophenol. Compare your IR and ^{1}H—NMR spectra obtained with the given spectra. Identify the significant absorption peaks in IR spectrum and analyze the ^{1}H—NMR spectrum of your product.

(8) Write the experimental report.

References

[1] Experiment 4.5 in this textbook.

[2] Mirafzal G A, et al. J Chem Edu. 2000, 77(3): 356.

[3] Barl S S, et al. J Chem Edu. 1992, 69(11): 938.

Chapter 6

Investigative Experiments

6.1 Studies on Synthetic Conditions for Preparation of Isopentyl Acetate (乙酸异戊酯)

Fundamental Knowledge and Principle

Isopentyl acetate, which has the scent of bananas, serves as one of the components of honeybee response pheromone. In this experiment, you will prepare isopentyl acetate from acetic acid and isopentyl alcohol by means of esterification reaction with concentrated sulfuric acid as catalyst.

$$CH_3COOH + (CH_3)_2CHCH_2CH_2OH \underset{}{\overset{H^+}{\rightleftharpoons}} CH_3COOCH_2CH_2CH(CH_3)_2 + H_2O$$

acetic acid   isopentyl alcohol   isopentyl acetate

Furthermore, you will investigate the effects of reaction conditions on the yield of product.

Procedure

To 21.7 mL isopentyl alcohol in a dry 100 mL round-bottomed flask, 25 mL glacial acetic acid is added. Slowly add 4 mL concentrated sulfuric acid and a few boiling chips. Heat the reaction flask under reflux for 1 h. Remove the heating source and allow the mixture to cool to room temperature. Carefully pour the cooled reaction mixture into a 250 mL separatory funnel. Rinse the reaction flask with 50 mL of cool water and pour the water into the separatory funnel. Shake the separatory funnel for a few minutes and then allow the water-insoluble isopentyl acetate to collect on the surface of the water solution. Separate the lower aqueous layer from the upper organic layer. Extract the isopentyl acetate solution with one 50 mL portion of 10% Na_2CO_3 solution. After the Na_2CO_3 extraction, allow the separatory funnel to stand in an upright position for a few minutes. Again drain off any lower water phase. Dry the isopentyl acetate for 10 minutes with anhydrous $MgSO_4$. Further purify the isopentyl acetate by simple distillation. Collect the fraction that distills at 138~142 ℃. Weigh the product yield. Record the IR spectrum and ^1H—NMR spectrum of your product and compare them with the given spectra of isopentyl acetate.

Research Interests and Requirements

（1）Investigate the effect of the amount of concentrated sulfuric acid on the yield of the isopentyl acetate.

amount of concentrated H_2SO_4/mL	1	2	3	4	5
yield of isopentyl acetate/%					

（2）Investigate the effect of molar ratio of isopentyl alcohol to acetic acid on the yield of the isopentyl acetate.

molar ratio of isopentyl alcohol to acetic acid	1 : 1	1 : 1.2	1 : 1.5	1 : 2
yield of isopentyl acetate/%				

（3）Investigate the effect of reflux time on the yield of the isopentyl acetate.

reflux time/h	0.5	1.0	1.5	2.0
yield of isopentyl acetate/%				

^{1}H—NMR Spectrum of Isopentyl Acetate in CdCl$_3$

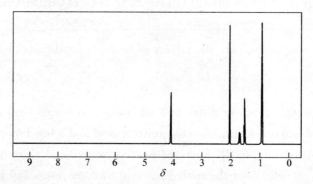

IR Spectrum of Isopentyl Acetate Using Liquid Film

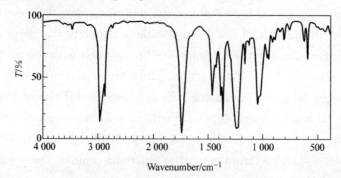

References

［1］周科衍，高占先. 有机化学实验教学指导. 北京：高等教育出版社，1997.

［2］麦肯济. 有机化学实验. 大连工学院有机化学教研组,浙江大学有机化学教研组,译. 北京：
人民教育出版社，1980.

6.2   Preparation of α-and β-D-Glucose Pentaacetates（五乙酸葡萄糖酯）

Fundamental Knowledge and Principle

Carbohydrates are one of the large and important groups of compounds found in nature. Emil Fischer, who was born near Bonn, Germany in 1852, was one of the great pioneers in the development of carbohydrate chemistry. The elucidation of the structures of glucose and other known sugars is regarded as Fischer's most important contribution to science and earned the Nobel Prize in chemistry in 1902. The monosaccharide D-glucose exists in an equilibrium involving an acyclic structure and cyclic hemiacetal forms in solution. The cyclic forms are designated as α-and β-D-glucose.

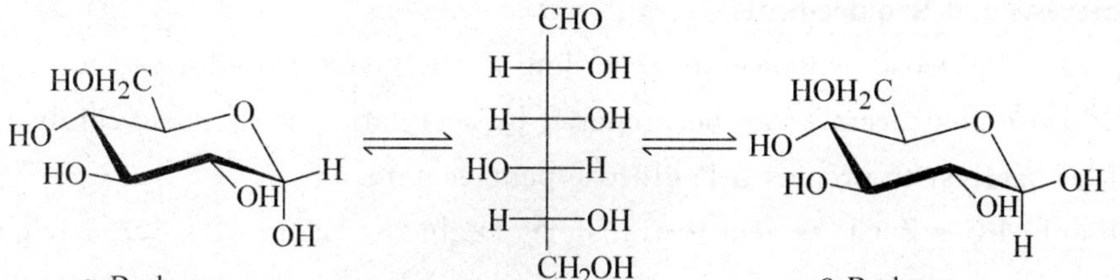

α–D–glucose   β–D–glucose

In this experiment, you will learn to prepare α-and β-D-glucose pentaacetates and investigate the isomerization between them.

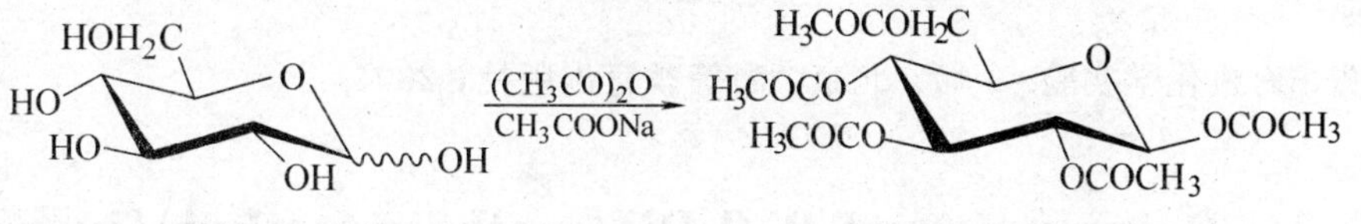

β–D–glucose pentaacetate

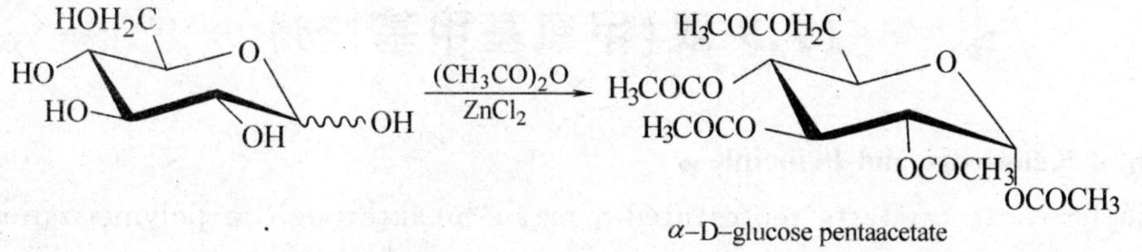

α–D–glucose pentaacetate

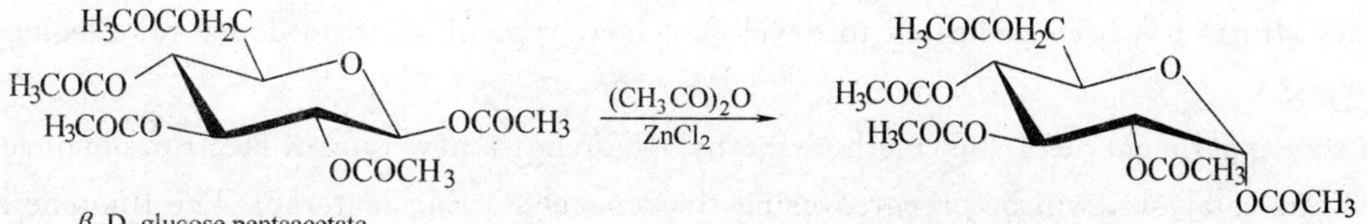

β–D–glucose pentaacetate   α–D–glucose pentaacetate

Investigative Experiments

Procedure

Preparation of β-D-Glucose Pentaacetate   Grind 0.9 g of anhydrous glucose with 0.5 g of anhydrous sodium acetate in a mortar, and then transfer the mixture to a 25 mL round-bottomed flask and add 5 mL of acetic anhydride. Heat the mixture under a reflux condenser on a steam bath for 1.5 h with occasional vigorous agitation. Pour the warm solution in a thin stream, with vigorous stirring, into 50 mL of ice-cold water in a beaker. Disintegrate any lumps of the crystalline precipitate and allow the finely divided material to stand in contact with the water, occasionally stirring it, until the excess acetic anhydride has been hydrolyzed. This will require about 1 h. Collect the crystals with suction and press them as dry as possible with a clean cork or flat stopper. Transfer the crystals to a beaker, mix thoroughly with about 50 mL of water, and allow it to stand with occasional stirring for about 2 h longer. Collect the crystals with suction and press them as dry as possible on a filter. Recrystallize the crude β-D-glucose pentaacetate from about 5 mL of methanol. The yield of purified product is about 1 g. The recorded melting point of the purified compound is 135 ℃.

Research Interests and Requirements

(1) Prepare β-D-glucose pentaacetate according to the given procedure.

(2) α-D-glucose pentaacetate can be prepared by acetylation with acidic catalyst. Use anhydrous $ZnCl_2$ as catalyst to prepare α-D-glucose pentaacetate.

(3) With anhydrous $ZnCl_2$ as acid to transfer β-D-glucose pentaacetate to α-D-glucose pentaacetate.

(4) Write the experimental report.

References

[1] 高占先. 有机化学实验. 4 版. 北京：高等教育出版社，2004.

6.3   Preparation of 9,9-Bis(methoxymethyl)fluorene (9,9-双(甲氧基甲基)芴)

Fundamental Knowledge and Principle

The Ziegler-Natta catalysts represented a major breakthrough in polymerization chemistry because they produce a variety of commercially important polymers. At present, one of the significant efforts has been dedicated to developing new type of electron donor for Ziegler-Natta catalysts.

In this experiment, 9,9-bis(methoxymethyl)fluorene, a new type of electron donor for Ziegler-Natta catalysts, will be prepared using fluorene as starting material. The fluorene can be converted to the desired product by hydroxymethylation and etherification reactions as shown in the following equation. The active hydrogen atoms on the methylene group of fluorene readily react with a strong base to generate a carboanion, which then react *in situ* with formaldehyde to form 9,9-bis(hydroxymethyl)fluorene. Etherification of 9,9-bis(hydroxymethyl)fluorene by dimethyl sulfate, dimethyl carbonate or methyl iodide gives the final product 9,9-bis(methoxymethyl)fluorene.

fluorene   9,9-bis (hydroxymethyl) fluorene   9,9-bis (methoxymethy) fluorene

Study on the Preparation of 9,9-Bis(hydroxymethyl)fluorene
Procedure

Equip a 3-neck round-bottom flask with a mechanical stirrer and place it in an ice-water bath. To the flask add 4 g of polyformaldehyde, 0.7 g of sodium ethoxide, 3.5 mL of anhydrous ethanol and 50 mL of dimethyl sulfoxide (DMSO) in order, and mix the reactants by stirring. Then add 8 g of fluorene dissolved in 50 mL DMSO to the flask within 30 s. Quench the reaction with 1 mL of concentrated hydrochloric acid after the mixture is stirred for 3 min. Some white solid is deposited from the solution when 200 mL of water is added. Extract the mixture successively with 80 mL, 40 mL and 20 mL of ethyl acetate, and combine the extracts. Add a proper amount of water to the extract and distill the azeotrope of ethyl acetate and water. Filter the crude product and recrystallized it from 50 mL of toluene. 9,9-Bis(hydroxymethyl)fluorene is obtained as needle crystals. Air-dry the product, calculate the yield, and measure the melting point of the product.

Research Interests and Requirements

(1) What is the function of the solvent DMSO? Is it possible to replace DMSO with other solvents?

(2) Identify the structure of the product by IR and ^{1}H—NMR spectroscopy.

(3) Qualitatively analyze the compositions of the crude product by TLC with ethyl acetate and heptane (4:1, V/V) as eluent or by HPLC.

(4) Separate each composition from the crude product by TLC or column chromatography and identify each composition.

(5) Optimize the reaction conditions (including selection of a proper strong base).

(6) Some substances in the crude product are not soluble in ethyl acetate and hot toluene. Try to figure out the reason and find a method to solve the problem.

(7) Discuss the mechanism of the reaction.

Study on the Preparation of 9,9-bis(methoxymethyl)fluorene

Procedure

To a 3-neck round-bottom flask add 5 g of 9,9-bis(hydroxymethyl)fluorene, 0.125 g of n-Bu$_4$NHSO$_4$, 50% aqueous solution of 10 g sodium hydroxide and 30 mL of toluene in order. With stirring of the mixture, add 5.6 g of dimethyl sulfate in toluene (30 mL) to the flask within 2 h. Stop stirring after the mixture is stirred for 5 h. Two layers appear in the flask after the mixture stands for a while. The upper layer is clear and light-yellow, and the lower layer is a milky-white suspension. Separate the organic layer and wash it with water for several times until it is neutral. Decant the organic layer to a flask, add a proper amount of water, and then distill the azeotrope of toluene and water. A yellow solid is filtered and recrystallized in 15 mL ethanol. 9,9-Bis(methoxymethyl)fluorene is obtained as needle crystals. Air-dry the product and measure its melting point.

Research Interests and Requirements

(1) Try to use dimethyl carbonate as methylation reagent to replace dimethyl sulfate according to reference [4].

(2) Identify the structure of 9,9-bis(hydroxymethyl) fluorene by IR and ^{1}H—NMR spectroscopy.

(3) Qualitatively analyze the compositions in the crude product by TLC or HPLC.

(4) Separate each composition from the crude product by TLC or column chromatography and identify each composition by NMR spectroscopy.

(5) Find the influence of the reaction temperature on the yield of the product.

(6) Optimize the reaction conditions (including selection of phase-transfer catalyst).

(7) Discuss the mechanism of the reaction.

(8) Write the experimental report.

References

[1] Giampiero M, Antonio C. EP 728727.

[2] Ti Koji, K Koji. JP 09,95460.

[3] 高占先，等. 中国发明专利，01132630.1 2001.

[4] 许招会，等. 石油化工，2007，36(7)：686.

6.4   Preparation and Resolution of Racemic 1,1′-Bi-2-naphthol (1,1′-联-2-萘酚)

Fundamental Knowledge and Principle

A racemic mixture means an equal mixture of two enantiomers. As you already know, enantiomers have nearly identical physical properties except for the direction in which they rotate plane polarized light. Therefore, the enantiomers of a racemic mixture can not be separated by physical methods like distillation or crystallization. However, if the enantiomers are converted into diastereomers, they can be separated because the diastereomers have different physical properties.

Enantiopure (R)-and (S)-1,1′-bi-2-naphthols (BINOL) and their derivatives are one of the most efficient chiral inducers and they have been widely used in various asymmetric syntheses. Although there were many reports on the asymmetric synthesis of an enantiopure BINOL, the resolution of racemic (±)-BINOL is still used as a dominant method to get an enantiopure BINOL.

The racemic (±)-BINOL can be conveniently prepared by oxidative coupling of 2-naphthol. In this experiment, you will prepare the racemic (±)-BINOL by following synthetic routes: make an oxidative coupling of 2-naphthol using $FeCl_3$ as oxidant either in aqueous solution or in the solid phase, and in the latter case the reaction can be facilitated by microwaves.

There are more than 20 resolution methods reported in literature. In this experiment you can use following two resolution methods:

(1) Resolution of Racemic (±)-BINOL Using N-Benzylcinchoninium Chloride as Resolving Agent

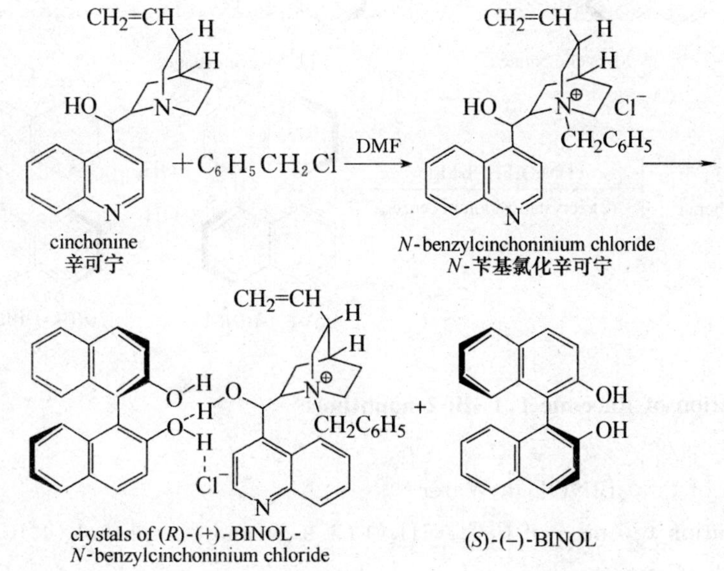

cinchonine
辛可宁

N-benzylcinchoninium chloride
N-苄基氯化辛可宁

crystals of (R)-(+)-BINOL-
N-benzylcinchoninium chloride

(S)-(−)-BINOL

crystals of (R)-(+)-BINOL-N-benzylcinchoninium chloride $\xrightarrow{\text{HCl}}$ (R)-(+)-BINOL + N-benzylcinchoninium chloride

(S)-(−)-BINOL (in solution) $\xrightarrow[\text{(2) HCl}]{\text{(1) evaporate the solvent}}$ (S)-(−)-BINOL

Investigative Experiments

(2) Resolution of Racemic (±)-BINOL Using (S)-Pyrrolidine-2-Carboxylic Acid as Resolving Agent

$$i-\text{BuOH} + \text{H}_3\text{BO}_3 \xrightarrow{\text{reflux and segregate water}} (i-\text{BuO})_3\text{B} + 3\text{H}_2\text{O}$$

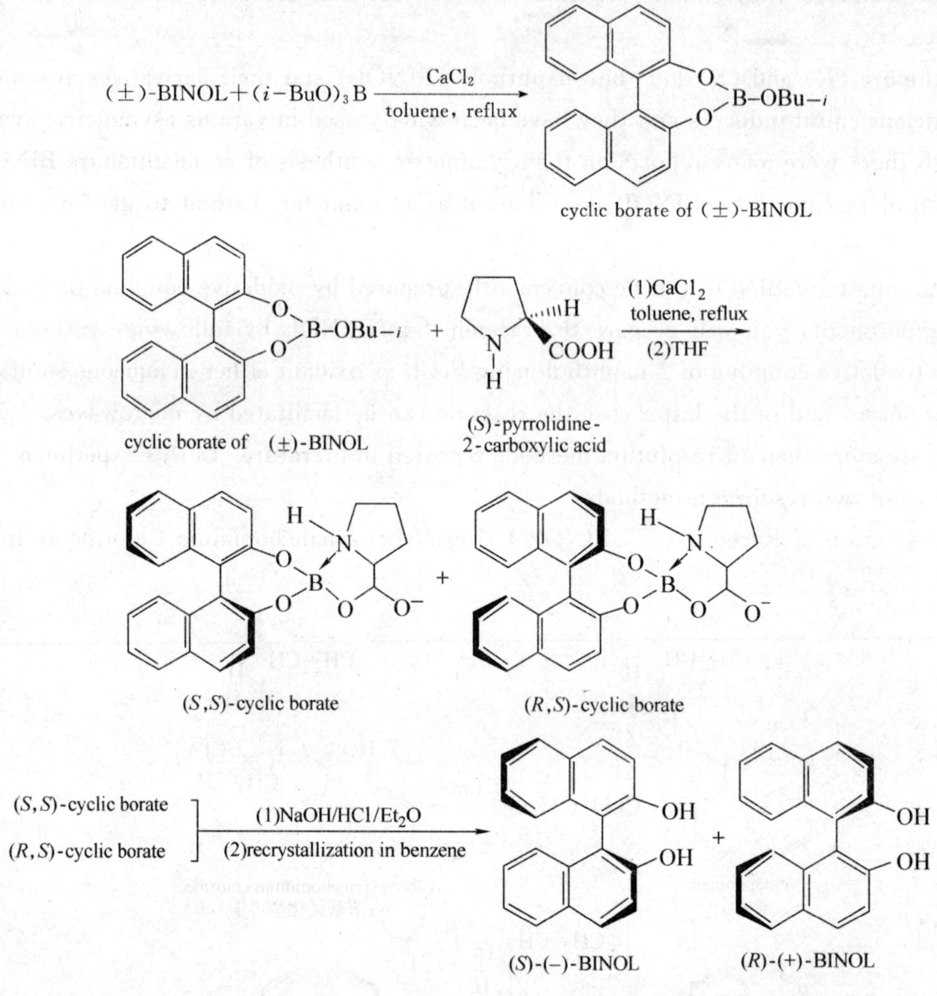

$$(\pm)\text{-BINOL} + (i-\text{BuO})_3\text{B} \xrightarrow[\text{toluene, reflux}]{\text{CaCl}_2}$$

cyclic borate of (±)-BINOL

cyclic borate of (±)-BINOL   (S)-pyrrolidine-2-carboxylic acid

$$\xrightarrow[(2)\text{THF}]{(1)\text{CaCl}_2 \quad \text{toluene, reflux}}$$

(S,S)-cyclic borate   +   (R,S)-cyclic borate

(S,S)-cyclic borate
(R,S)-cyclic borate
$$\left.\begin{array}{c}\end{array}\right\} \xrightarrow[(2)\text{recrystallization in benzene}]{(1)\text{NaOH/HCl/Et}_2\text{O}}$$

(S)-(−)-BINOL   +   (R)-(+)-BINOL

Studies on Preparation of Racemic 1,1′-Bi-2-naphthols

Procedure

(1) Preparation of (±)-BINOL in Water[1],[2]

An aqueous solution (20 mL) of FeCl$_3$·6H$_2$O (3.8 g) and 2-naphthol (1.0 g) is added to a round-bottom flask. Equip it with a reflux condenser. The mixture is stirred at 60 ℃ with a water bath for 4 h. After the resulting solution cools down to room temperature, filter the crystals and wash them with a small amount of water to remove Fe^{3+} and Fe^{2+}. Air-dry the crystals and then recrystallize them in 10 mL toluene to afford colorless crystals (ca. 0.93 g). Measure the melting point of the crystals obtained.

(2) Preparation of (±)-BINOL in the Solid Phase

Finely grind 3.8 g FeCl$_3$·6H$_2$O and 1.0 g 2-naphthol in a mortar and mix them well. Transfer the ground solid mixture to a flask. Place it in a 60 ℃ water bath for 3 h. Afterwards add a small amount of water to the mixture with vigorous stirring. Filter the solid and wash it with water to remove Fe^{3+} and Fe^{2+}. Air-dry the solid and then recrystallize it in 10 mL toluene to afford colorless crystals (ca. 0.93 g). Measure the melting point of the crystals obtained.

(3) A Microwave-Assisted Preparation of (±)-BINOL in the Solid Phase

Finely grind 3.8 g FeCl$_3$·6H$_2$O and 1.0 g 2-naphthol in a mortar and mix them well. Transfer the ground solid mixture to a small beaker. Cover it with a watchglass and place it in a microwave oven. Set the heating button of the oven to low power. Take the beaker out of the oven and stir the mixture after each 0.5 min. The mixture is heated in oven totally for 1.5 min. Afterwards add a small amount of water to the mixture with vigorous stirring. Filter the solid and wash it with water to remove Fe^{3+} and Fe^{2+}. Air-dry the solid and then recrystallize it in 10 mL toluene to afford colorless crystals (ca. 0.91 g). Measure the melting point of the crystal obtained.

Research Interests and Requirements

(1) The methods to identify the structures of the products. You can use NMR and IR spectroscopy.

(2) Qualitatively analyze the crude product, for example, using TLC with ethyl acetate/heptane (1:4, V/V) as developing solvents, or using HPLC method.

(3) Monitor the reaction with TLC to observe the changes in the components of the mixture during the reaction, so as to determine the time needed for the reaction.

(4) Try to find optimal reaction conditions for preparation of (±)-BINOL in a large scale, for example, using a mixed solvent of water and other organic solvent.

Studies on Resolution of Racemic 1,1'-Bi-2-naphthols
Procedure

(1) Preparation of the Resolving Agent N-Benzylcinchoninium Chloride

To a 25 mL round bottom-flask, add 1.18 g cinchonine, 0.76 g benzyl chloride, 8 mL N,N-dimethylformamide (DMF) and a magnetic stirring bar successively. Equip the flask with a reflux condenser. The mixture is stirred at 80 ℃ with a water bath for 3 h. After the mixture cools down to room temperature, filter the white solid and wash it twice with acetone (5 mL× 2). The yield of the resolving agent: 1.28 g. Measure the melting point and the specific rotation [α] of the crystal.

(2) Resolution of Racemic 1,1'-Bi-2-naphthols

To a 25 mL round-bottom flask, add 1.02 g (±)-BINOL, 0.87 g N-benzylcinchoninium chloride and 13 mL acetonitrile successively. Equip the flask with a reflux condenser and heat

Investigative Experiments

the solution under reflux for 4 h. When the resulting solution cools down to room temperature, some precipitates appear gradually. Let the flask stand at $0 \sim 5$ ℃ for 2 h, and then filter the crystal and wash it twice with acetonitrile (5 mL×2). Combine the acetonitrile layers with the mother solution and keep it for recovering (S)-$(-)$-BINOL. The crystal thereby obtained is the 1:1 molecular complex of (R)-$(+)$-BINOL and N-benzylcinchoninium chloride. Measure the melting point and the specific rotation $[\alpha]$ of the crystal.

Isolation of (R)-$(+)$-BINOL: Add the white solid obtained to 25 mL hydrochloric acid (1 mol·L^{-1}) and stir the mixture vigorously for 30 min. Then filter the solid, wash it with a small amount of water and dry it. Recrystallization of the solid from benzene affords pure (R)-$(+)$-BINOL. Measure the melting point and the specific rotation $[\alpha]$ of the resolved (R)-$(+)$-BINOL in THF.

Isolation of (S)-$(-)$-BINOL: Remove the acetonitrile from the above-obtained mother solution by distillation to afford a solid residue. Add this solid to 25 mL hydrochloric acid (1 mol·L^{-1}) and stir the mixture vigorously for 30 min. Then filter the solid, wash it with a small amount of water and dry it. Recrystallization of the solid from benzene affords pure (S)-$(-)$-BINOL. Measure the melting point and the specific rotation $[\alpha]$ of the resolved (S)-$(-)$-BINOL in THF.

Recovery of N-Benzylcinchoninium Chloride: Combine all aqueous hydrochloric acid solutions from the above two procedures. Neutralize the solution with solid Na_2CO_3 until no gas releases. As a consequence, some precipitates appear in the solution. Filter the solid and recrystallize it in methanol/water. Calculate the yield of the recovered N-benzylcinchoninium chloride.

Research Interests and Requirements

(1) Repeat the resolution experiment and optimize the procedures, to obtain the higher yields of (R)-$(+)$-BINOL, (S)-$(-)$-BINOL, and ee values and to enhance the yield of recovered N-benzylcinchoninium chloride.

(2) Resolve $(\pm)$-BINOL by using (S)-pyrrolidine-2-carboxylic acid as resolving agent via cyclic borates. Compare the two resolution methods.

(3) Learn how to designate the R/S configurations to such enantiomers containing a chiral axis.

(4) Look up the literature to find a catalytic reaction using enantiopure BINOL as chiral inducer.

Notes

[1] The melting points of related compounds reported in literature:

$(\pm)$-BINOL: mp $216 \sim 218$ ℃;

N-benzylcinchoninium chloride: mp 256 ℃ (dec.);

The crystallized complex of (R)-$(+)$-BINOL-N-benzylcinchoninium chloride: mp

247～248 ℃；

(R)-(+)-BINOL：mp 209～211 ℃；

(S)-(−)-BINOL：mp 209～211 ℃.

[2] The specific rotations of related compounds reported in literature：

N-benzylcinchoninium chloride：$[\alpha]_D^{27} = +165.9$ ($c = 0.50$, H_2O), $[\alpha]_D^{22} = +164.8$ ($c = 0.72$, H_2O)；

(R)-(+)-BINOL：$ee > 99\%$, $[\alpha]_D^{27} = +32.1$ ($c = 1.0$, THF)；$ee > 99.8\%$, $[\alpha]_D^{21} = +34.3$ ($c = 1.0$, THF)；

(S)-(−)-BINOL：$ee > 98\%$, $[\alpha]_D^{27} = -33.5$ ($c = 1.0$, THF)；$ee > 99\%$, $[\alpha]_D^{21} = -34.0$ ($c = 1.0$, THF).

References

[1] Ding K, Wang Y, Zhang L, et al. Tetrahedron, 1996, 52：1005.

[2] Famio Toda, et al. J Org Chem, 1989, 54：3007.

[3] Wang Y, Sun J, Ding K. Tetrahedron, 2000, 56：4447.

[4] 单自兴. 综合化学实验：武汉：武汉大学出版社，2003.

References

[1] 高占先. 有机化学实验. 4 版. 北京：高等教育出版社，2004.

[2] 薛思佳，季萍，L Olson. Experimental Organic Chemistry. 2nd edition. 北京：科学出版社，2007.

[3] J C Gilbert，S F Martin. Experimental Organic Chemistry：a Miniscale and Microscale Approach. 4th edition. New York：Saunders College Publishing，2006.

[4] D W Mayo，R M Pike，P K Trumper. Microscale Organic Laboratory with Multistep and Multiscale Syntheses. 4th edition. New York：John Wiley & Sons, Inc. ，2000.

[5] C F Wilcox，M F Wilcox. Experimental Organic Chemistry：A Small-Scale Approach. 2nd edition. New Jersey：Prentice-Hall Inc. ，1995.

[6] H D Durst，G W Gokel. Experimental Organic Chemistry. New York：Mcgraw-Hill Book Company，1986.

[7] K Williamson. Macroscale and Microscale Organic Experiments. 3 th edition. New York：Houghton Mifflin Company，1999.

[8] A M Schoffstall，B A Gaddis，M L Druelinger. Microscale and Miniscale Organic Chemistry Laboratory Experiments. New York：McGraw-Hill Inc. ，2003.

[9] Akio Yamamoto. Organotransition Metal Chemistry：Fundamental Concepts and Applications. New York：John Wiley & Sons. Inc. ，1986.

Appendix

(1) Atomic masses of commonly used elements

	symbol	name	atomic mass		symbol	name	atomic mass
银	Ag	silver	107.87	锂	Li	lithium	6.941
铝	Al	aluminum	26.98	镁	Mg	magnesium	24.31
硼	B	boron	10.81	锰	Mn	manganese	54.938
钡	Ba	barium	137.34	钼	Mo	molybdenum	95.94
溴	Br	bromine	79.904	氮	N	nitrogen	14.007
碳	C	carbon	12.01	钠	Na	sodium	22.99
钙	Ca	calcium	40.08	镍	Ni	nickel	58.71
氯	Cl	chlorine	35.45	氧	O	oxygen	15.999
铬	Cr	chromium	51.996	磷	P	phosphorus	30.97
铜	Cu	copper	63.54	铅	Pb	lead	207.19
氟	F	fluorine	18.998	钯	Pd	palladium	106.4
铁	Fe	iron	55.847	铂	Pt	platinum	195.09
氢	H	hydrogen	1.008	硫	S	sulfur	32.064
汞	Hg	mercury	200.59	硅	Si	silicon	28.086
碘	I	iodine	126.904	锡	Sn	tin	118.69
钾	K	potassium	39.10	锌	Zn	zinc	65.37

(2) Boiling points and relative densities of commonly used organic solvents

名称	name	bp/℃	d_4^{20}	名称	name	bp/℃	d_4^{20}
甲醇	methanol	64.9	0.791 4	苯	benzene	80.1	0.878 7
乙醇	ethanol	78.5	0.789 3	甲苯	toluene	110.6	0.866 9
乙醚	ether	34.5	0.713 7	二甲苯 ($o-$,	xylene ($o-$,	~140.0	
丙酮	acetone	56.2	0.789 9	$m-$, $p-$)	$m-$, $p-$)		
乙酸	acetic acid	117.9	1.049 2	氯仿	chloroform	61.7	1.483 2
乙酐	acetic anhydride	139.5	1.082 0	四氯化碳	carbon tetrachloride	76.5	1.594 0
乙酸乙酯	ethyl acetate	77.0	0.900 3	二硫化碳	carbon disulfide	46.2	1.263 2
二氧六环	dioxane	101.7	1.033 7				
				硝基苯	nitrobenzene	210.8	1.203 7
				正丁醇	$n-$butanol	117.2	0.809 8

(3) Commonly used acids and bases

solution	relative density	mass percent/%	content /(mol·L^{-1})	mass concentration /(10 g·L^{-1})
concentrated hydrochloric acid （浓盐酸）	1.19	37	12.0	44.0
hydrochloric acid at the azeotropic point （在共沸点的 盐酸，252 mL concentrated HCl＋200 mL H$_2$O, bp 110 ℃）	1.10	20.2	6.1	22.2
10% HCl （100 mL concentrated HCl ＋ 321 mL H$_2$O）	1.05	10	2.9	10.5
5% HCl （50 mL concentrated HCl ＋ 380.5 mL H$_2$O）	1.03	5	1.4	5.2
1 mol·L^{-1} HCl （41.5 mL concentrated HCl is diluted to 500 mL）	1.02	3.6	1	3.6
hydrobromic acid at the azeotropic point （在共沸点 的氢溴酸，bp 126 ℃）	1.49	47.5	8.8	70.7
hydroiodic acid at the azeotropic point （在共沸点的 氢碘酸，bp 127 ℃）	1.7	57	7.6	97
concentrated sulfuric acid （浓硫酸）	1.84	96	18	177
10% H$_2$SO$_4$ （25 mL concentrated H$_2$SO$_4$ ＋ 398 mL H$_2$O）	1.07	10	1.1	10.7
0.5 mol·L^{-1} H$_2$SO$_4$ （13.9 mL concentrated H$_2$SO$_4$ is diluted to 500 mL）	1.03	4.7	0.5	4.9
concentrated nitric acid （浓硝酸）	1.42	71	16	101
10% NaOH	1.11	10	2.8	11.1
concentrated ammonia （浓氨水）	0.9	28.4	15	25.6

(4) Relative densities and compositions of commonly used acid and base solutions

Hydrochloric Acid

HCl mass percent/%	d_4^{20}	HCl/(10 g·L^{-1}) (aqua solution)	HCl mass percent/%	d_4^{20}	HCl/(10 g·L^{-1}) (aqua solution)
1	1.003 2	1.003	22	1.108 3	24.38
2	1.008 2	2.006	24	1.118 7	26.85
4	1.018 1	4.007	26	1.129 0	29.35
6	1.027 9	6.167	28	1.139 2	31.90
8	1.037 6	8.301	30	1.149 2	34.48
10	1.047 4	10.47	32	1.159 3	37.10
12	1.057 4	12.69	34	1.169 1	39.75
14	1.067 5	14.95	36	1.178 9	42.44
16	1.077 6	17.24	38	1.188 5	45.16
18	1.087 8	19.58	40	1.198 0	47.92
20	1.098 0	21.96			

Appendix

Sulfuric Acid

H_2SO_4 mass percent/%	d_4^{20}	$H_2SO_4/(10\ g \cdot L^{-1})$ (aqua solution)	H_2SO_4 mass percent/%	d_4^{20}	$H_2SO_4/(10\ g \cdot L^{-1})$ (aqua solution)
1	1.005 1	1.005	65	1.553 3	101.0
2	1.011 8	2.024	70	1.610 5	112.7
3	1.018 4	3.055	75	1.669 2	125.2
4	1.025 0	4.100	80	1.727 2	138.2
5	1.031 7	5.159	85	1.778 6	151.2
10	1.066 1	10.66	90	1.814 4	163.3
15	1.102 0	16.53	91	1.819 5	165.6
20	1.139 4	22.79	92	1.824 0	167.8
25	1.178 3	29.46	93	1.827 9	170.0
30	1.218 5	36.56	94	1.831 2	172.1
35	1.257 9	44.10	95	1.833 7	174.2
40	1.302 8	52.11	96	1.835 5	176.2
45	1.347 6	60.64	97	1.836 4	178.1
50	1.395 1	69.76	98	1.836 1	179.9
55	1.445 3	79.49	99	1.834 2	181.6
60	1.498 3	89.90	100	1.830 5	183.1

Nitric Acid

HNO_3 mass percent/%	d_4^{20}	$HNO_3/(10\ g \cdot L^{-1})$ (aqua solution)	HNO_3 mass percent/%	d_4^{20}	$HNO_3/(10\ g \cdot L^{-1})$ (aqua solution)
1	1.003 6	1.004	65	1.391 3	90.43
2	1.009 1	2.018	70	1.413 4	98.94
3	1.014 6	3.044	75	1.433 7	107.5
4	1.020 1	4.080	80	1.452 1	116.2
5	1.025 6	5.128	85	1.468 6	124.8
10	1.054 3	10.54	90	1.482 6	133.4
15	1.084 2	16.26	91	1.485 0	135.1
20	1.115 0	22.30	92	1.487 3	136.8
25	1.146 9	28.67	93	1.489 2	138.5
30	1.180 0	35.40	94	1.491 2	140.2
35	1.214 0	42.49	95	1.493 2	141.9
40	1.246 3	49.85	96	1.495 2	143.5
45	1.278 3	57.52	97	1.497 4	145.2
50	1.310 0	65.50	98	1.500 8	147.1
55	1.339 3	73.66	99	1.505 6	149.1
60	1.366 7	82.00	100	1.512 9	151.3

Appendix

Sodium Hydroxide

NaOH mass percent/%	d_4^{20}	NaOH/(10 g·L^{-1}) (aqua solution)	NaOH mass percent/%	d_4^{20}	NaOH/(10 g·L^{-1}) (aqua solution)
1	1.009 5	1.010	26	1.284 8	33.40
2	1.020 7	2.041	28	1.306 4	36.58
4	1.042 8	4.171	30	1.327 9	39.84
6	1.064 8	6.389	32	1.349 0	43.17
8	1.086 9	8.695	34	1.369 6	46.57
10	1.108 9	11.09	36	1.390 0	50.04
12	1.130 9	13.57	38	1.410 1	53.58
14	1.153 0	16.14	40	1.430 0	57.20
16	1.175 1	18.80	42	1.449 4	60.87
18	1.197 2	21.55	44	1.468 5	64.61
20	1.219 1	24.38	46	1.487 3	68.42
22	1.241 1	27.30	48	1.506 5	72.31
24	1.262 9	30.31	50	1.525 3	76.27

Sodium Carbonate

Na$_2$CO$_3$ mass percent/%	d_4^{20}	Na$_2$CO$_3$/(10 g·L^{-1}) (aqua solution)	Na$_2$CO$_3$ mass percent/%	d_4^{20}	Na$_2$CO$_3$/(10 g·L^{-1}) (aqua solution)
1	1.008 6	1.009	12	1.124 4	13.49
2	1.019 0	2.038	14	1.146 3	16.05
4	1.039 8	4.159	16	1.168 2	18.50
6	1.060 6	6.364	18	1.190 5	21.33
8	1.081 6	8.653	20	1.213 2	24.26
10	1.102 9	11.03			

(5) Saturated steam pressure of water

temp. /℃	steam pressure /(mmHg)[①]	temp. /℃	steam pressure /(mmHg)	temp. /℃	steam pressure /(mmHg)	temp. /℃	steam pressure /(mmHg)
1	4.926	9	8.609	17	14.53	25	23.76
2	5.294	10	9.209	18	15.48	26	25.21
3	5.685	11	9.844	19	16.48	27	26.74
4	6.101	12	10.52	20	17.54	28	28.35
5	6.543	13	11.23	21	18.65	29	30.04
6	7.013	14	11.99	22	19.83	30	31.82
7	7.513	15	12.79	23	21.07	31	33.70
8	8.045	16	13.63	24	22.38	32	35.66

Appendix

Continued

temp. /℃	steam pressure /(mmHg)	temp. /℃	steam pressure /(mmHg)	temp. /℃	steam pressure /(mmHg)	temp. /℃	steam pressure /(mmHg)
33	37.73	50	92.51	67	205.0	84	416.8
34	39.90	51	97.20	68	214.2	85	433.6
35	42.18	52	102.1	69	223.7	86	450.9
36	44.56	53	107.2	70	233.7	87	468.7
37	47.07	54	112.5	71	243.9	88	487.1
38	49.69	55	118.0	72	254.6	89	506.1
39	52.44	56	123.8	73	265.7	90	525.76
40	55.32	57	129.8	74	277.2	91	546.05
41	58.34	58	136.1	75	289.1	92	566.99
42	61.50	59	142.6	76	301.4	93	588.60
43	64.80	60	149.4	77	314.1	94	610.90
44	68.26	61	156.4	78	327.3	95	633.90
45	71.88	62	163.8	79	341.0	96	657.62
46	75.65	63	171.4	80	355.1	97	682.07
47	79.60	64	179.3	81	369.7	98	707.27
48	83.71	65	187.5	82	384.9	99	733.24
49	88.02	66	196.1	83	400.6	100	760.00

① 760.00 mm Hg = 101 325 Pa.

Index

Index

Vocabulary

A

Abbe refractometer 阿贝折射仪

absorbent 吸附剂

acetaldehyde 乙醛

acetanilide 乙酰苯胺

acetic acid 乙酸

acetic anhydride 乙酸酐

acetone 丙酮

acetonitrile 乙腈

acetophenone 苯乙酮

acetylamino 乙酰氨基

acetylation 乙酰化

acetylsalicylic acid 乙酰水杨酸

acid anhydride 酸酐

acid chloride 酰氯

acrylonitrile 丙烯腈

acyclic 非环状的

acyl chloride 酰氯

acyl halide 酰卤

acylation 酰化

adapter 适配器，接头

addition funnel 加料漏斗

adipic acid (hexanedioic acid) 己二酸

adsorbent 吸附剂

aldehyde 乙醛

aldol condensation 羟醛缩合

alkali metal 碱金属

alkaloid 生物碱

alkane 烷烃

alkene 烯烃

alkoxide anion 烷氧基负离子

alkoxyl 烷氧基

alkyl aryl ketone 烷基芳基酮

alkyl halide 卤代烷

alkyl hypohalite 烷基次卤酸

alkylation 烷基化

alkyllithium 烷基锂

alkyne 炔烃

alumina 氧化铝

aluminum chloride 氯化铝

aluminum foil 铝箔

aluminum hydroxide 氢氧化铝

amide 酰胺

amine 胺

aminophenol 氨基苯酚

ammonia 氨

ammonium carboxylate 羧酸铵

ammonium salt 铵盐

ampere detector 安培检测器

amphoteric 两性的

analytical balance 分析天平

anhydrous solvent 无水溶剂

aniline 苯胺

β-anilinopropanal β-苯氨基丙醛

anode 阳极

anthracene 蒽

antipyretic 退热剂

arene 芳烃

aromatic 芳香的

arylamine 芳胺

asbestos pad 石棉垫

aspirator pump 抽气泵

asymmetric synthesis 不对称合成

auxochrome 助色团

auxochromic effect 助色效应

azeotrope 共沸物

azeotropic distillation 共沸蒸馏

azeotropic point 共沸点

B

barbituric acid 巴比妥酸

barometric pressure 大气压

beaker 烧杯

benzaldehyde 苯甲醛

benzene 苯

benzoic ester 苯甲酸酯

benzyl alcohol 苯甲醇

benzylic alcohol 苄醇

benzyltriethylammonium chloride 三乙基苄基氯化铵

9,9-bis(hydroxymethyl)fluorene 9,9-二羟甲基芴

9,9-bis(methoxymethyl)fluorene 9,9-二甲氧甲基芴

blue litmus paper 蓝色石蕊试纸

boiling chip 沸石

boiling point 沸点

boric acid 硼酸

brine 盐水

bromoacetone 溴丙酮

bromobenzene 溴苯

Büchner flasks 布氏烧瓶

Büchner funnel 布氏漏斗

butanal 正丁醛

butanol 正丁醇

butanone 丁酮

butene 丁烯

butyl acetate 乙酸丁酯

butyllithium 正丁基锂

butyraldehyde 丁醛

butyrate 丁酸盐(酯)

C

calcium chloride 氯化钙

calcium hypochlorite 次氯酸钙

calcium oxide 氧化钙

capsanthin 辣椒红素

capsorubin 辣椒玉红素

carbanion 碳负离子

carbene 卡宾

carbocation 碳正离子

carbohydrate 碳水化合物

carbonyl 羰基

carboxylate ion 羧酸根离子

carboxylic acid 羧酸

carcinogenic 致癌的

carotene 胡萝卜素

carrier gas 载气

catalysis 催化作用

catalyst 催化剂

cathode 阴极

celite 硅藻土

centrifugation 离心作用

chemical shift 化学位移

chiral 手性的

chiral axis 手性轴

chloroethane 氯乙烷

chloroform 氯仿

chromatography 色谱法

chromic acid 铬酸

chromium trioxide 三氧化铬

chromophore 发色团

cinnamic acid 肉桂酸

Claisen head 克氏蒸馏头

clamp holder 夹持器

column chromatography 柱色谱

concentration 浓度

condensation 冷凝

conjugate 共轭

cooling condenser 冷凝器

correction factor 校正因子

coupling constant 偶合常数

cuprous chloride 氯化亚铜

cyclic borate 环硼酸酯

cycloaddition 环加成

cyclohexane 环己烷

cyclohexanone 环己酮

cyclohexene 环己烯

cyclopentanone 环戊酮

cyclopropane 环丙烷

D

decarboxylation 脱羧

decomposition 分解

degree of unsaturation 不饱和度

dehydration 脱水

dehydrator 脱水器

dehydrogenation 脱氢

dehydrohalogenation 脱卤化氢

deprotonation 去质子化

desiccant 干燥剂

desiccator 干燥器

deuterated solvent 氘代溶剂

developing solvent 展开剂

dextrorotatory 右旋物

diastereomer 非对映体

diazo-reaction 重氮化反应

dibromocarbene 二溴卡宾

dibutyl ether 二丁基醚

dichlorocarbene 二氯卡宾

Dichloromethane (methylene chloride) 二氯甲烷

diene 二烯烃

dienophile 亲双烯体

diethyl ether 乙醚

diethyl malonate 丙二酸二乙酯

differential refractive index detector 差示折光检测器

1,2-dihydroquinoline 1,2-二氢喹啉

dimethyl carbonate 碳酸二甲酯

N,N-dimethylformamide (DMF) N,N-二甲基甲酰胺

dimethyl sulfate 硫酸二甲酯

dimethyl sulfoxide (DMSO) 二甲基亚砜

dimethylurea 二甲基脲

dinonyl phthalate 邻苯二甲酸二壬酯

dipole-dipole interaction 偶极-偶极相互作用

disproportionation 歧化作用

distillation 蒸馏

double-blank manifold 双排管

drying tube 干燥管

E

electrolysis 电解

electrolytic 电解的

electrophile 亲电试剂

elimination 消除(反应)

eluent 洗脱液

eluting solvent 洗脱剂

enantiomer 对映体

enantiopure 对映体纯的

enolate anion 烯醇负离子

Erlenmeyer flask 锥形瓶

ester 酯

esterification 酯化

ethanol 乙醇

ether 醚

etherification 醚化作用

ethyl acetate 乙酸乙酯

ethyl 2-phenylacetate 2-苯基乙酸乙酯

ethyl acetoacetate (ethyl 3-oxobutanoate) 乙酰乙酸乙酯

ethyl benzoate 苯甲酸乙酯

evaporation 蒸发

exothermic 放热的

external standard method 外标法

extract 萃取

F

ferrous sulfate 硫酸亚铁

filtration 过滤

flame ionization detector 火焰电离检测器

flask 烧瓶

fluorene 芴

fluorescence 荧光

formaldehyde 甲醛

formic acid 甲酸

fractional distillation 分馏

fractionating column 分馏塔

fractionating head 分馏头

functional group 官能团

fused ring compound 稠环化合物

G

gas trap 气体收集器

glacial acetic acid 冰醋酸

glasswool 玻璃棉

glucose 葡萄糖

glutaric acid (pentanedioic acid) 戊二酸

glycerol 甘油

goggles 护目镜

graduated cylinder 量筒

Grignard reagent 格氏试剂

H

halide ion 卤素离子

haloalkane 卤代烷

halogen 卤素

halogenated 卤代的

heating mantle 电热套

hemiacetal 半缩醛

Hempel column 亨佩耳(蒸馏)柱

heptane 庚烷

heterogeneous 异相的

hexane 己烷

hexanedinitrile 己二腈

Hickman fractionating head 希克曼分馏头

Hickman stillhead 希克曼蒸馏头

high-performance liquid chromatography (HPLC) 高效液相色谱

Hirsch funnel 赫氏漏斗

hood 通风橱

hybridize 杂化

hydrate 水合物

hydroboration-oxidation 硼氢化-氧化

hydrobromide 溴化氢

hydrocarbon 碳氢化合物

hydrochloric acid 盐酸

hydrochloride (hydrochloric acid) 氯化氢

hydroformylation 氢甲酰化(反应)

hydrogen peroxide 过氧化氢

hydrohalic acid 氢卤酸

hydrolysis 水解

hydrolyze 水解

hydrophilic 亲水的

hydroxyl 羟基

hydroxymethylation 羟甲基化(反应)

hygroscopic 吸湿

hypoiodite ion 次碘酸离子

I

immiscible 不混溶的

index of refraction 折射率

infrared (IR) spectroscopy 红外光谱法

integral trace 积分曲线

internal standard method 内标法

iodate ion 碘酸盐离子

iodide ion 碘离子

isomerization 异构化

isopentyl acetate 乙酸异戊酯

isopentyl alcohol 异戊醇

K

β-ketoester β-酮酯

ketone 酮

L

lachrymator 催泪剂

lead dioxide 二氧化铅

levorotatory 左旋的

lipophilic 亲油的

lubricant 润滑剂

M

magnesium sulfate 硫酸镁

magnetic stirring 磁搅拌

maleic anhydride 马来酸酐

malonic acid 丙二酸

manometer 压力计

mechanical stirring 机械搅拌

melting point 熔点

merbromin 汞溴红

methane 甲烷

methanol 甲醇

methyl 甲基

methyl butyrate 丁酸甲酯

methyl iodide 碘甲烷

methyl t-butyl ether 甲基叔丁基醚

methylation 甲基化

methylene blue 亚甲基蓝

methyltrioctylammonium chloride 甲基三辛基氯化铵

mobile phase 流动相

molar absorptivity 摩尔吸收率

molar extinction coefficient 摩尔吸收系数

molecular sieves 分子筛

monochromatic light 单色光

monosaccharide 单糖

Vocabulary

N

naphthol 萘酚

neutralize 中和

nicotine 尼古丁

nitrate 硝化，硝酸盐

nitrating agent 硝化试剂

nitration 硝化(反应)

nitric acid 硝酸

nitrile 腈

nitroacetanilide 硝基乙酰苯胺

nitro aromatic compound 硝基芳香化合物

nitroaniline 硝基苯胺

nitrobenzene 硝基苯

nitrogen oxide 氧化氮

nitronium ion 硝鎓离子

normal phase chromatography 正相色谱

normalization method 归一化法

nuclear magnetic resonance spectroscopy（NMR）核磁
共振谱

nucleophile 亲核试剂

nucleophilic 亲核的

O

ointment 药膏，软膏

ophthalmologist 眼科专家

organoaluminium 有机铝

organolithium 有机锂

organomagnesium 有机镁

organometallic compound 金属有机化合物

oxonium ion 氧鎓离子

ozonolysis 臭氧分解

P

Pasteur pipet 滴管

peroxide 过氧化物

petroleum ether 石油醚

phase-transfer catalyst 相转移催化剂

phenanthrene 菲

phenol 苯酚

phenolphthalein 酚酞

phenylmagnesium bromide 苯基溴化镁

2-phenylpropane 2-苯丙烷

phosgene 光气

phosphoric acid 磷酸

phosphorus chloride 氯化磷

phosphorus pentoxide 五氧化二磷

phosphorus tribromide 三溴化磷

pipet 移液管，吸量管

plane-polarized light 平面偏振光

polarimeter 偏光计

polarizing filter 偏振滤波器

polyformaldehyde 聚甲醛

polymerization 聚合

potassium carbonate 碳酸钾

potassium hydroxide 氢氧化钾

potassium iodide 碘化钾

potassium permanganate 高锰酸钾

primary alcohol 伯醇

propanol 丙醇

proton 质子

protonate 质子化

protractor 量角器

pycnometer 比重瓶

pyridine 吡啶

pyridinium chlorochromate 氯铬酸吡啶鎓盐

pyrrolidine-2-carboxylic acid 吡咯烷-2-羧酸

Q

quaternary ammonium salt 季铵盐

quinoline 喹啉

R

racemic 外消旋的

rearrangement 重排

recrystallization 重结晶

reflux 回流

reflux condenser 回流冷凝管

resolution 拆分

resolving agent 拆分试剂

retention factor 保留因子

retention time 保留时间

reversed-phase chromatography 反相色谱

rotary evaporator 旋转蒸发器

S

salicylic acid (*o*-hydroxybenzoic acid) 水杨酸

saline 盐水

saturate solution 饱和溶液

secondary alcohol 仲醇

separatory funnel 分液漏斗

silica 二氧化硅

silica gel 硅胶

singlet 单重峰

sodium adipate (hexanedioate) 己二酸钠

sodium benzoate 苯甲酸钠

sodium bicarbonate 碳酸氢钠

sodium bisulfite 亚硫酸氢钠

sodium carbonate 碳酸钠

sodium dichromate 重铬酸钠

sodium ethoxide 乙醇钠

sodium hydroxide 氢氧化钠

sodium hypochlorite 次氯酸钠

sodium phenolate 苯酚钠

sodium sulfate 硫酸钠

sodium thiosulfate 硫代硫酸钠

solubility 溶解性，溶解度

solution 溶液

solvent 溶剂

Soxhlet extractor 索氏提取器

spatula 小勺

specific rotation 旋光率

spectroscopy 光谱学

spectrum 谱图

spin-spin splitting 自旋-自旋裂分

standard-taper ground-glass joints 标准磨口玻璃接头

stationary phase 固定相

steam distillation 蒸汽蒸馏

stillhead 蒸馏头

stillpot 蒸馏釜

stirbar 搅拌子(棒)

stirrer 搅拌器

stopcock 旋塞

sublimation 升华

substituent 取代基

substitution 取代(反应)

sulfur trioxide 三氧化硫

sulfuric acid 硫酸

support stand 支架台

T

tautomerization 互变异构

terminal alkyne 端炔烃

tetrabutylammonium bisulfate 四丁基硫酸氢铵

tetrahydrofuran 四氢呋喃

tetramethylsilane (TMS) 四甲基硅烷

thermal conductivity detector 热导检测器

thermometer 温度计

thin-layer chromatography 薄层色谱法

thiol 硫醇

thionyl chloride 二氯亚砜

thiophene 噻吩

tincture of iodine 碘酒

titration 滴定

toluene 甲苯

tosylate 对甲苯磺酸盐(酯)

toxicological 毒理学

transesterification 酯交换

1,3,7-trimethyl-2,6-dioxopurine 1,3,7-三甲基-2,6-二氧代嘌呤

triphenylmethanol 三苯基甲醇

two-way cock 两通旋塞

U

ultraviolet (UV) lamp 紫外灯

ultra-violet-visible (UV-Vis) spectroscopy 紫外可见光谱法

ultraviolet-visible light detector 紫外可见光检测器

α,β-unsaturated acid α,β-不饱和酸

urea 尿素

V

vacuum distillation 减压蒸馏

Vigreux column 韦氏分馏柱

W

water segregator 分水器

west condenser 直形冷凝器

Periodic Table of the Elements

Atomic masses are based on ^{12}C. Atomic masses in parentheses are for the most stable isotope.

Legend:
- 6 — Atomic number
- C — Symbol
- 12.011 — Atomic mass

Group																	
IA	IIA	IIIB	IVB	VB	VIB	VIIB	VIIIB	VIIIB	VIIIB	IB	IIB	IIIA	IVA	VA	VIA	VIIA	VIII

Periods

Period 1																	
Hydrogen 1 H 1.0079																Hydrogen 1 H 1.0079	Helium 2 He 4.0026

Period 2:
- Lithium 3 Li 6.942
- Beryllium 4 Be 9.0122
- Boron 5 B 10.811
- Carbon 6 C 12.0115
- Nitrogen 7 N 14.0067
- Oxygen 8 O 15.9994
- Fluorine 9 F 18.9984
- Neon 10 Ne 20.183

Period 3:
- Sodium 11 Na 22.9898
- Magnesium 12 Mg 24.312
- Aluminum 13 Al 26.9815
- Silicon 14 Si 28.086
- Phosphorus 15 P 30.9738
- Sulfur 16 S 32.064
- Chlorine 17 Cl 35.453
- Argon 18 Ar 39.948

Period 4:
- Potassium 19 K 39.102
- Calcium 20 Ca 40.08
- Scandium 21 Sc 44.956
- Titanium 22 Ti 47.90
- Vanadium 23 V 50.942
- Chromium 24 Cr 51.996
- Manganese 25 Mn 54.9380
- Iron 26 Fe 55.847
- Cobalt 27 Co 58.9332
- Nickel 28 Ni 58.70
- Copper 29 Cu 63.54
- Zinc 30 Zn 65.37
- Gallium 31 Ga 69.72
- Germanium 32 Ge 72.59
- Arsenic 33 As 74.9215
- Selenium 34 Se 78.96
- Bromine 35 Br 79.909
- Krypton 36 Kr 83.80

Period 5:
- Rubidium 37 Rb 85.4678
- Strontium 38 Sr 87.62
- Yttrium 39 Y 88.9059
- Zirconium 40 Zr 91.224
- Niobium 41 Nb 92.9064
- Molybdenum 42 Mo 95.94
- Technetium 43 Tc (98)
- Ruthenium 44 Ru 101.07
- Rhodium 45 Rh 102.9055
- Palladium 46 Pd 106.4
- Silver 47 Ag 107.807
- Cadmium 48 Cd 112.40
- Indium 49 In 114.82
- Tin 50 Sn 118.69
- Antimony 51 Sb 121.75
- Tellurium 52 Te 127.60
- Iodine 53 I 126.9044
- Xenon 54 Xe 131.30

Period 6:
- Cesium 55 Cs 132.905
- Barium 56 Ba 137.34
- Lanthanum 57 *La 138.91
- Hafnium 72 Hf 178.49
- Tantalum 73 Ta 180.948
- Tungsten 74 W 183.85
- Rhenium 75 Re 186.2
- Osmium 76 Os 190.2
- Iridium 77 Ir 192.2
- Platinum 78 Pt 195.09
- Gold 79 Au 196.967
- Mercury 80 Hg 200.59
- Thallium 81 Tl 204.37
- Lead 82 Pb 207.19
- Bismuth 83 Bi 208.980
- Polonium 84 Po (209)
- Astatine 85 At (210)
- Radon 86 Rn (222)

Period 7:
- Francium 87 Fr (223)
- Radium 88 Ra (226)
- Actinium 89 **Ac (227)
- †Rutherfordium 104 Rf (261)
- †Dubnium 105 Db (262)
- †Seaborgium 106 Sb (263)
- †Bohrium 107 Bh (262)
- †Hassium 108 Hs (265)
- †Meitnerium 109 Mt (266)
- 110 (269.1)
- 111 (272.1)
- 112 (277.1)

*Lanthanide Series

- Cerium 58 Ce 140.12
- Praseodymium 59 Pr 140.907
- Neodymium 60 Nd 144.24
- Promethium 61 Pm (145)
- Samarium 62 Sm 150.35
- Europium 63 Eu 151.96
- Gadolinium 64 Gd 157.25
- Terbium 65 Tb 158.924
- Dysprosium 66 Dy 162.50
- Holmium 67 Ho 164.930
- Erbium 68 Er 167.26
- Thulium 69 Tm 168.934
- Ytterbium 70 Yb 173.04
- Lutetium 71 Lu 174.97

**Actinide Series

- Thorium 90 Th 232.038
- Protactinium 91 Pa 231.0359
- Uranium 92 U 238.03
- Neptunium 93 Np (237)
- Plutonium 94 Pu (244)
- Americium 95 Am (243)
- Curium 96 Cm (247)
- Berkelium 97 Bk (247)
- Californium 98 Cf (251)
- Einsteinium 99 Es (252)
- Fermium 100 Fm (257)
- Mendelevium 101 Md (258)
- Nobelium 102 No (259)
- Lawrencium 103 Lr (260)

†Tentative names for elements 104-109. Elements 110-112 have not been named.